Sallie J. Hancock

The Montanas: Or, Under the stars

A Romance

Sallie J. Hancock

The Montanas: Or, Under the stars
A Romance

ISBN/EAN: 9783337064778

Printed in Europe, USA, Canada, Australia, Japan

Cover: Foto ©Andreas Hilbeck / pixelio.de

More available books at **www.hansebooks.com**

THE MONTANAS:

OR

UNDER THE STARS.

A Romance.

BY

SALLIE J. HANCOCK

OF KENTUCKY.

"A day, an hour, of virtuous Liberty
Is worth a whole eternity of bondage."

NEW YORK:

Carleton, Publisher, 413 *Broadway.*

M DCCC LXVI.

THE MONTANAS.

CHAPTER I.

"Spontaneous joys! where Nature has its play,
The soul adopts and owns their first-born sway."

GOLDSMITH.

IT was one of those spaces that ensue when Nature, wearied of the convulsions from which spring mountains lofty and grand, hills "rock-ribbed" and broken into ranges vast and far, comes down to repose for a while on smooth lawns and crystal streams, whose currents dash in wildness adown the steeps, then tamely ripple through an interval of gentle gliding on their journey to the distant sea. There, in one of those vales of quietness in which nestled the town of Wayburn, where, after having given up our handsome house in New York, we came to live in a little cottage, around which the snow wrapped its great white arms in winter-time; while the cheerful fire glowed and crackled on the hearth within, from which arose a genuine old-fashioned chimney of the Puritan times, where the swallows hold their summer revels to this day. I wonder if they missed me, for my childish hands had often fed them, when after our brief sojourn we three went away—one to the sunny, and two to the silent land? Or if in their calendar there may be found any record of the time when first the echoless space reigned there grimly, as if in constant reminder of the voices that had ceased to speak as they were wont to speak, and now uttered words in tones that made the home music cheery to other time and place than these, when the merry cricket sang his season song by the hearth-side? Even now I never see a band of swallows cutting the sunshine with their dark wings but I think of Raphael, and how they were his only companions in the solitary house, where he lived with his memories of a beauteous love-lighted past; and how he fed and cared for them at the last, just before his great soul—emancipated—mounted the blue stairs to heaven where Julia was, with a footstep light as "swallows on the wing."

The thoughts which come to me to-day are not alone of him or the swallows that he loved; though I too loved them, for they were long the only tenants of my broken home. A memory lies far back amid the great billows of the past; a calm space beneath a sky that was sweetly, brightly blue, and each season's sun arose on flower-strewn banks. The tides of life broke stilly on those morning shores, and the golden days rippled by with a gliding tread that was half rest, half dream. I have often wondered if other homes were like this one of mine in the feeling and the presence; time has not answered my question satisfactorily. I know now how the bright links in the chain are apt to fall apart when misfortune comes, cutting into them with the sharp sabre of her discipline. And how wide asunder the hearts of the hearth-circle may become, when spaces of the outside world come in between. But I thought not these thoughts then, as I lay in the stilly nights looking from the windows of my little room, breaking the course of the moon from the first pale cold flicker of her empty cycles, to the full glory of her perfection; or pondering of the great untried world outspread under the stars; and of the heaven that seemed so vast and so far. I never felt that we were poor, for I was so rich in all those attributes which tend so much to brighten life, and make it treasured in whatever sphere its altitudes may be cast. There was a genial warmth in God's sunshine, and a glory in all things His hands had created. Oh! now for the worship of that childhood time!

My father marvelled that I never repined at our change of circumstances, he was himself so sore at heart; and when I saw him bowing lower day by day, I began to feel very wicked that I did nothing to take the sting from his crushed spirit; and grasp by one effort of the will all he meant, when he said to me that his "last venture had failed him." There was no change apparent in our household, yet my father came to be a laborer for his daily bread. Wayburn had its manufactories, as have all Northern towns, and at one of these he worked, growing each day more gloomy and morose.

My gentle mother, too, suffered; how good she was to hide the pain that was gnawing at her heart, and appear to sympathize with my gaiety of mood, which seemed only to wound and irritate him. Men so rarely understand their young daughters, though they often forgive the wildest freaks and the gravest incursions upon authority, if the error is perpetrated by a son.

I had one female companion, Leah Eldridge, of whom I was very fond; we often ran riot in our garden grounds while my father sat silent, and mother looked on with an expression I shall never forget. There was such charity for our shortcomings, and such tender love in it.

Oh! where in after years do we find the heart that will hold for us these things like a mother's?

At such times Leah left me early in the evenings; then
I would brush my father's scattered hairs, and pressing a
good-night kiss upon the lips of each, would steal quietly
to my little room and count the stars, until sleep came
so softly to my pillow I half imagined I numbered them
in dreams. Then at morning I would watch the sun, as
with golden fingers he knocked at the portals of Mr. Kingswell's great square house on the slope, just beyond our
grounds, with its white colonnade, and mantling ivy, and
broad sides encrusted with the lichens of years. It was
pleasant to see the mists as they rolled like sheets of crystal
ether from the summits of the New Hampshire hills, with
their forests of cedar rising dark into the sky.

In the early evenings, too, I loved to watch life at the
great house; its ebb and flow; its lights flitting to and fro,
and shining in the darkness like my stars. How strangely
came about my acquaintance with its inmates. I first met
Mrs. Kingswell at the house of Captain Bob Eldridge; so
he was called by everybody in Wayburn. Everybody
seemed to know him; the smallest child could have pointed
out to the curious stranger the eccentric seafarer's abiding-
place.

It was a tall, rickety, old domicile, very barn-like in appearance, with very steep roof and weather-stained gables,
to which were attached martin boxes of a peculiar style of
architecture, around which the wind shrieked and howled
most piteously in the chill seasons; and a greenish slime
choked the few simple blossoms that dared to lift their
trusting heads, and look for summer shine in the atmosphere of such dense thickets of arbor vitæ and box, whose
lower limbs ran together in dense masses on the ground.

Notwithstanding the exterior was thus unprepossessing,
within were the marks of thrift visible everywhere; for

Mrs. Alice was a tidy housewife, and Leah was swiftly growing into the ways her mother had striven to teach her; so, despite one lowering shadow, this too was a happy home.

Mrs. Eldridge had been for years an invalid. She seemed spirit-broken like my father. The ways of sorrow are common ways, and we fall into them very readily.

Captain Bob was a cheerful fellow, very full of jokes and stale aphorisms. He came often to our house, and his visits seemed to cheer my father though they were short, and the evenings usually long; yet his presence, however brief his stay, was a source of comfort to the old man. We love to have those about us who are well and strong, when we are weak and suffer. I say old, though my father was still young in years; I did not then know that time is the last thing to blanch the cheek and silver the hair. There are bypaths to age much shorter than those through the years which we live upon earth; those of grief and sin are briefest of all.

Mrs. Eldridge was suffering more than usual, and Mrs. Kingswell spent much time with her. Even then I had a vague presentiment, which afterwards became a certainty, that kind as was this lady to his wife, her visits annoyed Captain Bob; and that he, of manner usually off-hand and careless, was restive and uncomfortable in her presence. Though I was surprised at the brusque tone of his declination of a courtesy so gentle, when she suggested that her husband would come down with her " in the evening for awhile," the Captain very gruffly thanked her, saying he would prefer, 'since she chose to come, that she came *alone!* The lady's face flushed for a moment, but she checked herself in the manifestation of the slight feeling of resentment for the— " eccentricity" of the old sailor. Yes; she was actually charitable enough to attribute his manner to this source, and her face settled again to its usual sweet placidity when she saw the deprecating, pleading eyes of the sick woman **fixed** earnestly upon **her.** " I will come this evening, as I promised to do," she said, and left the house.

Mrs. Eldridge ventured very timidly to expostulate with **her husband after** their guest had departed, saying:

"**It is** too bad, she has been so kind; it was only this **day** she said it gave her such an unaccountable pleasure to **be** here. I was almost tempted to tell her why it was so. In my younger days I **was** much **like** William. There may yet be enough left of the old manner to have attached her to me. I wanted to take her in my arms and proclaim the tie that existed between us, but I dared not."

Captain Bob was **usually kind** and patient towards his wife, but now he seemed in danger of losing his temper, quite.

"Alice, are you a fool? Excuse me, but have you no **pride**; what would you receive from that man? Did he not, **in his** letter of scathing reproach, bid you 'whatever came to pass, never speak to him, or seek to have him recognise you, for he should feel degraded by the contact?'

"Do you expect me to receive here, in my house, the man who used such insulting language to my wife? Am I to humble myself before this proud aristocrat? He is rich! *I am poor!* But my self-respect equals his, and I would rather die in want than play the despised suppliant to any nabob in the land. Just count *Bob* Eldridge out, will you? Not even for you would I do this; and you well know that during our life together it is the first thing I ever refused which you asked of me, or even hinted would give you pleasure."

His voice had softened much before he uttered the last

words. They were unaware of my presence in an adjoining room, where Leah had left me while she went above stairs to fetch some prints they had brought from China. I felt guilty in thus listening to what it was not designed by either I should hear; and was just on the eve of withdrawing when the wife's gentle tones arrested me, so earnest were they:

"You have always been good to me, Robert, and kind; but you are *unjust to William*. He, too, was good to me once, as he is to the whole world now—of his friends and acquaintances. Those words of his—those written words, which struck us both so cruelly—were hasty; they were unlike any others that came from him; and I have no right, knowing William as I do, to lay them up in anger against him. They were prompted by the first heated impulse upspringing from a deep sense of injury. Ask yourself if you would not have said more had you been in his place and he in yours?"

Captain Bob hung his head, and though he did not admit that she was correct in the assumption of this truth, he certainly did not feel called upon to assert that she was wrong; he remained very sensibly silent while his wife proceeded:

"You are proud, Robert, and self-respectful. So am I; but it has not been pride that has kept me, Alice Eldridge, from William Kingswell. Oh! the bitter, bitter memories that have made such barriers between us. I only remain asunder because I could not early bear to be near him. Could I look him in the face, and have his eyes always saying to me, though his lips were never so silent, 'Ah! Alice, there are two graves at your old home which, but for you, had not been made so early?' I could never bear this, and that is why we have not met; that is why I have blindly obeyed your mandate. Yes; believe and forgive me, Robert, *the only* reason."

The Captain was visibly moved, and said in a tender tone, "And did you love me, Alice, and are you *sorry* that you went away with me!" She turned her tearful eyes upon him; the same dear love for him that always shone there was shining still. "No, Robert! not sorry I went, but sorry I *stayed*. I was so vainly happy in your love. I never thought how my poor, blind mother's heart was breaking for her wayward child. After I became a mother I could understand those things, and that was why I wished to come back, but it was too late; they were gone, and the old home desolate. Though I would see William, Robert, before I die—go away never to come back; just one word to tell me you consent."

He sat thinking, with his head upon his hand. I was thinking, too, perhaps it was better not. Sympathy cannot take the sting from the remorseful heart, however potent in alleviating sorrow. Leah came back at this juncture, and I heard no more save a few broken sobs at intervals, and then a heavy, low, deep sigh from Captain Bob; from a soul that refused to be loosed from the torture-rack of its error. These are the most galling spirit-bonds, where reason and judgment assert a premise which will and inclination utterly disclaim. Oh! had he but known, that rough, though kind-hearted man, how one little word fitly spoken would have opened wide the gates, through man's pardon, to a just God's; have taken off the dragging weight of a terrible life-long suspense from the wings of a noble spirit; unsealed the close-shut fountains of tenderness in the heart of a worthy man; taken girlish feet from out the ways of temptation, where the lines of her life might chance to fall, and the possibilities of sin, to place them on the heights where principle would hold them firm, and those, too, his child's—his young daughter's feet. And more perhaps than all this, taken a thorn from out his dying wife's side; and strewn with beautiful flowers even the darkness of that death in whose lowering shadow he then groped. All this *one little word* might have done, and yet the summer went by for them. The harvest of its golden days was ended; and that one word, under sun or stars, was never spoken.

I remember one evening Captain Bob came round as usual; he had left Mrs. Kingswell with his wife. He and my father sat talking, or rather he talked and we listened, until it was far into the night. This was his story, told feelingly at broken intervals, interspersed with such aphorisms as he always chose to season his discourses. Some strange caprice had unlocked the floodgates this night.

"I think, Mr. Montana, a man should think long and seriously before he takes a young girl from her parents' roof into the rough world with him, no matter how dear his love for her, or what the feelings which prompted him. It may do very well while the money lasts, but when wealth is gone, and health is gone—aye! sir, 'there's the rub.' When I was able to support my wife in a style to which she was accustomed before, I was happy and she was happy; but now, since we have fallen from that estate, she droops, and I have to see her failing day by day, and I cannot help her. Oh! it is very hard, Mr. Montana; very hard, sir."

He bowed his head, and I could see by the light of my stars that there were tears upon his cheek. Then he proceeded as if talking in justification of himself:

"Though, in sooth, a less susceptible man than myself would have loved my Alice, for she was a beauty and no mistake. Our acquaintance was so romantic, too. I sat singing one afternoon as I watched the lowering quay—our ship had just come into port—one of my wild sailor songs, when she, chancing to pass that way, paused to listen ; perceiving the motion I sank my voice to its most melodious tone, and chanted rather than sang one of those old ballads which I had heard the Italians sing when steering their gondoliers by moonlight on the Arno. The song concluded, she passed on. I, charmed by her wondrous beauty, followed her at a respectful distance to see where she lived. Then I sent her flowers every day ; then it came to pass that she recognised me, and we exchanged notes at stated intervals ; and I knew she loved me, though she never invited me to call.

"I was not far wrong in my suspicions as to the true cause of my exclusion. She had many suitors—one, who was accepted *by her parents ;* and she well knew they would never look with any degree of favor on me. My pride was hurt at this, for Bob Eldridge was one whose conduct had never been such as to exclude from him the right to stand up as the equal of any *honest* man, whatever difference circumstances might make in their conditions. So I said to myself, 'There are pretty women in every port ; do not make a fool of yourself, Bob, about this one ;' but I had grown to be twenty-five without having really loved any one, until Alice, with her sweet face, crossed my path. And the more I tried to forget her, the more impossible I found it to do so. I was man, too ; and there were both revenge and vanity in my nature. I resolved to marry her at all hazard. Her haughty friends would have looked down on me and called me plebeian, and I for this meant to set their authority and scruples at defiance. Then there were two or three young men, each of whom fancied himself the favored suitor of Alice. I just thought **how** charming it would be to play a Spanish trick upon the whole ship's crew of them; and Alice readily consenting to my proposals, we were married on the vessel the very morning she sailed—Alice merely leaving a note behind to say she had 'found a protector who was better suited to her than any they could have selected.' We neither of us thought what false construction might be and was put upon **her** hasty flight, until William Kingswell's letter came to us beyond the seas. He **should have known** Alice better than it seems he did. No; we never dreamed of this, **we** were so happy. I felt very like a prince to have that beautiful young thing clinging to me, all my own; I, as she said, 'her only protector.' And at evening, sitting on the broad deck with my arms around her, and the great sea heaving round us both, I sang to her the old songs **under** the stars, and thanked the Master who had held the helm in all the storms through which I had passed for His **gift.**

" I had always spent money very freely, but I had saved a very pretty sum, and for years Alice never wanted a luxury ; and it has been my pride to say that even in the darkest days of our reverses she never lacked a comfort. We might yet have been happy and prosperous in our home beyond the sea ; but after she heard of the death of her parents— she was tenderly attached to both—more especially her mother, who had been blind from birth, she seemed possessed of an uncontrollable desire to return to her native land. Then when we came to her old home, she could not bear to remain there ; so we drifted out here, and somehow we have been going down hill ever since ; for now I see that she is leaving me from day to day ; I have little heart to work, and seem to care very little about prosperity. True, there is Leah; but what will I do with the girl, and no mother to train and teach her?"

Captain Bob looked down here. Again I saw his tears swift falling in the still, white moonlight, but he soon recovered himself, and then went on to say as though he had never ceased his narrative : "I wish, though, that Alice had never insisted upon my coming to Wayburn. I did not know until recently it was because William Kingswell had located here."

"**Does** he suspect," said my father, "that she is——"

"No, no! and what is more, I do not intend he shall. My pride is too strong for that. **His** wife seems an **angel**, almost, and Alice is very fond of her. And they two **have** well-nigh upset my plans several times; but why am I talking idly on and on of the things which oppress me from day to day? I must be going. You will not betray me, I am sure. Come **back to work as** soon as **you are able.** We want you; the hands need a *master*-spirit." Here Captain Bob laughed a rather hollow-sounding laugh at his **own** joke. As there was **a heart of tenderness, so was** there a broad, sunny area in the nature of this man—very commonplace, yet possessing attributes that isolated him from the majority of his kind. It was one of his most marked peculiarities that he never failed to see the point of his own jokes, however blunt and imperceptible they were to others. Now he bade us adieu, and went singing down the road, thinking, perhaps, the effort at gaiety might take the weight from his spirits. Men are strange creatures; they turn the by-paths to avoid sorrow, and when **they must stand** face to face with it, how they seek, by many an idle subterfuge, to escape from its circling influence.

It so happened that I was ill for several weeks, confined at home; and when I was able to go abroad, Captain Bob made no longer a pretence of singing away the dreary weight that oppressed him; surely, now, there was nothing left him but to face his woe.

Poor old man, how I pitied him, sitting alone with Leah in the solitary house. The wife and mother's chair was empty; from her earthly dwelling-place she had been transferred to a house whose roof was low and narrow, and long and dark—close shut within four walls. There she slept, out under the clinging sunshine, under the stars—in her last house—*the grave!* The house for which the rich and mighty of this world must exchange their "castles full of splendor," and the weak and the weary find their first, long, dreamless rest. Ah! as surely, too, was " that vast sea which rolls round all the world," bearing my loved ones on its bosom; and upon the shores of youth and morning wave meeting wave, and the circle that runs its round with the race of man, came into itself again. To those that were going, gone, there was the boundless area of an immortal destiny; while to me, who loitered playing with the golden sands—and to the desolate old man in his solitary home, his motherless child clinging to him, and the waves, fiercer than those he had often ridden at half-mast, when the storm-clouds were dark and tides ran high, lashing him as he sat on the barren, beaten shore—this house was alike long and low and narrow and dark, when those we held most dear were locked in its grim silences; and of all that had been to each of us, only this green-growing door, shut close until the resurrection morn, to drop tears upon.

There the soul of youth and the soul of age kept tireless watches of memory under the eternal stars.

———o———

CHAPTER II.

"Love is not in our power,
Nay, what seems stranger, is not in our choice;
We only love where fate ordains we should."

FROUDE.

I ROSE quite early one morning, and walked out to my favorite haunt on the strand. The sun, just rising, had stained to amber the current of the bright-flowing river, with its flood of golden beams. Long I sat in the still glory, as I was accustomed to do on mornings like this, tracing names upon the sand, and watching the light waves as they came up to wash them out. Soft gliding down the stream came a small sail-boat, light and airy as a swallow, cutting the smooth surface with her painted prow, in which sat a youth of most striking appearance.

Turning his skiff half round, resting on the left oar, he floated with the current near to where I sat, then sprang lightly on the sands. There was a grandeur on his face as he stood, the bright morning reflected from waves that kissed the shore at our feet, girding him about as with a retinue of sunbeams. He regarded me with a look half amused; as he bowed with a grace so winning and courteous, I was undecided whether it were best to treat him with the frankness due a boy, or the reserve with which I would have received a man whose years bespoke for him a man's prerogative of earnest civility.

He wore a suit of spotless linen, silken half-hose, and slippers of shining leather, panama hat with broad black band; his collar and wristbands were fastened with buttons it dazzled my eyes to look upon. These little details of dress I mention because they form a part of the strange mystic impression that fixed itself upon me then as presenting so striking a contrast to the sober, drab-apparelled youth of Wayburn.

"I fear I have interrupted **your very** pleasant occupation," he said, naïvely. "It is a favorite pastime of *mine;* I love **to trace names** upon the sand, yet how soon the tides wash them out." I am sure I blushed, for I was so confused I could make no reply, but sat heaping up the shining particles, my hands dripping with the surf. He added, apologetically :

"I have few lady acquaintances in Wayburn ; I wish we could be friends ; **I am sure that I** should like you, now that I have found you here the presiding genius of wave and sunbeam—tracing names **upon** the sand. Why not write your inscriptions **where they will** be more lasting? **Nature is** an inconstant jade, for ever ringing in the dirges **of her seasons.** Do not trust her, she is faithless ; she will not teach **us** the lessons which, as sweethearts and lovers, we should **know.** **They** should wear the insignia of eternal truth."

I looked at him very quizzically, forgetting how embarrassed I had been, thinking he must be a very precocious fellow to talk about love in any sense. I was as romantic as young ladies given to star-gazing and romance-reading are expected to be in their pinafore days. Yet it was difficult for one of my ardent temperament to detect in the form of my cavalier one feature in accordance with my standard of a hero, who would probably talk about "*wooing* nature," or "sweethearts," or "lovers," or "eternal truth." Nor in my humble estimate had an individual any right to aspire to such distinction who had not arrived at the dignity of his first beard, even though he wore diamond buttons of first water and lifted his panama hat to a simple rustic like myself with the grace of Adonis. I imagine he

divined my thoughts, for he said, half seriously, half play-
fully :

"Your ideas of love are circumscribed. To what age or
condition does it specially belong? What power has ever
yet encompassed its vast range? To childhood and youth
it is one thing, to philosophers another, to painters and
poets yet another, to the great heart of nature and humanity
still another. There can be no standard sufficiently just
and accurate to measure what is illimitable. Again, can
love, a thing itself infinite, be reduced to system involving form and law?" I felt that this youth, at whom I
should have sneered five minutes ago, was entirely without
the pale of my ridicule; being disinclined to measure
lances with him, I terminated a brief fit of musing with the
question, "Do you live here?"

"No; I am only sojourning at Wayburn with my uncle,
Mr. Kingswell. New Orleans is my native place, and there
I reside a portion of each year."

My feeling now was more than mere surprise! It was
the wrapping about my Northern proportions the garb of
sectional sanctity, in a manner that said, "I am holier than
thou!" From that land, reeking with the curse of Ca-
naan; that far away Sodom, which I had been taught to
regard with horror, not by my parents but by teachers and
ministers of the gospel, who looked at the evil through the
spectacles of a fanaticism which lent no enchantment to the
view. I pursed up my mouth with a very self-righteous
expression, and bade my cavalier a cold good-morning;
with the same graceful alacrity that marked his demeanor
on landing, he fastened his boat and was by my side, ere I
was aware of his intention, to accompany me home.

"Do you live here?" he said, as I halted at the piazza
of our vine-covered cottage, the dimensions of which he

had compassed in one hasty, indifferent glance. Now I had asked of him a similar question previously; he responding politely and kindly. Why could not I do likewise? Because my eyes were blinded to one of those grand truths luminous as the sun in heaven. One of the lights shrouded with the dark mantle of prejudice might make for us, were reason and judgment permitted to rend the veil in twain, the radiance of a great peace in the glooms where a nation lies struggling, bleeding, *under her stars!*

Perhaps, too, it was because I contrasted my humble sphere with his evidently superior position that I answered him with such bitter asperity.

" Yes, and my father is a day-laborer in yonder factory. You who are taught to look upon work as beneath the dignity of *ladies* and *gentlemen*—regarding those who in your esteem degrade themselves necessarily in the performance of any duty, as slaves are menial, I presume would scarcely have taken the trouble to escort me home had you known me as the daughter of such a one."

" Then you mistake me very much," he answered, with sudden dignity and not a little coldness in his tone. " I was taught by my parents not to recognise between the people of any locality or the representatives of any race, distinctions, save those traced by the hand of God. There is no superiority save the majesty of mind, which gives dignity to any system, and asserts itself in any condition. It was this I saw shining in your face when we met. My mother was a Northern woman, my stepfather and present guardian is a Northern man; believe me, we in the South think much less of these things than you affect to do. I fear, however, I am guilty of unpardonable intrusion; I hope you can forgive me; I will promise not to offend again. Good-morning!"

Strange, strange, in the days that came and went, go often as I would to my old trysting-place, I saw him no more; but that one golden morning, with its brightness circling about him, shone in my life for ever after. Several times I saw him lying under the shadow of the great trees on the terraces of Ridgely.

Time passed. I traced names upon the sand and the waves washed them out, until the summer was quite gone and the amber **glow of** late October was on the New Hampshire hills. Still my golden river glided on—on; now under the bright **sky of** morning, now under the stars. Whither was it **bearing me in my** dream? Why was it I sang no longer through **the** days, but pondered more frequently about our change of circumstances, and grew more into the home ways with a gentler care for all?

Even now as I look back I can find no place in the far sunbright memory for what **came next.**

My father went one morning **to his** work as usual, but **soon** returned pale and **ghastly as a** corpse. He sank fainting into a chair. My mother's shriek brought Eleanor, our maid of all work, to her aid; while I, stupified, lent my assistance in the application of such restoratives as we could command. **We soon had the** happiness of seeing him so much revived that by noon he was enabled to sit against a prop of pillows, and talk very calmly to my mother **about** the things he wished, and **what it** would be needful **for us** to do when he was gone. **At length, after a** long interval of sobbing, my mother said brokenly:

" **May I not write to Clifford** James, **and** tell him your true situation? Perhaps, after all, it has not been the want of brotherly affection that has kept him from you; it may be that the cares and the responsibilities of his Southern life have so multiplied about him, he finds no leisure for the duties that once were pleasures. Let me tell him how your final venture has failed you, and the last effort is fruitless."

"No, no, wife; he neglected me when my position was equal to his. I know not who was most to blame; but I do know that one of those sectional barriers grew up gradually and strong between our brother hearts. I railed at his slaveholding. He has requited my interference with years of silent, contemptuous indifference. I cannot now be brought to force my broken life upon his remembrance. He would not like to hear the sad story."

Oh, pride! thou who dost build barriers between brother hearts and other hearts that love, in all the highways and byways of this earth! thou shouldst have no place here— where one broken, sorrowing man is coming down with weary feet to the border-land of death—where his brother, too, shall come one day—down from the high eminence of wealth and position, lowly as he should stand now by his side—though one should stay, and one go out into the unknown alone.

Unable to combat these thoughts, for I had often regretted my father's estrangement from his brother, I passed to my own room, where I could weep in solitude. Unconsciously I walked to the low window and looked out through tears of silent bitterness upon my bright river, golden still, in the autumn noonday. A light-hearted child, should I ever play upon its banks again? Echo answered " again?" —my heart responded—never, any more.

I was closing the blinds when the Ridgely carriage passed with the Southern youth and Mary Kingswell, lounging gracefully on the cushions. Her fair face was shaded by a jaunty hat, and he held her hand in his. Why not? —she was his cousin. Though somehow, the sight hurt

2

me. I shrank back peevishly, closing the blinds with a snap of the clasp, and returned to my father's room.

There I found Mr. Kingswell sitting by his side. I knew my father had sent Eleanor to his place of business for him, though I had not expected such promptitude in answer to the summons.

"You are not well, Mr. Montana," he said kindly, wiping from his brow the perspiration that chill autumn day, for he had come hastily, not knowing what need there might be.

"No, no—it is almost over," answered my father composedly. "I sent for you, sir, because I know you are the friend of the widow and orphan. I am sure you will comply with my request. I have a brother in the South; there is no kindly tie between us. For myself I will ask nothing, but when all is ended for me here, you will write to him; will you not, in behalf of my wife and daughter, solicit from him a home which I shall not be able to leave them? There is a mortgage on this cottage which would more than cover what it would bring if disposed of now. That was the money I lost in my last unlucky speculation. You will be kind enough to attend to the sale for me; there may be enough left to pay you for your trouble; if not, God will reward you, sir; I am sure of it."

"You trust Him then," said Mr. Kingswell, searchingly. The answer came tremulously:

"Yes, though only through Christ's mercy have I hope."

"Who of us dare hope for pardon on the score of our own questionable merit?" said Mr. Kingswell again, with true humility. "Trusting and feeling this as you do, my friend, while you hope for forgiveness through God's great mercy, have you shown mercy and forgiveness to your brother?—have you left any evidence that he was pardoned; that the bitterness has passed away from your spirit?—if so, ask of him these things yourself. I will transfer your messages, verbal or written, to Mr. Clifford Montana—whose wife was one of my earliest friends—through my nephew, Clyde Ingram, who leaves for New Orleans to-morrow." There was some pre-occupation in Mr. Kingswell's manner, and the light of far-off memory in his patient eyes, as he added:

"I hope you will rest easy, my friend; I will arrange all things as you have suggested." He took my father's hand with an expression almost divine resting like sunshine on his noble face; he held it in that strong firm clasp which always springs spontaneously from great hearts, adding— "You will try and write your brother, if only a few words, will you not?"

There was pleading in his tones now, and my father promised; he could not do otherwise. Who else with so few words could have effected a reunion between those widely severed hearts, and how was he able so to do? Only because there was that in his daily life which convinced men, thinking men like my father, of an eloquent fact: he was striving humbly and patiently to do God's work on earth; every word and deed gave strength to the conviction. From his apparent earnest desire to do good to his fellow-man, came the power with which he swayed my father.

He left us then; with my father's last remnant of strength he wrote the letter to my uncle. When he had finished, a great peace came to him, and never left him any more—the issue was with God.

Later in the afternoon Mrs. Kingswell came, taking from her carriage—the same carriage in which Clyde Ingram had ridden out with her daughter at noon-time—a basket filled with delicacies to which we were unaccustomed; for our home fare was very frugal. With her own hands she made the tea, and beguiled my father into drinking a cup, which refreshed him very much. When she took her leave, carrying with her the letter which her husband's nephew was to bear with him on his homeward journey to the far South, there were many sunbeams glistening in the room, which I had not observed at her coming. My poor father looked after her, a bright, sparkling tear fell on my hand, holding his own, as he exclaimed:

"She is one of God's angels of mercy! Oh! if her arms were long enough to embrace all she loves, they would be thrown around the whole world. How many come within the range of her care it is impossible to know, for she goes everywhere; her husband's means, without limit, are at her disposal. Many among the poor in this quiet town can attest her goodness. Some that lie cold on yonder hill died blessing her; many more live, saved by her timely aid and kindness."

Day after day she came and ministered. Night after night I sat looking out sorrowfully at my pitying stars, and the pale, cold moonbeams as they gathered around the New Hampshire hills, around the sheltering house of Ridgely; its terraces sloping down to where the river, not golden now, glided slow and grey between its locks and falls, until the liquid track was lost in mist and foam below; —thinking of this death.

It came at last. My father was borne along the shadowy road—shut in from our sight by the new-made grave in the cemetery just above Ridgely. I kept ceaseless vigil at my mother's side, until she too, worn by anxiety and sorrow, sank to rest.

After that I knew no more, for so long it seemed; and even now, as I look back to that dark time, the events are confused. Of my mother's going to sleep one cold, grey night, when there were no stars shining; no music in the

roar of the rushing river—going to sleep very soundly, while
I watched—I have an indistinct remembrance. Then of
Mrs. Kingswell coming at morning trying to arouse her,
talking meanwhile to some strange lady about me, and how
she said " Poor stricken child" as she took my hand away,
for it was locked tightly in the cold death-grasp of my mother. I seemed to hear the crashing, too, of the great door
of destiny which shut me out into the world of loneliness
and orphanhood.

After that the weeks seemed a blank, for I struggled with
brain-fever, and it left me no power to remember. I am
very thankful the sorrow of that summer season has not
lingered with me ; for oftenest when I go back to the days
when I lived with my parents in the cottage at Wayburn,
the same blue sky is over them, and at nightfall I looked
to see the old stars shining, with their gentle, then sorrowful radiance. I can recall too, the dark, earnest eyes of the
handsome youth, who even then looked into the deeps of
my soul with the eyes of destiny. At other periods the
sky of memory is overclouded; then I see only two graves
and a lot cast amid the richer flowers of a southern land.
Flowers that blossomed brightly once. Now they will
bloom no more ; for a deluge of blood has swept them
away. With hearts young and warm and brave, which, too,
have sunk beneath thy crimson tides, O revolution !

Can it be that upon the darkness which shrouds their
last sleep, a nation's stars refuse to shine ?

Aye ! but God's stars do not withhold their radiance, and
I will, of many, keep bright and glowing the memory
—for I loved them—still love them—and feel assured
that he is able, and will awaken them to all the beatitudes
of a perfect peace.

CHAPTER III.

"Oh! there are tones and looks that dart
An instant sunshine through the heart;
As if the soul that minute caught
Some treasure it through life had sought."

MOORE.

A GREAT blank succeeds in memory; the sky of stars and river gliding goldenly under the bright morning and calmly under the clear arching noonday. An overwhelming consciousness of desolation succeeded the long journey which I made in company with Mrs. Montana, who I could scarcely realize was my uncle's wife. On arriving at her magnificent home I was ill again for a long time; when convalescence came lingeringly, it was difficult to grow familiar with my new surroundings.

Every tie binding me to the old life seemed utterly broken. I was sensible through the misty dimness of the presence of many who were kind to me; but my poor heart was dumb as my lips, and made no response to any save the lady who had taken my hand from a dead mother's clasp—it seemed to me—ages before.

Among the visions which floated up in the strange bewilderment, there was one with form and curls that clustered like morning light about the beautiful head; a sweet face bent over me often, and cherry lips called me sister; but as yet I could make no answer, the old wounds were bleeding too profusely.

One afternoon I seemed to waken, soul and sense, as from a long, restless lethargy. Windows were wide open, and the delicious aroma of a thousand flowers came to me like the resurrection of buried summers. I could only weep in unison when I heard the fall of a fountain near with a liquid murmur like trickling tears. I was puzzled:

could it be that I had slept while that long winter of grief had passed into the spring? While I mused, a face—the face of my morning dream at Wayburn—appeared, to look, as he thought, upon my unconscious rest. At this juncture a bright-eyed mulatto girl came from her post of duty to inquire if I wanted anything. I did not; nothing that she could give me: I only wanted to think and to be rid of her presence. I dismissed her by saying "my head ached, and I should prefer to be alone."

"Lord bless you, Miss, I wouldn't dare to leave you for a single minnit; Miss Stanley rode down to town with young Mars, and she gave me my orders to stay right here in this room until she came back."

I was about to inquire who Miss Stanley was, when the lady herself looked in at the open door. She wore a jaunty riding-cap of blue velvet plumed with white, and her curls rippled in waves of gold upon the rich blue of her habit. With light footstep she came to where the mulatto stood, and spoke softly in tones as silvery as the murmuring fountain without: "Has she been quiet since I left, Hawsey, and have you waited upon her well? Are you sure?" she added, surrendering to the girl her whip, gauntlets, etc. "Yes, marm," was the creature's only response to the several inquiries of her mistress.

Stanley retired briefly to her own apartment for the purpose of changing her costume; she reappeared clad in a dress of flowing white. Coming to my side as I lay with my thin hand shading my tear-wet eyes, she kissed me, supposing me to be asleep. The little caress thrilled me through and through; I clasped her in my arms; my heart had broken the chains of its stern silence; henceforth, from that day and hour, she was my best-beloved, my soul sister.

From her lips I learned that she was my cousin, the daughter of Uncle Clifford Montana. She had one brother, with whom she had ridden that afternoon; she called him Ray; and another, who, though no relative, was in truth all of a brother and more: her mother's stepson. I asked her mother's former name. *Edith Ingram.*

I lay quite still now, holding her hand in my own, which trembled a little, from physical weakness of course! Edith Ingram, the face I had seen at my window, then, was no dream. The odor of flowers, and murmur of the fountain; the soft luxurious atmosphere; the almost fabulous splendor of the room in which I lay, was so strange! Yet the break in my life was still yawning widely at my side; a gulf never to be recrossed. But the flower-strewn vistas of a new life were open to me—outstretching where? Ah, who could foresee that!

I closed my eyes, still holding those tiny hands of Stanley, saw my stars arise from that long night of pain, counted the sands upon far-away shores that I had left, and the youth who came adown the stream in the morning light; saw my golden river gliding—gliding as it chimed its ripple with the murmuring fountain, flowing outward until it seemed to mingle confusedly with the roar of the sea.

All these things were present with me often; and during that tardy convalescence Stanley was beside me always. When I was strong enough to walk, Clyde Ingram came to escort me below stairs. Upon his young arm I leaned during those first tottering steps about the beautiful grounds of Claremont. He had adopted a singular system of retaliation for the hospitality I had manifested towards him in my own land. I saw that he remembered it; for he really seemed to take pardonable pleasure in thus heaping coals of fire on the defenceless head of his ancient enemy.

He was too generous, however, to vaunt his triumph in my present weak state of mind and body; that would not have been politic. How handsome he was! more so, even, than I remembered him; and the light of genius, grand and glorious, beamed from every lineament of his classic face, and burned in his deep, clear eyes. Afterwards, whenever I walked, Clyde or Raymond was at my side. That summer was like a wandering amid the flowers of fairy-land. Old misunderstandings, arising from prejudice, were forgotten, and oh! we were all so happy together. In the autumn we separated; Stanley and myself were sent away to school, Raymond and Clyde went to a German university.

We met not again for four years; years of study, of mental and physical development for all of us; to Clyde and Raymond, years of classic research amid time-stained records of the ancient masters for treasures that other years could not dim. Meantime, Stanley and myself, busy in acquiring more superficial accomplishments, thought most of their return.

To Claremont those four springs came soft and dreamy as the first one I remember there. The summers, too, glided by with calm quietness as by-gone summers at Wayburn were wont to do. Autumn came gently to the last of these. October had kindled her fires in the dark line of forest rising high into the lurid sky, tinged with the gleam of boughs glancing brightly in the red sunshine; rich flowers, preceding the fall, blossomed everywhere. The birds sang gaily as in spring-time; voices came softly from beyond the grey expanse of sea, so plaintive and subdued, they seemed the echo of golden harps swept by the fingers of unforgotten dead.

This was the season in which Clyde and Raymond came back. I had parted very tenderly from my young cavalier

2*

four years previous. He had told me, with a look in his
great, earnest eyes which I shall never forget, "how he
would miss me when the sea rolled between us." I had
treasured those words till the coming back. Now they
were returned, cousin Raymond—our frank, handsome
Ray—had taken me into his arms and kissed me again and
again; Stanley and Clyde greeted each other, meantime,
no less warmly, yet when the latter came to me holding out
his arms I could not for my life have gone into his embrace.
There was something in the face and manner of the tall,
elegant young man, so removed, so different from the boy
with whom I had parted, abashed, I shrank back in silence.
The same earnest eyes pleaded, " Have *you* no greeting for
me ? " Only for an instant, then the look of surprised inquiry passed ; then one of pain was succeeded by an expression of wounded pride. He glanced at Raymond—his
face flushed, then grew white. Well I knew how his sensitive nature had withdrawn into its own grand proportions,
though these mute evidences were all that he gave of having felt a slight that cut him to the soul. This was not our
first painful misunderstanding—would to Heaven it had
been our last !

Winter came and passed, just touching with frosty finger
the flowers and grasses ; but the ice-king found no welcome
in this balmy tropical clime when he would have girded it
about with frozen chains.

It was morning, dewy and crisp, in the spring succeeding. How fragrant the aureole breath ; how the amber
sunshine wrapped us in its folds as we stood in the grand
arcade of our Southern homestead waiting—Stanley and I,
patiently as even the most exacting might expect us to do,
while holding in strictest remembrance certain innuendoes
which a gentleman, Clyde Ingram—of whose tardiness we

were the amiable victims in the present instance—had cast at us in days that were gone for delinquencies of like nature; which even those **most** addicted to fault-finding could but decide was not a circumstance compared to the delay which had kept us in an urbane state of "durance vile" for the space of half an hour; during which probationary season we had paid due court to sundry reflections and refractions of our persons in the mirror of the escritoire; each succeeding glance only serving to confirm the original impression that no improvement was necessary. Being thus fortified with the opinions of two ladies of taste and judgment, we cajoled ourselves and each other into the belief that we were looking quite as well as it was possible to do, the style of each subdued by a drab travelling suit surmounted by a hat of similar hue, when Clyde made his smiling appearance, announcing his entire readiness to depart.

The astounding fact would under other circumstances have called down upon his guilty head a tirade of raillery —an indulgence quite dignified and fashionable in these days. I cannot tell how it happened, the aforesaid scolding Clyde did not receive upon that day or any other; for each had its own record of such enjoyments on his part, yet I am sure he remembered gratefully long afterwards that he was minus one tongue-lashing. Perhaps it was because we knew he had been in Aunt Edith's room in close conference with her, for we saw tears upon her cheeks when she came out to us; scarcely less dear than her own manly boy was to her *this son of his dead father.*

Then came the adieux upon which I will not linger; suffice it to say Stanley and I were in imminent danger of having our self-sustained verdict reversed; for a gushing shower of drops had almost washed the roses from our cheeks ere we became conscious that this time Clyde was

the martyr, not the patient one we had been either, as he
stood tapping his patent leathers with a spray of catalpa,
and whistling an air from Lucia de Lammermoor, in the
interval of directing servants who were *loading* the
baggage.

I speak advisedly; for so ponderous a quantity of lug-
gage rarely falls to the honest portion of two unpretending
young misses of the modest dimensions of Stanley and myself.   Finally the last article was safely deposited; from the
two-story trunk, in a capacious corner of which we might
have buried ourselves after the capricious fashion of Ginevra
—should fancy have dictated so *grave* a course—to the
brown paper parcel quite *Dickens-onian* in appearance, containing sandwiches and other elements of comfort wrapped
in a snowy napkin which peeped suggestively from the
willow basket which Stanley persistently refused to abandon,
influenced by private injunctions of mine, and fortified with
a colored legion headed by Aunt Dinah, who I think
religiously believed that travellers' salvation depends upon
sandwiches.   I am furthermore assured, upon the best
evidence, that the old lady's idea of the peace and comfort
of heaven lies in the hope that she may find plenty of
sandwiches there.   She had been the faithful slave of the
Ingrams during a long lifetime; yet I do not believe I
should be doing her injustice to assert that should a shadow
of doubt regarding the truth of these views, in strict adher-
ence to which her head had grown white, cross her mind,
she would prefer remaining for ever within the immediate
vicinage of these creature comforts, to being emancipated
in a region where they were not.

Our cavalier rebelled at the sight of the basket; but all
his protestations and the most comforting assurance of
coffee by the way, could not annihilate one of Aunt Dinah's

blunt straightforward arguments in favor of the sandwiches; so he yielded reluctantly and came back to where Aunt Edith stood. After pressing the last kiss upon her lips, he entreated her again and again to take good care of herself—she was not so well as she had been—and expressed an ardent hope to find her better on his return; a hope which found a dim sad echo in my heart, for I had a presentiment that in this world Aunt Edith would never be strong and well any more.

"I will not forget," he said, in his deep, rich voice, "what you have said to me this morning, mother; I shall treasure your words—I will take my place in the world's front ranks, and cause you yet to feel that your tender care of my infant years was not misplaced."

He spoke these words with his strong arm around the frail form of the woman who had held him in her true heart, and loved him as her own; somehow he seemed the only tie between buried years and a love whose loss she mourned still—a tenure yet so strong; though the mists of another separate life had fallen, the radiance was not wholly dimmed. A fitful gleam of the old fire was in her heart, and the light in her eyes was for him alone; Stanley and I had no share in it. He saw it too and felt it, for he caught her in his arms again, as though he would keep always the love that was pouring out its last riches upon us on earth. But ah! the angel love that would be ours for ever!

Perhaps it was the electric power of this sympathy—my part of a common grief—a joint sorrow, that caused the touch of Clyde's hand to thrill me as he handed me after Stanley into the carriage, and took his place beside me. I never have seen him look as he did then; the dim shadow of future years was in his deep eyes; a sure foreboding of impending bereavement shone from out their depths. He neither saw nor felt our presence—of course we chose not to remind him of facts so apparent—only waited with an undefined perception that a world of ambition was belted by that little space of thought.

As we passed the curve in the road, and the trees which one by one like silent sentinels of the morning hid Claremont—dear, lovely Claremont, and the pale spiritual mother-face from our view—the face that had shone as the sun in his childhood, we ceased to remember it would not always shine for us. When the full glory of the day burst upon us, the shadow was gone; for youth is buoyant and sanguine, prolific of many sources of enjoyment. We turned our faces towards the city, whose spires stretched heavenward to the God who looked upon it, all astir in the morning light; and the blue gulf stretching far away to its ocean boundary, the river with its myriad fleets paling in the sweet May sunshine—heard the drowsy murmur of the breeze, the hum of bees, and the distant song of the lark from groves of palmetto and larch, reaching a dim wilderness of sea-green from the east windows of Claremont to the gate of Sunrise.

Crushing the shells of the beautiful lake-shore road beneath the wheels of our ponderous carriage, we soon found ourselves upon Canal street, incorporated with vehicles uncompromising as our own. We waited some time in front of my uncle's bank, surrounded by the tumultuous din, ere the august dignitary made his appearance. During years of Southern life, he had not become a devotee at the court of its customs, or learned to take things easy. At length he came out, a pen behind his ear, spectacles upon his head, his hand full of exchanges which he transferred to Clyde for our joint benefit. He then bid us a hasty good-by, adding the pleasing information in anything but an amiable tone—Raymond tired of waiting for us, and had gone somewhere, he knew not where; but of one thing he was certain, we should miss the train if we went to look for him. He thought, however, it would be well enough to call at the Saint Charles, then drive speedily to the depôt, as though such a thing were possible, until we had been emancipated from that thronged thoroughfare—Canal street. We did not find Raymond; we scarcely succeeded in reaching our destination, having girded on an armor of the defensive and "run the blockade," successfully edging our way through jostling crowds, almost deafened by the sounds of preparation for departure, undergoing the necessary preliminaries—passing through the routine with the pleasant consciousness of having left one of our party behind.

Scarcely had we taken our seats, when Ray sauntered into the car whistling with that air of careless *abandon,* half reckless, half self-dependent, which sits so gracefully upon Southern youth to the manner born. His face was radiant beneath the *leghorn hat,* sitting jauntily upon his curls. He crushed the tendrils of my hand in his firm grasp, and kissed Stanley vigorously, as a brother might be expected to do such a sister.

"Just in time," he exclaimed, as the sharp click of the engine drowned the thunder-tones in which the conductor vaunted to us the startling fact, that we were "*all aboard!*" the clang of the bell reiterating an assertion which was barely a verity, so far as our party was concerned.

Raymond remarked how very narrowly the pompous individual in shining hat had escaped telling a fib. Then we all laughed merrily as participants in the earnest drama of a *frantic rush* could laugh, whose triumph was so hardly won. Our mirth was succeeded by a pensive quietness; as the train crept softly through the suburbs, we with one accord turned to take a last view of Claremont.

The May day was very full of memories of our days together there, never to be forgotten ; there were long loiterings upon the bright green hillsides, and flower gatherings in the valley sunshine ; there were hand-clasps remembered, and words of kindness from those who had so brightened my orphan life, treasured in that season during which we four had lived and loved together ; to whose dewy morning time, weary and awed by the greatness of the after-pilgrimage, we turned so often back from the dusty highway, upon which a burning sun of actualities had risen to that period, when with fresh hopes and fresh hearts we enjoyed lifetimes in the lightness of one summer's radiance and the fragrance of its flowers.

On and on we passed, more swiftly now ; and when the sun of that day of our departure from Claremont was merged in noon's fierce heat, the loved home with its groves of bright-winged birds, its shadowy walks, and the lonely mother's eye wandering through them ; the city with its towering spires and gilded domes ; the river with its painted fleets, and gulf, whose mists were all cleared away, blazing like a silver sheet passed to the ocean—all these which we saw at morning were soon far behind us, so we cast dreaming to the winds and surrendered ourselves to the pleasures of the moment. The monotony was varied by snatches of sweet carolling from Stanley, interlarded with fragmentary bursts of eloquence from Raymond ; varied by an occasional recitation from myself, who, for the most part, was delighted to play auditor while Clyde recalled some trifling though interesting incident of their life beyond the seas. I was very often interrupted in my quiet enjoyment, to parry for Clyde, who was shrinking and sensitive, some acrimonious shaft aimed by Ray in his merriment; though oftentimes for hours together my strategy was held in strictest requisition to defend my unoffending self against some merciless prank perpetrated by this common enemy of our peace.

How charming we found the little incidents of travel, including sandwiches, lemon pies, etc.; and the strangest thing of all, was to observe how much Clyde enjoyed them, notwithstanding his torrent of opposition, which Stanley and I had bravely stemmed in order to bring them. But then he could not have heard Aunt Dinah mutter in her triumph, at the close of the successful contest with Mars Clyde, the very plaids of her turban starting from the fabric, and quivering with separate wrath :

"Sense he done been of to dat German Varsity and larned to be so grand as to do widout etin' hisself, he thinks everbody else ort to do it to. Them are chillen haint been raised to no sich notions; lor' knows ole Dinah hopes de'll never git no furrin' larnin' in their blessed heads ef it makes 'em kind o' crazy like."

No! he could not have heard at the time this aside of the old lady's, or, in very respect to her memory, he would surely have desisted; if not in consideration for our pampered stomachs, at least in charity to himself.

And thus time passed during the pleasant days of our journey until the mornings, with quick, sharp breath and atmosphere altogether new and strange about us, proclaimed that we were in a northern land—the land of bright rivers and calm skies; of brisk, busy life for old and young; of patient work alike for all.

Our pathway lay for miles along the shores of Seneca Lake.

"This," said Clyde, "is the lake storied in song. I re-

member, during a season north at my uncle's, hearing a
strange legend of this little body of water. Owing to its
cold, crystal purity, which preserves bodies from decompo-
sition, *its dead are never raised*, but held firmly in those
pristine deeps awaiting the final resurrection. In direct
contrariety to scriptural affirmation, 'Dust thou art, to dust
thou shalt return.'"

"Which assertion is verified in few instances," Raymond
answered; "for illustration: do you remember, Clyde,
what we were told by that old monk when we visited a con-
vent on the Seine? He said the poorer classes of the Pa-
risians were permitted to rent graves for their dead only
during the space of three years; at the expiration the
bodies were exhumed to give place to others. In those
long contested battles during the Napoleonic conflict which
convulsed all Europe thousands were left to blanch upon
the field unburied."

"God grant the red hand of war may never fall upon our
nation," exclaimed Stanley, fervently. From the depths of
our four hearts in chorus came an earnest amen.

We fell into a reverie befitting time and place. We saw
the sun go down into the deeps, smooth, glassy, and diamond clear; it seemed as if no storm of earth could ever
mar it, or even the tiniest ripple break its halcyon calm; I
thought it like some natures whose capacity was unrevealed,
externally placid, yet far down lay power strong enough
either to madden or destroy while thirsting for gifts they
never seemed to care for. The natures that are always mis-
understood rarely love, because ever feared; the natures
which never appear to suffer, yet suffer most. Such was
Clyde Ingram—our brother Clyde.

That sunset was like the waning of the sun of some gorgeous dream! Each separate beam multiplied by a hun-

dred others upon the silver surface, until the face of the deep was lighted by a glow of crimson, curling into waves of molten sapphire, then melting away into mists of opal and amethyst. Ah! how rarely and radiantly beautiful it was under the enchanted spell. We gazed upon the picture until the forms of the trees lengthened and the shadows of twilight gathered about it; then from behind those same trees, whose proportions in the still gloaming lay dark upon the water, the bright moon of May rose up in her splendor, mirroring palaces of amber whose tall spires glittered and quivered, broken by the waves in the sharp breath of evening, growing less and less as the night queen climbed higher up her ladder of stars, until at last the shadow of summer, of woodland, was quite gone; then there was only the moon with her night train full orbed, shining from the heavens and from the crystal surface of the deep.

How mute were the spirits of the morning! For a long time silence reigned almost audibly. Stanley's fair brow rested on Ray's shoulder, and moonbeams were playing with her bright hair. There is in my memory to-day a picture—that summer lake and sweet moon beaming around above, below, and the strange look upon Clyde's face, which I did not rightly interpret then nor fully understand until years had dragged by their slow length of days that were each burdened with the anguish of a fearful mistake. When he turned to me, holding out his arm in intimation that I should rest as Stanley had often done in its clasp, I thought he only did so from pique that she had shown this preference for Ray, who was so wont to prefer him to her boisterous brother; so I turned away as though the motion and the look in his dark, soul-full eyes was unseen, to the landscape dark with fir and hemlock, for we had left the lake with its mirrored stars and summer moonshine far behind us. I drew my victorine closer about me and shuddered in the night gloom. I might have seen him shudder, too, if I had not felt the chill of other memories which had their birthplace in the region of our present touring, creeping into my heart. Into those darker musings there glided a shadow, one which, as Dickens would say, lay on my heart with no dark and shuddering chill, but was cast by an object in itself so pure and holy that the shade seemed only a subdued brightness and the light which cast it a glory. But a shadow it was, whether it had its origin in fact or only in my thought—of unrequited love.

Clyde sat wrapped in the impenetrable armor of reserve into which my caprice or Stanley's indifference had plunged him, looking out upon gliding forests so dark that not even one ray of a May moon's brightness could pierce their gloom, with a far-off gleam on his fine face, like a statue of the old time, the dim light from car lamps falling in spectral glamour upon sleeping forms about us. Stanley too was sleeping, smiling through her dreams; the brightest beams gathering where she sat, and wrapping her with a chastened glory like the robes of the redeemed.

On the morrow we arrived at Wayburn. There, half hid by the vines, was the cottage, and just beyond the red square brick house, with dark solemn firs dotting the terraced grounds; below, the town outspread with its neat yards and daintily set fencings; afar off the New Hampshire hills with agricultural products climbing their steep sides. Everywhere were these little white nests of homes so close beside, yet each eloquent of individuality and redolent of that sweet presence without which the most costly and elegant structure is but four walls and a ceiling.

The sun was hanging on a sharp spire of the tall church

balcony when our train arrived, passing all dusty and panting into the depôt. We occupied the carriage which we found awaiting us, and were soon en route for Mr. Kingswell's.

———o———

CHAPTER IV.

"Know then this truth (enough for man to know),
Virtue alone is happiness below."

POPE'S ESSAY ON MAN.

THE shadows of twilight descending tinted into flame with rays of the sinking sun of the far away South, with its groves of orange and palmetto, had enwrapped Claremont in their misty folds when we came in this same twilight up the slope to Ridgely. It is impossible to imagine two localities more utterly at variance in point of style than were these two. Wayburn and its vicinage savored of the brisk Northern presence which creates more than enjoys; hospitality is regarded in the light of social duty rather than an impulse. The atmosphere was one of business.

Mr. Kingswell came to meet us down the tan-bark walk with its neatly shorn sides—a handsome man still; and there was in his greeting such brisk heartiness which made us feel he must once have been fiery and impetuous like the youth in whose charge we repined and suffered. We were met on the threshold by his ladylike, self-possessed wife, who did the honors gravely yet cordially. Her kind eyes lingered upon my face, seeming to say, "You have changed a great deal;" but they had not; they looked exactly as on the morning when he lighted the sweet torch of peace which illumined the mazes of the estrangement between my father and Uncle Montana, in whose house destiny had made my home in the sunny land far away from old scenes and friends.

What pleased us most **was the perfect** understanding existing between Clyde's uncle and aunt, manifest in many **ways beside the** mute suggestions **for** our personal comfort. **It was evident to** us that between **these two,** who **had loved and wed** in youth, there was **but** *one heart;* **and** that same love-light and youth-light **was on** their faces still, subdued and chastened, the after radiance which comes when the storm and conflict with the world **had been** triumphantly **passed—this** calmness the victory. Stanley and I made this disclosure to each other upon retiring to our chamber for the purpose of refreshing ourselves with bath and siesta, being weary and travel-worn with the long journey; which, to our everlasting credit be it said, we did upon that occasion with remarkable dispatch, making our appearance promptly **at the** late tea which had been arranged for our convenience. We found the young gents on hand as they usually were, sitting with father and daughter within the radiance of the home-light on the piazza.

Mary Kingswell was lovely; fair like Stanley, with the sweetest face **it** has ever been my pleasure to see; there were roses, northern roses, upon her cheeks, and the home-light too was in her beautiful eyes **as** she came forward to greet **us** with **a soft,** deprecating grace so far removed from the languishing hauteur of Southern manners—modest, timid, yet there was earnest truth in it.

Raymond's quick eye observed it, and Stanley, too, with that delicate intuition by the aid of which we recognise kindred attributes, saw it as readily. Conventionalism is well enough; there are many persons in intercourse with whom it would be intense pain to go beyond forms; they are a safeguard in many instances, a refuge from the servile element with which emancipated minds could not assimilate, any more than a ray of sunshine could be a part of the dusty highway it warms and brightens. The puerile resort to these to disguise native deficiency; yet true character has a self-centred sustaining dignity above such commonplaces. It towers supreme, lofty in the consciousness of man or womanhood, far removed from such necessities.

It was thus in this instance, ere twelve consecutive sentences had been spoken by any one of us, Mary had taken her place in our four lives—separately, yet relatively—an individual though a joint possession, to have and to hold, to joy and trusting and love to the uttermost. Grovelling spirits cavil because unable to understand that mysterious system of blessed recognition which binds the lofty of the earth in one glorious brother and sisterhood; who behold, flaming in the higher radiance, signals marking God's chosen, when they hear the mystic watchword spoken; ties grow strong in one short hour, as though riveted with trust, and cemented by an intercourse of years. There is in truth a freemasonry between those who wear the insignia of that higher life of the soul; who have unfettered thought, and come to hold converse with spirits of sublimer truths than the world in its every-day reaches can grasp or fathom; who look upon life from the stand-point of a higher purpose, meaning nothing more than doing God's work on earth, with a patient, steady out-look of will and energy, creating while they perform; thus filling full the measure of each day with good deeds and generous actions. The kind of life which infuses serene content, and has in it something of the spirit of the Great Master. Thus it was in this family.

When we sat down to our first tea with them at Ridgely, we felt as if we had always been acquainted.

I learned, in the course of the evening, that Captain Bob Eldridge was living still, all alone, in the rickety old house. Leah, it seemed, had been deceived by Fred. Seaman, a young fellow in Wayburn, of whom I had often heard her speak during our childish life together. The father, hard and unforgiving, had shut close the doors of his home and heart against the poor, motherless girl, who had gone out into the wide world friendless. Bitter tears fell that night, as I lay looking upon the little white cottage from the windows of Ridgely; for her who had been my childhood's friend, thus fallen and forsaken. Winding my arms about Stanley's neck I fell asleep, not counting the stars as I had so often done, but I knew they were shining still, as of old; then prayed, even in my dreams, that poor Leah, betrayed and stricken, might by their sweet life find way to some quiet nook of peace, far from the broad highway of sin, into which her feet had strayed.

Ah! those were sunny days, and sunny are the memories of them. It was May then, it is May now; though between the reality and the memory, six long weary years are lying, yet not one golden beam has gone from their primitive brightness. I feel assured they will shine on until we all shall meet, perchance, in some sweet *Maytime of the hereafter.* The snow lies cold upon the May flowers to-day, but has blighted none of those blooming in that fairy past.

Each hour was full of enjoyments; those two calm spirits planned every species of amusement for us. One day we made a pilgrimage to the hills opposite, the river lying between. Ray gave to Mary his strong arm, Clyde escorted Stanley, and it became my pleasant portion to be led up the rocky heights by the kind, firm hand of Mr.

Kingswell. I am sure I never passed a day so pleasantly; his wonderfully fine taste, blended with poetic impulses, was so heightened by his geniality, and tempered by correct judgment; his views on any subject, whether it involved the discussion of Fine Arts or the manufacturing interests of his section, were so far-reaching, so lucid, so characterized by sterling worth and sense, bearing unmistakably the stamp of sex, his society was to me a perpetual source of speculation and wonder. I was unprepared to find this degree of refined intelligence coëxisting with such thorough and efficient business capacity as I had always heard attributed to Clyde Ingram's uncle.

We were seated on one of the grassiest slopes, hundreds of feet above the level—crowned with sunshine like a diadem—observing the mist as it gathered about the spires of Wayburn, and gloamed in vales below; there was a shimmer in the air—it seemed as though the very rainbow danced; thus completing one of the most gorgeous scenes I ever beheld. Tears gushed from his eyes; not for the grandeur and beauty of what he saw, but because he loved and venerated the source from whence it sprang. We sat silent a long time. At length Stanley came to us, her young face radiant, wild flowers dimpling the waves of her sunny hair. "Mr. Kingswell," she exclaimed, "will you assist Jennie and myself in climbing this last slope? the boys are too indolent for further exertion, but I feel unwilling to rest until I have gained the highest pinnacle."

"You would have figured well as a politician, Stanley, upon my word, and would have appeared more advantageously than I do now; behold me, nephew," he added, turning to Clyde, "*a blush rose between two thorns.*" This he said with a quaint exhibition of humor, taking the hand of each of us.

3

"Thanks to the presiding genius of my lucky destiny for having transferred one of them from my side to yours, uncle," answered his affable and accommodating relative.

"Spoken with characteristic generosity; that spirit of self-congratulation would commend you anywhere," Mr. Kingswell said, with a shade of sadness in his tone. He felt, I question not, that he would rather face the universe at contrariety than feel the sharp wounds of those little friendly arrows. Men who know the world and understand the nature of true friendship rarely deal in them; they grow kinder, more considerate for the feelings of others with the passing on of time.

"I doubt very much if my nephew, notwithstanding his grave aspersion of the several attributes of these young ladies in whom he avows so reluctant a proprietorship, would under any consideration manifest a willingness to transfer said thorns to the side of a younger, handsomer man than I am," observed Mr. Kingswell sententiously.

I glanced at Stanley as our peacemaker closed his sentence; her eyes had wandered from the rainbow-tinted valley to the mists gathering in the dim distance beyond; seeming afar off as the future which is with us while we dream of its coming. How strangely witching she looked —like a wood-nymph she looked then; I wondered if Clyde felt her loveliness as I did. Yes, I think so; though he lay on the grassy slope looking so provokingly indifferent I half questioned if a score of handsome women could have moved him to animation, until he raised his face to mine; then I saw a look of faith, of doubt, and inquiry pass over it, the shadows haunting his "lucky destiny," which told him then and there the time would come when each would leave him—one from choice, the other from a cruel misunderstanding which would blight all her life; yet to the last how fearlessly in spirit would she cling to him. He arose finally, offering his arm to Stanley with mock pomp and hauteur; we made the ascent, enjoying the view more if possible than those preceding.

Descending after we had indeed climbed to the highest peak, my escort stumbled suddenly upon a shapeless mass of something—kind heaven, was it a man? I should never have recognised God's image in the mutilated semblance upraised by the firm arm of Mr. Kingswell, and supported tenderly as if he had been an infant while he led him slowly down the path to a house near the riverside. "I could not have done that," said Raymond, his voice betraying intense contempt for the man, who was beyond all consciousness of what was passing. Mr. Kingswell answered gravely:

"Ah! my young friend, when you shall have come to know this world as well as I; have felt its rough corners rub hard against you, and been pierced with sharp angles of its fate; realize how full to the brim of temptation it is, and snares and pitfalls for the unwary; when you have been brought in swift, unsatisfying contact with all classes of men for forty years, you will have learned to feel no contempt for any error generating in the weakness of those who know not the way of strength. Conscience at some time or other inflicts the reprisals of justice; inevitable suffering succeeds, and penance is the final result. I confess I have little patience with those who err when every vaster consideration is on the side of right, circumstances conspiring to hold them firm; but knowing as I do the heights from which men fall—from which that young man fell—the fearful odds against him, I thank my God that *I have not been tempted as he has been!* He too was upright once; only two short years ago. Let us not vaunt our strength; who shall say what wrecks we may not become, crashing amid 'stern rocks' on a 'pathless sea,' through which a worthy divine has told us lies the narrow way through mortal endeavor to immortal destiny. He loved a worthy girl who was poor and lived under the same roof with him, performing household duties for his parents, who were wealthy ; he wished to marry her—they refused ; he persisted—when with imprecations they drove her from their presence. Her father was old, depending entirely on the wages she received for his support. When he found she had lost her place through an ill-conceived attachment, he was very angry and sent her away. After having sought vainly for work, she left Wayburn in the hope of being more successful elsewhere. Fred followed her; but did not find her, I think, for he soon came back. Maddened by the injustice of his parents to the girl, and his own despair, he plunged recklessly into dissipation, and is this day what you have seen him."

"The girl ?" I asked, breathlessly.

"She has not been heard from since. But to return to this boy ; he is in truth a noble fellow, and has ever been a favorite of mine : I have wept tears over his downfall, and would give almost everything I possess, for power to reclaim and see him stand up God-fearing, self-reliant, looking the man that he is." Here we paused at the residence of Mr. Seaman.

"I shall leave you here, Frederick," said Mr. Kingswell, kindly. Somehow, the intoxicated man was not so stupidly unconscious as he appeared before. He turned towards his benefactor with an uncertain expression upon his bloated features, though mingled with the shame there written. I traced a gleam of grateful emotion as his swollen eyes encountered my own. There must have been horror in my look, notwithstanding all that had passed ; for I recognised the betrayer of my friend Leah with an anguish too deep for words.

Darkness was gathering upon the face of the waters as we recrossed the river to the home shore. Mrs. Kingswell sat waiting in the Ridgely carriage to take us home, where we found a fragrant tea awaiting us. How happy we were! how wretched those two wandering "without the pale." Oh! did not kind Father eyes from that far heaven look pityingly upon them—knowing how they had lost their way in the darkness? Was not His the heart which prompted the sublime response to sorrowing Magdalen— "Neither do I condemn thee, sin no more."

There were re-unions planned for us in which all Wayburn participated. The *élite* came by dozens to call upon us: very soon Mary's fragile card-basket was filled to overflowing with solicitations from every available source. We decided to accept an invitation from my mother's distant relative Mr. Solomon Hayne, who was occupying his summer place at Wayburn. While the rest talked of him, speculating upon the probable return from Europe of his bachelor son Warren, Mrs. Kingswell and myself, apart, conversed of my mother. I have so often thought of the good lady's words on that occasion.

"If on earth we truly love a human being, it is because we feel and know him to be worthy our affection. Esteem is a necessary appurtenance to the durability of affection: we have seen those whom, though brilliantly accomplished, we never could have loved, because their inner life held not this prolific germ. There are others—passed away, long hidden from our sight, of whom we never think without a gushing wave of buried tenderness, which calms the tumult of every-day life like a benediction."

It was thus we remembered my mother in heaven these

many years. I really felt grateful for the warmth with
which I was received and welcomed into strange house-
holds for her sake. Those who knew her best while living
in their midst, who were her daily associates—ever referred
to her as having been loving, patient; never faltering in the
hard way which fate had assigned to her. The circle was
held together by her memory as it had been brightened by
her presence. All was sadly changed since then: some
had prospered, others had not; some had grown grey in
the hard world's service: many I missed who claimed my
childish remembrance—who, like her, had "gone the way
of all the earth!" None, I rejoice, had grown so sordid or
avaricious with accumulated wealth and care, as to deny me
this one bright spot amid the vast wilderness of all the
past: in the land which held my mother's grave, the heart
of her orphan child was sunny and light.

We were ushered into the midst of a brilliant assem-
blage that evening, when the Ridgely carriage left us at Mr.
Hayne's. Our host and hostess, in consequence of urgent
solicitation on our part, had accompanied us, as we were
to leave them on the morrow. They were not participants
in the gaieties on this occasion; but did not object to having
their child mingle in the festivities. Christianity was to
them a divine power lifting itself above forms—wholly
independent of externals; religion that was bigoted or
intolerant, could not coëxist in the atmosphere of their
unpretending piety. How this simple goodness charmed
me! And what reverence I was daily growing to feel for
the inmates of this household, with the glorious spirit of
love in their midst; the great love which circles all objects
with its munificence—a power, a possession, which even
the least of God's creatures shared. In that family we
first learned to pray; at early morning and quiet evening-

time, the father had knelt with us—a calm peace on his brow; he wore it now amid these scenes: I think the greatest tumult could not mar for an instant the holy serenity of his spirit.

After we had paid our respects to Mr. and Mrs. Hayne, and interchanged the necessary pleasantries with that courteous lady and gentleman, we were moving away, when to my surprise and pleasure I beheld cousin Warren standing amid a group near the centre of the room. He joined me immediately after. A cordial greeting was the result, during which he held my hand between his slender fingers, his large dark eyes wandering often to Stanley, who was promenading with Clyde. That reminds me I have never yet essayed to describe my heroine. Perhaps I have delayed thus from consciousness of the extreme difficulty involved in the undertaking.

The sunbeam and sweetest strain of the thrush; the soft whispers of slowly coming spring, which steal upon you with lulling, indescribable charm, a thrill to the soul, a conviction to the sense—are things that may be felt but never delineated. Such was Stanley Montana's beauty; being of that rare type defying all description, whose charm is infinite variety—not so much a personality as a very subtle presence, which made itself manifest without the aid of any embellishment whatever. She carried with her and diffused her own peculiar atmosphere; all who breathed were filled with sweet exhilaration in her circle; the very essence of the charm crept stealthily along the fibres of their being—a sensation none were likely to forget. Her features were singularly perfect, though her eyes of dark ocean-blue were the most wonderful creations of all.

I had never seen her look lovelier than in the snowy-white which showered about the very essence it seemed of her spirit's virgin purity; white was Stanley's favorite dress. Now her curls fell over shoulders fair and round like waves of sunlight. Then her eyes—how I have gone down into their depths with my own, to find rest in that true soul as yet unwarped by earthly contact; a grand soul, the mirror of her woman's heart, where all of love and affection that . was divine shone forth; an avenue through which may be obtained glimpses of the immortal.

Warren said as he crushed my hand, "Why did you never speak to me of this peerless creature? I have never met one looking so youthful—empress-like as she appears."

"She is distantly allied to the Haynes," I answered, saucily; "that circumstance may in itself be sufficient to elucidate the problem of her surpassing loveliness."

He smiled his old imperious smile, which I loved best to see upon his kingly face; then answered while his eyes followed Stanley as she glided through the intricate mazes of a polka quadrille in progress, which she and Clyde danced admirably together. This diversion had been one of our favorite amusements at Claremont; it was strange to see it in vogue at Wayburn, so quiet and puritanical in its usages once.

"Some of the city fashions the Haynes had brought from New York with them," remarked Mrs. Seaman, the ill-conditioned wife of a church deacon, who had become sufficiently reconciled to *this fashion* to become a spectator in this instance. Warren smiled again as I remarked, "What cannot be cured must be endured."

"I observe you have not lost your propensity to be sarcastic, Jennie; as a child you were exceedingly cruel to me; I find you unchanged. Tell me, in your sunny home have you ever thought of our pleasant days together in New York? How uncle's decision that he would reside in Way-

burn broke into our arrangements; afterwards you became
a recluse. My friend Milverton has not forgotten you; he
speaks of you often, and has sent you messages through
the medium of my letters, to which you never once responded."

I heeded not his reminder; my heart had gone out into
that school-time with the bereavement which ensued; I
thought of the two graves in the cemetery near by, their
white stones gleaming in summer moonshine like spectres
of the old days. Warren had been so unfortunate as to
sweep these chords of bitterness. Now taking my hand
caressingly he led me towards the sitting-room; I made a
deprecating gesture when he would have taken me to the
piano; instead, we passed into the garden, treading its paths
in the shadowy night—through clustering dewdrops that
shone like diamonds, flashing back the starry radiance in
which we walked.

"Now, Jennie, you must tell me something more about
this Hebe cousin of yours. How long do you remain in
Wayburn; where will be your next halting-place; and
when will you transplant your southern lily to her native
bowers again?"

"You give me no time to answer one query ere you ply
another. Stanley is the only daughter of Uncle Clifford
Montana. We leave Wayburn to-morrow, go to Boston,
Nahant, and home in September."

"Who is the young fellow with whom she dances?"

"Clyde Ingram, her mother's stepson."

"Ah! yes, I understand; I learned from Aunt Hayne that
she was accompanied by a most devoted suitor, who really
monopolized her. Arrived at Wayburn I was regaled as
usual with the gossip of the place; heard the merits of
your beautiful cousin discussed before you came this even-

3*

ing. Tell me, Jennie, is it true that her father is seeking
to negotiate for her a marriage with *him* because he is
rich ? "

I felt that the pain at my heart was suddenly checked by
this trite conclusion to his interrogatory : something very
like angry defiance flashed into my face, when I saw the
lofty expression of triumphant disdain in the magnificent
eyes of my cousin Warren ; though in his courteous tones
there was moderate surprise affably expressed—nothing
more, in the words he spoke now :

" Her suitor, is he—indeed ? "   There remained nothing
for me save a course of repentance for my hasty wrath,
then to laugh immoderately at his diplomatic quietus upon
my intended defence of Clyde. Warren too laughed, each
knowing why the other laughed, though no further inter-
pretation of our risibility was vouchsafed by either. By
and by Warren said very tenderly :

" You are a strange girl, Jenny.   I shall be more cautious
about looking for my proposed triumph over this Quixotic
rival, if such I may consider him, especially when I have an
auditor who is ready to convert my glance into an imaginary
dagger—— "

" And your cool disdain into an impossible conquest," I
answered, thus concluding the sentence in a manner foreign
to his design.   Then we passed into the house.

Stanley was seated at the instrument, singing with Clyde
an invocation to the South ; words and music were her own.
We managed to get a position amid the throng of listeners,
near the singer. I have never since seen my cousins look
as they did that night. Stanley fair and beautiful as the
angel of a dream ; Warren showing how he felt all the
witchery and power of her loveliness. His soul bowed
down, wrapt in humble adoration, while those slender, child-

ish fingers swept its chords as none else had ever swept them—the wild, sweet strains would linger with him, doubtless, until he heard other strains very like them from angel fingers come over the cold, grey waters from bright harps beyond.

When she had ceased singing, he crept reverently to her side, thanking her in such courtly terms and with such manifest pleasure. As I looked upon my proud cousin, I could not help feeling keenly the distinction between what he *might have been, and what he was !*—a disciple of that selfish class of worldlians, whose higher impulses are invariably at the mandate of interest, who worship at the shrine of that inexorable Mogul—*Mammon !*

We met my cousin again; he joined us at the early breakfast prepared at Ridgely for our especial benefit, before leave-taking, in which he too participated. He went his way, and we went ours, missing very much the kind voice, genial manner, and handsome face of Warren Hayne.

———o———

CHAPTER V.

" In many ways does the full heart reveal,
The presence of a love it would conceal."
COLERIDGE.

ALMOST immediately upon our arrival at the Tremont, Warren paid his respects to us ; he had lingered at Wayburn only long enough to telegraph his intention to his father, who he knew could readily supply his place, in the event of a protracted absence. It was evident he had decided to become one of our party, though far too gentlemanly to think of monopolizing Stanley's society to the exclusion of

Clyde, who was her legitimate escort, though he never
failed to join us in the evenings, no matter where he went.
He invariably preceded us to the Opera. On entering, we
were sure to behold him in some conspicuous place, often
leaning against one of the sculptured columns, ostensibly
much absorbed in the performance. However, even through
his well counterfeited semblance, it was manifest that his
indifference was unfelt; that he was silently drinking inspiration from Stanley's mystic presence, while she, in her
touching girlish beauty, was wholly unconscious how this
world-serving man, with stealthy tread, was treading the
avenues of her young heart—a heart from her earliest childhood so loyal to Clyde. Thus, in a few brief days were
swept away " the ties of long, long years."

One afternoon, returning from a shopping expedition
with Raymond, I ran across the corridor to Stanley's apartment for the purpose of displaying some new purchase in
which she was interested. She stood before a mirror, rolling over her taper fingers the wavy bands of golden hair, a
picture of unconscious loveliness, her eyes lustrous—dreamy ;
such misty splendor, such trusting fondness, in their
depths. She turned suddenly, beholding me, cast her arms
about my neck, blushing with a consciousness that I too
felt, for I held no place in her reflections then. The room
was filled with the odor of jasmine clusters and tea roses.

" See my flowers !" lifting from the window-seat where it
stood without the Venetian blind, a goblet of silver elegantly
chased ; inclosed within a beautifully wrought device on one
side, was the little word " Stanley." Somehow there was a
blur in the air about me, as I inhaled the fragrance of those
flowers.

" From Clyde?" I asked with apparent indifference,
stifling the dull pain at my heart, to which of late I had

grown so accustomed, crushing it down as unworthy of me and of our friendship.

"I imagine they came from Mr. Hayne," she answered firmly, though with evident emotion.

"Was there a card?" I persisted.

"A blank one," was her reply.

My mental query was, why did she suspect him of having sent them? Only because in her secret heart she would have been pleased most that he was the donor of this beautiful gift. It was like his delicacy, I mused in pursuance of the thought; he would not openly address Stanley, thinking Clyde her suitor. Or else—a terrible suspicion crossed my mind—would he, by these indirect means, inveigle himself into her affections without making in return the slightest concession or giving her the faintest hold on his?

These were Warren's old tricks—heart-breaking had been his favorite pastime.

> "To kneel at many a shrine,
>   Yet lay his heart at none."

I could have brought forward numberless epistles from various members of the circle to which we were attached, to say nothing of the convincing and convicting record of his own lithe pen, recounting innumerable victories between the ages of seventeen and twenty-seven, as proof positive that my assertion was correct. I should have told her then and there to beware! There was a bright, bright structure forming under heaven that some cruel hand would shiver to atoms; gaudy tissues weaving which a breath of fate would scatter so widely, at the inevitable mandate of other time and place, that neither might ever again find that which was lost in the days whose golden sands we counted during the pleasant time of our sojourning there together. God grant such loss may not stand clear in heaven.

Clyde saw and felt this as I did, and fearing it was War- ren's intention to trifle with Stanley, he haughtily held him aloof as one unworthy his esteem and confidence. I attri- buted this feeling to the sorrow he experienced in Stanley's manifest preference for Warren. He spoke more and more coldly to his rival: with secret misgiving I beheld this silent antagonism growing up between them. I sym- pathized deeply with all parties, though fearful of being unjust to cousin Warren, whom I liked sincerely notwith- standing his many faults and ficklenesses; I resolved to keep my own counsel, leaving to God the issue.

One of my cousin's favorite pastimes was to promenade the long hall at the hotel, his princely head inclined for- ward, making the outline perfect. It was thus always, and thus I ever remember him—walking and waiting—in other days, when we came not in answer to his summons.

He often invited Stanley to accompany him alone to the theatre and other places of amusement. On such occasions Clyde invariably appeared restless and wretched. I pitied him, and sought to mitigate his suffering and cheer him with my simple songs and talk as I had often done at Claremont, when my endeavor was less vain than now. Once he seemed so grateful for the effort, which he duly appreciated, he was almost happy ; his face actually softened into the pleasant smile I loved so well and had not seen for so long. He was almost transformed one evening when I passed to his side, indulging in the old habit of shaking hands on bidding him good-night. He said suddenly, speaking with vehement eagerness:

" Aljean, have you ever loved ? " The hot blood rushed to my cheeks! What right had he, Stanley's sorrowing, disappointed lover, to question me thus? I was turning away when I caught the anxious expression in his face. I could not be unkind, so I answered, half recklessly:

"Yes! I have loved, but my love is unrequited; none will ever know——"

He shrank back into his wonted silence with the look of white anguish his face had often worn of late; then I left him, regretting the next instant my hasty avowal, since it had seemed to recall with such force and bitterness his own burden of wasted affection.

On the following afternoon Clyde accompanied me on a tour through the city in search of an article Aunt Edith had specially requested us, if possible, to find for her. Raymond was engaged in the execution of commissions for Uncle Montana; Stanley had gone driving with Warren. Clyde knew that there was no one else to escort me, otherwise I think he would have declined. His manner towards both Stanley and myself had changed very much since the acquisition of Mr. Hayne to our party. I sometimes fancied he imagined us both in love with Cousin Warren, who compelled us by force of example to treat him with due consideration—a belief which I rather encouraged than otherwise; anything sooner than he should come to know and feel my secret love for him.

Ever since that strange interview he had been more distant than ever; now he appeared very patient while I overlooked, assorted, matched, and purchased interminable parcels for the benefit of the household at Claremont. During the measurement of a robe designed for Aunt Edith, he selected a silk Marie Louise blue—just the color of her eyes—brocaded with tiny sprays of lilies of the valley, for Stanley. While it was being wrapped up, I myself having added the trimmings, I heard him sigh heavily once or twice.

"Are you not well, brother?" I asked, compassionately.

"Yes, very," he answered, in a strange, husky voice; "but, Aljean, I wish you would not call me brother ever any more. I do not care to have you mock me thus." I was speechless with surprise and pain; I could not even inquire what he meant by those strange words, until he added:

"There is a beautiful lavender of similar pattern; will you wear it?" Did he think by this assumption of the old manner to obliterate from my mind the memory and effect of his capricious and cruel speech? I determined not to let him see how deeply that one little sentence had wounded me; when I responded there was no pain manifest, only bitter sneering in my tones.

"No; I thank you, Mr. Ingram, I never wear lavender; it is unbecoming my complexion."

"Select your own color; here is any shade you wish."

"I shall not make a selection," I said, with angry vehemence. His sarcastic answer pierced me like an arrow:

"Who has objected to your accepting and wearing my gift? I have the right to ask, for some one has of late influenced you against me strangely."

"Your questioning, sir, I consider unwarranted by my refusal to accept what you offer. As this is from Stanley, you can compel her to answer you; she who has the right to object to your interrogating me, if she choose."

"My sister; yes, she has the right, but would not avail herself of it; she has more consideration for me. I shall be well content to feel assured Mr. Hayne has not the right to demur to her acceptance of the little purchase I made for her. Though, I am sure, I as her brother should not object to her receiving gifts from whom she choose—even from him, if he and she so willed it."

Did he really think to teach his poor heart to look upon her as a sister—nothing more? Then why his angry questioning words to me who was less to him even than this; how had I merited them? At the remembrance of all, my wrath flashed up again, and I answered excitedly:

"Granting the truth of all you say, Mr. Ingram, is that any reason you should speak as you have done to me? I have accepted your mother's charity—it does not necessarily follow that I should degrade myself by receiving yours, or that you should insult me by offering it."

Alas! I did not then know—for he had generously concealed from me, from all of us, the painful fact that to him and to him alone were we indebted, one and all, for everything; even the very bread we ate.

He answered very sorrowfully—I wonder now how he could have been so patient with me—with a forced resignation to his fate:

"I perceive you strangely misconstrue my motive, Aljean; I meant no insult to you; God knows I speak truly. I requested you not to call me brother, because it pains me to hear you call me so; why you do not comprehend, I see; so let it pass; some day you will learn to know me better; then you will readily forgive my hasty words."

"I have already forgiven you, Clyde," I answered, tremulously. Somehow that little sentence of concession had melted the wall of anger suddenly arisen between us. I too had been hasty; why did not I ask pardon of him as well?—because I was sure he would grant it whether I asked it or not; for how good and kind and forgiving he had been to me always!

Returning to the hotel, we found Stanley and Warren, who had preceded and were awaiting us. She sat beside him on a divan; her bonnet was of white cactus; there were clusters of blue violets and daisies in the face-trimming; these were so incorporated with waves and ripples of sunny hair, it would have been difficult to discern the exact boundary between them. On one point at least the beholder could be specific, fearless of being inaccurate: this was regarding the very beautiful roses encircled by the fairy garland which had that day been invoked by Warren Hayne. They were Christian roses, and manifested no spirit of interference or encroachment upon their surroundings, even while they bloomed thus brilliantly, mute symbols of his triumph. I had seen it from the first all along, though I think Clyde had never realized it until that interview. To avoid meeting his eyes, I took my seat beside her, took her tiny, trembling hands in mine, and sought to turn her beaming face away from his searching gaze.

Very soon Ray came back, and the three gentlemen joined us at dinner, at the conclusion of which meal, at the suggestion of our *brother*—Clyde was not our brother any more—we repaired to the parlor; the gentlemen, excepting Warren, who never smoked, decided to forego their cherished cigars in lieu of the "family chat" which they proposed. Warren was in full force that evening; it was the next thing to impossible to avoid growing genial in his presence; ere the conclusion of the second glass of champagne he became exceedingly voluble, saying some very witty things with true Southern dash, and many friendly winning ones with such heartiness it was, as I before hinted, akin to impossible to resist their influence: even Clyde apparently became pacified and companionable.

During the course of the evening the conversation assumed a political form; that quicksand Stanley and I, as cicerones, had hitherto sought to avoid; our endeavor in this instance had been worse than useless.

I really feared for Ray, who blurted out his opinions without stint or reservation. He expressed a conviction that the " Republican candidate for the Presidency would be elected by a sectional element, not by the voice of a united people; in almost any event he fancied the Republic would be dismembered, and dissolution be the final result. This he had long apprehended, an event which never seemed so likely to ensue as now. The institution of slavery had ever been a pretext to agitators, an eyesore to both North and South. It is a question of vast import to the South in estimating the value and interest of the Gulf States, where white labor is unavailable; though it should be a consideration of little moment to those North, who are the first to cry out, 'Down with it! let slavery be for ever extinguished!'"

" You do not, you cannot, even though you maintain slavery to be right, and justifiable in the sight of God and man, claim the premises that it is advantageous to any community, in whatever section their lot may be cast," remarked Warren earnestly. " I hold it to be a festering evil, a chasm bridged over by custom, sustained by the pillars, now rotten and crumbling, upon which it was reared—an institution fit only for the darker ages; a structure whose foundation-stone came from heathendom. The world has made gigantic evolutions, from generation to generation, through vast areas of progress, with this Gorgon of the feudal period clinging to the power-wheels of civilization. The scales have dropped one by one from the brightening eyes of nations, each of whom has been born again into a glorious realm of freedom! America stands alone. Even the universal revolution has long since crossed the ocean; the North rose up in its strength, as one man; humanity, with probe and knife removed the moral cancer from her vitals—

shook from the strong limbs of the people, in at least one portion of the Republic, the lethargy that had bound them in a state of inactivity. By her magnanimous example the bondman was made free.

"But your country, that vaunted, boasted land of the sunny South! the canker is yet in her glorious heart, the poison of this system in her veins, retarding every attempt at progression, a malaria binding her to the rack of feudal deformity—a lamentable condition of mental and physical inanity.

"Russia stands stronger to-day than when the structure of her national pomp and pride was reared upon the pillars of serfdom; so would it be with you, if from your system of government this evil was purged out. It is prolific of convulsions! for the giants in intellect among you, and these are comparatively few, there are thousands who are helplessly and hopelessly dwarfed, cringing in vales of wretchedness, ignorance, and poverty. It is a diplomatic and adroit process of sifting the rights of the small from the wrongs of the great! or rather *rights* of the few from the wrongs of a multitude! This is your boasted system of human slavery. The iron heel of its pernicious usages grinds the white laborer down to a condition infinitely worse than that of the most abject servitude."

"You are right there," Clyde answered blandly; "the blacks enjoy amenities and privileges from which the poorer class of whites are debarred. To those who chancé to be personally acquainted with these facts, your argument in favor of improving the condition of the negroes sounds strangely inconsistent. In nine cases out of ten they are satisfied with their condition, and would not exchange their present state for all the immunities of a freedom the significance of which they have not the power to comprehend.

I understand the subject well, and realize how much superior in circumstance and destiny are those held in lineal servitude to the poorer class of whites. In nine cases out of ten, as I before remarked, you would nôt better the condition of the slave."

"That may be so; I am not pleading the cause of the negro at the tribunal of these fair arbitresses; it is only the cause of humanity. By your own admission, the condition of nine-tenths of your net population is infinitely worse than that of the lineal bondsmen. Oh, were this crushing, binding burden but taken from the shoulders of these poor men, that they might come up gradually from the mazes of their ignorance—come to feel that they are in truth men among men, and learn to comprehend in its fullest significance all the dignity and power implied in the term, to stand as freemen, shoulder to shoulder, heart to heart; then there would be a new order of things. Avenues would open as if by magic; through those shining portals vistas of a higher destiny would become visible; feet now wandering in poverty, faltering in obscurity, would soon learn to walk firmly and hopefully the sunnier life-track.

"There is a work, a great work for the present age to perform; the pathway to it is beaten and blood-stained: toiling up from the stand-point of black-pinioned doubt millions of freemen will come scattering life and treasure, the nation's bone and sinew, by the way, to the goal of this end.

"I am convinced, as well as him who sees the end from the beginning, that the liberation of the slave, the white man's advancement towards the civilization in which posterity will rejoice and thank us for, united under the flaming head of freedom, will be triumphant."

"Then it will be a triumph dearly won," answered Clyde, with flashing eyes. "Even the *cause* which you vaunt as a pretext must elude you; for the South, rich and poor, great and small, bond and free, will stand up as one man to defeat your purpose; high hearts will bleed and break, and their death-throes will shake your government to its very centre and convulse the material universe ere this shall come to pass."

I have often since recalled this prophecy of Clyde's, though none of us seemed to feel or scarcely to heed it then, and by some adroit strategy on our part the conversation was changed. They talked now of the beautiful countries through which they all had passed; where Warren Hayne, more especially, had grown rich in those mental treasures which made his society a resource so prized by all—invaluable to a young enthusiast like Stanley. On that occasion I remember he talked magnificently; there was such power in his eloquence, coupled with the lofty charm of his manner, such grandeur in the personality thus asserted. I too was captivated, and appreciated my cousin more than ever before; he possessed a strange capacity to magnetize his auditors. Now, while he spoke of Germany, we listened to the chime of Bohemian bells and heard the sounds of the rushing Rhine: he glided on to other themes, themes world-wide and comprehensive; we beheld spheres rhetorical and metaphorical spheres evolving through the mystic spaces of his thought, bathed in sunlit mists, embalmed in the fragrance of their flowers; we seemed to hear two sweet strains of soul music while he thus grandly swept young heart-strings that were twining into the recesses of his own, with what power and effect only God knew.

I scarce knew whether I most joyed or sorrowed for the

turn affairs had taken; I could not but listen sometimes
to the deep voice of hope in my own being whispering,
it is best; but when I looked on Stanley's face, which
darted occasional glances of unrest into my own, owing to
some undefined cause, or upon Clyde, who was at times so
moody and watchful, I felt it would perhaps have been
better for all if we could have had the old time back without the added sunshine of this new presence.

Cousin Warren made one of our party to Nahant; to
my surprise we there encountered the Soulés and the Aus-
tins from New Orleans. Now I had just cause for disliking
Retta Austin; she had been a pupil at the same academy
in which Stanley and myself, as Ray jestingly remarked,
had "climbed the hill of science;" there I had held her
aloof, after the fashion of school-girls, though now, with
characteristic littleness, she deemed it politic to avail herself of the acquaintance in consideration of the gentlemen
attached to our party, though it was easy to see and feel
she had not quite forgotten or forgiven the old score.
From her first introduction to Warren she persisted in
claiming a portion of his time, even at the expense of her
delicacy and his manifest preference for Stanley.

The days passed very charmingly in this ocean-girded
retreat; each was full to the brim of that busily-idle precarious life of pleasure, which is ever succeeded by a sense
of loss or a consciousness of wanting something to occupy the
void they leave behind them. Such seasons of exaltation
are ever followed by periods of corresponding depression.

Meanwhile, mists were fleecing and thickening on the far-
rolling sea; sunshine mellowing on the paths in which we
often walked or drove; summer song-birds drew feathery
mantles closer about shivering little forms, wet with ocean
spray, and trooping, chattered of their southward voyage.

We, too, began to think of returning to Ridgely, often wondering, as many a summer party has done before, if we should ever meet again. Aye! perhaps. Ere we came, the life journey ended to a darker ocean-side, if not beyond seas.

Warren's friend, Milverton, too, had joined us at Nahant. We found him a valuable acquisition to our party; so genial, so quick in his perception and comprehension of things; so witty and voluble, we could scarcely realize that we had actually existed previous to his arrival. He saw there was something amiss, and set himself at work to discover and amend it. I knew not how it all came about, but Clyde was feeling better, I found, as the days went by. Pride had served him in good stead; he was strong, and in my secret heart I honored him for his triumph and dignified submission to what was apparently inevitable. I was very kind to Clyde, more so than I had been for months. Once I caught his eyes fixed upon me with a queer expression of inquiry—timid, yet full of meaning—which I dared not interpret according to the dictates of my own feelings. Stanley's deportment towards him was that of a sister; he rarely caressed, never repelled her. Raymond was the brightest spirit in our midst; he permitted nothing to mar the harmony of our days together there, now rapidly drawing to a close.

One early evening I sat with Clyde beside a low window, listening to the crashing waves beneath. Afar out upon the trackless deep a solitary ship was ploughing her fearless pathway into the unknown. Clyde spoke no word, only pointed to the isolated sail—in the swift breeze fluttering like a thing of life.

"Clyde," said I, after a long pause, "will you tell me why you will not let me call you brother?"

" Aljean, I have asked myself that question many times ; you answered it once *for all time.*"

" When—where ?" I asked, in my eagerness.

"In the parlor at the Tremont one evening when we were alone together."

What, because I had avowed my unrequited love, was that sufficient reason why he should refuse me his brotherly affection ? I was growing restive and uncomfortable. I was very glad when Raymond joined us and commenced talking to Clyde on some business matter between them, and Warren, sauntering that way, claimed me for a promenade ; he held my hand, as he always did when we walked together. I imagine Cousin Warren was well aware of the fascination which his presence exerted ; I even, I who often warred with him, could not wholly resist it ; however vindictive and resentful in his absence, I was invariably amicable when he was by my side. This influence was extended to all who came within the circle of it. How he contrived, under the semblance of his kingly indifference, to comprehend my struggle between liking and disapprobation—to assimilate these contesting elements and cause me to forget everything save that his full dark eyes were upon me in cousinly affection and confidence—is more than I shall ever be able to account for. Upon the occasion above referred to, he said earnestly :

" One more week of bliss, such as the gods might envy, and then—oh ! how desolate I shall be when you are gone !" Accustomed as was Warren to this phraseology, wrapping rhetorical tissues about empty words, oftentimes with no other object than to conceal an indifference he really felt, I believed him to be serious now ; though for once fact was stronger than fancy ; though I replied in a jesting manner : " Ha ! ha ! my anchorite has decided to play the sentimentalist! Well, the character becomes you, trifler that you are. Oh! cousin, you are so wretchedly fickle there is no trusting what you say. You will go to Cape May or Atlantic City and forget us all in a fortnight; in anticipation of this melancholy oblivion I forewarn you, Stanley, and I may follow your illustrious example in that regard."

"Jennie, you are unjust to me as usual. Even you, wilful witch that you are, I could not forget if I were to try, Stanley—" lowering his voice at the mention of her name, until its tones were rich, full, almost reverent—"to forget her would be to forget the world of women, the universe of glorious nature, its birds, flowers, and sunshine; its light and music; the heaven and hope beyond; in short, a total oblivion of all things, for she is all of these; she is life itself to me—the only perfect woman I have ever known. You may look surprised and incredulous, as I see you have a mind to do, but if I had lived among such women I should never have been the heartless cynic, the male flirt, the world esteems me to day."

"If Stanley has faith in your words, I should be insane to doubt their truth." I looked into his face; he seemed moody and reflective, sad withal; then spoke more in response to his own thought than in answer to my adroitly worded suggestion:

"She does not know it yet; shall never know, unless her own heart first teaches her the beautiful truth."

Quick as lightning a conviction crashed through my heart-strings. I looked at Warren; there was a strange set firmness about his mouth so unlike the expression upon Stanley's pure face, with its roses and frame-work of falling curls, as she passed us in the promenade, all radiant in the twilight, leaning on the arm of Milverton. Would Warren dare to trifle with her? A bitter rejoinder sprang to my lips, but the mist

cleared away from before my eyes as I felt the magnetic
pressure of his hand, and felt his own reading my thoughts,
while the serenity that was habitual to both resumed its
empire again.

"No, Warren, you will not miss our party; even here
there are some pleasant people, two or three whom you
may find sufficiently charming to beguile the hours of
our *lamented* absence. I am sure you will not lack for
entertainment; then there cannot exist the faintest pretext
for *ennui* within the circle of your favorite, Retta Austin.
She has spirit enough to animate a whole party; she is
highly combustible, however, and may at least endanger
your broadcloth. No one can tell to what length she might
go in her wild pranks, if Jane was not constantly checking
her. I am sure you will not be permitted to grow tame in
such company."

"Miss Austin is not a favorite of yours," remarked Cousin Warren loftily, as though he held such trifling variances
far beneath his gentlemanly consideration. I appreciated
his exclusiveness, and in this instance, so I answered
carelessly: "Oh, no! if I cared anything at all about her I
should do violence to my sense of justice if I did not dislike her very much. I understand her thoroughly; could
not avoid conning the distasteful lesson during my daily
contact with her in our school days. Her assumption of
artlessness, which she vainly seeks to vaunt under cover of
versatility, is but another cloak for her wilful and intricate
designs. During our residence at the Academy, I have seen
these dangerous qualities brought to bear upon many a
guilelesss school-girl who had chanced to incur Retta's
haughty displeasure by excelling her in some pursuit, rendering the probability of her missing the first premium almost
certain. In such cases she would not scruple to forge and

fabricate, until she had amassed evidence sufficient to cause the young lady's dismissal. Being a favorite with the preceptress, she usually succeeded in any undertaking upon which she had set her head and heart. Now you will understand why I say it is dangerous to deal with her, and why I repeat the assertion. If I had any feeling other than perfect indifference for her, it would be one of distrust and dislike."

"You are evidently not a favorite with her?" he answered, seeming to grow more interested in my narrative, smiling meantime at my warmth, "and she is at least frank enough in this instance to make no effort to conceal the fact."

"It is a palpable case. I unmasked her once, and she, measuring my spirit by her own very narrow one, vaunts her revenge as an offset to the contempt she imagines I feel for her, which I am astonished that I do not feel, though I do not hesitate to express the opinion hitherto asserted, that Retta Austin is a dangerous woman—even as a friend—treacherous as Iago!"

"Precisely," said Cousin Warren; "and this is the woman into whose false fair clutches you would have me surrender myself in the event of your absence."

"I retract, Warren," I answered, with mock symptoms of relenting; "it may be dull for you here, but you have many resources independent of her or any other woman. I have accused you of being fickle in some respects; but in this instance the impression will last beyond the hour. I do not think it will fade before the snow has fallen to chill the life from your beautiful summer-flowers."

We scarce lifted our eyes in recognition as a beautiful woman swept by us with a lofty glance, and just the pretext of a nod in my direction, though I saw her own bent in pride and passion on Cousin Warren; it was Retta Austin; from that hour I knew her secret well.

At this juncture Stanley joined us; Warren offered her his arm. I laughingly remarked that I should leave them, through fear of relapsing into a *terrible third*.

"Not at all," answered Warren rapidly. "I have nothing to say to Miss Montana which I should not say fearlessly if all the world stood listening."

True! I had seen it in Stanley's face in those days at Boston; the pleasant drives to Haverhill, Melrose, and during long quiet lingerings upon the velvet turf of the beautiful common, with that bright young face by his side, had taught her to love him, and in return he had *no words* for her *which all the world might not hear*. We three were silent for a long time; Warren was the first to speak.

"Whither will you bend your course from here? though really I shall know whether you take the trouble to answer me or not. Satellites invariably gravitate towards the one great solar centre. It will be thus with all Miss Montana's friends and admirers; there too in that bright orbit I shall run my destined circle, whether to bliss or misery who shall say. Emerson, I think it was, whose definition of fate was 'free will.' I will demonstrate the truth or falsity of his assertion." Stanley's cheeks hung out white signals of pain! For her sake I answered for us both.

"We are not to delegate to ourselves the slightest compliment in the appropriation of your well-meant gallantry, cousin, since in obeying this recognised law of 'gravitation' which forces you into our orbit, insomuch as you are so unwilling a victim to the martyrdom imposed by the science which governs the centripetal and centrifugal forces of our being; leaving you no alternative but submission." Next instant I repented having said so much. Warren was too wretched to make any response to my raillery; I sincerely pitied him without knowing why it was he should suffer thus.

On the morning following we drove upon the beach. Raymond had gone up to the city on business; Warren took his place in the carriage—so there was only we four. Clyde escorted me; he and Warren had, it seemed, enjoyed a much better understanding of late; when Stanley and I left them to dress for the drive, they locked arms, much to our surprise, and walked to and fro together in the morning sunshine. There were many things that to me were utterly incomprehensible, only because all this while I had regarded Clyde's passion for Stanley in the light of a stubborn fact, had grown to accept it as a matter of course, attributing to him feelings foreign to his nature or intention; though by look or word he had never, save in my estimation, revealed more than a brother's affection for her. What an inexorable tyrant love is! often rushing us blindly into some conclusion which brings upon its swift wings only misery. He and Warren had never been other than kind to each other, except in my thought; barring that first bitter suspicion of Clyde's that Warren might prove traitor to Stanley's pure young love.

Adown the beach we passed—we four together in the bright morning sunshine. What cool and refreshing breezes from the sea! what exhilaration in the very air we breathed! Our steeds struck fiery sparks from the pebbly road while bearing us along with a motion so rapid it left us no time for thought. Stanley and Warren were so happy they asked of the Infinite nothing beyond this day and its glory; no hope, no promise for the morrow. Between Clyde and myself there was *only silence!*

> "There is a silence which hath been no sound,
> There is a silence which no sound may be."

I could find no word—he sought none; we two sat thus

with eyes wandering out upon the sleeping deeps—very stilly they were in the morning light, which caressed white-winged fleets in the far harbor—and hovered about the city with its surging tides of human life with a radiance like the widespread circling pinions of Deity.

We returned by way of a circuitous route, which brought us to another entrance of the hotel; as we were being handed from the carriage by Milverton, who anticipated our attendants in the performance of that duty, Stanley's dress was caught and held by a tack from a trunk which stood upon the steps, evidently but just dislodged from a travelling cab which yet stood in waiting.

"There is something in *your way,*" remarked our obsequious gallant, waggishly glancing from Stanley to Warren, who had lent his efficient service to disengage the fabric. He gave a start of surprise as the name on the trunk—that of a rich heiress in Philadelphia, at the shrine of whose charms he had been a devotee—caught his eye. He lifted his face to Milverton with a queer expression neither of us understood.

"Come, Warren, old fellow, you are to do penance henceforth. I will take my oath it is not me she is after," was Milverton's comforting remark to his friend, who escorted Stanley to the parlor, where he left her in a maze of fitful abstraction, bowing merely, without requesting, as he always did on leaving us, that he might soon be permitted to see us again.

We spent most of the day in our own apartment. How sweetly Stanley looked, with her curls gathered in a net, through whose silken meshes rebellious rings of gold would break from masses of the chestnut, seeming to mock in their sunny radiance the look of patient waiting on her lovely face. Milverton and Clyde attended us at dinner, Ray being still absent; neither was Warren present. When we came into the ball-room in the evening, he was there, the centre of a group, an imperious blonde hanging on his arm. Her form was perfect, though her features were almost expressionless; her blue eyes sleepy without being languid; her manner haughty, almost to sternness. They were conversing with a pompous grey-haired gentleman with very heavy watch-seal and gold-headed cane, who I readily suspected was her father, judging from their resemblance to each other.

It was evident she had heard of us, for she turned to take a survey of our party as we entered; Milverton, perhaps, had told her something, for her gaze, though well bred, seemed to grow pitiless and hard as it rested on Stanley. I read the secret of those haughty blue eyes as I had done that of another pair of eyes on the previous evening. The deduction was palpable. *Warren Hayne was engaged to this woman!* She had doubtless been informed, as I before hinted, of his apparent devotion to the Southern belle, and had come down to Nahant for the purpose of warning her captive to his chains again. This then was why his love for my friend had never been spoken; why he would wait until Stanley's heart had taught her the truth. The dead weight on my heart seemed crushing it into a far more fearful silence than that which hitherto had bound it.

Retta Austin went into a series of transports at the present aspect of affairs; looked all kinds of triumph—a process to which Stanley appeared entirely oblivious and impervious—as she swept down the centre of the room, leaning on the arm of her handsome brother, peerless, defying competition; a shower of white tulle falling in snowy waves about her person, swaying with each graceful undulation of her lithe form—the very impersonation of "Holmes's golden blonde." I had never been so proud of her as at that moment. "The arrowy light" seemed to follow and linger with her; a very spirit of loveliness "brightening the scene." If my darling was heart-sick, Warren Hayne should not know it. How in my soul I honored that brave little woman for the manner in which she kept this resolve! I saw how Warren's eyes followed her, the same deep mystery and subdued lustre in their depths which I had seen there in the morning.

Many of Stanley's admirers at Nahant, who had given way to him as to one having superior claims—partly from respect to Mr. Hayne, again because they cared not to come into open competition with that gentleman, in a race for favor involving certain defeat to themselves—now seeing his immolation, gathered about her in mute profession of the homage they felt. She appeared so gay, so brilliantly animated, even I was puzzled to decide if the assumption was real. It was strange to see how composed and self-sustained she was; while he was correspondingly moody, sullen, and wretched. The chain he had worn so lightly hitherto, now galled him bitterly. I had never known this polished man of the world so entirely at a loss as upon that occasion.

Milverton, considerate fellow that he was, charitably claimed Warren's fiancée for a polka; it was amusing to behold with what alacrity he resigned her to his friend and came at once to us. When within the enchanted circle of Stanley's pure presence "Richard was himself again." She smiled calmly, never once by look or act admitting that she felt his omission of the morning; for he had been so constant previously in his devotion to our party it could 'be regarded in no other light. He was piqued at her apparent indifference, and grew positively angry when some favored friend of Raymond's led her forward to the dance. Ah! how vain his wrath then! I smiled when my eyes

4*

sought those of our tragedy king, for I really enjoyed his
discomfiture.

"I imagine you have enjoyed a charming *tête-à-tête*
with your new-found friend," I remarked, as he came
nearer. With cool sarcasm he answered :

"To those who do not know better I might admit that
I had; but to *you*, who are informed that the contrary is
true, I do not hesitate to repeat *I have not.*" Retta Austin watched him from a distant sofa, never once taking her
black eyes, which shone like basilisks, from his face.

"Cousin Warren," I said again, more gently now, for I
pitied him, though with terrible meaning in my words, for
I also pitied Stanley, "you have two women's hearts
under your heel! Which will you decide to crush, one or
both?" He sprang hastily at the conclusion; speaking so
vehemently, I was really alarmed to see the cold, proud
man thus moved.

"Tell me frankly, Jenny—much depends upon my
knowledge of these facts—do you think Miss Montana
cares in the least for me, or does she love Ingram?
If I could bring myself to feel they really loved each
other, my course would then be clear; I should not
for an instant hesitate. In the other instance to which
there is reference in your meaning, I can assure you there
would be *no heart broken*, simply because there is none to
break. On the contrary, if I should crush Stanley's, with
it I should set an iron heel upon my own. I have not
spoken a tithe of what is in my heart for her, because in
many regards it seemed not quite honorable so to do:
though to none other am I bound by a *positive* promise.
Miss Strawbridge, in our New York circle, has been so
accustomed to receive my attention she has come to look
upon it as a matter of course to regard the monopoly as

her right rather than her privilege. Tell me, Jennie, before Miss Montana joins us again; I must know, and shall know sooner or later."

"Question your own heart, Warren, if hers has not long since taught her this lesson? follow whither this knowledge may lead you."

He gave his arm to Stanley as she came up flushed with the exercise of dancing; she leant upon it, paling slightly beneath his burning gaze. The atmosphere of the room furnished sufficient pretext for his leading her to the veranda that they might get a cool breath from the sea. When they passed the low window near to which I sat, I saw that he had taken both her hands in his, and heard him ask distinctly, in tones hoarse with suspense and suffering:

"Shall not this wretched mockery cease?"

I heard not the answer she gave, for just then I went to dance with Clyde. Once, as we again neared the window, I saw them walking to and fro. I could not forbear a triumphant leer in the direction of Miss Austin in retaliation for the glance she had sent after Stanley early in the evening.

The quadrille ended; we two, Clyde and myself, came out to join them where they stood looking out upon the broad expanse of water, over which the solitary ship with single sail had passed to the further tides. How deep and dark appeared that sea, outspread under the stars of heaven! A cold, white moon uprose in the sky. What should we prophesy? There was no speck or blemish in all its bright expanse. The ship was out of sight, swift gliding towards a port of the unknown. Again the bright river, as it ran through my morning dream, crossed my memory. A beam from the ghastly-faced moon, as she skulked within the gathering mists, cast of Stanley and

Warren a joint image on the sanded floor, "while pulse to pulse and heart to heart was beating"—one little shadow united, nothing more!

Was this the all of love immortal as Deity? We shall see.

Overhead God's stars were shining! Beneath their radiance we trod the pathway of invincible destiny.

———o———

CHAPTER VI.

"There is no future pang
Can deal the justice on the self-condemned,
He deals on his soul."

BYRON'S MANFRED.

"STAN, you little princess!" exclaimed Raymond, kissing her with great vehemence, when the engagement was made known to him; "Hayne is the best match in all New York! Half the women there are dying for him; he is a kind of Adonis."

"**How** sublimely selfish, Ray," I ejaculated, by way of response; "you expect to settle in this locality. I have not forgotten your *penchant* for Mary Kingswell."

"Neither have I," he answered, smiling. "By the way, **Jennie, how** does it happen you did not succeed in captivating some one of the legion beaux at Nahant? You might **well have 'stooped** to conquer' another so elegant a fellow as Warren."

I dared not look up—I was conscious that Clyde's eyes were upon me; when once for an instant I met his glance, it was so full of agonized tender regret (for Stanley's loss I thought), tempered with an appeal that was like gall to my spirit, remembered in after years.

Leaving Milverton and Hayne at the sea side, we came back to Ridgely in the grey gloaming of an early autumn morn. We four; the atmosphere of a nameless change about us, other than the one we knew of, into which had been infused the subtle essence of a new presence. Surrounded by love's delightful atmosphere, Stanley glided back into the quiet life so long forsaken. Somehow we all fell into the home ways at Ridgely, naturally as though we had never left them off; and the calm, broad, peaceful current had not been turned aside, and we tried our strength upon a deeper ocean of thought, feeling, and suffering. There were our mornings breaking in glorious light and beauty over the New Hampshire hills; and our evenings, when the father joined us in our walks upon the terrace or lounged with Ray and Clyde upon the velvet turf, whilst we wove acacia buds into wreaths and tied frail mignonette blossoms into garlands for their brows, thinking how the dead wife in Ike Marvel's "Reveries" had loved it; and what a sad thing it would be to exchange the beautiful world, with its flowers and sunshine, for the decay and darkness of that terrible realm of the unknown. There were no unquiet thoughts in this dreamy spot; we had left the tumult amid the gaieties of Nahant—in the heat and dust of the great metropolis. The glow came back even to Clyde's classic face, and a strange prophetic rest to my own tired heart.

How gradually, yet naturally, Ray and Mary came to withdraw themselves from our midst; and during long, golden afternoons, to wander off in shady by-paths to converse in gentler, deeper tones—in short, to love each other more than all the world beside. I have never known a couple so entirely assimilated in disposition, taste, and feeling. Love to them was a calm, placid stream, upon which to launch their bark of life, whose current was a deeper peace. To us was left the regal flow, over whose crystal deeps we dashed onward mid rocks, wrecks to the eternal sea outspread beyond. Is there a fate linking the least of these sentiments with the Infinite? and must the process needs be one of simple peace or deep, deep suffering, according as our natures require the chastening? Through the medium of these tender heart-chords does the Father seek to draw unto Himself again His world-wandering children.

I remember one evening, Stanley's head, with its wealth of golden brightness, was resting on my shoulder while the gentlemen talked. Mr. Kingswell conversed with them frequently and earnestly; he never opened his mouth but pearls of wisdom dropped from it. How sagely he dealt with life! Each simple stricture contained a lesson worth enshrining. We were fully conscious that his words were pervaded by a deeper, more subtle philosophy than sages usually propagate or men of God at all times practise. On this occasion their subject was one—a man who was esteemed among the great of this earth. Clyde remarked, cursorily:

"I truly sympathize with him; he has outlived his generation, or rather he has fallen behind the age in which he lived. Companions of his mid-life orgies are widely scattered; of all who revelled with him, very few are left; many who set out with him at the commencement of the journey have passed on. He walks the streets of his own city; the curious peer at him from every window; old, familiar faces one by one have gone further into the mists beyond; homes where he was wont to go at evening, an ever-welcome guest, bear strange inscriptions upon their door-plates. What must be his feeling to know the world that he has served through all his life has thus changed to him? The reflection must indeed be a melancholy one; for he too is changed and grown unacquainted with its simplest usages. I can think of no one more, deserving my pity, and that of all men."

"How few of our great men," remarked Mr. Kingswell in answer, "learn, until some unpleasant necessity forces upon them the simple truth—the world is Satan's taskmaster! Those who do most to deserve its favor are those who oftentimes incur its severest censure. Besides, this man was a faithful disciple of his tutor; he has been one of the most noted libertines of his day. How many a simple-minded girl, chaste and pure before breathing the dreadful miasma surrounding him, has taken then the first step in that downward path within whose mazes he, the last of all his victims, has lost the way; perhaps for all eternity. To such I accord my sympathy and regard as exceedingly unjust; a tribunal which would exclude from all charity his victims, while exalting and heaping its honors upon the man who has made these heartless triumphs, and consti-tuted them the stepping-stones to advancement within the area of his ignominious celebrity."

Raymond here observed between puffs of his Havana, omi-nously incorporating with white wreaths, blue ones of smoke:

"The vanity and self-love of some men are absolutely dis-gusting; judging from the manner in which they parade their debaucheries, one might imagine they considered every species of error in which they chose to indulge as being really exalted by their august participation. After having warred all their lives through with purity and uprightness, at last, upon the score of their very degradation, claiming amnesty from the God of truth and justice."

Mr. Kingswell then remarked:

"Ah! but they cannot do this; it is not in the power of

man to do.   Even those whose souls commune with and interpret rightly the commands and exactions of Deity—those
who are mighty in intellect—who can make stepping-stones
of mountain peaks, and move within an area of the stars—
cannot sin without coming down from those proud heights
for which they have toiled, thus nearing the everlasting
sun.   The spirit just begun to rejoice in its freedom is
dragged back to the dusty highway of **earth,** where it
grovelled first ere its fetters were rent in twain.   R—— is
one who has thus sinned in the face of Revelation and conscience, possessing the fine tastes of a mind **born to a**
higher heritage.   When the awakening comes, and these
faculties assert themselves, he will be of all men the most
miserable.   He may wrap gaudy tissues about the form of
sin; but she will one day shake them off, and appear before
him in all her loathsome deformity; a coarse, repulsive
courtezan, assuming a thousand disgusting and repulsive
aspects with which his higher nature cannot longer assimilate.   The soul will not trail its glory-tipped pinions 'mid
the dust of the senses; heavenward it soars; ofttimes then
is the affiliation but very mockery.   I think R—— has
come to feel this already!   The soul has proclaimed her
heritage of freedom; the sun is going down upon the last
slopes westward lying, yet is the mortal part still bound by
a thousand jagged tissues to the rack of past and present
transgressions; the age runs its round of days without him.
Hence, upon the earth, he who ever bent so ready a knee
at the shrine of her pleasures is now a stranger and pilgrim.
What account shall such a man render, not only of what
has been done, which it were better to have left undone,
but what might have been accomplished had he not permitted selfish indulgence to blind the true, far-seeing eyes
of immortal destiny."

Here a shadow crossed the starlight, sleeping on the grass-plat at our feet; and the figure of a woman, bearing in her arms a child, sank down as in supplication; the light on her clearly cut features—so wan, suffering, and pale—showed to me the face of Leah Eldridge, the friend of my childhood, now, alas, a mother, who bore still her maiden name! I uttered a sharp, shrill cry, as I recognised her. Mr. Kingswell stooping, raised the poor creature, who had sunk from exhaustion on the stone steps, had fallen really with such force as to cause a serious contusion on one of her temples. Those kind arms lifted and carried her into the house, while Mrs. Kingswell took up the baby, a bright little fellow of perhaps a year old, with dark-flowing curls, very pretty I saw at a glance; I also saw, when we came into the home light, not half a century of years could so thoroughly have changed my friend as that one year of sorrowing repentance had done.

Some lives can only be brought to sin by being borne out of their usual channels; when once the impelling force is removed that turned aside the pure, steady current, they surge back again to the upright course, and mirror the same beautiful soul-thoughts as before the beauteous spirit wings were trailed amid the dust and blight of the sunless way. I saw instantly how this was true with Leah. I hold with Mr. Kingswell that sin can never be exalted; it is a bitter draught to some who feel that they would rather toil, work, starve, die, than drain its cup to the bitter dregs.

This brave resolution was written where I readily translated it in the white look of anguished endeavor on Leah's piteous face; in the clothes she wore, the tatters that enwrapped her boy; in her readiness to face all, that she might find one who would aid her in coming back, one who would not simply tell her she had taken the wrong turning, but who would point out the way and means by which she might return to the forsaken path of right. Did Mr. Kingswell esteem himself too holy to do this for one so stricken and powerless as my poor fallen friend? All these thoughts came to me as I bathed the wan temples from which the life-blood was freely flowing.

"I think some angel must have guided me here," she said faintly, as if in a kind of dream. "How I prayed God he would take me somewhere, anywhere, out from under those cruel stars which seem to pierce me like the eyes of doom. I used to love them once, long ago, but stars are an awful thing to the homeless—shining afar off, like the light of joys we dare not hope to know again. Though henceforth I will say no harmful word of the stars; they brought me here; and oh! if you knew all: what I have suffered in my prolonged and painful struggle with the world for work, for life, for myself and child, I am sure you would not send me away. I will labor for you all my life through; I will be your faithful slave even, unless you really force me out into that wide, hard world again. I should faint in the heat of its noonday suns, with my sinful burden. I could stand it no longer; I can only die, should this last resource fail me, this appeal to you, Mr. Kingswell, who was my mother's friend." She wept here. I pressed her hand gently, and wiped away the blinding tears from her eyes; then she looked at me; a gleam of recognition overspread her wan features, but it faded swiftly as it came, for it seemed the sense of her true condition. Her shame so utterly overpowered her she could only exclaim, brokenly— "Aljean Montana, is it you? Oh! how wide the space between us has grown! yet I remember you well, as though it were but yesterday we parted. I know not your way since, but mine has been through an endless winter. I have fallen, Jennie, very low, but do not censure your poor friend; may you never know what it is to love as I have loved; forgive me, you do not know all; I am unworthy even to look upon your face, yet you hold my hand and bathe my brow—mine, poor, miserable, destitute as I am."

I heard a voice say—it was Raymond's, fiery, impulsive Raymond's—"Come away, Jennie." Then another voice— soft, tender like Jesus must once have spoken—"Let her remain; this woman was her friend! She needs her now." It was Mr. Kingswell's. Then both young men came and stood beside me while I bathed her brow, saying in turn to the host: "What shall you do with her?"

"What shall I—what can I do? The way of the transgressor is hard; we should not seek to make it harder. I feel I have no right to cast at her the first stone, if in truth I have a right to cast any stone at all." Raymond looked abashed and humbled; the more so when Mrs. Kingswell, in her soft, mild voice, came closer to Leah and laid her sleeping boy upon the couch beside her, saying gently: "Do not weep so, child; you shall not be sent away; we will try to find you a home of refuge from the cold, wide world you dread so much, which has in truth dealt very hardly with you. Now go to sleep and rest."

That wife had her earthly reward in the look which her husband bestowed upon her as we were leaving the apartment. It was the seal of her sacrifice.

On the following morning, at Mr. Kingswell's request, I walked with him to see Captain Bob Eldridge; to inform him of Leah's state, and her presence at Ridgely. The poor girl shook her head when she knew we were going, and said it would be of no use; she was sure her father could never forgive her, or receive her; we surmised that she was right in her conviction; but duty seemed to point in that direction, so we went.

It was a mournful spectacle that met my eyes; Captain Bob sitting still in the solitary house, as I had always remembered him sitting there after his dead wife was borne away—grimly, as though he had for companions the ghosts of departed fancies. He scarce raised his brow when we entered; and even in that faint effort there was no uplifting of the spirit to sustain the motion. In one brief glance I saw how his daughter's shame—that more cruel scourge than sorrow for the dead—had ploughed deep furrows down his cheeks, and burned a deep, deep record on his brow. His hair, grey and thin as I remembered it, was entirely gone now, saving a small patch on either temple. I was more affected by this speechless lethargy than I could have been by any words he might have uttered. I went nearer to his side, smoothing his bare crown with my ungloved hand—questioned him regarding his knowledge of the past and of me.

" Who asks if I know them?" he answered querulously; "I know no one; not even my own child." His voice, as he said those words of Leah, grew almost fierce; he stamped in rage upon the floor. I saw that he was almost mad; how terrible, and yet I had heard of his having been in this state for months at a time. The worst form of madness is that which never loses consciousness long enough to become cured of grief. Mr. Kingswell, thinking this opportunity as favorable as any that might occur, stepped to the other side of the old man, speaking very kindly but firmly of his wish and purpose:

" It is of that child—your daughter, the knowledge of whom you have this hour denied—that I came here to talk to you. She has found her way to my house after having suffered much; more than you and I, my friend, can ever know. Will you not pardon her? She is still your own; years of error on her part could never obliterate the tie that binds you to her; despite your course, a few bitter words could not break it—a few kind ones would make it strong again. She is yours still—yours and God's —who will not lose sight of her in her brave strivings to find the forsaken way. He will light her feet, and I myself righteously believe she means to walk in it, with His help, to the end. You, too, will help her; she will repay you, I am sure, by taking this sting of grief and shame from out your poor old heart. I ask in behalf of Christ who died for sin; in the name of her dead mother—in the name of the God who shall one day pass sentence upon us all—to take her into your home and heart again; there let your child find rest and peace!"

I could not fail to observe all the while Mr. Kingswell spoke how Captain Bob quivered like an aspen leaf; I thought him a prey to some revengeful emotion; perhaps he remembered still that his dead wife had said to him one day: "Robert, you are unjust to William." How like the eloquence of that long silent voice were the tones to which he listened now, I fancied with some sign of relenting; but the memory only served to gall him more. Almost any other would have been a more successful ambassador just then; yet the cause was a just one, and would triumph in the end.

"Are you here, William Kingswell?" exclaimed the old man, surprisedly—every fibre starting into new vitality, as his voice attained fresh vigor; "I have sworn you should never enter my door. That you have forced me to break my oath to the dead, is retribution dire. Leave me, I command you, or I swear anew you shall be compelled to go;

there is yet sufficient strength in the right arm of Bob Eldridge to expel you summarily." He would have fallen in his agitation, the poor, feeble old man, whom I knew strong and well, had I not forced him back into his chair gently, so gently, he was scarcely aware of the action. Mr. Kingswell faced him fearlessly.

"You mistake me strangely, my friend, if you imagine for an instant I came here to taunt or annoy you. I have told what I wish to say concerning Leah; you still persist in refusing to see and receive her; she is under my protection, and shall remain with me, since I must resign the hope of being able to place the poor girl under her father's roof. Since that may not be, I must not refuse to do for her what I can myself, and with God's aid I will." Finding his office of peacemaker at an end, he readily accepted that of protector.

The old man, thoroughly aroused by this unconscious assumption on the part of Mr. Kingswell, answered him in tones full of withering scorn:

"You can well afford to assume the office of general dispenser in cases involving the slightest omission of duty on the part of others, whose acts do not so much concern you; but have you always played the philanthropist, and been thus prodigal to your own flesh and blood? At whose mandate did one fair and beautiful and good go away from you, never to return?—for she went long ago to that bourne from whence no pilgrim may return. Who was unforgiving then? Who closed the doors of home and heart in that long-past time? William Kingswell, you have commenced too late."

I looked at Clyde's uncle; the old man's manner was menacing, and his tones were full of sneering, when he had hurled the last shaft at his ancient enemy. The dart had not reached its aim; Mr. Kingswell was impervious to keener shafts even than these; he was so accustomed to probe his own heart and lay it bare to his Creator. Unmarred was all the glorious inner life save by this mistake of his youth. He was calm as one who had triumphed over remorse, and the victory thus achieved was through long suffering, of which there was no trace now, however, only deep, painful anxiety in his tones, when he said tremulously:

"Tell me, my friend, if you know aught of *her*—that poor, erring child? I would give a world to know her fate, if I possessed one."

"What would you know, William Kingswell; more perhaps than I should care to tell you, if I could? Let me alone; I ask of you nothing, only that you will leave me." He pointed impatiently to the door. Feeling that nothing could be gained by remaining, we left the old man to his solitudes, and came sorrowfully up the slopes to Ridgely.

It was hard to meet the expectant look in Leah's face, and have no answering word of comfort to give her. She saw how it was—as it had been; tears trickled down the pale, thin cheeks, and fell upon the brown curls of her boy.

"Your effort has not been altogether hopeless, Leah; you shall stay here as long as you like; this shall be your home while you choose to make it so."

With one of those swift, sudden impulses which in the erring seem the upheaving of a better nature—hidden, but not destroyed—she threw herself at the feet of Mr. Kingswell; too full of gratitude, she held her benefactor's hands, while her tears fell down like rain.

"Leah," he said, solemnly; "do not thank me; there is one to whom your gratitude is more directly due." She understood him, and clasped anew her hands in earnest prayer.

And thus it came to pass that Leah Eldridge came into
the household at Ridgely, and took her place henceforth as
one of its inmates. How strangely such things come about!
We have never since had cause to regret what we did then,
though in many instances we could not have acted thus
with impunity. There is no standard by which to estimate
error in degree so true, so just, as that of manifest sincere
repentance. Then, again, we know that God is the God of
the wretched, and **Christ their Saviour.** Who shall hide
his glorious beneficence from the eyes of the world-weary,
whose sin by tears of bitter suffering has been washed out?

Once more into our season of content came the image
of Warren Hayne, bringing brightness, yet dispensing
shadows he **had left** in the void where his presence was
not.

But Clyde! I could not understand him, his conduct
seemed so strange. I was sure he loved Stanley, though
when her engagement had been first made known to him
he evinced little feeling, only I imagined I saw the agonized regret burning deep in his soul-full eyes. How I
worshipped this man! even though he seemed towering
high above me, as if his soul was set among the stars, in
whose light I walked, where his feet too trod on the hard
earthway beside me. His spirit seemed to soar and pierce
the dim ether, yet never for an instant ceased to be fet-
tered with the material part of life, or lose its hold upon
the **actual.** Often, often have I seen that gleam, spectral
as starlight, yet never once did I suspect or know until
long after what the glance portended. How blind is the
keenest insight at war with fate!

It soon became known in the circle at Wayburn that
Warren Hayne would marry the beautiful Southern girl,
guest of the Kingswells. Stanley very naturally shrank

from what seemed to her indelicate publicity of that which in her estimation should be held sacredly; but Warren manifested a strange desire to parade his triumph. He was one of those men who disvalue any gift the world does not share and set high estimates upon. Many marry as though they anticipated having numberless spectators to every domestic scene from youth to age, so eager a desire they manifest to conciliate society in the choice of a partner for life, and court its due appreciation of their selection.

Mr. Kingswell said little on the subject; he was too thorough a gentleman to obtrude the expression of an opinion which had never been sought; I knew he had learned to love Stanley very dearly, and would have been pleased if she and his favorite, Clyde, had chosen each other. I knew he talked it over with his good wife when they were alone together; for in each sober face I saw the verdict of their keener judgment than we possessed, which foresaw a time when the silver tides of this affection would sink amid the thirsty sands of after life.

'Twas thus the bright-browed summer passed, and in her stead came golden autumn showering treasures of crimson and amber; harvests fresh from the sickle were bound and stored; "the grapes were purpling in the grange," yet we lingered at Ridgely—lingered because we had no courage to break the airy tissues of our happiness and seek to weave them about other scenes, lest in the process they should vanish, leaving us in darkness. At length a letter arrived which turned the balance in favor of Claremont. Aunt Edith was ill; Uncle Montana, embarrassed by an unlucky speculation, required the services of his sons to set him right. I overheard Mr. Kingswell and Clyde talking softly about the matter, and judging from fragments of the conversation which reached me, I

was more than ever convinced that the suspicion I had
hitherto entertained concerning Uncle Clifford's original
investment was correct. I also knew that both Raymond
and Stanley were ignorant of this fact! therefore to no
human ear did I breathe the knowledge which had unavoid-
ably come to me. Some things were clearer now that
before had appeared so dread a mystery. The scales were
dropping from my eyes! I thought I knew now why
they had been so anxious to forestall matters in that regard
and negotiate a marriage between Stanley and Clyde ; just
then I was feeling sufficiently malicious to rejoice in secret
that their plan of bargain and sale was prospectively
thwarted by her anticipated union with Warren Hayne.
Though for Uncle Montana, in any event, I foresaw trouble
in the future. Austere, uncompromising man that he was,
loving money as his God, it was very natural he should
wish to wed his only daughter with great wealth. As for
Warren, beyond a decent competence he had only his
fine business capacity and indomitable energy, which were
in themselves the surest avenues to future wealth and
honor.

At length we came back to Claremont. Aunt Edith sat
up, wearing her sweetest smile with which to greet us, but
there was so marked a contrast between the almost transparent whiteness of her complexion and the hectic glow on
either cheek, as she rested them alternately against the
purple velvet lining of her luxurious chair, we were startled !
Then the hand she held out to us was so thin and wasted,
the look of it pierced our hearts with remorse. Why had
we left her to eke out the frail remnant of her vitality in
utter loneliness, while we pursued our pleasures ? How
cruelly selfish we had been ! I knelt beside her; pressed
the poor wan fingers to my lips, choking down the anguish

that would not drop its weight in tears; while Stanley, her own child, her best beloved, unable to look upon the change which had struck us all so painfully, went to her own gorgeous apartments, tapestried richly and draped in blue and gold, tasselled and mirrored in a style which would have rivalled the boudoir of an Oriental princess. 'Twas thus I found her, an hour later, her face buried in a rich couch in her chamber. Warren Hayne's beloved! yes, and Clyde's too! they both loved her. I loved her, and would soothe her pain; and I did, breathing in gentle words a hope which I felt to be hopeless; meanwhile picturing a future which would be hers even when this bright sun of her youth was gone down in the darkness, and only the star of his love shining.

I do not think Raymond really understood or duly appreciated the change in his worshipped mother. Very soon he sat down to tell her of Mary, of his engagement and his happiness, she smiling calmly—a sympathetic recognition of his joy; but when he went on to speak of Stanley and her love for Warren Hayne, she questioned until he told her all! Then a shadow fell upon her face—a shadow as of disappointed hope—while her eyes sought Clyde, whose misery was so proudly still; only she and I guessed how he suffered and how heavily the blow would fall on him.

How wondrously does the social atmosphere affect and influence the physical! Even that insidious foe, consumption, will relax his hold oftentimes for a little season, and allow his victims to linger securely in some sunny place by the wayside, even when most intent upon hurrying them to the dark shades beyond. It was thus with Aunt Edith, who was so happy in having us home again, she rallied and gained strength sufficient to take her place at the table which, being physically unable to preside, she had been compelled to abandon weeks before.

Aunt Dinah too was present, who declared it was "as solemn as a meetin' to have nobody to come to de table 'cept massa, who et nothin' hisself—hardly enough to keep a fish alive ; all de cookin' was done for nothin' while we was gone. As for Hawsey, she had pined after Miss Stanley tell she was no more 'an a shadder ! Pity young miss couldn't a tuck the child along wid her; but I 'spose it was dangerous, dem folks up Norf is so mighty medelsum 'bout we niggers."

Aunt Dinah's feelings were almost abundantly poured forth in behalf of any one who ate little ; this, in her estimate, was a state approximating the very climax of misery. Even in ordinary conversations, not in the slightest degree pathetic, it was Aunt Dinah's habit to shed tears. They were as natural to the old lady as sun and air to plants, or as Raymond mischievously remarked, as "water to a duck." They were the invariable tribute of her susceptible heart on occasions either grave or gay. Now, however, the old lady was entirely excusable for her indulgence of the emotion she felt at seeing her mistress well enough to resume her old place in the reunited family, and Hawsey, the apple of her tearful eye, reinstalled at her post of honor again. Said Hawsey was a faithful little creature, notwithstanding her propensity to regard the boys slily from out the corners of her bright eyes, and really attached so much importance to the performance of her duty as dressing-maid, regarding her service as so indispensable an adjunct to Stanley's comfort, it was amusing to witness her transports on our return. I verily believe she imagined Stanley's hair had not appeared well once during her long absence from home; good, kind, and indulgent as her young mistress was, she really permitted her to enjoy this belief, which she did even with the evidence of well kept glossy ringlets to the contrary. Hawsey's idea of a land where people waited on themselves was anything but flattering to the proprietors of free soil.

———o———

CHAPTER VII.

" Be wise to-day, 'tis madness to defer ;
Next day—the fatal precedent will plead ;
Thus on, 'till wisdom is pushed out of life."

YOUNG'S NIGHT THOUGHTS.

CLAREMONT! our fairy land! How very lovely it was— with long, cool verandas, shaded. by stately magnolias of dark shining foliage, and green slopes swelling southward to the gulf and westward to the sunset. Whether in the light of morning or the garish brightness of noontime, the gradual waning of golden day or soft shadows of evening, descending gently as the footfall of angels, it was beautiful, and its atmosphere was one of perpetual spring. Autumn had flitted caressingly over its shady groves and flowery walks, just touching with more gorgeous hue verdure and foliage, when Cousin Warren came to visit us. He appeared in a transport of rapture; actually put aside his stately politeness—assuming the elegant *negligé* ot Southern manners—took his place in our home circle naturally, as though he had been bred and born to the position he then occupied, and was self-constituted sole proprietor of his mystic surroundings. Often he would tell us over and over how very happy he was. One of his pet indulgences, I remember, was to pluck the fairest flowers, toy with them, then pull them to pieces, just for the pleasure of seeing them borne afar off on the misty wings of breezes which

came up softly from the gulf; again, he would strew them
in the path before him as he walked, and trample upon the
dissevered petals with a careless indifference that wounded
Stanley. One day she spoke to him of the strange habit.
I sat upon the upper veranda and could not avoid hearing
their conversation. He had woven a wreath of orange blossoms and set it afloat upon the surface of water inclosed by
a marble basin which held the fountain's falling spray,
talking languidly as he watched golden minnows leap to
catch them or trace their shadows underneath. She said,
softly, it seemed an answer to her thought :

" You may decide that I am fanciful, but I never see a
leaf cr flower detached from the parent stem without a
sensation akin to the keenest pain."

He responded in his usual *blasé* manner:

" They are among the bright creations made to be enjoyed while they last ; " his look said : Then put aside to
make room for others.

> " Gather the rose-buds while you may,
>   Old time is still a-flying ;
>   And the same flower which blooms to-day,
>   To-morrow shall be dying."

" Herrick is wise ; he has propagated a very comforting
sort of logic, which I never fail to adopt."

" Yet," said Stanley, " it is a very sad philosophy which
teaches men to speak and act thus; they would be inex-
cusable for the promulgation of such sentiments were not
word less culpable than deed ; men of the world affect a
species of bravado in adopting them. I should scarcely
expect you could be brought to endorse a theory or prac-
tice so chilling in its effects. Many poets, whom fortunate
genius has lifted above its severest casualties, seem to take

an insane pride in thus braving life and scattering its treasure by the way. I can never recall some of Moore's defiant lines without a shudder. Little by little we come to
extend this selfishness to animate as well as inanimate objects, which is apt to lead to practices very pernicious!
And were such indulgences unanimously adopted, the
result would be to sweep all generosity from the universe."

"The attribute of selfishness is more general now than
you seem to imagine. I have already learned to endorse
the theory—as every one must sooner or later in his intercourse with mankind; though truly it is a deplorable era
in the history of an individual—the first faint realization of
the fact that self-interest is the motive-power which impels
the machinery of society.

"Beyond one glorious truth, I hold all the world to be
false as it is fair; I am sure if I should learn to doubt this
fact I should not want to live! The blight would cover all
my life, and the charred remains of the structure in which
I have enshrined its hopes would blacken all the pathway
to that golden realm of light shining yonder—a goal in
the blue distances of coming time—and shroud in darkness the very canopy of heaven. This is the one great
truth whose existence I feel within the area of my heart's
pulsations. There is only one—there can be but one love
such as you have inspired—and since your little feet have
walked in the hollow wastes of my life, I have known no
other joy—

> "'With thee conversing I forget all time,
> All seasons and their change do please alike.
>   I love thee and I feel
> That in the fountain of my heart a seal
> Is set to keep its waters pure and bright
> For thee.'"

Ah! when other seasons, with their changes dread, came
on, did one inky drop of the sad blight succeeding stain
the crystal waters of the one pure fountain in his heart—
whose golden seal was crushed and broken in obedience to
a mandate of the world—the same world of which he talked
so contemptuously, yet whose voice was stronger than the
voice within?　Yes, out into this same world he passed,
leaving the bright golden love-life afar back in its glory!
The pearly gates closed after him with a crash that shook
the solid earth; on he went through desert ways, joyless
amid the seasons, gliding swift from flower to snow; that
same world lying henceforth all between his heart and
hers.

> "Oh love! what is there in this world of ours,
> 　That makes it fatal to be loved?　Ah! why,
> 　With cypress branches hast thou wreathed thy bowers,
> And made thy best interpreter a sigh?"

When in Warren's far away home autumn was wearing
the faded garlands of departed summer, the winter sky of
a fearful strife between brother and brother, friend and
friend, was darkening underneath the heavens.　The political contest of 1860 terminated in the election of Mr.
Lincoln to the Presidency, which event was succeeded by
the withdrawal of all Southern members from the repre-
sentative hall of the nation, which course resulted in the
secession of South Carolina, which was quickly followed
by other States.　Our hero began to grow restless, and
longed for the busy world again.　A system of pleasant
dalliance by the wayside may bring feverish ecstasy to a
man of active habit, but it can never wholly satisfy or insure to mind and heart lasting peace.　Life is a steady
current, ever rushing on, on; we must sail or drift with its
swift flow, and work our passage that we may come into

the channel which joins the ocean tides, which will bear us to golden portals of the bright beyond.

Warren proposed that with the consent of all parties concerned, he and Stanley should be married at once and return to the North together; she hesitated, from disinclination to leave her mother in her present feeble health. Was it a dim foreboding in my heart that, if deferred, the result would be misery for both, that caused me to speak as I did?

"You are wrong, Stanley, you should go with Warren; he wants you. Aunt Edith shall be well cared for; besides, you know not what might come between you to prevent the ultimate consummation of your hopes. Should the national Union, as we have reason to fear, become disrupted, Warren may then be considered an enemy to your land! Would you wish to marry him then? Again, his former enchantress may yet win his love from you: most men are stigmatized as fickle, you are well aware; he might not prove an isolated exception." An expression of deep pain passed over the features of my friend, though she answered not a little proudly:

"I do not anticipate the first event to which you refer as though the occurrence were almost certain. Our national league is too strongly augmented by the sacrifice of years to be broken by the guilty efforts of a few shameless partisans. As regards Miss Strawbridge, I do not fear her! However, if the result which you intimate be probable or possible, it were better I should know it at once; I could not so thoroughly appreciate his homage were it less exclusive."

Since I have grown older, in justice to mankind I do not hesitate to express a belief that so called fickleness is only refined exclusiveness. Man cannot lay his heart at

· 5*

every shrine to which he bows a willing knee in amusement or courtesy. Warren was not really unfaithful to Stanley in the test which followed; his waywardness was wholly the result of events so complicated—so directly bearing upon his destiny and hers—he found it impossible to break the chain of irascible circumstances.

When Mr. Montana became aware of the pending issue involving his daughter's preference for Mr. Hayne, he urged no grave expostulations, only evinced a pettish displeasure; which was manifest in his expressed wish to have the marriage deferred: "Wait," he said; "Stanley was scarce more than a child!" He could make no other objection, knowing how his daughter's heart was in the projected union; he repeated in the interval of deep hard breaths: "Wait."

Again, when Warren in person knelt with Stanley beside the pale-faced mother, asking the precious boon of her child's love, she could only clasp her trembling hands over that golden head with its falling curls; while her white lips, too, said "Wait." Why should those tears have fallen then and there, upon the flower-garden of her daughter's youth and hope? Only I knew how dear to each parental heart was the project of uniting her and Clyde, who was the sole inheritor of Claremont and Brightland. His mother held nothing, now that he was of an age to claim them; not even the slaves, except by suffrage: hence they looked forward to this consummation of their scheme as to a final adjustment of pecuniary affairs, of late so complicated and uncertain. At this particular juncture, if compelled to repay large sums of money frequently borrowed from Clyde's ready capital, the result would be utter ruin. It was because he felt he was not strong enough to breast the waves just then, that he said to Warren and Stanley: "Wait!" and the pale-faced mother repeated after him the one touching, comprehensive monosyllable. I thought I detected in the dark, splendid eyes of Clyde a gleam of tender appeal that, too, suggested—" Wait!" And my suffering, feverish heart responded with sad echo to the joint burden of that of the household—" Wait!" and we waited, but not long.

There was one person who advocated Warren's claims with great vehemence. Ray was the exception to the general expression of deference. He often repeated his assertion of a former occasion; that Warren was the most fitting match in all New York. Then perhaps he knew nothing of the league in favor of Clyde; or if he did, considered that young gentleman abundantly able to assert and advocate his own claims. But of some other things he was well aware, which we in our blindness did not know until long afterwards.

Notwithstanding all that Raymond said in favor of a speedy union, it was decided that the marriage ceremony should not be performed until the coming spring.

One morning, a few days later, it was arranged that I should drive down to the city with Clyde to do some shopping. I shall never forget the picture which met my eyes on going to Aunt Edith's room to receive special injunctions concerning her proposed purchases; she sat in a large chair near an open window, while Hawsey combed her soft brown hair; Stanley rested from her embroidery on an ottoman beside her; and a few feet distant, Miss Ellis, with her knitting-work. By the way, I have not yet had occasion to describe this very interesting personage; whose most prominent characteristic was the aforesaid knitting-work, which was ever present with her. She was possessed of many family details, which she had repeated until we knew them word for word, though the lady in our household was a " sarcophagus " of silence. She rarely spoke unless some one addressed her; then, if possible, answered the question or remark with as few words as possible. Again Miss Ellis, or Miss Phœbe as we usually called her, was well versed in the complicated record which held dates of every marriage and death which had occurred in almost every family of note in the section, for years and years agone.

How she came in possession of so varied and valuable a stock of information, was a fact utterly incomprehensible; for she never asked a question, unless, as we surmised, it was by some adroit process of storing what she learned incidentally; and by the exercise of the rare faculty she had of putting this and that together in the prolific soil of her own memory, which yielded in case of any emergency an abundant harvest of uncontrovertible testimony.

This little lady, with her quiet ways, had been the lineal heritage of Claremont long before the Montanas had lived there. During the lifetime of the first Mrs. Ingram, Clyde's mother, she had been employed to superintend the arrangement of the household. Upon the occasion of the instalment of Mrs. Ingram second, she had been permitted still to hold her place. Then when the father and master had died, and Mrs. Montana assumed the direction of the establishment, she was still held one of the humble retainers. Through all these vicissitudes she had been so constant and patient in her duty-doing, step by step she had mounted, until now she stood upon the topmost round of the ladder, from which high eminence of hardly-won confidence it would have been difficult to precipitate her, for she prided herself much upon this distinction. It was not a habit we children had acquired in our bringing up to like Miss Phœbe much! She so persistingly kept upon the track of our waywardness, and brought to light all our little mischievous schemings; she was sure to unravel our

mysterious confidences during vacations spent at home, **and**
report them in her quiet way, so that we really stood much
in awe of her in those days. Now, however, the feeling
had passed away, and we had grown to appreciate and
esteem her. It was easy to perceive she was yet a source
of annoyance to Hawsey, upon whom she kept a sharp eye,
though by day she never ceased her endless knitting. I
watched her now curiously as she sat weaving into the web
of counterpane upon which she worked, together with the
notes of birds singing from their stately perches amid the
foliage of magnolias; these mingled with the uncouth
croakings of Stanley's paroquet! All these were bound in
long white meshes that fell from her wax-like fingers slowly
as a moving shroud. Now and then was a square with
which were interwoven the golden threads of hope—like
those running through Stanley's bright years. Stanley had
ever been a favorite with Miss Phœbe! Again, with the
dream of Clyde's young manhood, some darker threads
streaked the fabric—running strongly and steadily as the
current of life that was ebbing before our eyes—though we
scarcely realized it now. How blind we were to the sad,
solemn truth! All save the observing, kind-hearted, soft-
voiced woman, who seemed so little likely to observe the
fact, and yet who knew it first of all. There was no trace of
the knowledge in her face; only now as I recall the many
incidents of that time, I remember too how her manner
grew more subdued, and then she manifested as unaccountable indifference to many of Hawsey's shortcomings! and
was seen much less frequently at her post of observation on
the lower veranda, where her glittering needles were brought
to bear upon the servants in their daily work. Aunt Dinah
held undisputed sway in her realm; and every morning after
having washed the china, trimmed the lamps, brightened

the silver with a piece of chamois leather, and dispatching
a little dusky emissary to Miss Phœbe with the keys of the
sideboard, descended thereafter to her own domain—oftentimes with full an added inch of turban on her woolly head.
Her importance expanded each day?   And in proportion
as her greatness increased, her severity to those in regard to
whom her jurisdiction was faithfully exercised, grew more
insufferable.   Aunt Dinah's philanthropy had also dilated
astonishingly ; her tears, usually so wont to flow, now gushed
forth without the slightest provocation.   In short she cuffed
the little kinky heads below stairs, and wept penitently for
the offence whenever she came into our higher realm of
expiation.

Of many things that were amusing in our household, and
some that were very sad, I stood thinking while tracing that
picture of the morning preceding the last evening which we
all spent together, when I heard Stanley's voice calling me
to come in from the veranda where I had stood musing long
and abstractedly.

"I wish, Jennie, you would call to see Retta Austin
and procure for me if possible the pattern of that worsted-
work; I cannot go on with this until I familiarize myself
with the original design ; you will confer a favor by so
doing, for which I will be very much obliged."   She
hummed a little snatch of melody from Trovatore, which
Paroquet repeated in a hoarser voice.   I promised to execute her commission, and hearing Clyde descend from his
dressing-room, I passed out on. the front veranda to let
him see that I was in readiness.   I soon received his signal
as the horses came sweeping round the curve, with proud
manes flashing and coats like autumn sunshine.   How very
gallantly, almost tenderly, he assisted me into the buggy
and took his place by my side.   We had long since ceased

to address each other save in the presence of others; now on this particular occasion silence was a luxury: the bright, bright river of my dream was gliding on; the golden water seemed to touch my feet as we went whirling along its margin with a speed that almost made me hold my breath, yet scarcely kept pace with its current. I was unable to decide if my fancy was not a reality, so strangely had this habit of musing grown upon me. At length I broke the spell of our silence by remarking, with enthusiasm:

"Life seems a dream, Clyde, so blended with the Infinite that I can scarcely separate the real from the unreal, the life here from that I hope for."

"I once thought," he said, a shadow coming into his fine face, "that life was a dream! but the dream is over. Now it is a cheat, a delusion, a show, full of sound and fury 'signifying nothing!' an autumn of reality in whose atmosphere wither and fade the bright things it brought from the depths of that great mystery in which it came— into which it shall be resolved again. I am shivering through a long November, which is fast darkening into an eternal winter. I have sowed—others will reap; the harvest is not my own."

I saw the shadows darken on his face where the morning light had been. I wanted to ask why it was so; if it was because he felt he could have no life apart from Stanley's love? Yet how bravely and quietly he accepted his sad destiny! There was no despairing, no faltering of his life purpose in the path where duty lay, no frittering away of energy and integrity, because of that departed May of life and love whose mortal sacrifices are as so many tabernacles reared to the Infinite. The interstices of passion lie above its downward paths: these should be avoided by the far-reaching vision of a love that may soar beyond!

enduring as the immortal power whose essence it is—regenerated, purified.

Yes, with the inspiration of his presence round about me, in behalf of that other love, that love of his for her, I could have said all this and more, had not Lane Austin come alongside our vehicle returning from his morning drive.

"I was coming out to Claremont this morning, Miss Jennie," he said, in his cheery voice. "I have intended doing myself that pleasure ever since we came back from the North. I am actually dying to hear the sound of your voice; I have heard no music worth listening to since we left Nahant; you were kind enough to sing for me there on one or two occasions, I remember."

"And we will either of us sing for you again should you come to Claremont for that purpose; moreover, we will welcome you gladly." He tipped his hat gracefully and passed on as we drew up in front of our stopping-place. I requested Clyde to come back for me. I looked upon his fine face for the shadow when he handed me out of the buggy; it was there, still deeper than ever, and with the resolution to chase it away if possible as we returned, I started on a journey to perform what Aunt Edith had given me to do. I went first to a dry-goods establishment in Canal street. Upon inquiring for certain articles I was instructed to walk to the further end of the store. Passing a row of assiduous clerks, I came at last to one who furnished me with numberless specimens of flosses, gay-colored worsteds, and fancy articles of every description, talking busily meantime of the merits of the goods in question, while I made my selection, caring little for what he said; Clyde's face, with its shadow, was at my side, and the bright river flowing far away.

In my preoccupation I was just on the point of having him tie up the wrong package for me, when my attention was arrested by the sound of a haughty, imperious voice, belonging to a lady who requested, or rather commanded, to be shown very many things—goods of every style and quality—as though she had been appointed chief inspector of new fabrics, with an air that showed plainly she thought she was conferring a great favor by deigning to examine them at all, even with no design of purchasing.

It chanced that Warren Hayne passed that way. She saw him, and immediately ordered one of the clerks to recall him. When he came she seized his hand with more than her usual warmth; whereupon he expressed in courtly terms his unexpected pleasure in having met her. Cousin Warren was never at a loss for fashionable badinage; now he told her he had never seen her looking more charmingly, even during the palmy days at Nahant. She thanked him cordially, and proceeded to ply a score of inquiries which sprang forth with the sharp vivacity of bullets from a seven-charged revolver. Firstly, "if he was quite well;" secondly, if he came South immediately after taking his face from their pleasant circle on the Ocean shore; if he purposed remaining long in New Orleans, and how he had passed the time since his arrival? He answered that he had not come South immediately after they parted, but had remained long enough to arrange his business, so that it might not suffer in his absence; that he was quite well—in short never better, and had passed the time at Claremont so very delightfully, it was a source of deep sorrow and regret that he should be compelled to return North during the winter; but so it was, he should leave on the morrow.

"I thought we passed you, Lane and I, as we were driving a few days since."

" Eh !—I was on the road with Mr. Ingram ; went with him to his place ; fair locality—Brightland."

"I presume," answered Retta, with an offensive and haughty leer from the corners of her sharp black eyes, almost hissing the words through rows of pearly teeth ; " that is, I am sure you must have passed much of your time with Miss Montana. She will be married very soon. Father remarked the other day—' Unless Mr. Montana's daughter married Mr. Ingram he was a ruined man. The investments in the business, together with Claremont, Brightland, etc., are the exclusive property of Mr. Ingram. The estates came by his father ; Mr. M. has held them in trust for many years—now his stepson is of age, and will probably want his capital for other purposes.' "

She said much more, which I will not here repeat ; she went on talking in that gross, unlady-like fashion, in a conspicuous place, of our family concerns, as though she had a personal interest in them, and the information favored that interest ; talked on utterly ignoring the fact of Warren's preference for Stanley. He said no word, however ; an occasional answer couched in monosyllables was all the response he vouchsafed to other queries when she had closed her harangue on this subject.

" By the way," added Retta, appearing to have forgotten until then the very purpose for which she had called him in ; "I suppose of course you are aware that Miss Strawbridge has arrived in the city ? I have not seen her myself; it was Lane who informed me her father had grown anxious concerning the ability of at least *one* of his Southern patrons to meet the requisitions of creditors in this severe season of almost universal suspension ; consequently he came to satisfy himself they would be sustained by efficient backers in the event of failure. Mr. S. and his daughter are at the St. Charles. I shall call there this morning. Perhaps," she added, turning carelessly from the piles of gossamer which an assiduous clerk had arranged for her inspection, "you will call with me. At all events I hope to have the pleasure of entertaining you this evening, the last of your stay in the city."

"I should be most happy," Warren answered—though it must be confessed he did not appear so just then—"were I not previously engaged, to accept your kind invitation, granting the exclusive right to monopolize me for the evening. However, I may see you this afternoon."

He took her little snow-flake of a hand—it was one of Warren's tricks—into his own, relinquished it, and was going, when she said again, assuming an expression of artless simplicity—

"Mr. Hayne, I have purchased recently an elegant floral album, and would like so much to have an acrostic or something of the sort above your autograph. Really, it would enhance the value of the trifle very much." Now who could have guessed the double purpose that lurked beneath this apparently single request! Firstly, perhaps, it was influenced by her secret love for Warren Hayne; secondly, it boded no good either to Stanley or himself. He answered, smiling:

"I shall copy an extract for Miss Austin with great pleasure, provided she makes the selection; but I have outgrown the habit of extemporizing on paper for the delectation of my friends."

The truth was, Warren was in love! and could not so readily divide his sentimentality with the world of women as he had been wont to do; they could have gallantry at his hand, it was their due, but he was chary of anything more than the merest lip service.

Again she turned a little uncomfortably to the examination of rejected laces. Again he endeavored to take his leave, though at the very door of the establishment he encountered Miss Strawbridge. A mutual salutation ensued; then a consultation, in which Miss Austin joined delightedly, leaving the assiduous young man to put away his goods without so much as thanking him for the effort to find for her what she really did not want. From my post at the further end of the store I beheld these proceedings, the finale of which was, Cousin Warren offered an arm to each of the ladies, and the trio passed together into the street.

I was aroused from a fit of musing by the voice of Clyde, who inquired if I was ready to go home. I gladly replied in the affirmative, speedily rectifying my mistake concerning the packages; then we too went forth into the broad, bright noonday, and the city outspread—a map of busy life, its fluctuations and its vast concerns—through shady avenues, streets dusty and sun-beaten, towards the home-way. After what I had heard my ideas were so confused, that notwithstanding I traced the shadow still upon his face, I had neither mind nor heart to ask him why it was there, and no spirit to make the faintest endeavor to chase it away. So we two rode on in our accustomed silence back to Claremont.

The same evening after I had listened to the conversation which took place between Retta Austin and Cousin Warren in the store in Canal street, Raymond came in—our bright, handsome Ray—tossing his brown curls and threading them with his fingers, having previously sailed his broad-brimmed Leghorn hat upon an imaginary sea; which, being the most accommodating of hats, having, doubtless, imbibed the spirit of its owner, came back in a circle to the sofa in the upper hall upon which he had ensconced himself; uttering a shrill whistle, meant to illustrate the temperature of the day, suggesting furthermore that his gentlemanship was very much fatigued and would take it in high dudgeon if no one came to fan him and inquire how he did.

Stanley and I were sitting in front of Aunt Edith's room on the veranda, enjoying the soft breeze which came up from the lake with the lulling, indistinct murmur of waves breaking on a distant shore. Ray's whistle was unheeded very soon he called out, in tones of gay reproach :

" Girls, you are inexorable to-day ; however, I happen to be possessed of a piece of news which I am sure will startle you very much. Jennie, bring your fan ; come sit here, Stan, I want to lay my head in your lap and have you guess who is in the city." I kept silence, waiting for Stanley to speak. However, after several attempts and failures, Ray answered his own question volubly :

" To-day, about noontime, I sauntered into the St. Charles, thinking to meet a friend who is stopping there. While in waiting I chanced to glance through an open door leading into the ladies' dining-saloon, when I saw Hayne sitting at table with an old gentleman whom we met at Nahant, and two ladies. I was aware Hayne's stopping-place was the Veranda. I was surprised to find him here. A second inspection elucidated the mystery. The ladies in question were Retta Austin and Miss Strawbridge ! Now what in the name of St. Cecilia do you suppose has brought her to this city ? and what would she accept from Warren after his open rejection of overtures from that quarter on a previous occasion ? Ah, me ! poor Hayne ! I have an undefined conviction she will yet carry off that fellow and marry him against his will !" After which charitable speech our sage Raymond composed himself gently to sleep. I fanned him patiently until the hour arrived which I had appointed to see Miss Austin, if possible, for the purpose of executing Stanley's commission.

I drove down with a servant that afternoon; Clyde
came later, behind his ponies. I met both Warren and
Miss Strawbridge at Mr. Austin's. That haughty young
lady bowed very formally indeed when Retta pronounced
my name, as though the accent insulted her or was associ-
ated in her mind with something very unpleasant.

She absolutely frowned as Warren said to me, when,
after having obtained the samples for Stanley, I rose to
depart: "Wait a bit; I will drive with you;" then glancing hastily at his watch, added: "I forget I have an engagement to meet Ingram *precisely at six;* I will come out with
him." This word, and the accuracy of his emphasis in
speaking it, were peculiar to Warren. When I had taken
my seat in the carriage he said again:

"This little affair will not occupy me long; please say
to the ladies I will do myself the honor to join them early
this evening. *Au revoir.*" He went his way; and again I
passed from the heated city into the shades of our consecrated home.

He was true to his word! he came early. I sat with
Ray upon the veranda, when we saw them coming out on the
shell-road, he and Clyde in a light buggy together. How
handsome they were! How radiant they appeared, wafting
graceful salutations to us as they came round the curve,
caressed with slanting sunbeams. The blush of red autumn
was upon the landscape and waves of the lake. The roseate
hue deepened as the sunlight paled in shadow; but the
flush was in our memory long after, whenever we recalled
the day upon which our fate came to us in the form of Miss
Strawbridge.

Clyde sent his cream-colored ponies and buggy with his
groom back for Uncle Montana; then joined us in the west
parlor, where the glow of sunset was lingering still. That

was a happy evening. By tacit consent no one spoke or seemed to think of Miss Strawbridge. We were very gay; even Aunt Edith joined us. It was only one of a series spent thus in the same manner, but there was a strange charm in it; I know not why, save that it was the last we were to have like it on this earth. Aye! was it the last of clear bright sunsets and shadowless moonbeams falling through dark green foliage of fir and palmetto; the last circle of smiling faces at the sumptuous board; the last musings and tender whisperings as evening waned? Ah! yes; the last of everything as it had been; of all things saving the farewells—one for a long time, and the other till eternity.

Before Cousin Warren left us that night a chill autumn rain fell. It seemed to pervade all things like a dense gloom, and wrap its vestments around the sufferer. Which one? is now the query of my heart as I write after the lapse of a few years which seemed to have been ages. We heard the sound of falling rain upon the house.

It was over; Warren was gone! but the rain and autumn leaves were falling still, with a dreary sound which drowned the music of the fountain. Vapors thickened about the Gulf, slowly descending and wrapping the harbor fleet like a shroud. I kept my watch at the window of my own apartment for a long time; then I went to Aunt Edith's room and found Stanley sobbing on her mother's breast. Alas! how many tears she shed in after time, when there was no bosom for her but her Saviour's and her friend's. My own was always faithful.

When silence brooded in the great house and the world without; when slumber descended upon bright eyes, love-lighted with hope and joy, and eyes weighed down and weary with the long out-look; when there were tears in the eyes of the stars—I saw the orange-wreath that Warren's hand had made, as it lay blighted in the misty night, beaten by the fountain's falling spray, cast hither and thither by the drifting rain. A moan came up from the wide grey sea, as if in its great deeps the gusts of a hidden storm were breaking.

I went and sat by Stanley's side while she slept—a smile upon her fair young face. I knew she was dreaming of days that were like golden ripples on a sea which was shaken as by a presaged convulsion, whose moans were like human voices—agonized suffering in the changeful night.

———o———

CHAPTER VIII.

" For all that in this world is great or gay,
  Doth as a vapor vanish and decay."
                              SPENSER'S " RUINS OF TIME.'

THE flush was gone from the red autumn ; leaves fell sorrowfully with sharp sprinklings of snow that fell glistening like frozen pearls upon the grass; scarlet bèrries hung in clusters looking sweetly picturesque, with their frame-work of nut-brown foliage flaming amid palmetto and larch. I had never seen a Southern winter look so gloomy and forbidding ; the orange wreath lay withered where the fountain fell, and that bright river which had hitherto kept pace with my life, was no longer a part of my musings. I seemed to have been brought nearer to a dim space, shrouding the vast ocean with its tides, in the two months that had elapsed since Cousin Warren left us. The winter gaieties were fullfledged ; old courtiers were wont to say they had never known a season so filled with attractive entertainments.

We, being novices, were compelled to participate, and were courted and flattered with attention from all quarters beyond our power or desire to retaliate.

Thus the days passed, and we out into the unknown. Winter was drawing to a close. No word from Cousin Warren since he reached home. Once or twice he had written by the way, and that was all. What could mean his cruel silence ? Alas, its consequences were plainly visible ; Stanley drooped. I scarcely know how she was enabled to pass through the ordeal of her formal introduction into society, yet she glided with her habitual queenly grace through scenes bewildering enough to have quite dazzled one less firmly poised. I remembered the words Warren had spoken on first beholding: "I have never seen one so youthful appear so empress-like." I have beheld since, how that same expression trembled on the lips of many within the circle of her own home. What to her were words of adulation ? They did but mock her, secretly pining as she was for the faintest sound that told of him.

One sad day the mystery was explained in a manner which struck me dumb with astonishment. I chanced to pick up a Northern newspaper Clyde had let fall as he came from the breakfast-room. Glancing briefly at the contents, I was about to throw it aside when my eye fell on a marked paragraph, with Milverton's initials below traced with a pencil. *Warren Hayne and Miss Strawbridge were married !*

It was this intelligence that so amazed and shocked me. I could not for some time avail myself of a single idea ; at length, however, I found myself possessed of a vehicle through which I could transport my thought to the startling truth, uprisen in all its vast proportions, where the flowers of the old hope lay crushed and fallen. It all seemed so strange, so new and dreadful ! I made my way to Stan-

6

ley's apartment, entirely unprepared for the sight that met me there. *Was that white, fixed figure, so still and cold, with glaring eyes of ocean blue, our joyous, merry-hearted child— our Stanley?*

I never should have been able to identify her but for the sunny hair falling in golden masses over her rich dressing-robe. She rose to receive me calmly, very calmly, so much so that I, in my agitation, was brought to doubt that she was yet aware of the strange, incomprehensible fact. Still no word from her lips, only that fearful, fixed look in her white face. My heart seemed burning within me—the room was reeling. I must speak. In as steady a voice as I could command, I said: "Stanley do you know—have you heard——?"

Every precaution failed me here; I burst into tears. I would have clasped the poor stricken bird to my heart, but that look on her face, so white and stony, repelled me. My eyes were dry now; she was first to speak. As she did so, a look of wildness came into her beautiful eyes, but no glow to her marble cheeks. The red current seemed to have ebbed from sight with the tides of that bright dream and the shores of the old time. How strange and far back in the past it seemed; after all, it was only one of those exquisite shapes which float in the dim air about us, yet find no likeness in stern truths of every day. How many bright tissues we weave about the forms we love and hope to clasp so fondly; yet at last, how they elude our eager grasp and float beyond our reach. Then we go our way through the semblance of things, our better, nobler, higher selves lying in the grave of some vain endeavor. I saw it would be thus with Stanley; all heart and tenderness seemed utterly gone; all that was fairest, loveliest, and best, sat mourning the far-off time by the mortal remains of her bright, beautiful dream. Her words came slowly and hoarsely :

"Yes, I know ! I have better authority perhaps than you have ; he was kind enough to *forewarn* me in a letter which arrived this morning. I should have taken your advice, Jennie, which was, I believe, to clasp the chain about my captive when the effort would have cost me less and the distance have been more convenient. *I envy you your relative.*"

I was cut to the heart by her cool sarcasm ; so wounded by this unnatural taunt, I forgot at that moment her suffering and her wrong—everything. I now think that the burst of passion to which I gave vent was her saving ordinance. My words relaxed the heart-strings winding more and more tightly around the swift coil of fate for a final terrible crash.

"Stanley, I think now you should have married Warren when he wished it ; you loved him and he loved you ; it was owing only to caprice that you did not go with him when he willed it. But for this delay you might both to-day have been happier. You may have been the chosen instrument to save himself and others ; you rejected the office. Has conscience no voice in the matter ? I have no word to offer in extenuation of his conduct ; but I do say I believe it will be much modified when we come to know all the influences that impelled him to this hasty course."

"I never wish to know more than I know now ! All the gilded tissues in the world could not disguise the horrible distorted fact. The very thought of extenuation is abhorrent to me. Loved him ? Ah ! yes, as I, poor silly child, loved him he will never again be loved. That love was the glory of my life ! It lighted the earth by day and the heavens by night. I came to womanhood with no other

thought or hope than those which circled about and cen-
tred in him, my ideal of all that was high, generous, and
noble. How it is fallen and lying in the dust at my feet!"
She sat for some time so still-looking into the dark space
that had opened into her young life so soulless and cold, I
was really alarmed. She added, with a bitter mocking smile:

"He said he loved me, that he lived but for my smile;
he called me tender names, but now—oh! I believe I am
mad! for Warren Hayne's kisses are burning on my lips,
and his tones of endearment ringing in my heart! Oh! if
I could only strike them from my memory as he has rifled
my hope! Could I but tear his image, with its earnest
eyes—yet reading my soul—mocking me with that false
one of his—from my life, and die. Ah! yes, death, decay,
darkness; anything is preferable to this agonized torture.
Oh! why do I feel as if there was no truth on earth, and
even God were false! For is not he, Warren Hayne, now
pouring into the listening ears of the woman he has chosen
the story of the miserable little dupe who thus loved him!
whom he deceived and trifled with! And she is gloating
o'er her triumph!—the triumph achieved through her paltry
gold." She arose and walked the apartment slowly; she
was not agitated, on the contrary she was still so preterna-
turally calm I really feared her; to arouse gentler thoughts
I spoke of her mother.

"Oh! my mother," she exclaimed, something like terror
rising in her white face—whiter than before, but motionless
of muscle and fibre as a tablet which marks a grave; "she
must not know this, Jennie; it would kill her outright. Let
no word on this subject to any one escape your lips. I
will fight this battle with myself alone." She emphasized
the pronoun *singularly*, that *other self* she meant; she
seemed to be seeking to discern it through new dim spaces

—backward lying in her life—as she continued: "Never name it even to me. I have done with it utterly as though it had never been. I regret nothing so much as the crushed idol fallen on the dusty way which I must tread." She was tearless still, but there was a look of such utter weariness on her beautiful face that told of a great soul-sickness within. My heart bled for her, poor stricken bird, but I could only wait until the ice was broken up. I recalled Warren's words the last evening at Nahant. I saw as then the great sea with its waves crashing near, and the storm rising in its heart. Far out through mist in the depths of that immeasurable space into which she had drifted I saw the lone ship cutting her silent way, waves lashing her gilded sides, wind crashing through her sails, driving onward to the dim unknown. Ah! could Warren, lashed to a dull shore which she had left, do cheerfully his work of life with eyes fixed on that timid sail fluttering white in the distance, which grew wider every hour? I felt then that his would be a drearier task than hers in the time to come; so I spoke hopefully:

"Stanley, you are young and beautiful and *proud*. Rise above this thing; strength will be given you to do so, I firmly believe. It will be hard. I know what it is; for I have not myself been without sorrow. I tell you this, that I may claim the privilege of enduring with you; we will bear together in silence, yet in sympathy, this heavy burden, until we come to a calm resting-place in the great journey."

"Thank you, Jennie, my true, true friend; I will accept what you so kindly offer—confidence, sympathy, everything —any other time; but to-day I am better off alone. Leave me, dear, and go to mamma; she will miss me, and she must not know!"

There was both appeal and warning in her face: in it I traced a gleam of the old self—the childish, guileless self—

looking through the eyes of this strong woman, who had so proudly mocked the image of her idolatry a few moments earlier.   Seeing this, it was hard to leave her; but she wished it and I went.   I heard her bolt the door; then all day long she paced to and fro; I, waiting in dumb anguish, served her meantime as best I could.

Aunt Edith inquired for Stanley.   I answered her with as much cheerfulness as I could assume; telling her Stanley was suffering from an attack of nervous headache; had not slept the previous night, and wished to remain alone in her room; she would soon be with us again.   Then I **gave** Hawsey private instructions not to disturb her young mistress by going to her room; she was sleeping, and would not come down to dinner.   There was no one present when that meal was served, excepting Miss Phœbe and myself. Aunt Edith did not appear, and the gentlemen were not home until evening.   Aunt Dinah was enjoying her usual state of tearful solicitude about members of the household in general: her sympathy was manifest in effect.   She consumed herself a double portion of the viands left untasted on the table, abundantly grateful for the blessings of Providence, among which was health and strength to enjoy what was prepared for others.

I carried a dainty little repast to Stanley's room; but she entreated me in tones of such broken suffering not to force anything upon her, that I descended again to the dining-room with her food untasted.   Aunt Dinah's bandana was brought into solemn requisition.   She had fears for "Miss Stanley, poor child."   My heart echoed faintly, "Poor child!" yet I felt no sorrow for her in that guise, loving, simple, trustful, hopeful—like that I now felt for the woman, full-grown, developed in suffering—to whom these qualities were lost, and could never be restored.

All that long, drowsy afternoon, with a secret knowledge how the spirit of this woman, stricken and proud, was striving with itself, I did my duty as usual; I read aloud for Aunt Edith while Hawsey brushed and plaited her long brown hair. Miss Phœbe sat knitting, gentle and still, while the sunshine came in, barring walls and pictures, the bookcase, and bed where Aunt Edith sat propped by pillows—bringing upon shining wings the odor of flowers—faded and gone like the summer the murmur of the fountain—all were alike to what they were on a certain morning when I noted them before. The group, wanting one figure, was likewise the same. I heard the words of Hawsey in her idle talk, mingled with the steady rattle of Miss Phœbe's needles as she knitted into the fabric of other strange occurrences, the broken threads of this broken dream of Stanley's. Its crash had not yet jarred upon the household, which moved in the routine habitual to it. The harmony was still unbroken. Golden ripples of sunlight crept lower on the wall; at length the shining track grew crimson and disappeared entirely. Grey twilight came softly; then the dimmest of darkness fell upon the picture and broken dream. The sun was gone down into a great, wide, inexorable sea.

I heard Raymond's voice in the hall calling, as usual, for his sister. I was amazed at the black, lowering brow with which he received the intelligence that she was not well. He gave me a piercing look, which I answered with a glance of assurance to him that she knew all and would bear it bravely. He drew me with him into the dining-room, in obedience to some little words of caution which I dropped concerning Aunt Edith. There he drew from each pocket a revolver, burnished and glittering, with silver-mountings flashing in the dim light.

" *In the name of Heaven*, Ray, what would you do with those terrible engines of death ? "

"*In the name of Heaven*," he answered, "I shall kill that contemptible villain who has deceived and wronged my sister." There was, indeed, murder in his eyes! I could only shrink and tremble; I was powerless to do or say anything that would turn him from his purpose. Poor, poor Stanley! Our pet, our pride, our sunshine! It was upon her that Warren Hayne had put this bitter insult. I saw it now in that light. Before, I had only thought of the suffering she must endure. My tears fell fast and burning, though I gulped down the hump in my throat and went to Ray, her brother, so stricken at the thought of her grief, lifted the matted curls from his fevered brow, and running my fingers through them, as was his custom, I essayed to speak—with poor success. He promised, however, to aid us in keeping the knowledge of what concerned us all so nearly from his mother. He did not relinquish, yet did not repeat the threat of vengeance: I saw his purpose deepening as the darkness gathered without—growing more solemn and certain of fulfilment every hour. Yes, I saw it, trembling with dread.

It was a strange, dismal meeting round the tea-table that evening. My uncle was not present; Clyde was moodily silent, as usual; Raymond's brow wore somewhat the aspect of gathering thunderbolts. As for myself, I was thinking of Stanley's strange words in the forenoon, and did the honors constrainedly. Ray pushed his plate away, to the discomfiture of Aunt Dinah, who had broiled his quails to the nicest shade of brownness, leaving them untasted, and **went slowly up-stairs. I heard** him knock once, twice, thrice, at the door of Stanley's apartments. He was admitted, and remained a long time; finally, when he came down, looking softened and subdued, the thought of his threatened vengeance passed out of my mind. I carried a cup of tea to Stanley to please poor Aunt Dinah, who was growing more and more wretched and tearful every hour for the shortcomings of our degenerate household.

I found my friend lying on a couch, her beautiful hair streaming wildly over her white pillow. Hawsey followed with a lamp, but Ray had lighted one of the wax tapers which stood on her toilet, so I motioned the faithful girl to leave us; she obeyed with tears in her eyes; they were in mine too. I prevailed on Stanley to drink the tea; she was very pale, but I was rejoiced that no trace of the haughty woman, who had so sternly looked her desolation in the face, remained. She was tearful and silent, yet appeared patient and gentle as a child. She wound her arms about my neck and kissed me; well I understood that silent caress. She was mutely asking my pardon for what transpired in the morning; I looked my forgiveness *all*, but not a tithe of the great love which made her a possession of my own. I told her I was vain enough to feel that I had a place in her heart which no one else could fill, and that when the wheel went round and she came back to the place where she had left me, she would want me then and would not hesitate to let me know it. And so it happened from that hour—in every conflict with herself she achieved a victory over that stern, hard usurper of the morning all alone.

On the following day Stanley arose and went about her ordinary life as usual; dissevered from the life that was ended, yet never looking back; no, nor forward to that which was to come; she took her place at her mother's side as though nothing had happened. The severest mandate of grief is that we are ofttimes forced to wear a mask with which to hide its gnawings.

Stanley's embroidery was resumed; the knitting was in a comfortable state of progression. Hawsey combed Aunt

Edith's long hair, whilst I read from the great volume. The father did his work of life in the city, assisted by Raymond and Clyde; in our household everything was going on as it was wont to do; only I observed with pain how Stanley grew whiter, more silently taciturn day by day. She often spent hours by herself; during which seasons, with the effort of keeping from Aunt Edith and the servants the knowledge of her sorrow, my energies were taxed to the uttermost.

One afternoon she sat for a long time listlessly looking into space. I think she was unconscious of her attitude of deep pre-occupation until aroused by words of her mother:

"Where has been my sunshine of late? She seems to have taken refuge behind an overarching cloud of silence and reserve. Stanley, my pet, what is the matter?"

"Nothing," the white lips answered.

"Nothing, dearest, are you sure?"

Again the white lips moved, though now 'twas only an echo, repeated more faintly—"Nothing."

The swift fingers of Miss Phœbe entwined the disavowal with her record of events. Hawsey's bright eyes were full of unshed tears as she trailed the coil of rich brown hair into a Grecian knot, then went out to shed them in secret.

Aunt Edith's head drooped lower on the pillow; her heavy lids fell dreamily upon two sunken cheeks. To her life was a spirit fetter, nothing more; yet to Stanley——

Ah! was it nothing that the strong stay had failed her when most loved and trusted? Nothing that the ivy tendrils of her sweet affection had been rudely torn from their support, and lay crushed and withered on the earth? Nothing that the universe was changed and the light of day gone from the face of heaven? Ah! nothing; the white lips said so. My heart repeated the echo of other words

spoken by other lips in other time and place, when the
chain was cemented, and two shadows blent in moonbeams
on the sanded floor; as Warren Hayne led Stanley forth
one evening long ago. The world, which seemed now so
narrow and blank, then was wide and fair, and life was beautiful; but now, all this was nothing! I repeated the word
in the depths of my spirit many times. Only another
stricken heart deprived of its anchor, hope; from a twin
bark dissevered, drifting out with the great tides of human
destiny. The orange wreath lay withered where the fountain fell—the beautiful river was lost amid barren sands on
a desolate shore; its golden ripples broken to ebb no more,
and a solitary ship driving on through mist and darkness,
outward to the far-lying sea. I began to feel it my
duty to inform Aunt Edith what had occurred to make
this change in Stanley. I signified to her my intention of
imparting something of importance; she bade me send
Hawsey out of the room. Miss Phœbe was to remain; she
was one of us. I had commenced my narrative of sorrowful events, with which the reader is fully acquainted, when
Retta Austin dashed into the room like a domestic tempest.
She took great liberties in our household, so she informed
us; half expecting we would gainsay a fact of which we were
all too sensible. She excused herself, however, upon the
ground of her anxiety respecting Mrs. Montana's precarious
health. It was this which induced her to avail herself of
the opportunity of coming out with Lane, who was on his
way to Brightland. Her quick eye caught Aunt Edith's
look of depression, and my own of inattention, as she rat-
tled on in her voluble fashion for a while; then inquired of
Miss Phœbe for Stanley. The gentle little woman replied
by looking hopelessly in my direction; which appeal I
readily interpreted, and replied that Miss Montana was

suffering from a severe attack of headache, and requested to be excused to visitors.

"How long has she been thus affected?" she answered, with sarcastic coldness. I saw the drift of her thoughts—knew before the reason of her coming; Miss Austin never did the slightest thing without a concealed purpose. I replied, with a haughtiness which equalled her own, "that Stanley had lain down since dinner." She sat for some time biting the fingers of her dainty glove; at length she said, sharply :

"I presume you were all much surprised to hear of Mr. Hayne's marriage !"

Miss Phœbe's knitting-work actually dropped from her fingers. I answered Aunt Edith's glance of inquiry with an affirmative gesture, merely signifying that this was what I meant to tell her. She composed her face with an effort for which I blessed her in my heart, and replied that she had felt very little emotion on the subject.

"Oh, no, of course not; the difference to any one at Claremont would be very slight, whether Mr. Hayne were married or single in one sense; though I supposed his friends"—she emphasized the word—"and relatives"—here she looked at me—"would naturally feel some little interest in his welfare, if only to rejoice in his having secured to himself so fortunate an alliance. Miss Strawbridge is a great beauty, you know, besides being a *millionaire.*"

I was only consoled in our joint endurance of this last palpable insult, to feel how these words had ploughed through Retta Austin's haughty heart and left their furrows there. I felt I never could have been brought to retaliate in the spirit which prompted her to say these things; for she too loved my cousin Warren with all the strength and fidelity of which a nature like hers was capable. Both

Aunt Edith and myself were silent. When the black eyes were brought to bear on Miss Phœbe she merely said, "Indeed; I was not aware he had been so favored." Her speech referred merely to the money arrangement, after which she resumed her knitting with the usual quietness.

After a few cursory observations, each pointed and significant, Miss Austin took from her pocket a tiny rose-colored note, sealed and scented, which she left with Aunt Edith for Raymond, remarking merely that it contained commissions which he had promised to execute for her in the East.

I fear my face must have expressed the terror I felt; I knew I was pale; the life-blood was sinking slowly, and a coil of agony seemed tightening around my heart. I answered quietly as I could:

"Of course, he will take great pleasure; he goes, let me see, when?"

"This afternoon, I think; he told me he thought he should leave on the five o'clock boat to-day. I called at the bank, but failing to find him, I came this far with Lane. Of course you will see him ere he departs."

I was agonized beyond expression; Miss Austin, without designing to do so, had been of infinite service to me. There was no time to lose. I rang the bell and ordered the carriage hastily; left Aunt Edith with a promise to return speedily as possible. I then went to Stanley's room and informed her what must be done, and done quickly. She was lying listlessly, her slender fingers clasped over her white brow, from which her golden hair was flowing. It seemed cruel to bring this new terror upon her, though she was prompt to feel the force and exigency of the case. When the carriage came round we were ready to depart. Swiftly down the road over which Clyde and I had passed

on that bright morning in the autumn-time we glided now.
On through busy thoroughfares and avenues all shady and
fragrant with the breath of exotics, and by streets crisp
and sere, teeming with life that was warped and withered,
we passed to Uncle Montana's banking-house. Raymond
was gone.   We threaded our way through the busy
throng on the levée, in imminent danger of being swallowed
up in the tumultuous din, when Lane Austin, who had
come down to superintend his father's shipments a moment
before, **rescued us** with great suavity. In answer to my
inquiry **he said,** "Raymond **is on board.** I saw him
standing with Ingram **on** the upper guard. I will endeavor to secure his attention for you." So saying, he
conducted us aboard, and after a few inquiries at the office,
led us back to an apartment near the ladies' saloon, in
which sat the truants for whom we were searching. The
door was partially ajar; I saw **at** a glance that Clyde's
attitude was **one of** eager appeal, while Ray, our bright
sunny Ray **of** old, now he was moody and still, his brows
knitted in angry, gloomy defiance. How changed he was
of late ! He started slightly on beholding us, but recovered
himself instantly ; he endeavored to carry off with a high
hand the part which he meant to play in this new, strange
drama, though he found the effort very difficult beneath
the calm scrutiny of his sister. She bent her white face
over him with a look from which there was no escape ; she *would* speak, and he must listen; and he did,
though the look of firm determination did not leave his
glorious eyes even when he resolved to hear all that she
wished to say.

There was no visible emotion when she did speak in her
face or voice, only she crushed my hand until the little
plain gold ring, my love-gift of childhood, was almost

buried in the flesh. My eyes followed the donor—once a brother, now so no more—as he passed through an outer door to the guard, and stood watching the sun-bright surface of the calm, still river, and the winter sun, half hidden in its heart. Bright beams gathered round, seeming to caress him with their sheen, while their fiery fingers toyed with his dark-brown locks, and danced to fairy music in the clear depths of his splendid eyes. How strangely Stanley's words broke on the spell with which I contemplated him— his attitude and expression.

"Ray, why did you leave us, with never a word of farewell?"

The brother was silent; he did not tell her it was because he had seen how that silent sorrow was daily making inroads in her young life, and he could not bear to meet the look in her white face, mute evidence of the change a few short hours had made. He who loved her did not tell her what was in his thought and mind; how we had in her home seen the orange blossoms lying crisp and withered; and through the crushed and broken dream no golden river glided. The rosy current, like the last tint from the sunset sky, had faded, and there were only the white, still waters of her young existence bearing the fragments of a morning hope to the far sea. Our hearts bled at the sight; we could not bear to look upon it, though there was majesty in those depths of woman-nature thus revealed by the sudden sorrow—the majesty of one ready for the journey—equipped for the warfare with life and with fate. In answer to this new-born strength and power, profound respect was added to her brother's fondness for his sister. The recognition of these attributes trembled in his tones when he answered her:

"Stanley, I did not tell you, because—because I go to

settle a terrible account with one who has wronged you."
He broke down here utterly; the faintest flicker of color,
like the tinge of crushed roses, came up in her white cheeks
for a moment, then sank again; a wave of the old life
touched once again the desolate coast where she was
stranded. She did not falter in her purpose. I have heard
such words but once, and hope I shall never hear them
again. Oh! the eloquence of woman's lips, trampling
pride with every selfish consideration beneath her feet; she
can only speak as Stanley did when pleading for the life of
him she loved, who was so far and yet so near. Ah! so
near, his presence in her own home—walking its paths
with his kingly tread, crushing the flowers he scattered
there. Nearer still, enshrined in her innermost heart of
hearts, yet smiling peacefully from out blue spaces lying
misty and far—distant beyond an eternal gulf, immutable as
the shining heavens and the *word* that "shall not pass
away."

"Raymond, once for all, if you love me—if you have
ever done so—hear me now. You must not go to Warren
Hayne as the champion of a proud woman who would not
thus admit and acknowledge his slight, if I died for locking
it in my heart. Do not cast this stigma upon me. His
life could not bring back my trust if he lost it, neither
could that atone for what I should suffer in the knowledge
that my name was bandied, the plaything of careless sport-
ing tongues, as one whom he had won, betrayed, and forsaken. You have not thought earnestly of this thing, else,
even in your just desire for vengeance, you would not render
me liable to what I should incur in the event of his death
at your hands. Besides, you mistake me; I do not regret
Warren now; 'tis only what perished with him—my glorious
ideal of manliness, my former self—that wasted year, and

all the other things that would never come back to me in this world, if he should die a thousand times over.

"Besides, again, he may not be so culpable as we deem him; the tenor of his brief letter I do not comprehend; it is ambiguous. What can he mean by this sarcastic reference to miserable misunderstandings that have occurred, and the letters he has written me that have remained unanswered? Why, because they were never received; then his closing benediction: 'I hope you will be happy in your choice. Perhaps it was all for the best.' What *can* it mean?"

"I regard that as a miserable subterfuge; nevertheless, yours is perhaps the right view of the subject. It shall be as you say. Now I wish to speak to you of other things, of which Clyde and I have talked this morning; matters are arranged for your acceptance or rejection."

I left them here, and passed out through the door, and stood beside Clyde in that strange silence which of late was with us always.

"Were you aware of Raymond's purpose of visiting the North?" I asked, at length.

"Yes," he answered, somewhat drily; "though I imagine his main object was to meet cousin Mary; though I believe he would have held Hayne accountable for his recent conduct towards our sister."

Our sister! I was *not* his sister; he had told me so once, and I was thinking of it as he stood looking dreamily at the water, then at the far-off sky, where it met and embraced the sea. Again the silence; I thought now it would never end. What if it should last from gliding age to age throughout eternity? Yet better this than the words which dropped slowly like molten iron on my heart, and hardened as they fell.

"Aljean, I believe you love me as a sister, though sometimes I have been led to doubt even that. Now I want to ask your advice on a subject of vital interest to all concerned in it. My step-father, who, as you know, has ever been indulgent and kind to me, has long ago set his heart upon having us married—Stanley and myself. He has frequently referred the subject to me indirectly. Until recently I have set the issue far from both of us. Now she is unhappy; if I, in my sad way, can do aught to make the thorny path a little smoother for her feet, I will endeavor to do so if I assume the sacred duty. Let me hear what you have to say ; what I offer her rests with you entirely."

Reader, I thought he was mocking me ; and my answering words fell seethingly from lips that were rigid and cold.

"And you submit this to me, Clyde Ingram? How could weak words of mine weigh against the voice of your heart? It would be as a faint echo amid its sounds, a thing of air. What is my poor opinion worth to a man that stands so far beyond me—up among those rising stars yonder? Yet you have asked it, and you shall have it. Marry Stanley by all means! She is not particularly fond of you, to be sure, but you, who have loved so long and so ardently, can allow for the lack on her part. If she can unlearn some other lessons of her life, she may come in time to love you."

"According to the evidence of your words and manner it would be an exceedingly difficult task," he answered, with bitter calmness; "as regards what you say concerning my life-long devotion to her, I should certainly deem you insane did not other passionless utterances convince me to the contrary. You have clearly forgotten, I see, what it gives me both pain and pleasure to remember; but that is far back in the past. I too will try to forget it has ever been, since you have not only outgrown the memory but have chosen to ignore the fact that the truth ever existed. Mine will not be a long life ; I have a prophetic assurance that you will survive me many years. Some time, when the grass is growing through and through my heart, or the snow lies cold upon it, you will count its throbs of these silent days and know why I submit to you this last appeal under so strange a semblance. You will know it all then, and in the solitudes of coming years the burden of a prayer gone by will come to you, from which you turned to-day. Yours must be the final fiat. These months of silence are your wish and will; I have taken no appeal from them save this; you can take none upon the silent ages that ensue."

For answer I drew the little ring, which I had worn so long, from my finger and placed it in his hand. I even tried to smile when I said, "It must be yours now, Clyde; you will soon be a married man, you know."

"There is one thing needful," he added, in tones whose bitterness was tempered with graceful humor—"Stanley's consent. Cannot you and Mr. Austin take the precedence?"

In my astonishment I never knew how it came to pass that Stanley, for her dear mother's sake, put her hand in Clyde's and murmured some words about doing her duty towards him. Ah! she never thought then of any vaster duty omitted in the very onset. A simple act of the State Legislature can legalize, but can it do the rest of many things involved in a marriage whose chiefest consideration is of duty that should be pleasure?

Lane Austin came to see us on the shore, appropriating me to himself naturally as though I belonged to him. Then we left Ray, charged with a kind farewell to his mother, standing on the guard; and when Lane saw us safely in our carriage, he, too, went his way, and we three in the winter twilight drove back to Claremont. Clyde silent, as usual; Stanley's head upon my shoulder, her beautiful hair all wet

with mist or tears, I know not which. It all happened so
strangely, yet we found ourselves sitting quietly in Aunt
Edith's room; Hawsey was sleeping bolt upright on a
cushion, and Miss Phœbe's busy needles were knitting into
the eternal mesh the events of this strange day. My past
life, as I recalled it, seemed like some wild, weird dream,
broken here and there by the gleaming of a golden river of
hope; but the bitter agony with which I too fought my
battle to its close and the victory achieved through God's
aid, that was not a dream.

A few evenings after I stood upon the veranda which
bordered the west parlor looking out upon the far sea, lying
cold and solemn and grey in the star-spangled starlight,
when a low voice beside me asked:

" Of what were you thinking, Jennie?"

I started slightly ; a shiver ran through my frame : a shiver that was half delight and half the chill of fate; but I
answered in low firm tones, with the voice that always came
to me in my childish days—

" I was recalling a portion of Maud Müller; you remember reading it to me one evening when we sat under the
cedars at Brightland—

> " 'For of all sad words of tongue or pen,
>   The saddest are these—' It might have been. ' "

" Whittier was wrong, Jennie. There are words sadder
far than these—of fuller, more bitter significance—' *It
could not be.*' "   _

To my death hour I shall never quite forget the tones in
which Clyde Ingram uttered these words. I can hear their
cadence still, and feel again the same wild impulse rising in
my heart, to ask—Why it could not be? Had I done so, the
barriers would all have been swept away; but some fate

kept me silent, and the struggle with which that silence was rife, Clyde Ingram never knew. Now at the close of years, which have rung their deep and solemn changes in between—I conclude that quotation as though he was this day my listener:

> " Ah! well for us all some sweet hope lies
>   Deeply buried from human eyes;
>   And in the hereafter angels may
>   Roll the stone from its grave away."

————o————

CHAPTER IX.

SPRING came—

> " Flowers in the valley, splendor in the beam:
>   Wealth in the gale, and freshness in the stream."

Its whisper was in the breeze, from the lake and the moon, from the sea. All its voices were sounds of gladness; flowers up-sprang where footprints were sunny through woodland ways. In our bright, beautiful home were flowers and sunshine everywhere, without and within.

> " The world leads round the seasons in a choir—
>   For ever changing and for ever new."——

> " Blending the grand, the beautiful and gay,
>   The mournful and the tender in one strain."

Though in our home there was a white face growing whiter day by day, we were happy that she lingered with us. Now there was no denying the fact—Aunt Edith was sinking slowly: the unfailing needles of Miss Phœbe told the story. During the oft-repeated recital we often saw how their lustre was dimmed with silent falling tears; the result was, they were a trifle more tardy in their round of duty than formerly.

Oh! it is dreadful to watch the slow consumption of vitality—a lingering death in life. It has ever been my prayer that to me or mine it should not come.

Stanley sat all day long now by her mother's side; yet when evening came—soft and balmy as evenings this season and clime are wont to do—when Aunt Edith slept a sleep of exhaustion, she would steal into her own beautiful room and sit thinking, with her eyes fixed on a little silver track of moonlight that always came and rested, brightened and faded at her feet. On coming one evening to her room, while she sat musing thus, I saw that the disc was overcast and the little beam paler even than usual.

"Stanley, darling, why do you sit here in the shadow? come into the piazza, it is very bright without," she answered sorrowfully.

"You are right; but I do not enjoy so much what is given alike to all the world. This little ray is mine. It seems a symbol of your dear generous love, Jennie, which always comes to seek me out when sitting lonely in the shadow at evening time."

I kissed the sweet, white face upturned to mine, lovingly as of old. The tears that were in my heart, despite my effort, would break hoarsely into my voice when I spoke.

"Yes, I come to seek you, Stanley; sometimes when I fear I am annoying you—often when I should leave you to yourself; but the house seems to want you, and then I too need you so much. It is from no merit of mine this love for you in my heart so constantly arises, and will not be put down. You yourself compel the sentiment by rendering yourself necessary to my happiness. I hope I shall never see the day that will separate us entirely."

" Nor I, Jennie ; you must live with me always after ; after this marriage, you know." She spoke resolutely—shudder-ingly. It was the first time since the evening of Ray's departure—in all our confidences—*this subject* had come between us. Now I trembled so violently, I feared lest she should observe my agitation and divine the cause ; I adopted the subterfuge of appearing to misinterpret her. I turned my face away as I answered carelessly, taking first the pre-caution to steel my voice against the pain that was rankling in my heart :

" Yes, I presume Ray and Mary will marry very soon. I imagined as much on first becoming aware of his intention to establish himself in business at the North."

It was long before she spoke. Eye and thought strayed from her little track of moonlight, out upon the purple space upwards, where worlds shone dimly and far off, like the dream and prayer gone by.

" No, Jennie, you do not understand me ; it is not Ray's marriage to which I refer, it is my own ; yes, *my own !* I have come to a point from which I can estimate very calmly things that must be ; they are in my destiny and will hap-pen ; I cannot avoid them—I shall try to do so no longer. It will make my sweet mother happy before she goes to see me marry Clyde and become permanently settled. It will save Claremont perhaps from strangers, and will require no sacrifice on my part. What little tenderness is left in my nature I consecrate to that brave, generous brother-husband, who will claim me. I will try very hard to make him happy ; with your help I think I shall succeed. But, Jennie dear, I always believed Clyde loved you, and sometimes have hoped you cared for him, until recently you have treated him so capriciously and coldly. Now do not curl your lip in that fashion, Jennie, and look at me so defiantly,

I am not going to censure you. I should not do so even if I felt I had the right. I meant no reproach that it is not so. These things are beyond the range of finite will; we have no power over them whatever."

All along I had found myself hoping that Stanley would not marry Clyde; now I sat quite still while she told me these things; my bright, bright dream was ended—passed away utterly as though it had never been. Oh, why could I not speak out and tell her all I felt, and all that I should suffer in such an event! No no, it were best not; Clyde loved her with more than a brother's devotion; she might in time learn to love him well. I at least would not deprive her of his strong, true arm, or grieve her with the story of an unloved, bleeding heart. Perhaps I should conquer it. My triumph would be one among the silent victories unwritten upon any record of earth. But oh, when tablets of the Infinite shall be brought into view, then will every leaf upon which the sacrifice that cost us most be unfolded. I should accept patiently my doom of loneliness; not even to my sister-friend would I tell what was in my thought then. Farewell bright dream, thou hadst been set among "stars that shine and fall," withered now like the smallest "flowers that drooped in springing." Again farewell, for all of earth and mortal time! As I speak the words, I hear their dim echoes resounding through all thy vistas, hollow, soulless world, and pealing through dim, unlighted vaults of the Eternal.

I thought of my golden river flowing only in the past, and the solitary ship out upon a broad, deep sea; but now, the bark was not Stanley's; another heart and life were in it, yet it drifted on and on, never resting, no anchor cast, no beacon burning on the further shore. Oh, that the winds which drove the tides should be gathered together for a little season of respite, in the hollow of one mighty hand, the same Father hand which held the threads in the complicated web that in one short year had been woven about us all so strangely.

Stanley came to me on the following morning, saying she had just heard from Raymond. He had entered the house of Mr. Kingswell as book-keeper, and designed remaining in Wayburn. He would be married in a few weeks, and wished us to come on immediately.

" He will take no refusal, Jennie," she added; " you must go. *I cannot go there!* Anywhere else. I shall not see Ray married, though I would love to do so."

" I think he cannot reasonably expect either of us, Aunt Edith is so ill, and——" She interrupted me.

" Mamma is no worse than she has been for months, Jennie. Miss Phœbe is with her night and day; Hawsey too is there; what can be done will be done without your assistance; that is why I ask you to go; some of us must; I cannot."

After all, thought I, it would be a change; that was what I most needed; my strength was fast giving way. At times my resolution almost failed me; I should go because it would be very hard if no one from Claremont should witness the marriage of our only brother and son.

I went quietly from room to room assisting and directing Hawsey, who was making necessary preparations for my departure. The mother's sad eyes followed me; there was a wistful tenderness in their depths. I knew she was thinking she might never see Raymond's bride; yet she possessed a strange unaccountable conviction that her boy had chosen wisely and would be happy. She had known the father of Mary Kingswell. Miss Phœbe's burnished needles appeared likewise to have caught something of inspiration

7

from the prospects of our eldest born, manifest in their accelerated motion.

Just one year from the time we first left Claremont—with its peaceful groves and broad expanses of sky and sea stretching far away—we took passage on a boat for Louisville, *en route* for Wayburn. We found things much as usual, Uncle Montana and myself, when we arrived. There was the same brisk atmosphere, the same white spires and New Hampshire hillsides—the same neat pavement leading up to the great square house, with its terraced grounds and ivy-wreathed columns; the Ridgely flowers and sunshine too were there as I remembered them; the family group and the home-lights beaming. When we came into their brightness, I felt the old choking anguish giving way and my heart growing joyous with its influence.

Uncle Montana was formally introduced to Raymond's bride elect. It was wonderful to witness the magic effect which Mary's simple beauty produced upon this staid, serious man of business; it was, as he himself expressed it, with a flash of the old gallantry which reminded me how I had seen my father kiss the hand of my sainted mother many a time; it was the very beauty of gentleness, goodness, and purity. We passed systematically as possible through the necessary greetings. Mary claimed uncle's attention for a time; when I had submitted to being vigorously hugged by that amiable bear Raymond, I ran off to find Mr. Kingswell. Oh! how I loved him! There was that in my soul which bowed in reverence at the shrine of his integrity, so lofty yet so blended with humanity that even the lowliest might have envied him the attribute.

"So you are come, Aljean; we are delighted to welcome you back; Ridgely sadly missed your presence when you left us, though we never forgot you in our morning or

evening prayer-time; when the sun was melting into shadow, and mists gathering about the far hills you loved so
well. Why did not Stanley come?"

He looked pained and grieved at my answer, so I wound
my arms around his neck and laid my head against the noble
heart that had a kindly sympathetic throb for all humanity.
Mrs. Kingswell, having disposed of uncle to their mutual
satisfaction, left him to the enjoyment of bath and siesta,
and came to join us. I said, as we took her into the circle
of our clasped arms:

"It is strange you find in your life a space that can be
filled by any of us who are so unworthy, when you have
her, so patient and so good, with you always."

He answered me, his eyes beaming with all that he felt
for this good true wife:

"She is my gift from God, for which I daily, hourly
thank him. I undertake no work but she is by my side to
do and bear her part; there is no task too difficult for
those hands of hers to assume—no burden of mine too
heavy for her heart; and we have sought to teach our child,
our Mary, who will leave us soon, that the end of life is not
here; that this is only a season of daily tasks; the circle
must be travelled—a circle that terminates in another
larger circle which holds other duties and other worlds in
its grand compass; and so the work of life must go on; the
strong must help the weak; those who do most are those
to whom the power so to do has been given. But of Stanley, why did she not come with you, Aljean?" He asked
me frankly, and I answered him in the same spirit.

"Aunt Edith was not well; in truth she is very poorly,
and then Stanley has had a hard trial recently. Cousin
Warren, you know"—I could not say deceived her; I could
not feel it thus, with all the evidence against him.

"Ah! yes, I understand; his marriage was purely a mercenary affair; I cannot tell what else could have influenced Hayne to sacrifice his happiness to this base end; though he told me once, Stanley had trifled with him! Averred that he only made the charge in justification of his apparently capricious conduct, which nothing could explain so well as her own written words. I thought he misjudged her, though he half succeeded in making the impression that he had been injured: whether he was suffering from pique that his truant game at hearts-for once had failed—he had lost and she had won, though he held the stakes."

"Warren deceived you!" I answered, vehemently; "I should like to tell him so; she it was who staked all, and lost; though, if I meet him, I will play the game to its close. He is conscious of having won that child's heart, and trampled its holiest feelings into the dust; but no one shall know this. Stanley will marry Clyde Ingram! And thus securely pin before the eyes of a discerning world the veil that he has dropped there in his wilful pleasure."

Mrs. Kingswell put up her hand with a quick gesture, as if to ward off an impending blow. I saw I had surprised and wounded them both, though I had only spoken truth. Without knowing just how to make amends, I withdrew from their kind clasp, and went out to seek Mary and Raymond. I found them sitting under the shadow of a dark fir, he twisting a cluster of *wegelia* into her brown hair. I kissed my finger-tips and passed them by, for I was thinking how treacherous hands had woven orange blossoms for Stanley's wealth of golden hair, and set them adrift; and how they withered where the fountain dropped its liquid spray—murmuring ever; and the great universe whirled its round as though they yet were fragrant, and her white brow wore not a crown of thorns instead.

Uncle Montana saw me from his window, and came forth refreshed to join me, offering his arm, which I accepted.

"It is delightful, here," he remarked; "seeing those happy children, Jennie, reminds me of the time when your father and mother were married." I led him gently along the hillside-path to the cemetery, till we came and stood by the graves of long ago. There were two grey stones—lichen-crusted and bowing—bearing each the name of Montana. At the feet of these, a plain, white marble-slab was erected more recently. We stood silently beneath a gilead tree, while the long grass whispered how peaceful had been their sleep; then he spoke so sorrowfully, his words cutting through my heart like a knife:

"I would give anything I possess, Jennie, if I had not suffered myself to lose sight of my brother and his young bride. I never saw them after I left home, first. It is the way of the world to grow so busy, we forget or eschew our heart duties; one by one we allow our old associates to drop from the circle we run—too much preoccupied, or too careless to retain them, until at my time of life, when we have come to a smooth place in the journey, and have leisure to look about us—we discover ourselves standing almost entirely alone, as when we first began the march. Then we miss what we have recklessly cast aside—what has drifted from us as the hurrying tide swept by. Oh! this constant struggle for wealth is a cruel thing; it rifles life of so much; even home-ties grow irksome amid its feverish toils."

"I presume, uncle, that no human being goes through life without some regrets clinging to him—sorrow for the lost, the treasured things he would have liked to keep. But you have been so kind to me, so considerate in supplying every want of my father's orphan child—you have spared no pains to make those you love comfortable and happy."

"And yet, outside of my own household, I have none to love me; I have done no deed of kindness to suffering humanity—thus writing my name upon hearts in which the hard strife with life would, at least, have left room for gratitude. I have toiled; but, oh! how selfishly. What I see and know of this man has put my poor abortive schemes to sorry shame! I look back upon my life to the structure I have erected; it was the work of years, yet it totters now upon the verge of ruin—will soon be broken into fragments—leaving me in return only the crushing burden of a miserable failure. Ah! better that quiet, unhonored sleep, than all this strife and tumult through years, to so little purpose."

"Uncle, your words strike a tender string very keenly; they grieve me; we never become acquainted with life, at least with its joys, until they are ready to leave us. The bubble has burst, and we relapse into ages of silence again."

"Even you, Jennie, and my own children, seem to fear me sometimes," continued my uncle, speaking as though my words had left no trace upon the thoughts which welled up within him. "I saw you embrace Mr. Kingswell as you never embraced me; is it that you love me less than this stranger, my child?" My arms were around his neck in an instant! At last I knew my uncle; the crusty covering had fallen off and his heart lay bare to my view; just as he himself had found it, after having stilled its longings, put aside its requisitions for years. As you will find yours, man of business, some sudden day; the little frail thing will ultimately grow too strong for you—it will rebound from the hard heel of your world service. It is God's voice speaking, and will be heard! The divine voice of love which is eternal.

"It is because Mr. Kingswell loves to have us caress him;

he is never too busy for this process; though we love you, my dear uncle, just as dearly as if we had taken the liberty of manifesting that love."

"I see it all. I have made a cruel mistake; but it will be so no more; by these graves, I make a resolution to have it otherwise."

Mr. Kingswell summoned us to tea. When we came up the walk Ray and Mary joined us. It was a pleasant gathering round the cheerful board that evening, barring the shade on Mrs. Kingswell's brow, caused by what I had told her concerning Stanley's intention to marry Clyde. They loved their adopted nephew, and the prospect of an unloving wife for him was like gall to their spirits.

After tea we took our places on the piazza, as we were wont to do in the previous summer, talking of many things; while the moon rose up, wrapping its silvery tissues around the form of her who on the morrow would be a bride, as she walked the terrace with Raymond at her side. I thought of another bride in her stately home, wondering if her young husband was as happy as we hoped Ray would be. Then again I thought of the fair, childish head, with its sleepless eyes watching the silver track of moonlight as it rested on a lonely pillow. I knew she was musing of us. Oh! why were some wreaths made to be blighted? and some blossomed into life, never displaced or withered? Last of all I thought of another, whose dark eyes seemed always seeking something through mist and space, thinking—thinking— Ah! nobody knew, for he never told us; a cruel silence sat evermore upon his lips. A chain of silence linking two lives, yet a barrier driving them apart.

————0————

CHAPTER X.

"But happy they—the happiest of their kind,
 Whom gentle stars unite, and in one fate
 Their hearts, their fortunes, and their beings blend."

EVEN an event, great, solemn, and mysterious almost as death, could not break the routine of duty and habit in this orderly household. Save a few extra preparations in the culinary department, and a few extra flowers in the several vases, the travelling trunk packed and strapped standing on the piazza, there was little change apparent; one might have thought it an everyday occurrence to have a bride leave home.

It was wonderful to see how the gentle mother bore up and spoke cheering words to Mary, who more than once broke down in the performance of some little duty for the household, or as fresh tokens of her parent's kindness came to her. To those who weigh and estimate it as they should, marriage is scarcely less solemn than death; it is putting off life, with its accustomed forms and usages, for the assumption of new duties; an exchange of the certain for the uncertain, parting with idols of childhood for a promise of love and care that are richer, more treasured.

It was not for long, however, that the faintest misgiving clouded the sweet face of Mary; when Ray, bright and handsome and cheerful, came down, the mists all cleared away; she ever had for him a greeting full of trustful affection. Once, I remember, as we threaded the terrace walks, he stooped to touch a sensitive-plant, saying to her mother as he did so—"This is like Mary."

"I am almost broken-hearted when I think that Ridgley will be her home no more," the mother said, with quivering lip; "when next she comes here it will be as a visitor."

It was hard; many a mother's heart has known a similar trial; the sun-beam that so brightened home scenes; the flower whose fragrance was emitted with every dawn till close of day, gone to lend their sweetness to another love-nest. In the old home there is only a vacant chamber; footprints lingering in the accustomed ways, marked less and less frequently by the little feet the mother has so tended in childhood, the presence fading from her view; the chair of age untended—this is what marriage is. Duties multiply in the new sphere of action, and the young bride will learn gradually to do without those whose care was once her greatest happiness.

Raymond and Mary were to live at Wayburn; thus to parents and child there came no pain of prolonged separation. Very bright and beautiful was the wedding-day. I was amused, when, in answer to the customary question of the minister, "Do you take this woman?" &c., Ray's clear, "I do," was articulated with such firm heartiness. I observed the smile go round; though it faded silently from lips that trembled slightly when they saw the father come to kiss his child. He could not speak the words he had meant to, only pressed her to his heart and left the room, weeping. Oh! what a brave, loving heart, was his; and how tenderly it had held and sheltered her in its depths for eighteen years. Mary had been a good girl, always dutiful; and the feeling between them appeared almost lover-like in its delicate manifestations of fondness for each other.

The mother never once lost her self-possession during the ordeal; yet in the silence of her own apartment, when the guests were departed, and we far on our way to a distant city, I thought of her, knowing that she was weeping and praying for her child.

Uncle Montana, being in haste to return to Claremont,

7*

left us at New York. I remained to see the young husband and wife safely ensconced within their new home.
We spent several weeks delightfully at the Metropolitan.
Among numerous cards of invitation came one from Warren Hayne, which we neither acknowledged nor accepted.
They seemed to anticipate such a reception of their courtesy, for, waiving ceremony, they called at our hotel. Raymond, his wife, and myself, were in our private parlor when
our unwelcome visitors sent up their cards. We consulted
about the matter, deciding that it was best, for Stanley's
sake, to exhibit no pique in consideration of his treatment
of her; therefore, the servant received instructions to show
them up : accordingly they came.

Mrs. Hayne, with her blonde hair, blonde face, blonde
eyes, and bland, insinuating manner, bestowed much con-
descending courtesy upon his beautiful bride, though she
greeted Raymond with haughty formality. I, in my dressing-room adjoining, heard Warren's full, rich tones, in conversation; they always thrilled me strangely, despite my
better judgment. Now he inquired in accents of well
affected indifference for the family at Claremont ; he was
not aware, it was evident, that Stanley had remained at
home ; for when I appeared, in answer to his wife's expressed wish to see also the young ladies—the Misses Montana—I
observed that her dutiful husband kept strict surveillance
over the door through which I emerged, doubtless expecting her to appear.

"She did not come," I remarked, maliciously, in response
to his frequent glance, my lips writhing half in amusement,
half in scorn. For answer, he fixed upon me his large,
brown eyes, in such reproachful sternness, I absolutely
quailed beneath their searching pride. Why did this man's
spirit thus ever vaunt its power over me ? When I raised

my eyes, there was something in his face of agony endured, and a look that seemed to say through mine he would read *her* soul, and know why matters were as they were.

Singular; for months previous to this anticipated meeting with Warren Hayne, I had arranged and rehearsed the amiable speeches with which I meant to lacerate his feelings. Now, why died the words unspoken on my lips? It was because in his one stern glance, I read a story of strife and victory, a spirit loftily poised, resting from the untold struggle. He rose naturally and offered me his arm; I accepted it mechanically: and again I found myself walking with my cousin the long corridor, my hand held fast as he was used to hold it, in other days scarce one year past. I wondered why he asked me no questions concerning Stanley; but he only talked in his usual courteous manner of things that were and things that had been; never once touching upon what was in my mind a constant thought. I did not then know man-nature as I have learned it since, or I should have accepted this avoidance of facts as the strongest possible evidence that he, too, was thinking of her, and the other time—gone; in *affaires de cœur*, the thing of which men think most they speak least. Other motives may have influenced his silence on this special topic.

He told me it was his earnest wish to have the pleasure of our exclusive entertainment for one evening at least, during our stay in the great metropolis. He would arrange it so that the entertainment should not interfere in the slightest with our previous engagements. He had previously spoken to Raymond and Mary, who submitted the matter to me. There was nothing left for me but an unconditional assent, which I gave.

We returned to the parlor. I sank upon a sofa in a

maze of strange reflections; I could scarcely realize the occurrences of that afternoon, even when I saw cousin Warren standing at a distant window, one hand resting carelessly on Raymond's shoulder, while with the other he held that of the young bride, to whom he talked gaily. I saw his well formed Grecian lips relaxing into smiles; I heard his deep familiar accents, but I could not distinguish the words he uttered, for my golden river again was flowing—flowing somewhere. I sat listening to the liquid music of its waves—perhaps the sound came up from the past, during this little ebb of time—I know not. I was unconscious of all things, save that I was dreaming impossible dreams—impossible of realization in this world, for their season had gone by.

Cousin Warren said, in his blandest, most insinuating tones, preparatory to their leave-taking:

"We have set Thursday evening for our party, Jennie; you will come—come early." We promised; at the appointed time we went.

Once in that stately home, with its lights and music and summer flowers, I could dimly realize the temptation which had beset Warren to secure Miss Strawbridge's fortune—with herself of course—after his accidental discovery that Claremont was a possession of Clyde Ingram's. Everything was in magnificent keeping; grandeur was apparent in the minutest details; every arrangement was perfect, from the elegant dressing-room, into which we were conducted by a neatly attired **maid who** gave **the** finishing touch to our **elaborate toilets,** to the supper-room in which was served a repast fitting for the most fastidious palate. Warren did the honors with his accustomed ease of manner, while Mrs. Hayne presided **chosen** goddess of the coffee-urn, in a manner which so entirely won my heart, I almost forgave her for having a blue ribbon twisted with her blonde hair, after the fashion in which Stanley was accustomed to weave it with those golden curls of hers. The wine was so fragrant we imagined it must have been distilled from roses. I think if I had not been fortified with a second glass of delicious Rhine, I should never have found courage to speak to Cousin Warren as I did that night.

We had returned to the drawing-room; guest after guest came pouring in—the tinted waves of fashion. I had passed through an ordeal of such frequent introduction to people for whom I cared not a farthing—whom perhaps I should never meet again—I was very weary; some way, the gay voices and sounds oppressed me. I was stealing off to the dressing-room—skipping lightly up the stairs to the music of a well timed *varsovienne,* when Cousin Warren called out: "Come back, truant!" at the same time, circling my waist with his coat sleeve, he drew me forcibly into the dancing apartment. Notwithstanding my protestations, he led me to a position. It was during one of the pauses in the figure that he remarked, somewhat sadly: "Although they were accustomed to have dancing parties every week, he had not danced once since we were at Nahant the previous summer." I waited to give him the opportunity to speak again before I said my say; but he did not.

"Ah! what a delightful season we had there! our promenades on those long, cool verandas overlooking the sea, all-mighty and vast, with the sweet moon shining on its troubled waves."

He changed his position slightly, put his hand into the breast of his coat; I felt his fingers tremble slightly against my own, which rested in the circle of his left arm; but he did not look at me as I went talking on:

"Cousin Warren, there is a picture in my heart to-night;

two figures standing on that long piazza overlooking the
sea—the moonlight blends their shadows in its silver fall.
One had played a part until his heart and soul were sick;
I see him take the hands of that beautiful girl in his own,
exclaiming: ''tis time this mockery should cease.' Trusting, she gave him her heart; but the mockery was only
then begun. The picture fades as it has done before;
other figures come between; in different lands, upon separate stages, I have seen each play a part since then. They
do well. This last scene in the melodrama is rendered
with special effect; I am enjoying it immensely. Ah! the
false has mocked the true, stealing its semblance the long
way through—wearing its regal hue; she has spoken, yet
no word from you."

His face was very pale, and the lines about his handsome
lips were drawn tightly. It seemed impossible for Warren,
usually so easy of speech, to syllable one word of the many
that were craving utterance from his "heart of hearts."
At length he said, hoarsely: "You are right! the mockery
was only then begun; now it must go on; I presume it
will last as long as life; she has willed it, so let it be. How
is she, and why did she not come? The sight of her could
not unman me now; I have lost the hope of that time.
This later phase of life upon which you comment so bitterly
has little connexion with the trial which preceded my
adoption of what doubtless seems to you a strange course.
Though through all I am conscious of having preserved my
integrity of heart." This was said with a proud loftiness
which, under the circumstances, could scarcely have been
equalled; though his accustomed blandness came into the
tones in which he added: "Will you be kind enough to
answer my questions concerning Miss Montana?"

If I had not believed he was feigning, I should have

driven the shaft less keenly than I did; as it was, I was merciless.

"'Tis easy to talk of 'integrity of heart!' Coming from you, it goes very far towards making up the sum-total of a lifetime mockery; however, let us speak of this no more. Stanley is well and looking charmingly. She would have come North this season, only we could not both leave Aunt Edith, who is quite ill. I came on with uncle; Stanley remained at home with Miss Phœbe and Mr. Ingram in charge of her mother." He turned upon me, a glance of angry inquiry flashing in his eye; I answered his thought as upon the occasion of our first meeting in New York.

"Yes; she will be Clyde Ingram's bride this coming autumn." The fingers seemed clutching at something that must have pressed upon his heart. Music again—brilliant, thrilling; through the mazes of the Lancers he passed as though trampling some imaginary substance underneath his feet; yet his manner was so proudly calm and courteous none would have guessed how in his heart there was an inner tempest raging.

The quadrille ended, Warren led me to a seat; then, in a voice which betrayed no excitement whatever, he spoke very indifferently, I thought heartlessly, of the persons about us, New York as a residence, and many other things which were far from our thoughts or feelings then, only he twitched my sandalwood fan nervously. I glanced at my watch—the evening was well-nigh spent. I went in search of Raymond, who sat with his bride in the drawing-room, listening to the recital of some old friend who sat in an easy chair, his face towards their sofa, his back towards the door. Judge of my surprise on coming over to them at being brought *tête-à-tête* with Mr. Milverton, our mirth-

ful spirit of Nahant, Stanley's friend, our joint admirer.
He sprang up with sudden alacrity, seizing my hand, asked
a dozen questions in the same breath concerning my health
and happiness; again of Stanley, whom he knew, and of
her family, whom he did not, saving Raymond, Clyde, and
myself. Said he had nothing earthly to do, at once proposed to accompany me home, a suggestion to which I
readily assented, though I told him I feared he would find
it very dull, the family were at Brightland; I should go
there on my return; his sojourn with us would be quite a
contrast to his life here in the great caravansary.

He answered me that nothing would delight him more;
he was tired of this locality, and deemed a change of climate, even at that season, a saving ordinance from death of
ennui.

"I am sure I shall revive the very instant I come within
the sphere of Miss Montana's presence. She has more
than once saved me from premature death by one of those
dazzling smiles of hers. You used to feel the force of
them, eh, Hayne? By St. Patrick, I once thought all the
powers of earth could not have dispelled the illusion which
bound you a willing captive to her side. How is it, old
fellow? Confess now, or I shall deem you already in the
leading-strings—afraid to own a former capture. How is
it, ha?"

Warren had followed me and taken his place amid our
group in the drawing-room. Thus appealed to, he assumed a tone of careless badinage in his answer.

"No one is more willing than I to acknowledge Miss
Montana's superior fascinations, though I cannot agree
with you in pronouncing her smiles a 'saving ordinance.'
I have reason to think they are calculated to *blight* rather
than exalt *mankind.*" The blood rushed over my face at

the conclusion of his unjust speech. Raymond's eyes flashed indignant fire! A gentle hand was laid upon his arm—the defiant spirit was rebuked. I should have spoken to Warren when he offered me his arm a moment after, but in his face there was the same reproachful look of fixed sternness that had hushed my clamoring heart more than once before; now his hand tightly clasped my fingers as we promenaded the drawing-room. He said at length :

"You think me harsh and severe, Jennie; I know women have an idea there are some things which men should bear without a sign or sigh of complaint. I have borne a great deal, but you have tried me to-night almost beyond endurance. You and Stanley play good hands at your double game! She won my love only to cast it aside as a worthless bauble. Not content with this, she has commissioned you, who are doubtless party to the transaction, to probe the wound and decide if it is deep enough to prove fatal. Yes, I feel assured this has been your chief mission to New York. You may say to your fair instructress, it does not abash me to admit that the wound is sore and bleeding still. I should not hesitate to tell her this if she had come. The thing which I most regret is that I did not do so in the beginning. I should have heard my sentence from her lips alone; instead, I listened to the voice of pride, donned this armor of reserve and indifference, hoping by such means to conceal from the world and from her what she had made me suffer."

I opened my eyes wide with astonishment! I actually for the moment thought Warren demented to talk as he did about the wounds that she had made. Then I remembered how, in that one letter to Stanley, he had accused her of deceiving him, and of having broken her plighted faith.

We had deemed his words only a subterfuge to free himself from an engagement which proved less advantageous in a worldly sense than it might once have done. Again, Mr. Kingswell had said Warren told him Stanley's written **words** were his proof of her falsity to him. A suspicion of foul play came over me like a flash ! though I knew not what I should say or do to detect it without compromising **Stanley** by the admission of **her** unchanged affection for **Warren.**

"Cousin," I said excitedly, " I am just now too intent on a purpose even to resent **your** insinuations concerning Stanley and myself—in league against you. There must be treachery somewhere. I think it will eventually be explained to our mutual satisfaction. To aid me in ferreting out the apparent cruel designs of some person or persons, I request you to send back her letters !"

"*Her letters ?*" he answered half contemptuously, profound surprise manifest in his tones and manner.—"For four long ,months after I left Claremont I heard no word from her ! At length, in answer to at least twenty wild appeals, there came from her just one curt brief missive, stating her engagement, requesting very coldly that I should discontinue my portion of the correspondence. In a fit of rage and pique at her duplicity, I resolved **that to** her, of all the anguish I felt, I would make no sign. **In** the silence thus imposed, I became—— ah ! well you know the rest. I see by your face you deemed her incapable of **this.** Once I should sooner have doubted all the world beside. **She** has since made me a sceptic regarding woman's truth. I congratulate Mr. Ingram upon the success of his suit ; he is to be envied, is he not ?"

"Warren," I exclaimed with some severity, "repeat your innuendoes either to Raymond or Clyde, at fitting time and place. I will assure you they will be responded to as they deserve to be. I shall not resent them, as I said before, because you have indeed been tried more than I had dreamed of. Now give me that note of Stanley's; I would have the evidence of my own eyes here. 'Tis not that I doubt you, but I have so believed in her I could trust nothing less than this."

He rose and offered me his arm with stately grace. I believe Warren could have been placed under no circumstances so complicated or disagreeable that he could have forgotten to deport himself with lofty elegance; though now the fingers which closed over mine, resting in the circle of his arm, were cold and rigid. He drew me into his private study adjoining the library, where he seated me in his large reading chair, during the process of unlocking a secret drawer in an escritoire, from which he took a note bearing Stanley's superscription and stamp. I knew her letters; it was easy to detect her style, which was uniform; I imagined I could be deceived as readily with regard to my own. The strangest of all was her chirography! I could have qualified it as hers, in a court of justice. It would have been difficult to counterfeit her peculiar hand.

My brain was reeling under the force of this blow. I was only conscious that Warren's eyes were upon me. I rallied, therefore, under his tones of cutting irony.

"I presume you are satisfied! at least you can doubt no longer the authenticity of letter or date." A bitter reply rose to my lips! I longed to tell him that I had doubts, but not of her; that I should not believe the whole world if they in one united voice declared Stanley false. But no, it were better not. I had no right to reveal one tithe of that long, hard struggle through which she had passed.   Accordingly I crushed back, in a deep, dark corner of my heart, my suspicions and convictions concerning a part some third party must have played in this drama.   I answered him falteringly—

" The evidence is certainly against her; until I am better fortified with strength to refute your charges, I shall not attempt her defence.   Do not think of her too harshly, Warren; remember those golden days at Claremont ; I am sure she has not forgotten them, they were so very bright." He sat with his eyes fixed upon the superscription of her note; mine wandered far off.   Shreds of my golden river came through the fissures of craggy rocks that loomed up, almost shutting out the heavens from view.   I saw the opal drops sparkling crimson, as ruby—then diamond clear, breaking into gem-like beauty through the tissues of broken dreams.   Warren's head rested on his left hand, while his right, within the breast of his coat, seemed clutching at some weight that was pressing on his heart.

We were each awakened from our painful reverie by the sound of an unwelcome voice which broke upon us very harshly, with a vivacity that was anything but pleasing. We raised our eyes to see—a blonde face, transfixed in green-hued wonder and indignation.

" I am astonished to find you *here*, Miss Montana ! Your brother has been seeking for you everywhere else. Mr. Hayne, you must have forgotten your duty and obligation as host in *my house.*   You have chosen to absent yourself during the entire evening—almost.   Now many of our departing guests await the opportunity and privilege -of paying their respects to you.   Will you come, sir, or shall I excuse you on the ground of this monopoly ? "

She said this with a withering glance in my direction. It did not reach me, however ; I was thinking of other things than her reproach, as I recalled and reviewed the wide, wide space that lay between those two—a difference uncancelled by pride of position! a difference which was God-created; neither years nor fate could abridge it, even though they were husband and wife. He felt it, too, just then, very keenly; I saw how the knowledge galled him; I hoped he would not resent her insult to me. I cared nothing at all about it—but he did.

"Perhaps, madam, you, who in *your own house* never lack courtesy towards any one of your guests—even those who are my relatives—might as well have extended your prerogative and denied your guests the privilege of dispensing adieus to their nominal host. You can do so still if you like; at all events, suffer them to await my pleasure." She rustled her indignant flounces as she left us. Warren again gave me his arm. I thought, oh! for one tiny ray of the sweet love life he and Stanley had lived to lighten the dark domestic atmosphere within this stately home. Oh! for just one atom of pure gold amid all the dross surrounding my cousin! Where should it be found? A voice within answered, far down in the deeps of that true, manly heart, whose strings were held by one little hand which he would never be permitted to press or fondle again. How trustingly it had once nestled within his own! I wonder if he was not thinking of it when those coarse, harsh tones broke upon his ear? If so, the recollection had melted somewhat the resentment within him; for as he spoke the fitting farewell to each departing guest, his tones were lower, richer, and seemed far off, like the sound of my golden waves. When we three took our leave, I saw upon his face the same absent expression, and he pressed my hand as though it might have been hers. We left him standing silently, moodily, on the pavement, within the shadow of his wife's stately mansion, his form so still in its faultless outline. I was thinking of him as we went whirling through the lighted streets, until our coachman let down the carriage steps at the Metropolitan.

———o———

CHAPTER XI.

" The highest hills are miles below the sky—
 And so far is the lightest heart below
 True happiness."

I **was** out when Warren called **on** the following morning; in the evening he came again, and while I was adding the finishing touch to my toilet, I could hear him as he walked the long corridor below with calm, firm tread, just as he **was wont to do in** the pleasant summer time gone by. Now he was gayer than I had seen him for a long time. There was **in his manner no trace** of the deep emotion manifest on former occasions. It was only the polished man of the world who greeted me, speaking with careless indifference, as though he would ignore the fact that he **had** ever been other than this. I was surprised and wounded at his levity, and thus expressed myself; **I shall never forget** his answer:

" Fortunately, or unfortunately, as you perhaps esteem the fact, we men have too much to do of life's busy work— too constant a strife with the world and its strong **necessi-** ties, to permit ourselves to grow habitually depressed. In the long, weary march from cradle to grave there are so many customs that not only wither the sweetest flowers **but set** an iron heel upon any impulse of generous emotion.

That stern dictator, duty, would make galley slaves of us all—even the most determinedly rebellious; reducing kings to the condition of serfs and minions. A tiny hand holds the feather that turns the scale of destiny; and from a sweet, sunlit way, where the brightest flowers lie, 'tis often but one step to deserts of darkness and misery. We mourn the departed glory, but soon learn to trim our torches and smile while we do the work of life in an artificial radiance—enduring calmly, hopefully, philosophically, all that we must. We cannot always suffer—the time so to do is not given us. I like Owen Meredith's definition of life:

> " 'Honest love—honest sorrow,
> Honest work for the day,
> Honest hope for the morrow.'

"I really like this aspect of the thing; there is a bravery in it which but few people realize. As regards the sorrow, that is an attribute that is real and wears no false hue, though as regards *honest love*—ah! there is little of that in this weary world."

It almost broke my heart to hear Cousin Warren talk in this strain. Oh! how I longed to look him in the eyes—to fix his conviction of what I uttered, and tell him there was at least one honest love in the Universe, stedfast and true as the sun, and how that loving one had sorrowed for this broken troth, as even he had not done—but I dared not. Oh, of all the idle words spoken, if I might have claimed just one little syllable with which to convey an intelligence of these things, it might have appeased the anguish in my heart—but it must not be! Loving as they two did, each knowing that the other loved, perhaps the frail barrier had melted away; then they, standing face to face, man and woman, might have spoken as they did at

Nahant. Could they have borne the heavy cross being aware of this most harrowing truth? I fear not.

As these thoughts flitted through my mind I sat carelessly toying with a little fillet of white and blue, a purchase I had made for Stanley. Warren regarded me so earnestly, I could not but feel that his tone and manner in the previous conversation were assumed.

"That is hers," he said at length. I looked at him with some surprise, answering in the affirmative. Then he went on to say :

"There is a peculiar atmosphere about everything that pertains to her. Even the most commonplace articles adapt themselves to her wearing, assuming this peculiar personality the moment they are purchased. I have a little gift here; it is justly her property, no one else could ever wear them. Will you give them, for me, into her charge?" It was a set of pearls: a necklace whose interstices seemed a glitter of frost-work, brooch and pendants of rarest style and finish. I took the shining bauble into my hand, letting the string slip through my fingers like cluster drops of falling water, saying as I did so :

"Warren, you very well know that, even under other circumstances, Stanley would scarcely accept these; now, she would be very far from doing so."

"I can see the drift of your fancy, Jennie," he answered quietly, though proudly, in a subdued tone of poignant suffering. "They are not my wife's, and can never be hers; they are no part of that contract, thank Heaven—they are Stanley's. All the romance and brightness of my life are entwined with them, and they must be hers, though she has put from her the beautiful dream and sweet thoughts that were mine, as I worked for them. But she cannot go back into the golden maze of the past, and blot out the time when she herself gave me the liberty to think these thoughts of her, and to build the hope of my life upon them. Better try to obliterate the suns that are shining on our childhood, and the stars in the past whose radiance never pales in growing spaces of after years."

"Warren, would you substitute these for the wreath you wove and left to wither in her own home? They will be valueless to her now—that has faded."

"Then lay them at her feet and let her crush them as she crushed the joy out of my life; only bear them to her, with a request from me that she will wear them on her bridal day. In return I ask of you that little band of white and blue. I want it; it will help me to learn to forgive her. I feel that I have almost done so already."

"Warren, you do right to forgive Stanley. Try to think of her gently and kindly, for she too has suffered. Just think what a dreadful thing it is to be surrounded by an invisible net of circumstances whose meshes could not be broken; it was fate! Stanley was not to blame! She will live to prove it to you."

"Jennie, why will you taunt me with these things? I knew the '*circumstances*' which influenced her to renounce me as she did. I, though not a poor man, was not a millionaire! Clyde Ingram was. Of course, I do not blame her; the difference was vastly in his favor; it is the way of the world. Jennie, we must all learn it sooner or later. There is no bitterness in my heart towards her; only a poignant sorrow when I recall all that was and is not, and all that might have been. But enough of this; it sounds too much like weak repining at a decree that is inevitable; the mandate is irrevocable, the fiat has gone forth. I shall learn to be happy in the knowledge that she is blessed. And now this is our last conference on this topic. To man, woman or child, saving yourself, I have never spoken these thoughts; and never again will I lay this portion of my life bare to any one. It was too bright and beautiful for the actual; it has drifted into dream-land, there let it rest. Suffice it to say, there **is** one word which I shall never take upon my lips again—the word *love*. It is among the sounds that are dead! Shut in a chamber of my heart that is locked hard; **the** key is in your possession; the walls are granite; at the touch of one little hand they would crumble into dust; but that touch will never come, and I must cease to miss and mourn it now; the season has gone by."

I stood gazing at him, with a deep pity in my heart, as he looked down towards the youth-land of romance as to a land of promise past.

He went to his stately, beautiful home, and we to the quiet shades at Ridgeley. It was so pleasant to feel ourselves in this quiet little home-nest once more. To rise at morning with the lark, to see the glorious light breaking into prisms far over the New Hampshire hills, and the mist in the valley gather **into purple** columns that shone burnished with long bars of sunshine which came down through the trees that grew upon the mountain-side, darting golden spars into the very heart of morning to a mellow music that seemed a refrain of wood-nymphs. Then followed a day, a **busy day, full** of life and work; the mellow grain fell before adroit sickles, and the harvest-season, with its rich, ripe melody, went gliding by; the task had been wrought—the reprisal garnered.

It was amusing during that period to see Milverton in a broad-brimmed hat of oat straw, gathering golden sheaves, humming fragments of bacchanalian songs—such as wreath the bowl, &c.—carrying his air of graceful nonchalance even into the harvest-field. He seemed always happy, living for the most part a surface life of pleasure, yet occasionally plunging into a vortex with a hearty will, as though this were all—this little narrow to-day, and there was no to-morrow, no eternity. I could not avoid laughing at his drolleries, though he always inspired me with a sensation as though I was falling from great heights.

The last evening, the one previous to our departure, came. Ray and Mary were comfortably ensconced in their new home. Mrs. Kingswell had dispensed the means that was the young wife's bridal gift with unusual tact and delicacy, and furnished their house to the very best advantage. It was a second edition to the home at Ridgley—a miniature edition, relieved with a few of the rich tapestries and brocatelles of Claremont; altogether as snug and elegant a nest of love as could be found in the country.

We were spending the last evening together—sitting, as we had often done before, on the broad piazza, in the light and smile of the young moon. True, there were missing ones to whose absence I was growing sadly accustomed of late. I spoke at length, and my words bore the burden of an inquiry made at many partings, yet never answered with the least certainty; for in that bright to-morrow of our thought may lie the event that may make or mar the remnant of existence. Impressed with this mournful truth, I said again:

"Uncle, life is a sad, hard thing, is it not?"

"Young people on first becoming acquainted with the actual facts of existence are ready to vote it so. I wonder, however, how many persons of your age could be brought to endorse your sweeping invective?"

"I know not what would be their verdict, uncle; but it seems to me, on the verge of constant parting with some one whom I love—a fever of fierce heat—an aimless warfare of body and soul!—a swift, sure death, and then——"

"Ah! Jennie, what then? Ask of faith what lies beyond this narrow stream of time—beyond the golden portals that bar eternity from view. Ask of that divine heart which poured its life-blood out, that upon the mortal tides we might be borne from the mazy darks of earth in the light of his great sacrifice, beyond the night of swift, sure death, to a morning of the Infinite. His love means more and is more than the material compensations which await the performance of our daily task. God is in our lives everywhere, my child; he will take us to his great heart when the labor and strife are ended. He will be with you when the sun goes down, as he was when you came into the world. Do not grow weary; live long in the days of your romance, drink often of those fresh, pure springs. Life is a circle! Age comes back at last to bathe its dusky, time-worn visage in the primitive fountain, and when the race is ended reënters by the same portal through which it first emerged. Keep a spirit untainted by weak repinings, and you will not have far to come when the flesh has grown weary and weak, for the crown of righteousness Christ has promised."

"Uncle, you make me feel strong to try, and I will."

"That is a brave, good girl, Jennie; the greater your effort, the more glorious will be your triumph in the end. Remember, 'the race to the swift or the battle to the strong' is not given. But to him that overcometh." How lofty shone that glorious spirit from his eyes, as he sat there, moonbeams falling on his silver hair! Ah! with a perpetual well-spring of youth in his loving, generous heart, he had conquered life and held its tissues in his venerable hand. How strong his words of encouragement always made me feel—equal to anything; so I returned home with a silent suffering deep in my heart, through which ran a wish to comfort Stanley and to school myself with looking on her happiness, thus assuming the heavy cross and sacrifice that must be mine.

The family, including all the servants save Aunt Dinah, who always kept house in our absence, were at Brightland. The old lady, with her ever ready comfort in the shape of a bountiful meal, entertained us very pleasantly, Milverton and myself, as she did the honors. How delightful we find the little details of home gossip to one returned from long journeying. We enjoyed catechizing Aunt Dinah, especially Milverton; who, between alternate slices of cold ham and lemon tartlets, asked many questions concerning Stanley, who someway constituted his whole conception of our family.

Once or twice the old lady essayed to adopt our policy, and venture a query concerning "Mars Raymond;" though this was done with the air of one who feared the answer might contain intelligence that would strike her dumb.

"Well and happy, is he? Lord save us! Who ever thought, when I was a raisin' dat are bressed boy, it would come to dis. Just think," she added, wiping from her eyes the ever ready tear-drops, "of his being happy away from old Mars, his dear mother, Miss Stanley, and the rest of us; it's too hard to bear, Miss Algy."

"It is the way of life, you know, Aunt Dinah; sons must go out from their father's home, take their places in the great world, and bear their part of active duty there."

"Yes; but jest think o' him, tenderly as he'd ben raised, goin' way up thar to live whar people has to work fur the' livin'. Why didn't he marry that purty young creetur, Miss Retty, and settle in town."

A shiver ran through my frame as I thought of Retta

Austin in Mary's place—Raymond's wife. The hasty comparison, while doing no credit to the former, did much honor to the latter.

"I presume Ray can best answer that question, Aunt Dinah; and as to his working for a living, we all do that in one sphere or another, unless we are fortunate as Mr. Milverton, and have a patrimony handed down to us with no thought or care, but to spend it pleasantly to the best advantage. In that case, one must needs be of a temperament that will exempt us from the endurance of those hard spirit-toils for others that accrue in bearing burdens for those we love."

"Well, God knows best—Christ bore one for us all," answered this faithful old bond-woman, solemnly.

Later in the afternoon, we drove down to the city. Accompanied by Uncle Montana, we took the train for Brightland. Horses and carriage awaited us at the station; after a swift drive of a few minutes only, we came to a plantation, extended for miles, bordering one of the famous swamps so noted in the annals of Mrs. Stowe. Surrounded by thick clumps of pine-trees, stood the white wooden house with long galleries circling around and dissecting the abode at right angles. In front, a long slope of yard with groups of woolly-headed children, playing; this was our home, or rather, Clyde's home. Here, many pleasant days of my childhood had been passed. With a great bound my heart went back to that old time. How natural it seemed that Clyde, who was sole master here, should come down the clay road to meet us, arrayed in an immaculate suit of snowy linen. The breeze strayed lovingly through his brown curls as he lifted gracefully his broad-brimmed Panama in answer to my salutation; then came forward to shake Milford's hand in the true Southern greeting. How my heart thrilled again when, stepping in front of his guest, he offered me his arm, leaving Milverton to follow. Pleasure beamed from every lineament of his pure Grecian face as he exclaimed:

"I am so glad you are home again, Jennie; you can never know how we have missed you."

I answered, vainly endeavoring to still my heart with a gasp:

"Many thanks, Clyde; it is kind of you to say so; I think *Stanley must* have wanted me; you would have been cruel not to have sympathized with her. I imagine it was nothing more than this—your desire to see me." I could not tell why it was—the radiance passed from his face, and again, then and there, between us, was inaugurated that cruel silence which so blighted both our lives. I saw the change instantly, and as usual attributed it to a source entirely foreign to the real cause. I was always wounding Clyde without meaning to do so. This time I thought to bring back the glad smile, so I said: "How are Stanley, aunt, and the rest?"

"They are much as you left them, thank you," he answered, in a hurt, chilled tone.

I, too, was grieved; I withdrew my eyes from the sorry face that I loved, to behold coming down the path an apparition which I felt to be Stanley; though I had never seen her when every ray of her glorious beauty seemed so concentrated. It burst upon me with such force; the cold, stony look had passed from her eyes; golden arrows danced and glittered in her sunny hair. I was in her arms—close to her fond, true heart, in an instant. We maintained long that firm clasp, leaving Milverton to himself, who proceeded to make the acquaintance of every dog and negro on the premises. Clyde stood looking over

those long, far fields with a dreamy, absent look upon his face
with which at Claremont he had been accustomed to watch
the waves roll in from a distant sea. Oh! it was so sweet
to have Stanley to myself again. Now that she was in her
old place, close to my well tried heart, I felt how much I
had really missed her all along. I was strangely happy
that evening as I knelt by Aunt Edith's bedside, and wept
that I was home again. Miss Phœbe, too, I think, was
really glad to have me back; she actually laid aside her
knitting-work, seated me in a large chair, bathed my face,
and combed my hair, while I told them about Ray and
Mary; the wedding festivities, etc.; and how happy they
were in their new home.

I unguardedly chanced to speak of the Hayne entertainment; I saw that Stanley drew her breath in quick
gasps, as though a stone lay heavy on her heart. I endeavored to change the current of her thoughts by referring
to the visible improvement in her mother's health; but
she said no word. With a regular motion the comb passed
through my hair; then Miss Phœbe answered: " Mrs. Montana is always better at Brightland; the atmosphere seems
to invigorate her." I soon learned the cause of Stanley's
silence, when her mother's health was alluded to; this improvement was the purchase of her sacrifice; yet for the
most part she was cheerful, and even assisted in the preparations for the marriage with the greatest alacrity.

Now came a message from the gentlemen that we should
join them, which we **did** on the grass plat 'neath the
arches of tall, dark cedars. Then we had a long, cheerful
chat about old times, during which Clyde gave utterance
to some caustic and witty things. As for Milverton, he
always made it a point to say the greatest number of droll
and humorous things. On this occasion he acquitted him-

self with unusual honor. Thus we sat after tea until chill
dews gathered from the swamps, and the notes of the
whippoorwill came in like a requiem. I saw shadows on
Stanley's beautiful eyes ere we separated for the night,
while in Clyde's manner there was that moody gloom
which always cut me to the soul! Often, in our horseback
excursions adown the shadowy road bordering the swamp,
he would ride by my side maintaining a silence so audible
I could hear the beating of his heart. Then, as by some
sudden inspiration, his soul would melt and come into his
eyes—hang dazzling there for one brief instant, then sink
back like the fall of some sweet song. Oh, if I had only
dared to meet that glance which always wandered from
my face out into the dim far space; perhaps even now the
shadow on my remnant of life had not lain half so darkly
or so inexorably.

Swiftly the summer days went by until the last were
gone—we lingered; ere the autumn rains set in heavy
and chill we took Aunt Edith back to Claremont; only
Clyde remained until the cotton was gathered in and he
saw his people comfortably settled in their winter quarters;
then Brightland was closed for the season.

It was pleasant to have Clyde with us again; he read to
us in the evenings; then he and Milverton arranged some
private theatricals for our special benefit, in which we took
the greatest delight. On one occasion Milverton inveigled
that staid, sedate Miss Phœbe to accompany us to the
opera; then absolutely gloated over his triumph for a week
to come. Clyde usually spent the day in the city. Milverton often accompanied him, though he returned to
luncheon, after which he lounged in the south parlor,
thrumming the piano or singing an amusing treble with
the harp, to the utter disgust of Aunt Dinah and the total

demolition of what little dignity Hawsey had succeeded in collecting during the short respite between pieces.

He absolutely succeeded in so far corrupting that young hand-maiden's morals that she accepted a bribe to furnish him the key to an apartment where old-fashioned dresses and bonnets were hung in state. Then actually assisted him while he proceeded to array his somewhat pursy proportions in sundry antique habiliments. In this guise he made his appearance at the door of Aunt Edith's sitting-room, where he stood for an instant endeavoring to look Cleopatra; failing signally, he gathered up his skirts with dainty fingers, and bowed himself out, leaving us convulsed with laughter. We were very sorry when Milverton returned to the North, I imagined because he did not wish to see Stanley married.

There were many things to do now; Stanley and I usually spent our forenoons shopping for the mantua-makers; we returned at noon much wearied. Once we were displaying our purchases for the inspection of Aunt Edith and Miss Phœbe; Clyde came in and stood looking upon the heaps of gossamer and laces with a stern fate in his indifferent face, which, with all my bravery heretofore, I could not bear to look upon. I cast down the baubles, going abruptly to my own apartment, whither Stanley came to seek me, as I had often done her when she left us to struggle all alone.

"I am sick and tired," I said, in answer to her questions; "very sick and tired, that is all." Oh! if I had only known what those few impatient words would bring forth I should have died sooner than to have spoken them. The color left her face, white as death—wildly rushing like a torrent long pent up, came her words; I could only shudder and be still.

"Yes, Jennie, I know you are tired of all this mockery. I am so, too. I should wonder if we were not. I intend this day and hour to put a stop to it. I do not love Clyde Ingram; he does not love me. What will be this marriage but a bargain and sale, which I am resolved must not, shall not go on. If the cards had gone out, I should recall them. I have chosen my course. I would rather be Clyde's slave than do a noble man the injustice to become his wife with this lie upon my soul. No; as the days go on which bring us nearer to the consummation of this fraud, I feel more and more the violence I should do to him and myself if I failed to retract this promise; therefore, I shall do so at any risk." It was useless to expostulate; I knew the feeling in her heart, for had I not beheld just such a look of soul-weariness in Warren Hayne's eyes when he took one of the little hands that were clenched hard together now and led her from the gay throng to the stillness without. As then, I heard the sighing sea, and it seemed to calm us both. After a long time I ventured to say, in defiance of my rebellious heart:

"Stanley, it will kill Aunt Edith to have this cherished project of life fail her at the last."

"No, no; you misjudge her. When she knows how I shrink from the fulfilment of this vow, she will say that I am right. I will go to her on my knees, and tell her all. She will forgive me—but——"

"But Clyde?" I rejoined, hoarsely.

"Ah! dear, noble Clyde, if I was sure he was quite happy, the sacrifice of my own feelings I would esteem very lightly; but he is not—he is wretched. It will be a relief to him to have this bond severed—it has long been irksome."

I know not how it was, but Stanley made her peace with

them all; and she and Clyde, in their changed relation, took their accustomed places at the tea-table that evening as though things had always been just as they were then. I afterwards learned from Miss Phœbe that Stanley had declared, in presence of her father, her willingness to sell herself, if needs be, for a stranger's gold, but never to Clyde Ingram, whom she loved as her brother. Clyde took his departure for Texas on the following morning. He sent **back** by his driver, from the city, a note to Uncle Montana, consigning Claremont to his charge. 'Twas thus it ended, ere the snow and the winter came again to Claremont. At **breakfast** there **was** only his vacant place. In our home and hearts, for many days and months, there was utter loneliness, for **we missed him very sadly.**

-------o-------

CHAPTER XII.

"The atmosphere of home! how bright
  It floats around us when we sit together,
  Under a bower of vine in summer weather,
Or round a hearth-stone on a winter's night."

PARK BENJAMIN.

AUNT EDITH was feeling better **as** the **spring** advanced. Affairs at Claremont settled back into their accustomed routine, though from our home-circle we missed Clyde and Raymond—oh! how much. It seemed so strange, so sad, to have, besides our own, only uncle's face at table; then in our evening reunions we were so lonely that we welcomed even Lane Austin pleasurably. He became our constant escort on all occasions, and was, in truth, the very *beau-ideal* of chivalry.

Thus winter wore away. There was much visiting in private circles in the great Southern metropolis; interspersed with the usual amount of heartiness and heartlessness in the society of New Orleans. Then there was the same cold grey look on the distant sea as its waves came rolling in with groan and sigh; the same pulseless trance of nature; the same bird-singing, grass-growing awakening from the spell ere spring in all her gladness burst upon us. Miss Phœbe's counterpane was laid aside, while her busy hands trained vines in the arbor and summer-house, where the boys went to smoke when at home. Beneath her touch, with the assistance of Hawsey, the flower-beds brightened, blushed, and grew fragrant.

Claremont wore its loveliest hues when we began to think and talk of accepting Raymond's invitation to go North for the summer. We could not go to Brightland for the summer. On account of his business, uncle could not accompany us. Clyde, who usually spent his summers with us on the plantation, was absent—we knew not for how long. There remained for us no alternative; so bringing all our eloquence to bear on Aunt Edith, for the purpose of inducing her to go with us, we decided to spend the summer at the North. I was sure a change of scene would benefit her, and it proved that my surmises were correct.

Stanley was passive; as for myself, I was anxious for anything that would in the least degree ease the quick, sharp anguish that always rang through my heart, when in fancy I canvassed the long life of loneliness outspread before me. True it is, as the Scotch divine has so touchingly said: "We can bear one day's burden at a time, but the weight of an hundred days together would crush the strongest."

Lane Austin proposed to be our escort, and, in the absence of our brother or Clyde Ingram, we accepted his kindness gratefully. The music of April, the flowers of May, the first rosy breath of June, were gathered into the category of nature's past treasures—into an echoless world of solemn silences—ere we took our departures. Then came long days of travel! The shrill voice that announced the leagues by which we measured distances between extreme sections, and each little detail—some pleasurable, others wearisome—by which we were made to realize this fact, were gathered into the record of experiences past and gone, like those sunbright days, to return no more.

A year had gone by; a lightsome, flower-garnished year of calm, serene joy to Raymond and Mary in their new home; a year of heart changes, soul-weariness, of vacant spaces, and unspoken pain to us at Claremont. We came into the new atmosphere gratefully, reverently. A gleam of the first morning joyousness came back to Stanley's face—so grave and quiet, save at sunny intervals, since that other summer time was ended—as she knelt beside the little crib and took the tiny velvet hand of her brother's first-born into her own; a baby girl—our sweet bird of immortality; she seemed lying there winking diamond eyes of blue as Stanley twirled sunbeams of golden hair that were half shadow in the shrouded room, upon the white brow which she kissed oftener than the cherry lips; it reminded her of another brow—but of this she did not speak.

Aunt Edith voluntarily established herself by this little crib—on duty at its post. It was strange, the interest and delight she took in her little grandchild. With more devotion even than was her wont, she prayed God that she might be permitted to see this little one grow strong to walk the hard earthway, ere she, frail as infancy, should be called to walk the ways beyond.

" What do you call her, Ray ?" I asked, kissing the hem of her snowy robes, which was the most I could do, for I felt the holy presence of angels hovering about that child.

" We have not yet decided, Jennie ; I wish you would assist us in finding a suitable cognomen for our little queen "— here the young father stooped and kissed his daughter's lips with dignity so tempered by love that was infinite, my heart bowed low down. Was this our Ray, so reckless, so rollicksome of yore ? Years of feeling with their purifying tides seemed to have passed over, leaving him an *earnest* man, reverent and God-fearing.

" Call her Stanley," suggested the calm-faced mother. We all acquiesced save her who was most specially interested. I was a little surprised at seeing Stanley turn her face towards Mary with the old white, stony look of anguish upon its fairness, as she answered in tones hoarse with suffering, crushed down by the burden of her life's one regret :

" Oh ! no ; not that name, please, it would almost crush the little thing; it is a sorrowful name to bear." Then, more gently, she added :

" I have a name in view; it is odd, and very sweet; I am sure you will like it, Mary—an artistic combination of two names, those of your friend and husband, Aljean and Raymond—Ala Ray."

It was beautiful, so we all thought ; even Ray, who drew his sister to his heart, and in one long, tender embrace, his consent and gratitude were expressed. Thus was our little angel christened Ala Ray by a baptism of joyful tears ! her little pilgrimage inaugurated by the loves of parents, sister, and friend. Might not these strong links which were woven with our heart-strings round her keep her upon earth ? Was the chain, all shining brightly as it was, sufficient to bind an angel to this weary world, or should those little feet first learn to walk the gold-paved streets where eternal sunbeams lie, while for us the sands fall, the morning flowers perish in the broad noon's heat, and suns sink daily into night? Mute lips have kissed thy rod, O Death, since the first golden morning dawned on Paradise, and will continue to do so until the last sands fall— the flower wreaths of earth shall perish, and the last suns go down.

But oh! we never thought of the failing glories of this world or its waning sun, while beamed upon us this bright morning star from the firmament of the immortal. We basked in its radiance, never seeking to know if it would set in the darkness of night, as other hopes had done before. We neither thought of nor feared the curse of idolatry. How strange and sudden sounded Mrs. Kingswell's solemn warning one day to the little circle gathered round the crib. Aunt Edith held Ala in her frail arms; Mr. Kingswell sat near, talking gravely to the little lady as though she was quite able to comprehend what he uttered, though I could see he regarded my aunt with as much tenderness as he did his grand-child and hers. The reverence almost with which Mr. Kingswell deported himself towards Aunt Edith and she towards him was to me a matter containing facts filled with grave speculation. I was puzzling my head about them when Mrs. Kingswell repeated her warning that we should not make an idol of Ala Ray. I saw that Raymond shared her apprehensions on this score, yet what availed their utterance then? The silken fetters were already grown so strong—then the object of homage was so sweetly fair, our worship was involuntary. We could not withdraw one tithe of the great love we had given her as time flowed on, even though the sands fell, the flowers perished, the golden

sun went down very calmly, and the night came on whose
stars saw our hearts lying in the dust beneath the smiter's
feet. The Haynes were occupying their summer residence
near to Ridgely. Though Warren was in Wayburn more
than once during our stay, he and Stanley never met in
private circles; it would not have been quite safe for
either. Notwithstanding the cold blue eyes of his wife,
which had looked her displeasure so severely, in consideration of his attention to me at a party one evening, he
would have sought us out and called to see Stanley, had I
consented that he should. I had grave reasons for my
refusal. There was that in the very presence of each to
the other, a spell which would have unsettled all resolu-
tions for silence and calmness, even while past grievances
were uncancelled, past wrongs unaccounted for. Ah!
when heart rose up to meet heart, each in their every throb
true to the summer music of old; when soul and soul
unmasked stood calmly looking beyond earth and time,
where would have been those frail barriers then? An act
of the State legislature has made it possible, by the strong
cords of society, law, and custom, to fetter a man physically with an external bond of marriage; but in the holy relation, can it do the rest? Can a few formal words uttered by
a minister of God make the music of his life and fireside?
Can rude hands of a custom that is universal unlock the
inmost doors of his being and bring the treasures forth?
Ask of those who vainly try to still these voices uplifted
above the hollow observance of rites sacred only when hallowed by a love undimmed as time flows on, consecrated
by a truth that never pales.

I met Warren several times during his stay at Wayburn.
There was ever upon his face an anxious look, as though
he sought something which he failed to find. I thought

how, with that faded wreath, had perished the flowers of
his life, and of the solitary ship cutting its way to the
heart of a lonely sea; but never more ran my golden river
now—a seal of fate was upon its lucid current.

Aunt Edith was so much improved, it was thought best
to remain at Ridgely until November, and thus another
summer rippled by. The few months from spring to
autumn had wrought in our baby a full, rich change,
though I often saw the light which is not of earth dancing
in her eyes; hence, in recognition of a fact, awful, solemn,
full of anguish, I could only bow my head and pray
dumbly that she might linger with us. Often in the glow
of autumn I pondered of these things, and marvelled why it
was so—that the fairest and brightest things that are given
us upon the earth should leave us thus.

Many a sunset found Stanley sitting on the grass-plot
with the child in her arms, watching the lingering light on
those far New Hampshire hill-tops, and the blue mists
gathering in the valley depths below; then again until the full
moon silvered them, and the stars took up their watch above,
has Ala Ray sat silently looking into space, and seeming
to feel a childish need of something we of earth could not
give her, something it was not ours to give, but the *Father's.*
Then she would sink into a deep, sweet repose, smiling while
she slept; the mother said she was talking with the angels;
and the father, calm, thoughtful, yet fearing he knew not
what, would kiss his little darling awake, and ask her over
and over again if she loved to sleep *under the stars.* Again
and again has he brought her back, as it were, from her
wanderings in Paradise, to lay her infant beauty to his
great, true heart, as if in that strong father-love he would
keep her with him for ever. We called her our spirit-child
—our sun-ray. When the little folks at Wayburn spoke of

her, they always called her Ala Montana, as though she
were half-grown, and not the infant she was.

"We must take her with us to Claremont," Aunt Edith
said; and her tones were full of pleasant curiosity as to
what Miss Phœbe and the servants would say of Ray's
baby; what rare exhibitions we would have of her infant
accomplishments. Thus we went on scheming for the
future, and making plans—as the sons and daughters of
men have vainly essayed to do from the beginning of
time. The little to-day is not deep enough nor broad enough
for the life we would crowd into it.

November came with its elections! Abraham Lincoln
was chosen President of the United States. A *Northern*
president! think of that, ye delegates to the Baltimore con-
vention! Think of that, ye dignitaries at Charleston, who
recklessly withdrew your support from the great Douglas
in favor of John C. Breckinridge. Ah! did they not
think of it in after days—angrily, defiantly, ere they cut
themselves aloof, with the states they represented, from
the body of the nation? The conservative heart went out
to Douglas! When wire-working partisans reversed the
current in his favor, why should they manifest surprise that
the faction to whom their act had given a majority should
have asserted its latent power, and gathered strength in its
triumphant course? Further still, when those Southern
representatives in Congress and the Senate of the United
States withdrew their voices from the legislative halls of
our common country, what right had they to be amazed
that the great machinery crashed on without them—whether
to glory or to ruin? Let those decide who shall write our
Nation's history—perchance, her epitaph.

Life in every department, in every grade, was a convul-
sive tumult, agitated by the approaching storm, which has

since burst, oh! how wildly! Hearts that were brave and true; graves where the clods are new, out-spread 'neath the heaven's bright blue; sad tears for me and for you, watching the long night through; all, all, save the weary few, lying out 'neath the crimson dew; red blood where the green grass grew; our loved ones, where shall we seek them? Yet they are everywhere save in the homes where their names are loved and cherished, where we shall miss them ever more. We may rebuild our national structure, erect pillars of her greatness that tower far towards the eternal heavens, yet we cannot mend the household altars that are broken into fragments in this strife, or bring back one tithe of that which has gone down beneath thy tides, O Revolution!

The sands are falling—bolts of death, the flowers perish and are consumed in the fierce fires of strife, which burn through long nights of anguish after the suns of many battle days have set in blood, which all eternity may not wash out.

But we are here to tell a simple story of the heart-trials of one small family of the millions that are unwritten—the God of battles, the Christ of peace has the record. When the reveille is sounded and the earthly roll-call has been vainly repeated, and those who were left sleeping by the way-side have failed to come in answer to the summons, we feel the assurance that many whose names were written among the "missing," **have** been folded to that infinite heart of the God of storm and refuge, who from out the battle tempest has taken them to himself.

Thus came November! a cold, bleak, northern November, of piercing winds and bare trees. I remembered that dear sojourner amid strange scenes had repeated to me, with such pathos in his tones, that thrilling poem of Hood's,

adding—"My life has been one long November!" I knew
and felt the truth of what he said then; the autumn previous, as we sat in the gathering shadows at Brightland—
the Promethean fires of genius burning in his glorious
eyes. Yes, he had his November as well as Hood, only
Clyde Ingram's, unlike the great poet's, was *unwritten*—his
genius was none the less immortal! an attribute that is
never at home with the commonplace on earth. If it finds
not the one haven which it seeks all through its world-
bound range, a love pure, glowing, and eternal, it is ever
with its possessor a stranger and pilgrim in the life-ways.
Perhaps it was the fact of my having grown to womanhood in the atmosphere of his presence, inhaling the invi-
gorating breath of grand silences and soul-thoughts shining through the few words we have need of, that has
given me in some measure a clue to hidden natures, such
as Clyde's. But certain it is I never hear any one say of
another "they are peculiar, I cannot understand them," but
I immediately divine there is something more than ordinary
to be comprehended, something to admire, to love, to
delight in, that the world knows not of, has not yet recognised; for it is slow to acknowledge, and has no innate perception of any grand truth, individual or general. Those
are the natures that always walk the loftiest paths of earth!
rarely coming out of their citadel of proud reserve; to learn
to know them well is to love them evermore.

And where was that life—that November in the cold
bleakness of our season at Ridgely? Not one word from
him since he left us the preceding autumn. Now that the
flowers were perished I often walked out 'neath a sky lowering and grey, repeating to myself a little poem I had
once read. I recall it to-day, despite the time and space
between; there is comfort, and hope, and promise in it:

" We meet at one gate—
When all's over. Thy ways they are many and wide;
And seldom are two ways the same, side by side—
May we stand at the same little door when all's done ?
The ways they are many, the end it is **one.**"

There has ever been a light in these little lines that has shown me the dark way, and taught me a lesson which but for what has happened I might have been long in learning.

I remember I was thinking of it the last evening of our stay at Ridgely. Clyde's uncle sat beside me, with his kind hand upon my head ; deep into my heart sank the words that he said.

"There is true happiness, Jennie, without alloy, **to be** found in the performance of duty. No matter what rugged paths we tread—through wastes of life, to the sunny plains beyond. In working for destiny we are working for God ; and the most direct route to Him and to heaven is one that is wrought by hands that are ready and willing to do **His will.** There **are** heroes and heroines in this world more worthy the name than those who are sung in story or storied in song ; brave spirits 'who find God in the thing lying nearest to be done.' The record of such **lives is** yonder, where also will be revealed that silent struggle **of** yours, dear, and hers and his. Trust God ; wait in silence—only work for the end and the victory ; it **will** come to you ; if not here, hereafter. Be strong, little one."

And listening to his words, I tried to believe him, for I felt he meant what he said—this practical Christian. **I saw** the radiance in his dear face shining like the sun over the far hill-tops that I loved ; further off from me in these long days and months of trial, seemed the faith of which he spoke, and the promise whose fulfilment he pictured.

There was only for me the weary waiting; yet I prayed silently to God in that November.

Ten days later the same circle sat by the parlor fireside in our own home. Besides our family, Raymond, Mary, little Ala, and Mr. Milverton came back with us to Claremont. The baby was delighted with everything she saw— the tropical plants, and winter birds singing in the boughs of evergreens, the falling fountains, the flowers that were everywhere; and everybody was delighted with her, even Aunt Dinah, who regarded her curiously between her spasms of tear-shedding as though she feared the little creature might take wings and fly away, exclaiming over and over again :

"Who would a thought I'd a lived to see Mars Raymond's baby ! at Claremont ? And the beautifullest creetur too ! with skin like them little white daisies in the cabin gardens, and eyes jest like the blue sky ! and hair jest like our own Miss Stanley's when she was a infant."

Hawsey was immediately installed chief protectress of her young mistress, and became so much enamored of her little ladyship, so won by her gentle ways, that she in her enthusiasm declared her intention of persuading Miss Mary and Mars Ray to permit her to follow the little blossom, watch and tend her even when transplanted to her Northern home.

"What !" said Aunt Dinah, "go up thar and be a free nigger ? Never ! De gal's gwine crazy plum."

When she found that her mother greeted the proposition with such lofty indignation, Hawsey, to all intents and purposes, relinquished her hope of becoming maid of honor to the juvenile Miss Montana. Though to all external appearance Hawsey acquiesced, I observed that she did a good deal of private wire-pulling through Raymond and the rest to gain her end.

Miss Phœbe knitted more persistently than ever now; she declared her purpose, before so vague and distant of fulfilment, had assumed a tangible shape. The counterpane had long been destined for Raymond's baby.

Uncle Montana was delighted with his grand-child. The third day after her arrival he brought home a handsome cup of gold with her little name upon its side. Presenting the pretty gift to her little grace with mock pomp, he told the story of the golden cup in mythology, and how the bearer stood at the gate. Miss Phœbe interrupted him with saying:

"It is my opinion that child will wait long at no gate; not even the golden one up' yonder; it would unclose of its own accord to let the little angel in. She is too bright a spirit for this dark world of sorrow."

We felt her words were true! We made no answer; how could we? What should we say? What was to be we left to time and God.

———o———

CHAPTER XIII.

"There's a Divinity that shapes our ends,
Rough-hew them as we will."
SHAKSPEARE.

I AM off for Brightland; who goes with me to-day? was Raymond's interrogatory when he appeared armed with whip and gauntlets, equipped for a drive, a few mornings subsequent to our arrival at home. Stanley had gone to spend the day with some friends in the city; Milverton had gone with her; Mary was doing some things for baby, sitting meantime in Aunt Edith's room, and preferred to remain with her during the forenoon. Accordingly, it became apparent that the pleasant duty devolved on me. With pleasurable anticipations I accepted Ray's proposition to drive behind Clyde's cream-colored ponies. The groom made a few observations as he gave the lines into the hands of his young master which amused me very much.

"They will take you that seventeen miles to Brightland and back, most as soon as the railroad, young Mars; Mars Clyde Ingram sot much store by dem hosses, so he did."

"Who ever heard of the *railroad* taking anybody any- where ! the cars do sometimes." With this amiable reflec- tion Raymond settled his patent leathers with a good deal of dash, gathered up the reins with a flourish of the whip, and departed at a rapid pace, utterly ignoring Peter's voluble retort to the effect that "*Mars Clyde never whipped his hosses.*" I glanced down at the arched instep so daintily encased in shining boots, remarking mischievously :

"Aunt Dinah has been sorely troubled lest, with your practical life at the North, you should feel called upon to dispense with some of the luxuries of living and elegances of apparel for which you were noted previous to your leav- ing home. I perceive you adhere to the old system in one regard at least; you always believed in being well shod." He answered readily :

"Yes, Clyde and I, when in Germany, formed a league within ourselves to support patent leather in extreme cases. My Marseillaise and linen suits have not been aired nearly so often of late. It has ever been my policy, however, to act upon the hypothesis that cleanliness is akin to god- liness; I endeavor to approach by that means as nearly as possible to the divine standard. The first thing I did last spring was to order a genuine Panama, to which I clung persistently throughout the summer." Then changing his

9

high tone for one of earnest meaning, he exclaimed impulsively, like the frank Raymond of old :

"I wish Clyde was here, Jennie. I cannot conceive why he wanted to go away leaving his business in town, and Brightland out of kilter, as it is. To be sure, he has an overseer, but that is not like having the supervision oneself. I repeat, I cannot conceive why he left; can you inform me?"

"No—yes—if you really wish it, I will tell you why he went. It was because Stanley refused to marry him," I answered, while a chill crept into my heart.

"The reason you assign involves another aspect of the case. Why did Stanley refuse to marry him; do you know?"

"I presume it was because she did not love him."

"No; it was because she felt Clyde did not love her, though for her sake, and to conciliate our parents, he would have sacrificed his personal feeling in the matter. Believe me, Jennie, could Clyde have given his heart to Stanley, noble, generous, and true as he is, he would in time have won hers in return; but it was otherwise. Now I am going to tell you a great truth, against which you have long shut your eyes. Clyde Ingram loves you, Jennie, devotedly and entirely, as it falls to the lot of but few women in this world to be loved. I only speak what I have known for a long, long time—since we were children together."

In my heart, now I believe Raymond spoke truly. I closed my eyes and clasped my hands tremblingly, while the glorious certainty of conviction, like waves of tenderness, swept over me. I heard sweet sounds from bowers russet and red, that girt us on every side. Out into the broad, bright light, streamed anew my golden river; its current piped the first hope-lays my orphan heart had sung in that fair land of promise. I was like one awakened from what seemed a long, troublous trance, though now the anguish seemed far off, as my faith had once appeared, when Mr. Kingswell told me once, the light ere long would break in glory. It had broken, and I could think only of my great joy, not daring to look up, lest it should vanish. Now I opened my mind's eye wide. Great Heavens! Was that my beautiful river, still rippling, gliding on?—*its current stained with blood!* Yes, the tides ran crimson now—its channel widening, deepening—as it flowed onward to an ocean of gore! I clasped my hands, exclaiming:

"Oh, Ray, this is horrible!"

"I sympathize with you, Jennie; this sudden revelation has bewildered you, but, for the life of me, I cannot see what there is so *horrible* about it. Clyde is a chivalrous, noble fellow, one of those grand souls who would unhesitatingly lay down life for his love. Why could you not give him one little corner in that great heart of yours, little sister?"

"Do not ask me, Ray, anything about it; some day I will tell you all I know."

Just then, we came into the avenue leading to Brightland. Ah! November, too, was here, sighing round the lonely house, brooding in the distant marshes, and in the bars and dots of mellow sunshine that came down through the tall cedars to play at hide-and-seek upon the nut-brown grass. Then in that solitary, loveless life of his—November always, from youth to age—one long November. Yet into my heart, illumined as it was with the light of the glorious truth that he loved me, none of the glooms and shadows about me could ever come again. Though I was happy in the knowledge of these things, I dared hope for nothing that promised the fulfilment of my hopes; for oh, those crimson tides were sweeping on, the channel ever broadening, deepening, while they ran.

The servants, all anxious and excited by our arrival, immediately bestirred themselves in the effort to make us comfortable and prepare for us a repast, as it was near noon. Meantime, I made a tour of the house, while Raymond talked over business matters with Clyde's overseer. I bathed my face, arranged my hair, and sat down for a breathing spell on the upper piazza.

Brightland was situated on an eminence; below were nut-brown swamps dotted with forests of pine, through which coursed the little stream by whose side we often rode or walked, in the golden days when my bright river ran cheerily; high over head the cold, grey sky arched over a November sea. I seemed to hear Clyde's voice and feel his presence everywhere; and my heart sent forth a cry—Oh, brother, come back to me; I am weary, and want you so much. I knew now why it was he could not bear to have me call him brother; knew also what he meant when he said "I loved one woman, but she loved not me." Yes, Raymond's words were true; Clyde's heart was mine—only mine—through long years, blind years, when I saw it not. When I thought I loved alone, pride kept me silent; now I felt that he too suffered—the barriers melted all away.

Ray came jauntily round the corner of the porch, talking in his usual off-hand manner to Clyde's overseer, Mr. Marley. This gentleman was of Northern birth, with red hair, coarse, wiry, red whiskers, and cold, black eyes; just the man to lord it over slaves; one who would draw the rein tightly, never sparing the rod. He said, with his quick, sharp accent:

"It has been some time since I heard directly from Mr. Ingram, though I hold weekly communication with his

agent in the city. He told me that Mr. Ingram spoke of
going to Australia, in a recent epistle addressed to himself.
Crops were very fine last year of rice and cotton ; sugar,
average. We shall cultivate largely next year, while we
have the hands. 'Make hay while the sun shines,' is our
policy. Do you know ?" he continued, squinting one of
his hard, black eyes until it was almost closed, " since people have become generally aware of the result of our elections, many of our neighboring planters have had trouble in
keeping down their slaves. Mr. Ingram's servants seem not
to have become affected with the malaria, for he is a good
master, and I believe if they had choice to-morrow, to go or
stay, they would remain to a man, though the elements of
dissatisfaction may arise here too, as they will, doubtless,
all over the whole country."

The man's words actually startled me. The storm had
indeed been brewing a long time; the crimson river was
fairly booming now, and I felt the issue to be certain and
near, and the end far off; yes, far beyond the blood-red
tides of years; as surely on that day as on this, almost four
years between.

"In the event of a *war* between the sections," continued
Mr. Marley, "your sympathies would be with *us?*" This
last was said with an insinuating leer of familiarity which
Raymond's recent democratic surroundings had not in the
least degree prepared him for; he drew himself up, answering very coldly, never once deigning to look in the direction of the hard, black, questioning eyes:

" It should matter but very little to you, sir, or any one
else, as regards the direction to which my sympathies tend.
I shall never permit them to sway me in the slightest, at
the expense of principles involving right and justice ; which
means duty to country as well as to my fellow-man ! "

Spoken like our own Raymond, I thought—little Ala's father. " Bless her," he exclaimed, while his eyes ran over when we were fairly on the way to join her.

"I cannot tell you half I feel for that little darling, Jennie; or how intricately day by day she is growing into my life."

"You need not seek to do so, Raymond; I know it all. Ala is precious to every one of us; but oh! brother, I feel it is wrong to worship her blindly, passionately, as we do. Supposing we should lose her? Then, if war should be declared, which is possible and probable, you may be called upon yourself to go—for your country to die—leaving her alone in this weary world. In that case, dearest brother, would it not be better that she went first? Remember, the golden portals are not closed against our Ala, Ray. Any time that God called she could go, and be welcome."

" Oh! don't," he exclaimed, as though my words were lances that cut him to the soul; "it almost kills me, Jennie, to think of this, even." He dashed the tear-drops impatiently from his face, and we came swiftly up the Claremont road. Where was my warning when Hawsey came out to meet us with Ala seated upon her shoulder, holding her dainty little hands while the child very demurely and quietly smiled to us a welcome home? Was it the slanting sunbeams streaming over her brow and face and hair that made her seem so supernaturally, almost divinely beautiful? I only know I never saw on any other human face the expression which her baby features wore very often nowadays.

A pleasant group sat dressed and waiting on the veranda in the Indian summer glow of a waning day, which I called my last day at Brightland. Tea was announced, which was spread in the most luxurious manner; broiled meats and game; hot biscuits with coffee, tea, and chocolate; a side-table bearing fruits of every description which the season and climate afforded. Lane Austin joined us in this meal, as was his custom to do at evenings nowadays. Though on this special occasion he startled us with a formal announcement that the Haynes had arrived in the city for the winter. I saw the very shadow of a crimson flush come into Stanley's cheek, then fall again; but she made no sign.

"Will you call upon them?" "No," Raymond answered abruptly and emphatically; thus the matter rested, though Stanley suffered, oh! how much: and I loved and sympathized with her, which was the most that I could do. I was powerless to help her in any way to bear her burden.

The misunderstandings which had driven Clyde and me asunder were nothing to this ban which made Stanley's pure love a sin in sight of God and man.

We met them the next afternoon as we drove down to the city. Stanley was looking radiant in a dress of cherry silk, trimmed with guipure lace, finished with point collar and cuffs; an ermine mantle, swinging by its snowy silken cord and tassel, partially enveloped her shoulders. Her eyes were sparkling, her curls flowing, cheeks glowing; this was the picture that met Warren's eyes as we swept hastily by them. I intercepted his glance of recognition of her, embodying a wild, passionate gleam that made me tremble; there was in it such an expression of reckless steadfastness which told he had suffered much, and in that instant was ready to do and to dare anything or everything for her; even to ignore his galling bonds—to come out from them to her pure side again, and vow in the presence of all the world the love that was consuming him. I knew that safety for either lay only in time and distance; in which even the frailest might take refuge. They were both upright in principle, but love was at the helm; and duty was a frail ship in which to combat the surging waves while the tides of fate set strong against them.

It was a hard winter for Stanley; we met the Haynes almost daily in our drives—occasionally at the theatre and opera; but never in our private circle; it was my policy if possible to avoid a *tête-à-tête* for those two—my cousins.

One evening, near the close of the season, there came a party of serenaders to Claremont from the city. I detected Warren's voice in the chorus to a full rich ballad, embodying a German air very pathetic and touching. Stanley brought me a card upon which she had pencilled these words—"Go Warren, and for my sake as well as for your own, never, never come here again." There was no signature, but I knew he would instantly recognise her chirography.

"I approve your measure, but I should have worded it somewhat differently; Warren is a gentleman, you know; this may lead him to fear you misconstrued his presence here." Her answer reassured me:

"No, no, he came thoughtlessly, I am sure, meaning no reflection whatever upon my name. There was in that plaintive song of his the burden of memories that will not be crushed down; he is haunted by a ghost of former joy, and forgets that I may not be strong enough to hear the hopeless voices that tell me of a by-gone time."

I spoke slowly and cautiously to Stanley, after having despatched a servant with the card addressed to Warren; much as I felt for her, I also pitied him. His manner in their meetings recently, brief and circumscribed as they were, had given her vastly the advantage; he had manifested all that he felt for her—the hopeless love and vain regret; while she was more than ever convinced that Warren had married for wealth. He never divined that she loved him still; he deemed her false and fickle—thought she had cast off Clyde from pure caprice.

I had never told Stanley of the evidence he had of her untruth to him; had not shown her the letter I held in my possession; I did not deem it best, just yet, to reopen wounds that had bled at every pore. I knew how cold and cruel must seem those little words of hers to him who already misjudged her. As we stood next morning on the veranda, a servant on horseback came up the carriage road from the city, bearing an exquisite bouquet, together with a note for Miss Montana. "There is no answer," she said haughtily to the man; then drew me softly into her own apartment, closed the door, and read as follows:

"You have bidden me come no more where I may look upon you; you have denied me the simple desire of my eyes; I will comply. If from all the past you will permit yourself to recall the one of my words that was most earnest and full of solemn meaning, believe that word to be true to-day as it was in that bright time. And let this be my apology for having annoyed you on the last evening of my stay. I leave for New Orleans to-day! let these simple flowers find a place somewhere near you—within the circle of your presence; they bear to you my long farewell—a farewell which I dare not speak; my lips henceforth are sealed."

I saw how it was; his patient words had smitten a place in her heart which she thought cold and hard towards him; ah! it was only her power of will that made it seem so. She tottered to where I sat, her arms outstretched, with a little sharp cry of anguish that was ere long broken by sobs that shook her young frame like a reed as she lay with her golden head upon my shoulder, and her white, cold arms clasped rigidly about my neck. Her emotional

9*

moments of late had been so few, I was surprised at her indulgence of feeling even on this occasion.

"How could you be so strong and hide all from him, when you have suffered daily, hourly, so much?"

"*It was from her I hid the pain*," she said, almost fiercely; starting up and petulantly bathing her face, as though angry with herself for the outbreak.

I mused for a long time, then said:

"Stanley, darling, has it ever occurred to you there might have been some counter current here—some tide beneath the tides, which has turned the current of two lives apart, when they should have flowed together? You believed Warren false; I believe that he has always been true; that his marriage with that woman, and the prolonged pain he suffers, are the inevitable results of a conviction that you yourself were not true, and cared nothing at all for him."

She made a haughty gesture of incredulity, but I proceeded fearlessly nevertheless:

"You have both been deceived—duped—cruelly, shamefully; take my word for it. I will not tell you how I know this; you might not feel inclined to listen; perhaps it is better you should not hear it. There is one thing, however, I wish you to understand; it is that you are very unjust to Warren Hayne when you cherish any feeling of resentment towards him. He is at least in every way worthy your esteem and friendship, if nothing more; kinder words are due to him than were those of yours last night. I am sure you will repent them some time. I wonder he bears them gently, patiently, as he does. I will leave you now; I must go to Aunt Edith; please join us soon."

But Stanley did not come. She remained alone throughout the day; she did not respond to her brother's special summons to dinner—excused herself upon the score of a headache. Ray gave me a piercing look of inquiry when Hawsey returned with her answer, then said in a quiet undertone, designed for my ear only :

"She has had a good many headaches recently."

"*Heartaches, too,*" was my mental suggestion, but he understood that too well. As I was going to my own room, I met her brother coming from hers, looking much pleased about something.

"She has promised to witness *La Fille du Regiment* this evening," he exclaimed, his face full of concern for the even transitory happiness of his dear sister. I thought often of that expression of triumph on his face in days that came after—when he was fighting on a broad battle-field that was far from our home and his.

I kept wondering all the afternoon if it were best to tell Stanley all that I knew concerning that affair of hers and Warren's; act as I felt, and express boldly my conviction that Retta Austin had intercepted their correspondence. Finally, I decided it was but just so to do ; whatever peace could come between them now, would aid in tranquillizing the mind of each, and could be maintained silently without encroaching upon another's rights ; at least, it would take the burden of a crushing doubt from the heart of my sweet friend.

I went to her room later in the afternoon; she was drinking a cup of tea, preparatory to making a toilet for the evening. She said languidly :

"Come, Aljean, I want you to help me. Ray says I must look my best to-night; do you know, since brother has been talking to me so earnestly about many things, I have half a mind to accept Milverton's hand, and go away with him anywhere—I care not—across the ocean, perhaps? I am reckless, and ready for anything and everything."

I quietly dismissed Hawsey, installed myself dressing-maid *pro tem.* to her young mistress, while she continued to talk on in that careless, hopeless strain, which cut me deeper than her words of anguish :

"It may as well come now, all that may happen in time. I presume I must get married; everybody says, how strange it is that we do not—you **and I, so** sought for and apparently desirable." She gave a little shudder here; she was too weary and heartsore to play well the part she had assumed.

"Lane Austin, Jennie, who worships the very ground on which you walk; let us make those two poor fellows happy. What say you?"

"And ourselves **miserable in** the meantime?" I said, interrogatively.

"There are **two prominent** barriers between Lane and myself; we lack the consent of the parties most directly concerned; he is not in the notion, neither am I; on that point we understand each other perfectly. Though were it otherwise, I assure you I should never outrage my soul by marrying any man whom I did not and could not love, even if he loved me ever so much; neither would you, though you were talking at random thus." She mused for some time, then resumed: "After all, what avails this weary waiting? It is aimless; rushing into that other association would not be wholly objectless; new scenes and new ties might wean me from some I find it necessary to eschew. Oh, Jennie! I am heartily sick of the whole pageant—this life I lead."

"If this were all, Stanley, we might well become so; but there is something beyond, when the pain and waiting shall be over. Uncle Kingswell has told us of these things many times. I did not realize his hope then; I have since felt the truth and glory of all that he meant. Life is but a trial season, a prelude to eternity."

"Ah! it does for you, Jennie, who have no secret pain to bear, to talk of life as though it was far away from you; I am thirsty, and feel its burdens are so real. It is much harder for those who are travel-stained and overcome with the heat and dust of the journey to come into that higher, brighter way that Mr. Kingswell talks so sweetly and hopefully about. Dearest, the pathway to that promised land lies through toil and tears and suffering; there are thorns in it, and I am too weak and powerless to pluck them out."

"If you cannot do this for yourself, perhaps you can for a fellow-traveller whom we once esteemed very dearly. He is your friend and mine. Do as I bid you, and the sharp arrow will be extracted; the act will be as balm to the bleeding abrasion." So saying, I took from my pocket a casket containing the pearls Warren requested so earnestly that I should give her. "You will wear them, dear, for his sake and mine."

She assented, doubtless imagining the gift came from Clyde, though with characteristic delicacy she forbore to question me on the subject, believing I would tell her all that was needful when the fitting season came. I rolled from my fingers masses of golden curls, then lifted them, fleecy and light, from her pure, beautiful brow, ran the little fillet of bright blue across the glittering mesh, and caught them by the pearl brooch at the side. I gathered the longer in a cluster, twisted with them a few half open orange blossoms, and caught the mass at the back of her Grecian head with a pure white comb, then clasped the pendants in her tiny ears, then stood off to witness the effect of my handywork. I had reason to feel proud of my effort and my friend. I

call her so, because in the category of terms there are few
dearer to me than this. She was radiantly lovely, attired
in a dress of Marie Louise blue, with an ermine victorine
caught by its cherry tassels. It was curious to see how the
golden rings of hair broke here and there from the mass
of brightness with no apparent design but to look what
they were, a part of Stanley's witchery. The household
greeted her with acclamations of delight when she came
below stairs; Milverton handed her into the carriage.

" Nothing could console your unworthy votaries in having
lost your society for the day, but the fact of your coming
forth so radiant this evening." Poor fellow, what else
could he say, he was so dazzled by this vision of loveliness.
Stanley thanked him kindly as we were being whirled
away; the buggy containing Raymond and Mary followed
swiftly in our wake.

We had scarcely taken our places in Clyde's box when I
observed the Haynes immediately opposite in the dress
circle. Stanley, too, saw them, though she seemed not to
do so as she sat playing abstractedly with the cherry tassels
of her victorine.

I caught Warren's eye just in time to intercept a look of
grieved tenderness which I had seen so often on his face
of late. The pained expression passed from his brow as a
vapor in the " *clear shining after rain;* " then an expression
of rest came over his features it was pleasant to look upon.
He turned his attention now to his wife, while the rich
swell of orchestral music rose and fell like the waves of
tenderness in those two souls who loved a love that was
hopeless yet deathless. Stanley was wearing his gift; she
did not then despise him utterly; it was for this evidence
of relenting and forgiveness on her part he had waited in
New Orleans another day. Now he could go home braver,

stronger to do his work in life. Strange, how even this
little manifestation that Stanley remembered him more
kindly, than her apparent slight and her words to him
the previous day had given him reason to believe, filled
his heart with intense joy.

We all felt happier, I think, for that evening's entertainment. We could look into the future with more clearness
and certainty—even Stanley, whose strange mood of the
morning had entirely passed away. She was more at rest,
and seemed to accept the destiny that was her life
patiently. She asked me no further question concerning
the donor of those pearls, and I told her nothing more just
then; the time was not yet come. I hoped I scarce knew
what for either her or Warren—only that God would help
them and bring them into His peace and His great love,
which was strength and might.

---o---

CHAPTER XIV.

"Then shook the hills with thunder riven,
Then rushed the steeds to battle driven,
And louder than the bolts of heaven
Far flashed the red artillery."

CAMPBELL.

Now come we to the saddest part of our story! The crimson tides sweeping through my fancy came nearer and
nearer. Through homes of the North and flowers of the
South ran their desolating course. Cold hearts sat shivering
by colder hearthstones as the blood-red current trailed.
Oh! whither would it bear our hopes and dreams? Who
could say, There is no face that I have kissed and loved

lying underneath the clods of a way since worn and beaten into dust by feet that bear our sacrifices to the funeral pyre, to await the fiery billows that should consume them. Ah! no; rapidly the keen darts are flying; you may encase your heart in a covering of adamant, they will yet pierce you through. Many a life-path to the far *eternal* lies through fields of gore, and our dead sleep not where home-shades may shelter them from the noonday sun that beat upon them in their last toilsome march.

The Haynes, as well as Raymond and his family, had returned to the North. There were summer flowers and warm bright suns that shone with a lustre that was mockery. The inauguration of Mr. Lincoln proved to be but another name for the inauguration of rebellion in the South, which involved our country in civil war. One by one those States had broken the old band of sisterhood, had seceded, and formed an antagonistic league under the Palmetto banner of South Carolina.

Ere March had sighed out her last days of peace, and April came cheerily with her bright wreaths and glad voices, " the guns of Sumter knelled in the war." Oh! with what agonized terror we watched and prayed, while the South with one accord, one heart, flew to arms, and were ere long enrolled as enemies to country and government. Men of the South, high and low, rich and poor, were soldiers in the broad field together. The fair, bright brow of many a mother's only son was crisped in the toilsome march to struggle for a phantom which they called liberty! The result of this infatuation was a tide of resistance, unquenchable as the life bounding in those young veins like the current of some inspiration, and a purpose that meant victory, success, but was only—death.

All through that long sunny summer we waited, for what?

We scarcely knew; listening to the rattle of musketry and the tramp of soldiers on drill. We often drove down to see the Crescent Guard, with their gay uniform, go through the manual of arms. There was such buoyancy in each young face, and jests passed carelessly from lip to lip. Ah! of that body of men how few have lived to tell the story of those days! Swiftly, to rise no more, they fell beneath the fire from battalions of the enemy; but they fought like men—brave men, who cared not for life when weighed against a purpose that was stronger.

I have since heard jeering lips scout the idea of Southern men, not inured to toil, being able to fight the long battle to its close. Horace Greeley, I remember, talked eloquently about "crushing the rebellion with a blow." But gradually that kind of thing has ceased to be, since we have learned the characters of the men with whom we war, and come to recognise in the Southern heart an attribute that fearlessly counts no cost, no sacrifice, unworthy the cause in which their energies were embarked—which meant resistance to the bitter end.

In late autumn came a letter from Clyde, the first syllable he had addressed to me since his departure. He stated briefly his views with regard to the war; expressed an opinion that the country would be invaded, and it would be better for us to go North to remain permanently until the thing was settled. This we decided to do, and had our arrangements completed when he came home.

We sat, Stanley and I, in the summer-house, talking of many things; of that past through which my bright river ran—of the solitary ship amid ocean tides—lastly, of our city circle, so changed and broken. There was a tempest in the social atmosphere, whose rain fell in blood-drops on the earth—whose fury was sweeping a generation of human

beings to their last account, when Clyde Ingram came and
stood silently before us.

I should have risen to give him my hand, as my heart
had risen to greet him, but there was neither trust nor hope
in the strange calmness of his manner—the look on his stern
face. The hard lines about his compressed lips softened
not for an instant, while Stanley plied many inquiries concerning where and how he had been, and why he had remained away without writing us one word.

"Oh! I thought you would not care to have letters from
me ; there was nothing to interest you in the details of my
life as passed in those forest wilds ; I considered the most
charitable thing would be to allow you a respite from my unwilling persecution. I should not now be home but for the
fact that my country needs me. On the first intimation of
her involved state, I left Australia with the intention of
offering my poor service in this hour of her peril. I felt I
had no right to withhold the little I could do."

My heart leaped into my throat ; the decision for my
future was *here and now*. I asked the question cautiously,
vainly endeavoring to still the throbbings of heart and brain
as I awaited his answer, which came slowly and solemnly.

"The die is cast, Aljean, without wish or will of mine ;
this armed resistance to the Government seems a rash pro-
ceeding ! but the present administration is at war with our
institutions. I am no man, no Southern man, if I give not
to the section in which my lot is cast, the work my hands
can do for the South. Had I been a member of Congress,
my sense of justice would have led me to occupy that place
until the trial season was over. Placing ourselves in a defiant attitude—assuming the offensive, was, I repeat, a rash
act, and furnished a pretext for many aggressions on the
part of the federal authorities since. God knows I love my

country, its starry flag and constitution, but I cannot turn traitor to the South—my section: see her bleeding at every pore of her haughty heart, yet raise no hand to help her. I cannot join with those who would desolate her; my all is here. I must preserve that—my property, if possible, from utter ruin."

Stanley spoke what she felt vehemently. "Oh, Clyde! for God's and country's sake, take no stand while patriotism and conscience are thus dissevered. Remember, if your property were gained, would it not be worthless if you sacrificed principle in the effort to retain it? Your *heart*, my brother, is not with those who have trampled under foot the Constitution and the old banner; then do not identify yourself with such! Come out from among them; take no part in the weary struggle! wait for the issue; God holds the balance; give not your life to assist in turning it one way or another."

"Stanley, my more than sister, you talk just like a woman! you do not seem to realize there can be no such position while we stand beside the seething caldron and see the fires are glowing. I must go in one direction or the other; after all, it makes little difference the position one occupies in this diabolical business. I hold that all war is wrong! God never intended that generations of human beings should murder one another, after the fashion of our doing. The glorious insignia of freedom and liberty are dimmed by the breath of ambition and party strife. We were growing too prosperous as a nation! this is our chastening! We had reached the climax of civilized arrogance; we are culminating towards barbarism."

Stanley again remarked—

" It occurs to me civilization is a mythical term of sectional strife and hatred in these days of miserable bickerings."

"True! it is a hateful age! As for myself I do not live in it. I have broken all bonds of companionship with those who do; have eschewed its petty commonplaces and requisitions; have learned to live above everything except its sufferings and desolateness."

I looked at him; the pallor on his face had given place to a glow of excitement which quickly paled and blanched, as do our blush roses in autumn. I saw burning in his eyes the great fires of genius, grand and immortal as his own soul. For this choice spirit was there only a lonely way, a constant reaching after companionship with a mind from which had been purged the drosses of every-day existence, one who could look upon its weird, distorted facts, carped and misshapen as they were, from the stand-point of a judgment coupled with foresight: a sense of justice that was far above all petty estimates and demands. He sat looking so grandly self-poised and self-centred, he did not need me; how could I approach him as he sat up among the stars—far, far above me, while he did the work of life in harness, struggling with the fetters he could not wear and could not break. My heart waited a long time in silence in the dust at his feet, then the words—Oh! Clyde, how we missed you—were forming on my lips when Milverton exclaimed at the entrance to our arbor:

"Upon my word, ladies, this is too much for even an amiable bachelor like myself to bear tamely! Just think of my having wandered about these grounds like a disembodied spirit, in search of these two young ladies since tea-time; now at last I find them holding a clandestine conference with you. By the way, notwithstanding an overwhelming sense of personal wrong in which you are involved with them to your discredit, I will say I am glad to see you! Welcome home, old fellow, I am glad to see you back; when did you arrive in the city, and how long do you purpose remaining?"

"I came two hours ago; I shall stay until I am ordered to depart with a regiment, the command of which has been tendered to me, now forming under the auspices of Lieutenant-Colonel Austin at Brightland. As regards the young ladies, having less claim upon their attention and courtesy than your more fortunate self, I will resign them to your charge until I have seen my mother." So saying, he arose to depart, but was prevented by Milverton.

"Oh! I beg your pardon, Ingram, I shall not be so ungenerous as to claim both; I will not play Shylock in return for your liberality. If Miss Stanley will favor me with her society, I will ask nothing more."

Clyde bowed and led me from the summer-house, into the night brightened by moon and stars, along the old familiar paths. I could feel his heart throb against my arm, though even in our home ways reigned the old silence which I could not break. Strange, I had resolved to say a thousand things to Clyde when he came home about the terrible mistake I had made. I meant to tell him, without his asking, that I did love him dearly and had loved him long; that my coldness and caprice were assumed to disguise the truth, because I thought he loved Stanley. I imagined it would be an easy matter to tell him these things, but it was not so. I waited silently until he spoke tremulously.

"Will you tell me of what you were thinking, Aljean?" I started, endeavoring so to do, but only succeeded in blushing quietly instead. Then his eyes wandered again to the starry avenues, as though my reply—even if I succeeded in making one—would affect him very little, and was something he had no right to expect. His aspect aroused my

pride, then enabled me to answer, though somewhat constrainedly and coldly :

"I was thinking of Brightland—quaint and old, hallowed by such thronging memories, yet desecrated by
the tread of unhallowed feet! of the tri-colored banner
floating there; coarse jests and oaths breaking the silence
of other days. I am glad we are going North. I could not
bear to remain here a witness to the enactment of such
scenes."

"Even if you stayed, you would not be pained by them
long," he said gently—very gently. I was ready to die of
shame at my petty outburst of an anger I did not really
feel. I hated myself for loving him, as he was so far above
me that even harsh words of mine had no power to touch
him. I wanted to retort, and should have done so but for
that calm, unapproachable look on his face, which said—If
kind words never come from you I can at least shut my
heart against those that are not so; they shall have no
power to sway me.

I went into the house to prepare Aunt Edith for this
surprise, leaving Clyde to follow. When I had informed
her of her son's arrival and calmed her agitation, I sent
Hawsey with a message to that effect; when he came in
I withdrew to the veranda, leaving them alone. I saw a
carriage coming up the lighted avenue, then heard gay
voices ask a servant if the ladies were at home. I arose,
went to my room to smoothe my hair. I paused a moment
at Aunt Edith's door as I was going to the parlor. The
scene in that apartment was too holy to be intruded upon.
A strong man kneeling reverently, his face full of tenderness, beside his mother, chafing her hands, telling her the
things long pent up in his heart. Miss Phœbe's needles
plied the task a little more reluctantly, for upon their bright-

ness was the mist of human tears, though no one saw them fall upon that night of our last reunion. Aunt Edith's voice was very sad and sorrow-burdened, though very gentle.

"Why have you left me so long, my darling boy?"

"I went because I could not stay. The why and wherefore of this fact is a secret which only God and my own heart know. I have never told it to mortal, because there was no one to hear it; therefore I went, that I might keep it to myself."

"And will you really go into the army, my son?"

"Yes, mother, I shall go; my regiment is being equipped and armed; and I must" —— he paused suddenly! a spasm of agony convulsed Aunt Edith's haggard face. I came forward here, sending Hawsey to find Stanley and inform her she was expected in the parlor, and took her place at Aunt Edith's side. Still I heard the gay voices below! how strange sounded the hum of their light talk while we listened, Clyde and I, to Aunt Edith's recital, which was very sad. I will only give the reader a portion of what she said that last night:

"My parents opposed bitterly my union with your father, Clyde, though I married him notwithstanding, because I wanted to come away from what had been to me the scene and season of a trying sorrow. They would never have consented either to my marriage with the only man I ever truly loved, because of some misconduct on the part of his sister. It was very hard for us both! He, too, suffered, if possible, more than I; though on account of the shame in which the affair involved him he was too proud to supplicate for my hand; neither would he tempt me to disobey them and marry against their will. Never, my children, hold any human being accountable for the sin or wrongdoing of another—even though that other be a near friend

or relative; it is cruel to make them responsible for what
they cannot help. Mr. Ingram came North with his little
son who was then but a few months old, in charge of Miss
Phœbe. I met him by accident; he courted me. I accepted him for the reason I have told you; though my
father entreated me earnestly not to do so.

" 'That little boy,' said he, 'will never requite your care of
him; one's own children rarely do that; he will do less.' It
so happened, providentially perhaps, we had no children
of our own. When your father died he gave you into my
charge. The man whom I had so loved, I heard was happily
married to a noble woman, and living in the region of my
old home. I did not wish to return there; neither did I
wish to assume the management of these estates during your
minority. Accordingly I appointed Mr. Kingswell guardian to you; for the sake of our past he accepted the charge,
and retained it even when I married Mr. Montana, to whom
I committed your property in trust. You owe much to the
kind guardianship of both these men; they are good and
true men.

" Do not misunderstand me, my son, I am not heartless;
though I did not love your father, I venerated him for his
integrity and high principle; we were mutually kind and
happy in our brief union. The father of my children I also
respect and esteem; but all the love of my heart was given
away before the duties of wife and mother came to me.
Somehow, all the pent up current of tenderness flowed out to
you; I would have given you since the most precious boon
in my keeping, my child, my Stanley; but you could not
love each other, it seemed, and I guess it was not to be. This
disappointment I bore silently, though my heart was set
on having you my own as long as I lived. But I cannot
bear tamely that your hand should be raised against my

son. Mr. Montana always loved best his own land. Raymond has inherited his father's preference. I think he will be with the government, right or wrong; as it is just that he should be.

"Claremont is yours! We remain here only at your option; once you take the position you have accepted in earnest, it becomes imperative that you should send us away beyond the lines. Now, my son, does it seem to you right that I, a broken-hearted woman, should suffer thus by the voluntary act of a child whom I have most loved and cherished? And that he in the days of her infirmity should place himself in an attitude where it will be impossible to afford her home and shelter? As for myself, I shall not need it long; but for Stanley and Jennie, my daughters, have I asked even this vainly of you, Clyde, who was ever before so kind to us all?"

"Mother, you really tax and try me very much indeed. I owe everything I possess, and more, to yourself and Mr. Kingswell; besides honor, respect, and love, which I feel I have given to the uttermost. As regards my real estate, including Claremont and Brightland, it is yours; it is to defend these for the sake of yourself and your children, against those who would desolate them, I stand where I do—an enemy to country and government!

"I am not responsible for Raymond's position any more than for my own. As regards your remaining here, mother, I am anxious to have you do so; though with your present proclivities that would soon become impossible; besides, it would not be pleasant in the event of an invasion, which we have reason to fear and to anticipate. I shall not meet Raymond in the field; we neither of us know, certainly, that he will go into the army; though even with the certainty that I should meet him face to face, yet would I not

10

fail in doing what I feel to be my duty in the matter." He bowed his head upon his hands, and wept! In all our lives together, I had never seen him thus moved. He was a child still in his feeling for her who had been a mother to us two, who were orphans. Clyde Ingram stood not now among the stars above me! By nature, he was not cold, but tender and gentle as a woman.

"Oh! my children, I have lived too long! How can I bear this last great agony!" It was, indeed, very hard to bear, though many women have borne this and more— their hearts lying in the dust beneath the grinding wheel of Revolution; awaiting the Almighty hand which alone can raise them up!

Miss Phœbe motioned us to leave the room; Clyde stepped into the veranda. I followed him tremblingly, for I had begun to realize there could be no wavering in his course now; upon the only ground which appeared tenable, I resolved to stand by him even to the last issue. He seemed to possess an innate recognition of my determination, for he took both my hands in his, saying very tenderly:

"Did you come to comfort me, Jennie? I have far more need of it than ever before; I am so weary! Oh! if you could only have found for me a resting-place in that great heart of yours, I should not feel so utterly alone and desolate in my sorrow now. Why could you not love me, Jennie, when I have loved you always so dearly, even though you would never let me tell you so."

Gracious heavens! the sky had unfurled banners of broad bright blue! The night was ended, perfect day had burst upon us. There was no lonely sea with the solitary ship ploughing through its watery heart; only the music of my bright river as it bore down from the first days of this hope! I saw no crimson tides staining its current in the morning of the new existence into which I had suddenly been launched. This sensation, however, was only momentary; when I raised my eyes to heaven, I saw the stars burning dimly, and the moonbeams fell with a cold flicker that was strangely unreal, though I scarce noticed these in my eagerness to tell him all; nothing should keep the knowledge from him now! I commenced, excitedly:

"Clyde, for long years I have,"——I heard some one speak my name! I turned as Retta Austin came upon the veranda in search of me. She bore a summons for us to the parlor. We could make no reasonable excuse for failing to comply, so she remained with us until we joined our friends below. Neither upon this occasion were spoken words of explanation that might have made us happy! or at least have saved us from days and nights of pain that followed.

————o————

CHAPTER XV.

"Easier were it to force the rooted mountain from its base,
Than force the yoke of slavery on men determined to be free!"
SOUTHEY.

THERE was a gay company assembled in the drawing-room; how handsome Clyde was! How princely he appeared beside the flippant young men whose thoughts ranged no higher than the badges worn to designate their respective ranks. There was Ella Soulé, Lane, and Gerald Austin, with their sister Miss Retta; who, as usual, commenced her garrulous tirade the moment we entered the room.

"We have not seen you for an age; Colonel Ingram—

how kind of you to refresh us with one first, last sight of your handsome face before going into the field. The first glimpse, as I said before, for an age! The last, perhaps for ever! Jennie, you are **not too** much of a Yankee, I trust, to admit that he is looking magnificently in his uniform— grey with scarlet trimmings," she added, turning to me.

"My opinion would affect him **very** little; **he is not the least vain** of his rank, **and would prefer** waiting until he has earned "——

——" Hanging at the hands of the Federal authorities," suggested Milverton mischievously, concluding my sentence in a manner entirely foreign to the original design. "**Your** pardon, Miss Jennie; be kind enough **to conclude your** speech, for the benefit of all. 'Until he has earned'"——

"The appellation of Colonel. When I lived North, it was not our fashion to deny to any individual a distinction to which his **conduct** entitles him, even if that be the one which **Mr. Milverton supplied**; though I sincerely hope the last named dignity may be conferred upon those better fitted to sustain and enjoy it. I should really feel sorry were I expected to designate all my old friends by some military title; though this war now pending is a fortunate circumstance for men who before in the social status were decidedly below par!"

"**For** examples, Lane **and Gerald**," suggested Retta maliciously. "Ella and I drove out to Brightland one afternoon to see the regiment drill; it did splendidly; though if our embryo **heroes** would **only forget their** dignity when **off duty!** Our young men have **inaugurated a** system of drilling and attitudinizing before **the parlor** mirrors. You should see them, Jennie; it would amuse you infinitely."

"Ah, poor fellows!" Milverton said, with patronizing pity in his tones. "**Once** in the field there will be little leisure for that sort of amusement. Perhaps the Yankees will cure them of vanity, by depriving them of these little luxuries. One or two hard rubs will take the polish from their idea of the service; the time they were wont to bestow upon their mustachios they will learn to devote to their fire-arms. Life at a post, in quarters, is delightful pastime; more charming than lying down to sleep, after a supper on hard-tack and bacon, with the enemy's shells bursting in your camp, setting fire to your commissary stores, and pirouetting gracefully about your ears. The Yankees are reserving for you petted sons of wealth many of these delightful entertainments."

"I am sure they are welcome, and will get value received for all the favors they choose to confer," Gerald answered pettishly, his black eyes flashing defiant fire. "I am longing to show them of what material our Southern army is composed; and to teach those who talk enthusiastically about crushing the rebellion, as though it were the easiest thing in the world accomplished, that there are human hearts piled up; these are its bulwarks of strength; let them try, they will feel constrained to charge their abolition President a pretty extravagant price for the task before it is complete. We will see that he pays it. You may expect to hear glorious accounts of us soon; true, as they plead, we are unaccustomed to hardships; our men were not raised to the profession of arms; but we can fight if necessary. We are ready and willing to do what we can; our allegiance and service are free as air; we can set no price on these, for our hearts are in the work. For a cause so glorious we are ready to sacrifice any and everything!"

It was on my lips to ask "*what cause?*" but a glance at Clyde's calm white face prevented me. Retta spoke instead:

"Were I Lane and yourself I should reserve my boasting

until the close of the war; it is much easier to anticipate
results than to face *causes* and work them out!"

"More especially such *piercing* causes as the enemy's
bullets may chance to prove," suggested Clyde. "I agree
with Miss Retta and the great poet, who bids us—

'"Learn to labor and to wait."

Wait! for how long? Until the war is over; until the
seceded States are subjugated; until that high wall of living,
throbbing human hearts is battered down? Ah, what then
would they do with an unloving people! Unloving they
were in all that Southern land; for long months I had heard
no voice upraised for our country's constitution and her
flag; the blood-bought banner that had sheltered and pro-
tected them by land and sea for prosperous years. And
those too were silent whose fathers had fought for it once.
I could look out from the parlor window and behold the
site of a battle-ground where it was planted January 8th,
1812. But they had torn it down, and trampled upon its
constellations; had come out from its shining folds; and
now talked of stabbing the Government, as though they
were really doing the age and the country a service. Even
the voice of my love was stilled in the sense of double,
treble crime, the expressions of which I heard almost constantly. I could only await the momentous crisis.

I said there was no voice upraised for the old flag. Ah,
there was one; over weary miles it came; like the chime of
silver bells the tones rang out upon this night of treason.
Lane Austin said:

"Well, Colonel, at your solicitation I wrote to my friend
Raymond, offering him the opportunity of filling an impor-
tant vacancy in our regiment. You shall have the decision

in his own words. I will read an extract from his letter of recent date which came to-day:

" 'Say to my brother Clyde, it is kind of him to consider me; even though I cannot for an instant think of accepting it. God knows how deep is my grief that he has done this thing. Between us it will be the subject of recurrence frequent of pain and bitterness, the existence of which was hitherto unknown; it will build a barrier that may be eternal, for, living or dying, I shall never falter in the course which I hold to be right, and I hope that my strong right arm may become palsied the instant I dare to lift it against the old flag. Should I ever fight, so help me Heaven, in accordance with every vaster consideration, I will leave all, to strike for God and for country *under its stars.*' "

For an instant, still as the grave was the night of treason and fierce rebellion that had closed about me! Then I beheld something, floating, flaming in the higher air: Ah! it was our banner, set clear in the unclouded heaven, held by a higher hand than man's! and its glorious stars were shining, no blight upon their lustre, no dimness in the folds that held them, no blood or blight upon the strong standard: but a white wreath of victory woven from the crushed flowers of dead brave hearts, who nurtured liberty with their last drop of life beneath those constellations of our country, who had stood and fallen, died under those stars of God's and the nation's. Was our boy, whose words came to us from afar, whose radiance beamed around us everywhere, of all their glorious brightness the one solitary *Ray?* Ah! in the light of morning, in the clear moon-times, in the darkness of succeeding doubts, that flag was still there, flaming high in the sky of my heart! try as I would I could not shut my eyes against it, even though love, stern dictator, made me try. Those stars upon our banner, like those I had counted in the heavens that bent above my youth, seemed constantly peering into my soul to see if the old feeling for them was there. Slowly from day to day into that self-same heart grew the conviction that fate and country had set their final seal upon the vast, immutable silences that were in it. Perhaps for Clyde or for me death with his icy fingers might unclasp them, but now—wider and wider grew the space between us; further and further apart our lives were drifting. Ah! should we two, when the battle was ended, pass over the silent way, and at the portals of God's peace stand firm together to part no more?

It was a relief when they took their leave. Clyde Ingram should carry with him into the broad field no knowledge of my love. In that moment of bitterness I could have renounced him for ever; him who for years had claimed me silently, and I had loved him with a love that left me no words to tell it. Words were not required to dissever an unspoken bond. Thus let it be, was the fiat of my heart; though next instant, crushed by the weight of its own resolve, it was powerless to act as a bird within bars.

I stood upon the veranda long after the carriage had passed out of sight, these maddening thoughts filling heart and brain. The cold night breeze came up pityingly from the distant sea, far lying bathed in shining mist beneath moon and stars. It was the same picture I had looked on in childhood when Clyde was by my side; now he was far away from me and from that old time. I heard his impatient cough on the veranda above, and knew that he too was keeping heart-vigil over a dead past. Oh! why had these legions come between us now that our love was no longer intangible and undefined? I went to my chamber, but not to sleep. I heard Clyde pacing his. How long I lay there I know not, I was only conscious that something great and momentous was happening. I heard suppressed voices speaking quickly; then a light footstep crossed the room, and Stanley stood beside me at the open window; there was a cold dew upon my face, and mist was dripping from my hair.

"Oh! Jennie," she exclaimed, "do you not know mother is dying? come to her quickly." I flew with Stanley excitedly to Aunt Edith's room. Clyde was there before me, kneeling just as he had done early in the evening. There were bright crimson stains upon the snowy counterpane, and Miss Phœbe wiped the blood drops from her pale, still lips. It was thus we passed the night; physician and watchers spoke no word until we saw that she slept from utter exhaustion; then we saw a look of peace come over her features! there was a rustle as of angels' wings in the air about us! Aunt Edith's soul had crossed the blood-stained river to the other shore.

It was a quiet, beautiful death! I thought of another death afar back in the years, and how I, a child, had looked out upon the stars and tried to count them, though countless they were as sands upon the sea. Oh! stars of evening in that youth-time, bright and glowing, oh! blighted stars upon our flag, and thou eternal sea! with thoughts of this pure beautiful death coexisted thoughts of thee. *Death!* was this death? ah! yes, it came to us with our first garments, and shall continue unchanged until the heavens shall be rolled together as a scroll! Thank God for death, since through death comes immortality. Those remembered words came to me with a pulse of promise for her who had crossed the crimson current that was coursing through our land. I thought of what one of the characters in Titan had said to the old man who was praying under a gathering tempest, though he knew it not.

"Pray on, thou man of God, to the all-gracious! and *go to sleep before the storm comes on.*" Thank "the all-gracious," she was spared the pain of seeing her home with its flowers laid waste in the battle-storm which shook all homes and hearts to their centre. Had the power been mine to charm that mother back whose life-task in this world was ended, I should have **said let her** rest in peace, which is denied to us as a nation and as individuals. What a change in our household since the previous evening! Clyde had come back, the mother was gone! **a few** fluttering breaths **had** passed, a heart had ceased to beat! in that little space **half** the world seemed to have changed to us. Ah, Death! hadst thou not enough to slake thy unrelenting thirst upon **the** gory fields outstretched in the land?

But this was no stern-faced death; it was a calm visage, garnished with fair **sweet flowers.** Many who loved her **came with** soft tread and lingered by the sleeper, until one sorrowful morning she was taken away **from us, and** then a long dark file wound over the road **to the** cemetery. **From** her magnificent home Aunt Edith had gone to bide in a narrow house, such as the wife of Captain Bob Eldridge, my father and mother, had occupied for many silent years. Aunt Dinah came up to arrange and close up the vacant room. She held in her hand a large bunch of keys.

"I wonder **who will take care** of these now," she said, piteously, between broken sobs; "old miss will never want em enny more—never, enny more."

"**No, no,**" I answered **consolingly**; "there are no locked doors in heaven, Aunt Dinah."

"Miss Jennie, do you blieve **dare is enny** *slaves in dat heaven where missus is?*"

"*Not as slaves!* We **are** told that in God's kingdom there is neither 'Jew nor Gentile—bond or free.'"

Next morning it was arranged that the family, including Milverton and Miss Phœbe, should go, within a fortnight, to Raymond's. We were to leave Uncle Montana, with the servants, at Claremont. For days we pleaded to be permitted to stay in the house, even with the vacant place there— by the new-made grave, but uncle and Clyde were deaf to our petitions. Our preparations were made with a view to procuring passes to go North, which we succeeded in obtaining with much difficulty. Little did we think, on taking leave, how many weary months would elapse before we saw our home again. We had bid adieu to every shrub and tree; to flowers, fountains, and the outstretched sea; we had taken our places in the car as on the morning of our first northward journey! Now there was no mother face to look a last, fond farewell through the gathering space! she was sleeping as the storm came on. When we passed Brightland, for the bitterness and sorrow in my heart I could not lift my eyes to see the Southern banner floating there. Apart and gloomy I saw a solitary figure stand! a white kerchief fluttered for an instant in the morning air: then the distance swiftly widened, and I began keenly to realize all that I was doing. Henceforth Clyde Ingram was my country's enemy. We should never, never meet again until, perchance, we should stand at the one little gate when all was over; and from ways that were many and wide, though their dust was stained with gore, we should come to bathe our souls in the fountain of love eternal.

In charge of Mr. Milverton we got on well. At the expiration of the fifth day three black-robed figures took silently their places at Raymond's board. His fair wife did the honors through her tears, when Ala Ray came to her, and in her little, clear tones inquired why "dandma" had not come with us! Then we all broke down and wept—

not more for the dead than to miss Raymond from the head of his usual cheerful table. But the battles of our country must be fought, and we will lay no cowardly, poltroon hearts upon her shrine in this her hour of struggle. I recalled Moore's glorious lines—

> "Oh, if there be on this earthly sphere—
> A boon, an offering heaven holds dear,
> 'Tis the last libation liberty draws,
> From a heart that bleeds and breaks in her cause."

In a few days we went to Ridgely. Like rain-drops on thirsty sands, upon our bleeding hearts fell Mr. Kingswell's words of peace and promise. Gradually we came to give Aunt Edith up, and learned to think of other things that were needful to be done in the world's work before us. Ala Ray was to us a perpetual sunbeam of comfort. Day by day she was growing in beauty and sweetness! her angel nature expanding like a rose beneath dew-kisses of an earthly morning. Never rested the little feet, nor seemed the little tongue to grow weary questioning of the strange things in the world about her. Oh! how we loved our little darling! In our idolatry we forgot how Aunt Edith had said. "the golden gates were not closed against Ala Ray."

In Milverton's first letter after his return to New York, he spoke of the Haynes—of having been entertained at their house. The wife, after her blonde fashion, was inspiring her usual sensation in their social circle. "Hayne," he remarked, "is magnificently stately, as it appears to him pleasurable at all times to be." I did not show the letter to Stanley; I inwardly prayed that she might not meet Warren: just now her cross was heavy enough. This was scarcely probable! his father had leased his summer residence in Wayburn : there was no reason why Warren should come down there, and Stanley would probably not see him, even in the event of her going to New York. Her bloom and light airy step were coming back. Youth is exuberant, and cannot be wholly extinguished : we gradually rise out of ourselves ! The self that mourned for the lost, the better portion of us, may dwell regretfully with the memory, but there is hard work in life for us all! and necessity compels us to come out from the shadow-land of grief into God's day. Nothing will so speedily dispel the cold damps of sorrow from our lot as patient duty-doing.

I was attacked with a malignant fever during the autumn. It was long ere the crisis came. Then, through days of convalescence, I lay in my bed at Ridgely, listening in fancy to the bugle-blast of victory; but the thought brought no exultation, for I knew how many hearts were bleeding—how many faces growing white and still beneath the blow of death on distant battle-fields. The work of the revolution had begun in earnest. Letters came frequently from Raymond, always cheerful, hopeful for the final issue. But no word from that other hero, nursed near to the same mother-heart, who, beneath scorching suns, toiled on—to what end? Let the future answer.

The winter came and passed—a long, cold, northern winter. We thought the spring would never come; but it did, at length, dotting meadows with cowslips and daisies; and the suns of April broke gloriously into prisms of brightness over the far New Hampshire hill-tops we loved so well. We had begun to grow accustomed to the old void in home and heart, though Stanley grew restive as the summer days lengthened, with nothing special to occupy her time. She formed a plan for taking a small school in the suburbs of Wayburn. Uncle Kingswell approved her project, suggesting that it should be an independent school, in which were taught only the higher branches. He thought it would prove an advantage as well as a diversion. I was not yet sufficiently recovered to assist Stanley, even had Raymond sustained her in her undertaking. When consulted by letter, he indignantly refused to allow his sister to do anything of the kind, and was actually wounded that she did not esteem herself as he considered her—entirely removed from the necessity of exertion for her support. What cared he if remittances from New Orleans had ceased to come? We could remain at Wayburn without them, until communication between the sections was reëstablished. Stanley appealed to her brother a second time. Her letter ran thus:—

"My Dear Ray : It is not that I feel myself an incumbrance to you; it is because Miss Phœbe and myself—since we must remain here—want a little home of our own. Jennie will remain with Mary. Mr. and Mrs. Kingswell approve my plan, and will help me to execute it. Now, give me your sanction, and I will be far happier than I have been since our dear mother died."

Ray could not resist her pleadings; and so the month of the roses found Stanley at work with her school. She and Miss Phœbe had gone to live at the cottage in which my parents died. Mr. Kingswell himself had purchased the property when the formal sale came off, whose management was wholly intrusted to him.

With a heart of poetry within, into what softened curves of grace and beauty grew the rough angles of that cottage home! Everywhere was visible the magic effect of Miss Phœbe's cleanliness, Stanley's flowers and perfume. We had some delightful reunions within those walls, when Raymond came home on his first leave, looking so handsome in his uniform of regal blue.

About this time, I received a letter from Ella Soulé, which filled me with secret anxiety. She had sent the letter through by hand; one paragraph contained a sneering taunt that was entirely unnecessary:—

" How should you like to see Claremont, Aljean, since it has been transformed into barracks for Yankee soldiers? I have grown to hate the very sight of a blue-coat recently."

She went on to tell me many sad things of the sufferings of friends, but nothing troubled me like this. To think of strange feet trampling down the flowers in our home, where a sainted mother's footfalls yet lingered; its groves despoiled by the profaning touch of a lawless soldiery; the trail of their devastation within those sacred precincts! I think if any one could bear patiently a reflection of this nature, he is possessed of more patriotism than I can boast of. Stanley was wise in acting for herself; we were worse than penniless. She toiled on, however, knowing nothing of this, nor we of Clyde. Oh, what would I not have given for one little word! But time passed on, and that word came not.

Still the tempest thickened, falling in blood-drops on the withered earth! Still the red tides ran swiftly to the crimson sea, through homes of the North and flowers of the South. The great heart of our nation grew sick and faint with constant gory depletion. Authorities at Washington had ceased to talk so grandly about crushing the rebellion. The plea was often one of resistance against the legions that bore down upon our shores, leaving their dead, grim and ghastly, side by side with our own. The record swelled, and the sacrificial list grew longer day by day. The great heart throbbed faster in its agony.

I sat thinking, darkly, vaguely, of these things one evening, as I rocked Ala Ray in my arms. The little thing talked dreamily of her dear papa, and how at night he lay down to sleep *under the stars*, adding earnestly: "Some of these times I, too, shall go out to sleep *under the stars*."

"My darling Ala, what makes you think and talk thus of such things?"

"Only because grandma did, you know; and my papa does so, too."

I pressed her closely to my heart, and told her how, some day, she would sleep on the breast of her good, kind father. For I felt she was drawing us with her to the little gate where she would take her leave of us.

Oh, little heart! that loved and twined your blossoms round, and little hands that wove into our coarse and tangled web of daily life the golden threads that bound its meshes to God's throne! Oh, dewdrop of celestial brightness, freshening the blossoms in our earth-worn souls, until they held something of ethereal beauty in their mystic depths! Oh, little feet, that came from their wanderings amid the heavenly ways, and left your impress upon our wilderness! Oh, sweet Ala Ray! What do we not owe to thee, during that dark season, of pure gushing joy here in our world! We listened to the music of thy little feet along their journey to its close, and then our hearts went with thee, darling, over the starry way, into the unknown land, while the birds sang, and bright waters ran. Then we lived—our body here, soul yonder—during the long night of grief which came after we had laid thee in thy little grave—to sleep under the stars of heaven.

When I laid her in her little bed that night, which gathered full of starry shadows, as I had seen many a night in our Southern land; below in the bosom of the valley lay the town, and the swift river running at the foot of towering hills, whose summits seemed to creep close to the Eternal Throne. With a sure tread of days whose memory would never die, I thought how Clyde and I had once stood together in the light of a bygone morning, with nothing between us save two children's vague hopes and dreams. Ah! the sorrow and changes since! The battle-cry, On to Richmond, struck on my heart like a funeral bell; crimson tides ran where the golden river flowed; and the feet that lingered once upon its margin had wandered through a rough wide world since then. The youth in my memory gave gradual place to a man chivalrous and brave, whose breast was bared to the shaft of every friend I had in the Federal army.

CHAPTER XVI.

"Farewell! a word that hath been, and must be;
A sound that makes us linger—yet farewell."
SHAKESPEARE.

STANLEY was succeeding well with her school; God had been pleased to turn the hearts of her pupils in love towards their teacher; she was very happy in her own home. "Oh!" she said to me once, "the rare luxury of being alone; of going down into the hidden places of one's own heart and learning the needs of our higher natures, fathoming our capacity for enduring all that life offers, be it joy or sorrow. I would not exchange this little domicile, with Miss

Phœbe to pamper and care for me,.for the elegant ease of
Ridgely or Raymond's more costly surroundings. I love
to be near you all; I should be wretched if I could not see
you daily; but there are times when I like best to be all
alone; I rely more upon myself, and feel my dependence on
God more."

"I think we all come to do that when we grow acquainted
with the world as it is. After successive disappointments
and humiliations we come to seek in our own thought all
that lay so vast and far away. I would by no means
depreciate the high and holy privilege of holding intercourse
with **our** fellow-beings; but, as men and women, we are
never quite happy unless we can come out from the social
world and find within ourselves the truest resources of
happiness. Though there was a time when my little Stanley
was not the philosopher she is now."

She started, **fixing her** eyes keenly upon my face; the words
struck her; she **had not forgotten** how Warren Hayne once
called her thus. She smiled a smile, bitter, yet serene, half
of memory, half of hope; a hope that had its origin in
higher things than the fleeting promises of youth, which
after time rarely fulfils; then answered me in the words of
an unknown poet:

"I have grown wise; the disciplines and trials
 Through which I have passed, with bitter groans and tears,
 Were but the shadows on God's golden dials,
 Pointing me onward to serener years."

She had gained them, but would this calmness stand the
trial test? I question:

"Darling, you are so young to give up **the** world thus.
Does it hold nothing for you? how do you appropriate the
long hours apart from your routine of duty spent in solitude
and loneliness?"

"I ask you, Aljean, what life would be expected to retain for me more than duty, when its crown of hope lay in the dust until the spirit-hand of a higher hope and life re-adjusted it upon a brow where the thorn-wreath sat; true, I spend long hours in solitude, but not in loneliness; I will show you how I fill them up."

She took from her desk a manuscript copy of poems, blushing timidly as I caught them from her reluctant hand. On and on I read; the beautiful thoughts, so elegantly chaste, were couched in language purely her own. Exquisite fancies trooped about me as I read my sister's heart there in those mirrors of the mind, in which I saw her glorious soul reflected, all radiant and glowing with the impress of Deity. I knew her then; I clasped her to my heart; the electric chain of eternal sisterhood was vibrating between us, as it would never cease to do henceforth; oh, how I loved her! In my enthusiasm I exclaimed:

"I would give worlds, Stanley, to be able to write like this!"

"There is this difference; you *live* your poetry—I *write* mine."

A few tender words at parting; I walked thoughtfully down the grassy home-road in the glistening sunshine, leaving her to herself; there was no society that could afford her such joy as these quiet communings with her own sublime and glorious soul. This was the woman whose love Warren Hayne had trifled away with capricious pride, had bartered for the gold of her rival. Ah, well! he had taken much less from her than she claimed from him; she could look down upon him from heights which he could never attain; for he wandered not from the shorn avenues of society. I was thinking of my cousin Warren, little dreaming how soon we should meet again.

On the afternoon succeeding I sought Stanley, to have her accompany me to my old haunt on the hillside. Miss Phœbe informed me that she was already there, and Mr. Hayne having called in her absence, she had sent him to seek for her in that locality.

"Cousin Warren!" I exclaimed with astonishment; "he here,—how long since he arrived?"

"He returned from Paris the first of the month, though he only arrived in Wayburn an hour ago."

Very moody and reflective, I took my way to the landing, untied the little painted skiff, and crossed the river to the opposite shore; then climbed the narrow pathway along the steep hillside until I came to a level space several hundred feet above the stream. I sat me down beside a cool spring beneath the shadow of a grand old tree—the same tree under which Clyde and I rested on the occasion of our first pilgrimage to this spot. I was thinking of it when a voice—sweet, plaintive—familiar to that old time, broke on the stillness and found its echo in my heart. It was Stanley singing. I wondered if Clyde, amid the din of distant battles, ever thought of her or of me now? I should have gone to her had I not beheld Cousin Warren ascending the steep, with a gloomy eagerness in his manner that I never observed before, even in the days of keenest suffering. I knew there was something on his mind, in his thought, which he felt it needful to speak! that he sought Stanley here for the purpose of seeing her alone. Though the undergrowth was profuse, I could not change positions without discovering to them my locality, thus preventing the interview: so I sat quite still, because I wanted that she and Cousin Warren should at last come to understand each other. I knew that he would be happier if such were the case; and it was only just to each that it should be so. I knew that Stanley Montana could never come down from her proud heights of principle to wrong his wife, even if the one's place had been given to the other. What had that civil contract, called marriage, that was loveless, to do with soul-bonds that were for time and eternity? Warren realized this when he spoke.

"I learned from Milverton all I know concerning you; he told me of the confiscation of your property, which was a cruel wrong. When I learned that you were teaching for a livelihood, knowing that your brother and Ingram were in the separate armies, I could not rest until I came to you: the reflection cut me to the soul. You, Stanley—young and beautiful—working at such toilsome business! I cannot tell why your friends allow it."

"My friends here do not regard this futile effort on my part to sustain myself, as a degradation in any sense whatever. It was my own plan; many of them approved it; my brother did not, though he never thwarted me in his life. My course was sanctioned by conscience, and that is the highest authority to which an orphan girl can appeal. The age is so full of work now,—sorrowing work for unwilling hands, and burdens for hearts that are bleeding! I should esteem myself miserably selfish if I bore no portion. Like the Prisoner of Chillon, I have learned to love my toils—'my chains and I are friends.' I appreciate all your delicate considerateness, Mr. Hayne, but there is nothing except kindness I can receive at your hands. Do not tempt me to change my decision; I am certain your respect for me will impel you to hold sacred the refusal of an offer made through sincere disinterestedness. I will do you the justice to believe naught else could have induced it."

He answered her in a grieved tone; I could hear his voice tremble as he said:

"Thank you! respect is a very cold word: but if it is the term you prefer, I will adopt it. But just now—holding you more sacredly, reverently, than ever before—I feel the time to be at hand when I must and will speak. When you were encircled by the peerless arms of society, I could look upon you unmoved, though I saw you day by day, young, beautiful, beloved by all. I will not say how one whose love you scorned, whose praise you set at naught, worshipped you more than any. Ah! you refuse to hear the story? well, it would not interest you; the time is long past; you have eschewed alike the passion and the memory of it. It is of other things I will speak now! other considerations are involved; commonplace ones of comfort have arisen, instead of the many things that have flown from you since then; there is little left! I wish to replace a small portion of what others have taken away. You must and shall hear me through."

She put back the words with an impatient gesture; half the ardor of her Southern nature flashed in the answer she gave.

"And I say that I *will not* hear you! Were I starving, Warren Hayne, I should accept no aid from you. Our conversation should end just here; in truth it never should have begun."

How that girl could speak thus to him, while her proud soul, thus racked and tortured, lay underneath his feet, is more than I can tell. Oh, world! for thee what will not mortals dare and do! Warren answered impatiently:

"Stanley, you will drive me mad! That you have not done so long ere this, was not owing to any omission in your effort. God knows how you have taxed and tried me; but let it pass; if the love on which I staked my life could awaken no answering throb, it were vain to expect that you would sympathize with the sorrow grown out of that early season of grief."

He bowed down his head, his form shaking with suppressed feeling, as she spoke again:

"Were it not for the ban upon your lips and life, which I would have you respect more than aught else, I should ask you to explain the meaning of your strange words of accusation? But now, there are griefs of my own which I would implore you to consider if you know how much I have suffered. For the sake of all that is past, which I have not forgotten, I ask you to leave me! What would the world say? Would it not cavil that you have offered me, an unfortunate woman, the means of support?"

"For God's sake desist! Is the world capable of sitting in judgment respecting my emotions and feelings, which it cannot know? Then, for the sake of one who loved and suffered before me, parade not the edict of that faithless thing. I hate it. I have as little respect for myself as for other votaries who have worn its livery and become its minions."

"And yet," added Stanley, "we hold society to be infallible! It is the world's voice, and we dare not disobey. Who has sufficient courage to brave the displeasure of that kingly autocrat, lynx-eyed, serpent-tongued?"

"*I have!* Society is not the world at large! It is the league of a fortunate few whom birth and position have placed beyond the range of circumstances; who look upon life from a stand-point far removed from its casualties, who presume to make laws for a portion of humanity whose toils and struggles they have never felt."

"God's law is the groundwork of society," humbly suggested Stanley.

"So it is, or was originally. However, there have been

wide deviations from the original standard and structure; religion deteriorated! Did the great Father intend that institutions of church, designed to perpetuate his love for humanity, should become as walls of granite to keep the poor and suffering out? When on earth, did He fill his temples with high-priests and judges, and empower them to make laws for the transgressor? What but those institutions have peopled insane asylums, and shut an iron gate against the wayward and the erring? Does not this same system set a cold hard heel upon every generous impulse, and ascribe self-interest to every pure motive? The world does this—the social world—the religious world! Not the lower million of humanity, but the world, with whose opinions and mandate you taunt me."

She answered slowly yet firmly:

"You are severe, Mr. Hayne; religion is not confined to the observance of any formula, or embodied by an institution! It is simply an intuitive recognition of God in the **heart.** Society has doubtless deteriorated, grown austere **and exclusive!** Yet in many instances within and without the church we find those who estimate life the weighty thing it is; who generously commend every struggle tending towards the consummation of its purposes; who look charitably on those wandering from the right—the feeling world, I meant. But it is not the world that **stands between** us to-day, at whose mandate we parted, a parting that came like winter to my southern home. I am glad you have learned its faithlessness since then! though all the while you conned this lesson, the tides, mighty and vast, were coming in between our lives, and the space growing wider there! Your friendly feet, even, may not cross it now; my heart is yet sick and sore; the smiter's hand was very careless, you know."

"Stanley, will you speak plainly? Your words are more cutting, from the fact that they are mystical. I, who have so much cause for complaint, could never be brought to speak thus to you. It is enough that you reject so bitterly my proposition of aid! Yet I will bear this patiently as I have borne other things before; only take that barrier from your thought, say that it is gone; this life is only a little day, and the evening shades are gathering fast; then there is the great to-morrow of eternity. Say not this great suffering must endure for ever; consent that we shall be friends—true to ourselves and to each other, steadfast evermore."

"The decision was your own, Warren; you must abide it. I repeat, *all the great world stands between us;* its tides have ebbed and flowed ever since my orange wreath was left to wither by the southern fountain. I have lingered on and on, have breasted tempests that were not so hard to endure as the hopeless calms. One by one the strong cords were rent asunder and the lights went out. Very sick of heart, I sought to prove myself, to try my own resources; I am stronger and happier in the effort. Delights of the mind are the only pleasures that do not leave us, when most we value them. When you grow discontented with your world, Warren, *your world*—you loved it once; open the windows of your own mind and soul! God's light will come pouring in, revealing many treasures within yourself, of which you were unaware. Now, go back to the life you have left; think not of me, except as one who tries to be brave, bearing her cross hopefully, patiently. Yes, you may think of me occasionally as sitting in the sunshine of a far-off time when there was between us two no mist and space; no faded wreath or broken trust."

"For God's sake, Stanley, let us not part thus, without

11

one word to sweep away this horrid phantom of formless change which has pursued me since we parted."

"Warren, I perceive there has been misunderstanding and misconstruction, which no words of ours can alter now; it is due to your lawful wife that neither should speak them—hence my silence. Now, farewell; nothing remains—that word is spoken."

There was a rustling in the sunshine of snowy drapery and falling curls, then she was gone. The brightness went with her. When he ceased to hear the music of her tones —so long silent—he unconsciously stretched forth his hands, as he sat there, powerless to move or to think. All his loving, pain, and struggle bore down upon him in that bitter moment, when Stanley left him thus. I rose to meet her as she came up the steep; she fell into my arms, uttering a sharp wail of anguish. The time was come to tell her all I knew. I spoke swiftly, certain of my ground.

"Stanley, my darling, do not take the responsibility upon yourself of so burdening a human heart. Warren Hayne loves you—has loved you all the time; some one intercepted your correspondence. Your letters and his were purloined by traitor hands; others substituted in their places. I have known this for a long time; that is why I wanted you to wear his pearls—the bridal gift, purchased in good faith *for you;* he would not allow another to wear them, because, he said, they were yours, though he believed you untrue. He has generously forgiven what he deemed perfidy in yourself. He has waived every consideration involving untruth on your part, suffering on his. He has offered you his friendship; accept it. Make peace with him; take the thorn out of his heart, darling. Come with me; speak words of comfort to Warren."

There was a strange brilliancy, as of delight, in her beau-

tiful eyes. After believing our idols fallen, it is so sweet
to find them occupying an exalted niche in the great temple of human destiny, even though they be high above us,
where love can never reach them. We came down the
hillside path to where Warren sat wrapped in gloomy
reflection. I laid my hand upon his shoulder, speaking
very gently :

"Do not think harshly of her ; she has good reason to
be severe. All along she has believed you false. She
received no written word from you, until the intelligence, couched in one brief, cold letter, informing her of
your intended marriage. We thought you had deserted
Stanley on learning she was not the heiress you believed
her. I have proved my trust in your further generosity by
telling you these things. I do not believe you will ever
betray her, or impart to any human being your knowledge
of them. Stanley has always been true to you." Brighter grew the light on his face as I spoke. He took her little
hand, kissed it reverently, as if it were a holy thing—
saying over and over :

"Ah, poor little heart, *it was true* to me, *thank God !*"

Then he told us how, after leaving Claremont, he had written all his lover-heart out to Stanley, and had waited long
months for an answer, which never came—only a letter
from Retta Austin to Miss Strawbridge, announcing her
intended marriage with Clyde Ingram, adding : " My man-
tua-maker is engaged in preparing Miss Montana's elegant
trousseau." We saw it all. Retta Austin, without promot-
ing in the slightest degree the purpose for which she dispensed with her integrity, had succeeded in keeping two
fond hearts apart. I was glad it was all explained away,
the haunting mystery. The world could not appreciate the
need of such a conference, and must not know it ; but there

is no shame in love that is pure and stedfast. We should only blush for the attribute desecrated and despoiled of its high nature. Between them now there should be *"no more bitterness—only fate and duty."* Stanley said bravely, feelingly :

"I can see, now, why this explanation was withheld from us until our affection had attained its clearest sight, which reveals to us danger and the prudent way to avoid it. I do not mean that our love could hold temptation to wrong, but you must respect its mandates, and shield me from the world, from even the semblance of evil."

We three came down the hillside together. Warren took one boat ; Stanley and I the other. Thus we crossed to the home shore. At her request, we took tea at the cottage. There was a sweet calmness in their manner towards each other. I saw how Warren felt her presence in everything about him. Once in his own surroundings, he would not feel it near so much. But now he certainly realized very keenly what was lost to him in losing her. When he was gone, she said to me :

"I can bear, Jennie, all that I must. But oh, if he had married some one else! Some one whom, in time, he might have come to love—who had power to make him happy—I, too, might learn to be content. But when I recall the hungry look of longing on his face, the face that I have seen love-lighted and radiant, I feel my burden is greater than I can bear—though I must try, for her hands make for him a home, while mine lie listless and idle, unless I strive to do God's work on earth."

Thus those two took up their separate ways through the wide world, while their souls and hearts in the presence of the highest Judge were wedded and one. The days wore onward to their close one by one until the summer was ended; the second summer of her soul-life was bound up with treasures time was garnering for her future yonder, where lights of summer never pale.

We learned from Milverton that Warren had gone abroad with his wife, whose health was failing. We heard almost constantly from Raymond; never from Clyde, though red autumn came and went. How swift are battle years, how long with agony and waiting; waiting for peace, which comes not until the twilight of death has closed out the fourth year!

———o———

CHAPTER XVII.

"Be thou as chaste as ice, and pure as snow,
Thou shalt not escape calumny."

SHAKSPEARE.

WAYBURN, like all New England towns, had its Soldiers' Aid Society, which met weekly at the residence of its friends and supporters. A few weeks subsequent to the events detailed in the last chapter, the circle met at Ridgely; I was sitting in the library with Ala, while she slept; a variety of subjects were under discussion; Mary was assisting her mother in household preparations for the entertainment of their guests; Stanley had promised to come with Uncle Kingswell when school hours were over. I held my breath with profound astonishment when I heard Mrs. Seaman in an adjoining room:

"I never in all my life was so mistaken in regard to any one; I wonder Mr. Kingswell should seek to impose that creature upon his friends."

"To whom do you refer?" inquired sharp-faced Mrs.

Cummins, in a weasel-voice, her black eyes twinkling with suppressed curiosity.

"Can it be possible you have not heard?—*that Stanley Montana* who teaches in town."

"Well, what has she done?" inquired the squeaking voice.

"We cannot exactly say what she *has* done, but we cannot answer for what she *hasn't* done!" answered malicious Mrs. Seaman, with the air of one who knew little, yet suspected a great deal. I remembered that her daughter had been a competitor of Stanley's for the school she had established. Mrs. Seaman added:

"I never had much opinion of those Southern women; there is something peculiar about all I ever see."

Mrs. Cummins's black eyes glanced vindictively as she turned them upon the mild-faced lady who addressed Mrs. Seaman now.

"If you know anything derogatory to the character or usefulness of this young female, speak, for my daughters are pupils of hers?"

"I don't know as it is exactly safe to speak about it *here;* the Kingswells are dreadfully bound up in her. Three or four years ago they came here first, them two gals and two young men; young Mr. Montana and another, his nephew I believe he called him. I didn't know as he was any kin to him, though I had often seen him here before. Well, they stayed all summer, flying round from one waterin'-place to another; they were part of the time at Ridgely, during which period young Mr. Hayne, son of Sol Hayne who owns the large place 'twixt here and town, and used to live there in the warm season, saw the one with all those curls, as is now a teachin', and fell in love with her, as she did with him. Oh, they were the lovinest couple you ever see!

To Mrs. Martin's party they wern't apart five blessed minutes the whole evenin'. Then after supper they went out into the garden; he pulled flowers and put them in her curls, and came leading her in to the parlor mirror, blushin' and simperin' after a ridiculous fashion, to look at herself. I have always tried to teach my daughter better than to go out walkin' with young men after night, even if the moon is a shinin' bright as day; or walkin' with married men either, for that matter, even though it be over the hills in broad daytime."

"Why did they not marry?" inquired meek Mrs. Moore.

"Well, as I was a goin' to say, I don't think he went as she did that summer, though he certainly followed her home, and was down there a'most all winter; when he came back he told his father they would be married, but he married a lady from Philadelphia instead. When I was in New York that spring after the weddin', Warren's mother told me her son had made a money match. Be that as it may, he's got the other now and ought to stick by her, instead of hunting up old flames to burn his fingers with!"

"Might he not have called merely for the sake of old acquaintanceship?" suggested Mrs. Moore; though Mrs. Seaman was determined to take no probable view of the case, so she answered somewhat curtly—

"If he wanted to see her, and she him, which was evident, why did they not go to see one another openly and above-board, instead of meeting secretly on the hill? Then he came over in another boat to elude suspicion. After having done all that, he went home with her. Yes, she actually walked through the streets of Wayburn with a married man!!! I saw her with my own eyes. I certainly think one should not be countenanced at all, who could with impunity set such an example to the young girls under her charge. As for myself, I shall show her no favor in future; she can expect nothing from people who pride themselves upon their character for virtue in society."

Indeed, thought I, it was wonderful; Mrs. Seaman's sagacity in beholding things that were to be seen! Yet why was she blinded that I was one of the party who walked through the streets of Wayburn with a married man in broad daylight—and that man my cousin, Warren Hayne?

"I have often heard that society in Southern cities differs very much from our New England towns. Married people receive and entertain, and go more frequently into company than young people do," ventured Mrs. Moore, timidly.

"Well! no wonder there is so much wickedness down there!—the Gulf States had to break out into rebellion : it was an escape-valve for their licentiousness. I have always heard the land was a perfect Sodom! I am more inclined than ever to believe it."

This observation came from a strong-minded female disciple of the Greeley school. Mrs. Seaman spoke again :

"Well, they should not want to introduce Southern fashions in a civilized country, where we don't indulge in such abominable practices. It is the fashion down there to hold human critters in bondage. But we don't intend to adopt such an ungodly usage in our Christian community. I'll insure it, if the truth was known, young Hayne had good reason for failing to keep his engagement with Stanley Montana. He would have married her if she had been worthy! for she was pretty enough, and rich enough, too, for that matter, to tempt any man."

Ah! how many of that virtuous, self-righteous social band would have trampled down a sweet voice in their heart, risen above temptation, and gone on in the way of duty, as had that brave young creature, whose name they bandied from

venomous lip to lip as though it were a worthless thing
—she who stood so far above their commonplace estimates
that their foul tongues might never reach her save through
the love of her friends! Yet was she subject to insult from
this virtuous clique. Virtuous because they had never
known temptation—harnessed, as they were, to the rack of
an every-day routine. I think the spiteful old woman felt
this keenly as I did; it was manifest in her tones as she
resumed—

"I repeat, it is a scandalous shame that Mr. Kingswell—
a deacon in our holy church—should not only suffer himself
to be thus imposed upon, but that he should extend the
imposition to us. I came here to-day for the express purpose of speaking my mind to him."

He arrived at the moment; before I could meet them at
the front door Stanley had bounded up the steps and was
in the parlor. There were Mrs. Mason and Mrs. Jones, who
visited her very frequently; who had actually courted her
society: why did they sit there hearing all, upraising no
voice in her defence? When will woman learn to brave
censure and be strong in the name of the good Samaritan
to defend the right and speak for each other? Seeing that
none of us were in the parlor, she merely bowed to the assembled company; their ominous glances and frozen counte-
nances chilled her to the very soul. She withdrew and
came to me, her face flushed, her eyes brimming, though
she kissed me as usual, saying no word of the palpable insult
she had received.

Tea was announced. When they were seated at table Mrs.
Kingswell said, addressing Stanley:

"My dear, you will preside, will you not? Ladies, I presume most of you have met Miss Montana? She has
promised to attend our circles regularly ere long."

11*

There came no word of answer to this kind speech of the hostess; there was an ominous silence, only broken by two or three affected coughs, a rolling up of Mrs. Cummins's sharp black eyes; then there was a suppressed groan of virtuous indignation, scarce audible, from Mrs. Seaman. Stanley's checks were glowing; hot drops swam in her eyes as she looked at me piteously. I answered her look significantly; whereupon she excused herself and left the table. I was about to follow her from the room, but Mr. Kingswell checked me by a look that sent the rebellious blood, uprisen in my face, back to its channels again. Mrs. Seaman cleared her throat once or twice; I think the manner of our host somewhat disconcerted her; while his unassuming integrity commanded her reverence, it held her in awe.

"Mr. Kingswell, do you know this young female to whom you have introduced us?"

"I do not clearly understand you, madam; though it is anything but flattering, the intimation that I would recommend as instructress of the young people in our place, a person with whom I was not thoroughly acquainted."

His tones of polite sarcasm cut deep, and the old lady's wrath waxed warmer in proportion.

"Then I must understand you; one of the leading men in our community giving countenance and protection to a person whose acts are shameless and disgraceful."

I was alarmed! Clyde's uncle was actually growing red with suppressed anger! Though he controlled himself, and spoke quietly in a low hoarse tone.

"In what has Miss Montana offended, may I ask? And upon what ground do you hold her, at an individual tribunal, responsible for said offence, even if she has committed one?"

I thought of the great Spirit who said to the woman of Samaria, "Who are thine accusers?"

"For the sake of decency and order we hold you responsible for having introduced into our midst a woman who is so lawless as to have secret meetings with an old lover; *a married man!* Is not this sufficient?"

The old lady was evidently disappointed in the effect of her intelligence upon Mr. Kingswell. When the matter assumed the form of an accusation against him, he cared very little about it; now he looked to me for an explanation of the charges preferred against Stanley. I addressed excitedly my vindication to him in their hearing.

"About three weeks since, as I was going out to walk I paused at the cottage; on being told by Miss Phœbe that Stanley had gone to our old haunt on the hillside, I lost no time in joining her there; soon after Mr. Hayne came over; he had much to tell us of our friends in the South. He said his stay in Wayburn must be short; his visit there incidental; so he sought us out, after finding neither of us at home. At our earnest joint solicitation he accompanied us to the cottage and remained for tea. When Mrs. Seaman saw Stanley and cousin Warren walking in the street, *I was with them!* She omitted to mention this fact, had forgotten it probably, it was so unimportant an item in making her statement to you. I cannot think she would willingly have done so; her narrative this afternoon, which I chanced to overhear, was characterized by a disposition to be entirely *just.*"

"Just!" he echoed with affable courtesy. "I am glad Mrs. Seaman is so; I should regret exceedingly to know that my lady friends were otherwise! or indeed that any should be so. There is nothing so hard for any human heart to bear as injustice; we should always endeavor to be charitable as well! but at least we should never fail to be just."

"We are oftentimes grievously mistaken in our estimates," remarked Mrs. Seaman, thoroughly disconcerted, fallen from her enormous height of fault-finding back upon generalities. She was beaten at her own game, and this was her only excuse for the shameless slander **she** had perpetrated concerning my cousins.

"Then," said my uncle, "the fault is not ours. **If we,** in good faith, take by the hand a fellow-mortal, brother or sister, in the great family of humanity ; if they prove unworthy to be so called, there can be no blame attached to us. We should not crush every generous, social impulse through fear that we might chance to bestow kindness injudiciously. Our reward shall be the same. God alone can decide. We have no right in this world to say to any man or woman, ' Stand aside, I am holier than thou.' "

"We can all know what we *do not do*," shrieked **the** little shrill voice of Mrs. Cummins, who came opportunely to aid the discomfited Mrs. Seaman. "I for one have always endeavored to live piously and keep the commandments."

This was said in a choked voice with an air of injured innocence ; and the black eyes looked round the table for a sympathetic confirmation of her assertion. Mrs. Kingswell now spoke in a calm, clear voice :

"We are none of us sinless. You say you have kept the commandments; my friends, how did you dispose of that little injunction, ' Love thy neighbor as thyself;' have you not worked evil to the injury of my young friend here without knowing her at all ? You have condemned her unheard ; your virtual decision has been, ' Stand aside, we are holier than thou.' I am less than woman if I raise no voice in justification of her evidently harmless act. Were it as you say, and she **was** in heart what you affirm, in Heaven's name *who constituted you her accusers ?* My husband shall tell you this young girl's story ; then, if you wish, you may decide against her, and those who are her friends." She looked the noble being she was, the confident assistant of such a husband. Oh! that of such men and women there were more in the universe!

"Her father was a banker in New Orleans, a Union man, and a high-toned gentleman; when the rebellion broke out his family came north for safety. On the acquisition by Butler and his forces of New Orleans, his property was confiscated with those who were supposed to be antagonistic to the government. Her beautiful home has since become a barracks for the soldiery. Stanley, born and reared in luxury and wealth, came here from the new-made grave of her mother. When it was no longer possible to obtain remittances from her father, she conceived and executed a plan for aiding herself. You are aware, Mrs. Seaman, that she—the lady whom you seek to defame—is the sister of my son-in-law."

"Indeed!" remarked the old lady in a tone faint with chagrin; "I have forgotten—that is, I think I never knew——"

"I presumed Mrs. Seaman was aware of the relationship," remarked Mrs. Moore, a little exultantly.

"I repeat," added Mr. Kingswell, "I am suffering no compunctions of conscience for having introduced my young friend into your midst. In our social circle she has no superior; except, perhaps, in point of *self-righteousness.*"

It was the most cutting speech I ever heard him make; though he had been very much tried that afternoon, there was a victorious look on his benign features as he led the way to the garden and conservatory. It was yet daylight; there were no young men in the party; Mrs. S. could not, of course, object to going too. I really pitied the poor old creature, as I do all those who cannot find resources of diversion and happiness within themselves, and, like vultures, must needs prey upon the characters of others to still the cravings of an active temperament. I imagine the disciples of Mrs. Grundy to be the most utterly miserable of all created creatures. I thought, too, if the poor soldier-boys, toiling in a distant front, could only know how many good names they cost, they would shudder whenever it became necessary to appropriate any article of apparel furnished by the loyal ladies—of Wayburn, for instance. Brave men would rather hear the music of a minie-ball than give ear to detraction in any form : they hate scandal-mongers, and avoid them as they would a pestilence. Returning from the garden, I met Mr. Kingswell. He said, ' I am looking for Stanley.' "

" That is my errand, too, just now ; I shall go further, however—I shall seek her at the cottage."

"I will come presently, when I have taken Ala home— when the house is vacated, and Ridgely is itself again."

He held the child in his arms, looking fondly into her bright blue eyes, while she smoothed lovingly his iron-grey hair. Afterwards, as I walked down the garden path to the cottage, I saw him leading his little human blossom among the flowers of that home.

Stanley sat near to the open window ; she had been weeping, and her face was very pale. Miss Phœbe was by her side ; a few silent tear-drops fell upon her knitting as I entered. There was an expression upon the faces of both that kept me silent ; so I waited for Stanley to speak.

" Jennie, I seek no explanation of the outrage my feelings received, and the insult to which I thoughtlessly exposed myself, a few hours since. I only know that my friends, for my sake, were subjected to the keenest humiliation. So far as I am concerned, the freaks of society affect me very little—I can live above them ; but this must have wounded Mr. and Mrs. Kingswell very much. I will see that there shall be no recurrence of the unpleasant scene."

I related faithfully all that had occurred in her absence, taking care to let the blame fall where it was most just it should fall, adding: "Poor, malicious, old woman, had I possessed no foreknowledge of the facts in the case, I, too, might have been one of her converts to the belief that you were really a silly girl."

"After all, Jennie, it was wrong—that conference with Mr. Hayne; I feel it so now."

"That may be, I will admit. From the stand-point of society, it does not appear to me exactly right; but what was I to do? In such cases we cannot be governed by standard rules of conduct; cannot make laws for any individual instance, and may scarcely abide by any, in such cases. I hold that your love for Warren Hayne is sinless. You loved him when he was free, and it was your chosen right so to do. Could you forget that love? Ignore the glory of it in a day, or an hour? No! I hold sinless the loves of both. His might have been otherwise, for he is a man of the world, Stanley, and they do not think of things as we do. That same world, so bitter towards an error in our sex, is more lenient towards them. Their sense of the nicer distinctions is necessarily somewhat blunted by the contact. I have faith, solemn, boundless, in you both; but 'dammed up passion is a dangerous thing.' The safest course was to throw the responsibility upon his honor, and trust him. I know Warren—know still that he will keep inviolate that trust."

Mr. Kingswell, as he entered the cottage, caught the last words of what I had been saying to Stanley. He laid his hands almost reverently upon her bowed head, remarking in tones which I can never, never forget:

" My child, there is some cross in life for every human being—this is yours. Bear it faithfully; ask God to help you, and he will."

He had some way, with his ready faculty, grasped what lay between Warren and Stanley. With what delicate tact he had administered comfort to her and to me, bearing my own cross silently !

" As regards the occurrences of this afternoon," he continued, " it is needless to ask that you will not allow them to wound you. We are all vulnerable to these things. There is one consolation, however: the shafts of envy invariably rebound from an armor of truth and high purpose. It is not the better portion of society that claim as pastime such indulgences. Whenever you see a female given to such diversions, you may be assured she is either very illiterate, or by nature very coarse. Refined society is more tolerant with regard to the faults and foibles of its votaries. Ignorance and prejudice go hand in hand in this covert field of action. That meant for section is often brought to bear in individual instances. You may regard yourself as quite a heroine, Stanley ; you represent the South, and must endure all the hatred and malignity directed towards her."

" I have heard these things before. But for this outbreak, I could utterly ignore the existence of any unpleasant feeling in the community towards myself: but I cannot bear that my friends should suffer humiliation for my sake."

" Oh, if that is all, leave that to us ; we will assume and bear it cheerfully. Never allow it to touch you again. Live above it; you are capable of doing so. Show Mrs. Seaman that she has no power to strike you. Truth and right are their own vindicators and avengers ; leave the issue to the arbitration of a higher power."

We watched him as he went down the path, the shadows closing round him; his glorious soul—the solitary radiance shining through the darkness—our messenger from the Infinite. I remained with Stanley that night. She sat up for a long time, writing. Then she came and sat beside me, saying:

"Oh, Jennie, how I long for the strong arm which should have been mine, yet failed me! How frail and powerless is woman to measure her strength with those of her sex who are foes to every effort outside the usual routine. Sometimes, for days together, mind is in the ascendant; but I am often made to think that the heart was only gathering strength, during the little respite, to utter its bereavement. Then a great weariness comes over me, with constant longing for a forbidden idol. And I long for death; the quietude of a Southern grave, beside my mother's. This is a hard world, Jennie, even were there no misconstructions, no perversions and injustice. But Christ bore all for us—and the death."

Death! True, it was our portion; for her, the bright-haired being at my side, with youth in every pulse of life; for him, who under the folds of the old flag, wielded the arms of his country's defence; and for another brave, whose battle-cry was: "Independence! the right of self-government for me!"—with the mystery of an invincible silence on lip and heart for ever. Alas! Clyde Ingram, for aught I knew, might lie cold and dead 'neath the bright flowers of his native land, whose far-away chimes rang through the watches of that solemn night!

We had, too, another cause for distress; we had reason to fear the safety of Uncle Montana. A few weeks after coming north our remittances ceased. From that time we had heard no word from him, nor received any intimation of his whereabouts, if living. Stanley was right! This was, in truth, a hard world, and its battle-days to us were full of suspense and anguish.

-----o-----

CHAPTER XVIII.

"What next? I know not, do not care;
Come pain or pleasure, weal or woe;
There's nothing which I cannot bear,
Since I have borne this withering blow."

Another summer went, its roses, sunshine, and perfume by; another autumn came—russet, crisp, and sere to her deserted haunts. One afternoon Stanley had gathered the last golden-rods from the hillside, and arranged them in vases on a table at the open window, near which she sat, reading aloud to Miss Phœbe, who as usual was occupied with her knitting. Ala Ray came in for her share of the brightness and comfort of this little nest. Ala had failed very much in health and strength recently. She clasped her thin arms about Stanley's neck, saying gently—she seemed to grow in gentleness as her strength wasted, and her little tones were like the chimes we often hear in dreams:

"Auntie, mamma wants you to come over to supper. We think maybe papa will be home, and we want all together; we hope to have all except grandma Montana; she is gone, you know."

Ah! there was another of the household absent, whose name the child had never been taught to lisp; he was held a traitor to his country, to the flag for which her father fought, and Ala Ray was too young to remember the days when it was not so! When they two were brothers, in heart and soul; as such they should have gone through life together. I saw a bright tear fall upon the sunny head nestled in Stanley's bosom. I know she was thinking of the time when it was otherwise; of our Southern home; how the hopes that clustered round it had been broken into fragments and scattered widely at the inevitable mandate at other 'time and place; would they ever be gathered up. Ala went on to say.—

"Oh! Aunty dear, if that papa of mine could only know how much I have wanted to see him, and how I have lain awake nights waiting for him to speak just one little word to me! And now that these solemn days are here, and the wind seems to be crying about this great war, I want him more than ever. I never want to give him up again."

Ah! many a time had that father thought and dreamed of the little face that looked to him through silent falling tears on leaving home, and the little heart that waited for him there. Oh! days that had been! days that were to be! Of which did we think most then; and on which lay the shadow heaviest as we came up the terraced walks dotted with autumn flowers?

"Auntie! I think of all the flowers I like the daisies best of any I know. They are so small and white, and lie so still on the grass in spring-time, as though waiting for God's fingers to gather them up."

We raised our eyes! A pair of manly arms were outstretched; his little daughter was held fast in a close firm grasp. Ala's head lay on her father's breast. Why did he hold her so tightly? He had heard her words, and feared God's fingers would pluck his daisy ere the springtime. The child wept for joy as though her little life would go out; all the while saying brokenly, how much she had wanted him, that she would never let him go again; then entreating him to stay with her as long as she lived. He promised her all she asked, as she smoothed his crisp curls and kissed his face over and over with her soft lips. Oh! how he had longed to be with them! And **how** could he ever leave his home-idols again! Poor man's weak heart fails him sometimes! No wonder; life and fate hold for him such hard trial tests.

"Mamma, don't you leave him?" Ala said.

"Yes, daughter; though you have given mamma no opportunity to **say so.** Stand down, and let papa look at his little pet."

"Why, how tall she has grown, and thin," he added aside to Mary, in a pained voice. "Oh, I hope she will improve now."

"I was so tired! so tired for you to come home, papa!"

So saying, she climbed into his lap and was soon asleep. He laid her in the little crib. Then we all knelt, while Mr. Kingswell thanked God for our hero's return in safety. When we were all seated round the tea-table, Raymond remarked:

"And so you are all here to meet me! This is pleasant."

"*All*, Raymond," Stanley asked significantly; "have you forgotten?"

"No, sister; I have not forgotten—I cannot forget who is absent, and how **he remains away.** Many a time since I have been a soldier in the service of my country I would have given a world, had it been mine, to have shaken hands with him under the folds of the old flag. I could better have borne to see him fall, as I have seen thousands, than to think of him as he is."

Then he talked of his campaign—of the Fredericksburg slaughter—of the thirty thousand braves sacrificed to so little purpose. Then of home and its concerns! Of Ala— very gently, with that feeling tremor in his voice, which I always fancied I could hear when I read his letters to

Mary, in which he never failed to say, "Take good care of papa's little daughter." Then we came and sat by her side as she lay sleeping. No more words now of storm and conflict. We felt that angels were on *guard* that night watching the soldier and his child.

The following day was spent by us all at Ridgely; the next with Stanley in her cottage home. During the afternoon I received a letter from Cousin Warren. He wrote briefly; yet in the few sentences of commendation I felt how much Stanley, going on from day to day in her round of patient duty, claimed his reverence. He, from his standpoint, traced her path, and felt how nobly and firmly she walked in it. He sent some books from Paris for our joint perusal, and begged that we would not forget him. He spoke of his own land, and the hearts in it that were bleeding to the death, and how he longed to be at home. The letter bore date just one year from his visit to Wayburn. That evening, as we sat together on the piazza at Uncle Kingswell's—Raymond playing with his little daughter—I remembered how, in the first summer days, we had sat there with those two present who were absent now. One beyond the sea; the other further off, beyond countless seas of ceaseless strife.

The next day brought Milverton to Ridgely. He inquired for me; on being informed that I was at the cottage, he sent down the letter he had brought. It was from Lane Austin. I afterwards learned how he obtained it; hearing that Gerald was a prisoner at Washington, he visited him for the purpose of learning something of Clyde. On being told that Lane was probably the only person who could give him any information, he wrote at once. By the exercise of considerable strategy he succeeded in posting his letter, and obtaining an answer addressed to me, which ran as follows:

"I will dispense with preliminaries, Miss Aljean, in telling you all I know concerning our beloved Colonel Ingram. I will say nothing of the preference that you manifested for him when we were all at home. How long since I have had a home save in the field. It was enough, in the days of hardship, to realize how much more worthy of your esteem he was than I. Had it been the fullest measure of which your woman's heart is capable, the boon was richly merited, for a braver man to work for country, for independence, and for God, I have never seen. But he is dead! I saw our soldiers weeping while they dug his grave in a Southern wilderness. I can never express a tithe of what I felt in that bitter hour. I would have died to save him, for I loved him better than any one else in the world!—than my own brother, who pines to-day in a Northern prison.

"Our Colonel went himself with a small detachment on a scouting expedition. They remained absent so long I grew anxious, and went in search of them. I met some of his men returning to camp! They reported a skirmish, in which the Colonel had been killed. I ordered them to pilot us to the spot where they had left him. It was difficult to keep the direction; a heavy rain was falling; we were attacked once and driven into our fortifications. We made another attempt, carrying a flag of truce; we determined, if possible, to recover the body of the Colonel at all hazards. So many delays were involved in the prolonged search, his face was unrecognizable! The faces of all the fallen men were marred and discolored by the drenching rains. He lay near to his faithful steed—one which he always rode when on his plantation; the creature's head was near his master's shoulder. There, in a wilderness of green, the blue sky over him, dust below, our soldiers made his grave and fired their volleys over him! I have seen many

fall, Miss Aljean, since that last evening at Claremont. I
have looked upon death in almost every form! I have seen
it in camp, in fort and hospital, by the wayside and on
battle-fields; have seen my near relatives—those who were
once possessed of thousands—starving for a crust, but
nothing ever affected me like this; he was my friend—
brother; on the march and in camp we had faced death
together. But the arch-enemy had come to him when I
was not near to claim a parting pressure of his hand and
treasure his last words. It was hard to think there was no
kind voice to break the last, long silence, as it closed about
him."

I was glad no one was near me. It chanced that I was
alone in Stanley's little chamber. The grim eternal silence
seemed closing about me, too; iron bars were pressing on
my heart; oh, it was bursting. I was reeling, suffocating.
I passed into the garden, found Stanley, gave her the letter;
she read it while I walked about recklessly crushing the
autumn flowers under my impatient feet. Stanley wept,
exclaiming in broken sentences:

"Poor Clyde, poor dear brother! Oh, Jennie, I am so
sorry that I sent him away that time, he seemed so solitary
and desolate; those whom he loved to him were stony-
hearted. Oh, why did not you care for him and save him!"
My heart grew hard as I looked upon her; then I could
speak the taunt, but not the anguish I felt:

"Stanley Montana, do not stand there mocking me; do
anything else you choose; pity me, *for I loved Clyde
Ingram*, have done so for years and years; loved him, and
he loved me; I shall go mad that I have lost him." I
threw myself upon the ground; there, lying on the crushed
flowers, I defied the smiting hand that had stricken him.
Yes, God forgive me, in that bitter moment I uttered a

tortuous malediction against the power that had bereft me. Night came down with its cool dews from the fountain of His immutable love; as they fell upon my thirsting soul tears came to my relief. As I lay there the autumn moon rose up—the moon that shone, and the autumn that dropped its leaves upon his distant grave. The heart of the universe had ceased to pulsate. His life-task was ended; he was gone from the canker that cuts into the soul with its slow charges and takes the bloom from life; gone from the sudden casualties, the sad possibilities and probabilities, which are but other names for the freaks of human destiny. Never more would they crash through his heart-strings with sudden desolation, as they had done through mine. He was sleeping, we were weeping. It was my cross in life, this death, and I must bear it to the end. The ponderous machinery of the universe crashed on as though he slept not.

We were to have company in the evening; how much the seal which had hitherto set upon my lips and life aided me in crushing down the inward strife. I went into Stanley's little bed-chamber, lay looking out of the window upon the widespread busy universe, which held for me nothing save its category of grim silences. By-and-by I saw Raymond and Milverton coming; how cheerful and indifferent they looked.

Captain Montana wore the uniform of our country—the insignia which asserted grimly and vaunted to my sick heart that he was the dead man's enemy. For an instant I could not look down into the deeps where the old brotherhood rested pure, unsullied by passion or sectional prejudice. Now I only thought how two countries, whose widely dissevered interests and aims had come between, and how one lay in his far-off sleep, with none to mourn him save the silent heart whose love for him was all untold. These thoughts were passing through my mind while I heard Raymond entreating one of their visitors, Miss Radway, to sing. I lay spell-bound, listening to the words:

> "When our boys come home in triumph, brother,
>   With the laurels they shall gain;
> When we meet to give them welcome, brother,
>   We shall look for you in vain."

Her voice was tremulous with intense pathos as she sang the closing half of the last stanza:

> "Surely we would not recall you, brother,
>   Though our tears flow fast and free,
> When we think of you as sleeping, brother,
>   Underneath that southern tree."

My heart melted as I looked at Raymond, who sat near the open door, for I saw a brother's sorrow under the calm exterior of the soldier. "Where is Jennie?" he inquired suddenly; when Stanley answered him he came and sat beside my sofa, talking casually of many things. At length, with the air of one who had long evaded what must be faced, he spoke: .

"Jennie, Mary, and I will go to Washington to-morrow; will you bear us company?" After a pause he continued: "I am very sorry, Aljeau——" the sentence was not concluded, for he saw how I shuddered as with the chill of that death. I think he now, for the first time, realized my love for Clyde Ingram. Notwithstanding my silent pain, which he felt as keenly as I did, he asked, while a beam came into his face:

"And is it true, Jennie?" Yes, it was true; one of God's truths, which time or change, death or eternity could not annul. Yes! I would go with them; I told him so:

I would see Gerald Austin myself, and inquire his brother's address, which Lane had omitted to give me.

The following morning found Raymond and **Mary**, Ala and myself, en route for the capital. We paused but a few hours in **New York**; grey mists lifted up their shadowy arms to salute the morning sun as it streaked the bosom of the Delaware while we crossed. Some Government boats were loosed from their moorings, and in the brooding stillness I heard workmen at the forge singing, "Maryland, my Maryland." I thought then, as I have ever since, it was the finest lyric poem of the age. In those wild, wailing tones of appeal, I caught the enthusiasm which must have animated many a heart to do and dare what those **southern hearts have** done for country and the love of it.

We soon saw the glittering domes and spires **of the** capital, bordered with its broad white sheet of Potomac, beyond which, upon the plains of Virginia, stood bulwarks of **a nation's** strength, in an attitude of appeal **to** the god of victory. What was Washington grown to be ? From halls **where** strong-armed, calm-faced Justice was wont to rise **and speak** his mandates, to the inheritors of **a** common country, were heard now **only the** croaking voices of demagogues, who instantly set hard heels upon any white **bud** of peace that dared **to** lift **its** modest head, **with** timid promise of blossom, amid the strife.

When we became settled at **our** hotel, I went with Raymond to seek Gerald. He obtained, through Captain Montana's numerous friends, **admission** to his prison. It was **a strange** interview ! He seemed as if he wished to talk of everything but what **my** heart most longed **to** hear. Yet in all he said, there **were** no broken sentences of repentance ; no regrets, **no** repinings—only a sullen persistence in his political fallacy, through which shone a dogged spirit

of resistance, which might be crushed but never wholly
extinguished, even within the walls of a dungeon. He was
kind, polite, respectful; yet we could learn from him
nothing more concerning Clyde's death than we already
knew. We failed even to procure Lane's address, which
was our chief design in going there. So we came back to
Weyburn after our hopeless journey. As we recrossed
the Delaware at night, the stars seemed to look down with
a pitying radiance into the troubled abysses of my soul!
and I heard a voice which said to the lashing waves—
" Peace ! be still."

---o---

CHAPTER XIX.

"For what is life? at best, a brief delight;
A sun scarce brightening ere it sinks in night:
A flower at morning fresh, at noon decayed;
A still swift river gliding into shade."

DURING our visit, Ala had pined for the atmosphere of her
own home. She seemed to grow weary of all things about
her, and said she wanted to rest. When we brought her
back she would lie ofttimes in her little bed so still that we
grew alarmed. We began to devise means by which we
could avail ourselves of medical aid, without having her
suspect we thought her really ill. Accordingly, Raymond
brought Dr. Berkley; ostensibly to dine—really to admi-
nister to our pet. She was a favorite with him, as she was
with all who knew her. He laid her golden head against
his cheek, adroitly examined her pulse, but his face gave
no sign that he thought our darling in danger. We were
reassured by his manner; our chilly fears took once more

the warm hue of hope; we caught the sunshine of the brief interval that was to elapse before we must give her up finally. For this we were only waiting.

Raymond had made his preparations with a view to returning to camp. His leave of absence was already expired; on the morrow he would go.

The eve before his leave-taking, he and Mary had a little conference—half sad, half hopeful—about home concerns and Ala—how she would bear the blow. I left them and went down to the cottage. Crisp leaves were lying on the garden path, and the autumn sky hung down its banners of crimson which shone through the swaying trees, reminding one of altar-fires lifting up their everlasting incense to the Creator, gratefully. I thought how on distant fields, where the dead lay white and still, gleamed other banners, red with the gore of our hearts' chosen idols. With these reflections pressing heavily, it was natural I should seek to avoid meeting Mr. Milverton, whom I observed coming up the path. I had special reasons for not wishing to see him, but there was no escape. We shook hands; then he said his say earnestly:

"I am very grateful, Miss Jennie, for this opportunity of seeing you alone before I return to New York. I have something which I must say, though you will doubtless think me a sorry old fool for having said it; but I am tired of what the gay world calls pleasure! I have money, friends, and health; but I want a home of my own. I am just beginning to realize how dreadfully selfish a bachelor is. Now here I am, roaming round, while you, a little frail creature, are moping, growing pale, for want of somebody to nurse you up and care for you. I propose to do that; I want you—your presence—in the home I shall make, want you here in my heart to still its cravings—to make

me a better, nobler man than I am. Will you be my
wife ?"

I raised my hand deprecatingly! his words jarred painfully a sensitive chord in my sore heart, that would never
again vibrate with tenderness for any man living. I answered him with energy, not a little amused despite myself.

"No, no, not your wife! Why, Mr. Milverton, you do
not know me, or rather you do not know yourself. You
care no more for me than for five-and-twenty other young
girls in your circle. I am as jealous by nature as a Blue-
beard, and could never consent to occupy such a tiny nook
in any man's heart, especially yours. Large as it is, I should
want the whole of it. Besides, do not want to marry me on
account of my paleness ; I may transfer that to you when
I tell you, that immediately on becoming mistress of your
prospective home, I should resort to a vigorous use of my
tongue, in order to induce you to abandon all your *innocent*
amusements, such as balls, *soirées*, theatres, &c., and settle
down demurely into quiet life. Then you would be compelled to stop flirting. One of the natural matrimonial results is, that a man shall give up kissing all the pretty girls
in his circle, even though that man were Mr. Milverton, a
gay bachelor of thirty-five. See what a martyr you must
necessarily become."

"Now, now, Miss Jennie, I protest most solemnly. By
the way, what has so suddenly sobered you? I have not
forgotten a few seasons since you were the most inveterate
coquette present at Nahant."

"Ah! my friend, the soul seems to have gone out of
everything since then : the land is full of sorrow. I am
desperately earnest now in all I say and do."

"So am I. I design quitting all my bad practices—get-
ting married, just for the novelty."

"Then let me inform you, that unless you have in the matter more genuine feeling than your tone and manner would suggest, matrimony will prove anything but a novel performance."

"I suppose you think one should be deeply in love— well, what is it? Let me define love for you: It is a flame that burns itself out with the ardor of youth. Refined intercourse in a social circle will produce a comfortable state of amicable feeling. In some instances, we find those whose companionship is a source of rare delight, and confers upon us, as individuals, a happiness which all the world beside would fail to supply. Beyond this there is little for men who have arrived at my age. I should give you as much tenderness, perhaps, as any of my sex."

"Oh, I am thankful for the privilege of looking upon human nature from my own stand-point! Throw away those spectacles, Mr. Milverton. Do not imagine all the world is looking through them, when it is only yourself. I am not yet so callous to the genuine attributes of mankind, that I can afford to dispense with love in my union. I want that something—a presence vast enough to cover all the earth, and in one little space where it is not, I want to feel as if impenetrable darkness had settled; a sentiment which came from God with messages of a hope that may be eternal, alone, enduring as the stars. Then, though there may be long, sad farewells, and heart-tears never dry; grim silences of death and separations that stretch through time to the white portals yonder, beyond those crimson clouds of sunset; yet, too, there may be something beyond those broad slopes of the everlasting life, in that heaven which is love's true abiding-place." I checked myself suddenly, as I felt the red flash into my cheeks beneath Milverton's

gaze of pitying scrutiny. The question fell from his lips
unconsciously :

"Have you ever loved that love, Jennie, whose hope is
here of fruition there ?"

"Yes; I did love! My heart attests the truth; it is
over now. He walked through earth *a king* among men;
he is dead! All the world cannot give me back what died
with him. I have told you enough; let the subject never
recur between us." I gave him my hand, over which he
bowed in silent acquiescence, then left me. I saw him
enter the gate at Ridgely ere I joined Stanley at the cottage. It was twilight; the lamps were not yet lighted;
the glow of the wood-fire was upon Stanley's cheek, and
golden rings of hair broke like beams of sunlight through
her net, and lay upon her dark dress caressingly. Those
tresses of hers would not bear confinement; they were
rebellious as her nature, for I saw tears upon her cheeks
which told me that she wore not her harness patiently that
evening. I gathered her head to my bosom and asked
her why she wept.

"I was thinking, dear, what a strange and wayward fate
has been ours! Of that love of yours whose glory was hid
in a tomb; and mine——. Oh, it is no light thing!—the
task of learning to live without some one to cling to, whose
love is all your own. Do not interrupt me; I am talking
of nothing, want nothing that belongs of right to Warren
Hayne's wedded wife. But I do so often miss what was
given me; that which, but for the treachery of *some*, would
have been mine."

"I know, darling, you miss what should have been yours,
and will do so more and more, as you go on through life.
There are many in the world who care for us, more or less,
but there are very few who *really love us.* Our mother

did—our brother—he leaves us to-morrow. Ah, here he is; another farewell!" Ray sat with us some time, affecting to talk cheerfully, though it was plain to see how the soldier's heart was bowed low; that the separation was inevitable. Of Ala he thought most of all.

"It will break her little heart to know that I am going. We must bring her down here. When she finds that I am really gone, you girls may be better able to pacify her than her mother. Poor Mary is herself so miserable. You will manage it, Jennie, will you not? I cannot bear to have her torn from me. This seems the only course left me."

"Yes; I will endeavor to do so, Ray, but you must promise me that when your term expires, you will come home to stay. Ala needs you more than your country, just now."

"Ah, that is a woman's view of the case! You would not make a good soldier, Jennie."

My face flushed; I saw he did not comprehend my meaning. I could not speak more plainly. I could not look that father in the face and tell him of the slow-breaking heart-strings of his only child, so I only answered:

"At all events, Raymond, should I send for you at any time, *come;* come quickly, at all hazards."

He promised then. As he was leaving the house he beheld a little white-winged something, that seemed to stir the moonlight, it was so light and airy, coming down the garden path. Raymond stopped still, breathless with suspense and anguish. As the figure came nearer we saw the white dress, falling hair, and spiritual face of Ala Ray; there was such tender love for him shining in every lineament of his daughter's face as she exclaimed:

"Oh, papa, why did you not take me with you? I have sought you everywhere. I have been so unhappy since you went, and left mamma crying dear—blessed mamma; and, oh, your little Ala was so miserable."

"Why, my little pet, do you think you could not get along without papa for a little while? What would my darling do if I should go away again to stay?"

She anwered musingly:

"I am sure I don't know, though I think I should die!"

Ray looked at me piteously, while the child glanced eagerly, apprehensively, from one to the other. She put her arms close about her father's neck, nestled up to him, lying quite still, as if in pain, her breath coming hard between her set teeth. No one spoke, no one could just then. At length Raymond said:

"My darling, your little dress is wet with heavy dew, you are cold, let aunty warm you and then put you in her bed until papa is ready to go home." With a strange silence, and obstinacy entirely unnatural to her, she clung closely to her father, refusing to be moved. At length she said in a grieved tone:

"Papa, why did you ask me what I should do if you were to leave me again?" Raymond understood from my face that he must tell her all about it.

"Because, my darling, papa is compelled to rejoin his regiment. He must leave you for a little while, but when the spring is here, and there are many flowers in auntie's grounds, adown the pretty garden way, I will come and stay with you all the time!"

There was no outburst, only she trembled a great deal, and the little face, down which the still tears trickled, seemed to grow momently whiter, more transparent; faster, harder came her breath through the quivering lips. Seeing that Raymond was unable to articulate one word, we besought her, Stanley and I, to remain with us; all in vain.

12*

In answer to our entreaties, she said in a choked voice, that surprised us for its calmness:

"No, no, I cannot leave my papa to-night! Now, auntie, do not take me from him at the last. If he must go, I will **try** and bear it as well as I can!"

Oh, it was so touching; the recognition of the exigency which separated them. Many a person who had grown saintly, resisting tribulations; who, in the hard service of **the** world, had become inured to disappointment; might have learned a lesson from that child, in her patient acceptance of what seemed inevitable; of the sorrow which almost broke her little heart. Raymond recognised it, and exclaimed passionately:

"My brave, noble child! you are more a hero than papa, little one; and you shall stay with him as long **as you** can, and papa will come back to you very soon."

"Before daisies blossom, papa? and the grass grows green again in the old church-yard, and myrtle upon the rough sides of **gilead trees, where** the little birds build their nests in daisy times? And you will think of your little daughter often when you go again to sleep under the stars?"

"**Yes, yes,** darling!" he answered, soothingly; "and papa will write many letters to his little girl; **won't** that be nice?"

"But then, dear papa, **you** will not be here to romp with me in the morning times. I could **bear to** do without you **through** the long days, but in the evenings, oh, I shall want you so much; how can I ever do without you?"

Ah! he could not tell her that; the father, **with** his broken voice and sinking heart. He rose, saying he would take the child to her mother, passed out into the wan light of the autumn moon, hanging just above the garden path; that home-way, where **the summer** flowers were faded and leaves were lying crisp, o'er which an angel's feet had come to guide him to the very portals where they should part, father and child, not to meet again in an earthly spring-time. Not yet, not yet, the bright doors unclosed; why? the keeper's hand was on the latch; was there yet some mission unaccomplished? Our hold of her seemed so frail that a breath might destroy it; yet oh, how our hearts clung to that little shape, that was so fair and heavenly.

Raymond was gone! Mary being unwell I was installed chief nurse to Ala Ray. Often during the day she complained of being tired, and would lie for a long time in my arms—still, as if death was already upon her; then she would start up and sing a little snatch of some song her father liked to hear. Then she would ask how long it would be until the daisies bloomed. Then settle herself as if she would *try* to wait patiently. Oh! country, bleeding at every pore through these reeking days of sacrifice, there was nothing more hallowed laid upon thy altar than what that child gave to thee thus uncomplainingly—the joy of her father's presence during those last days of hers upon the earth. Ah! sweet Ala Ray! There is no name for heroism like to thine; but God has taken the struggle of thy little heart into strict account. Thy offering was to country and to him. Brighter even than the hero's crown of glory shall shine thy white wreath of innocence in the father's peace.

Winter came, wrapping again its white arms around the habitations of this earth, tracking gently the graves of the summer flowers. There was no visible change in our pet, saving a constantly increasing languor, a gradual failing of vitality, which was replaced by a pallor whiter, more transparent. I grew so accustomed to having her little golden head upon my breast, I missed her when she asked to be transferred to her own little couch, with its drapings of the blue she loved so well. It seemed she daily grew more cheerful, more considerate for those around her, and would often say :

"Aunty, I am sure you must be tired holding me so long?" She was apparently unconscious that her light weight was no more than a pleasant burden to me.

Leah Eldridge had lived with Mary during Raymond's period of service. About this time Jamie, her little son, was attacked with a malignant fever. Ala would not rest by day or night until the little boy was brought in and placed upon her own silken couch. I assumed the charge of watching them both one night, that Leah and Mary might both be rested. Jamie slept ; Ala lay quite still in my arms a long time, then started, turning her eyes upon me with a delight that was quite new and strange to her of late. "What is it darling?" I asked.

"Did you not see them, auntie ; they came so near to you, their white wings almost touched your cheek, holding out their hands to me, and I wanted to go with them for they were very lovely, auntie ; but then I thought of you and dear mamma, and how hard it would be to leave you ; then that papa of mine came home, auntie darling, though the daisies were not yet bloomed. A tall, dark man, came with him ; it seemed as though I had seen him somewhere before ; and they clasped hands, papa and he, and talked of peace ; you looked so happy, and I heard such sweet music! Oh! auntie, I am sorry it was all a dream ; I should really love to go to that beautiful place."

My tears were fast falling as I pressed her closer to my heart trying to speak calmly, softly, that the mother might not hear ; but I could articulate no word of all that must be said.

"Auntie, you know how well I love you every one, but I think I must go there for a little while; I shall come back to see you many times, and you will all be happy when I am gone, for you will know that I am happy in that beautiful place. Auntie, *there will be no pain there.*" She unconsciously put her hand to her head; I felt her pulse adroitly, and found she had fever. I administered a cooling draught, which was the most that could be done. During the afternoon she often said to me:

"Auntie, have you told mamma that I am going away by-and-by, where this pain can rest? Oh! if it could only sleep for a little time! But I suffer so much." I choked back the tears at such times, but rarely answered her. Oh! how she suffered for many days! The eking out of that small remnant of vitality was indeed fraught with the accomplishment of a great mission. Not yet, not yet, was the little frail bark borne outward to the eternal strand. Not yet was the bright door unclosed; not yet the little fingers swept the chords of a heavenly harp.

-----o-----

CHAPTER XX.

"A truer, nobler, trustier heart,
More loving or more loyal, never beat
Within a human breast."

BYRON'S TWO FOSCARI.

IT came to pass in course of time that Jamie grew better, and during the days of his convalescence our darling was stretched upon a bed of death. Physicians, friends, and nurses by the score came and went with noiseless steps, but their errands availed naught for the little sufferer, who was happily unconscious of all. There was nothing in the every-day routine to break the stupor of our great grief. I went myself to the office and telegraphed for Raymond, when I found there was no hope of her lingering long. I stood at the gate a few moments on my return. A stranger trudged wearily by, taking the broad road to Ridgely. My heart beat quick. That form was like unto another's, who had been bowed and stricken by a battle-blast! I was so agitated I found it necessary to recall a Southern grave, and the sleeper there, in order to calm myself. As I entered the hall I could not avoid hearing the loud, harsh tones of Mrs. Seaman, who was in the reception-room holding solemn converse with some one concerning a very suspicious charac-ter who seemed to be entirely at home with the Kingswells. "He had been there for upwards of a week, and was, in her estimation, a deserter from Lee's army." I passed boldly into the room. Mrs. Seaman started, blushed guiltily, and said deprecatingly :

"We came to ask if we should be permitted to see the little girl; I hear she is much worse; what a pity! the father should be sent for. Of course you anticipate the worst results. In my experience this malady has invariably proven fatal, though it is a disease which takes a long time to kill. Well, I'm sorry for Miss Kingswell, she was so fond of the little thing, and as I said before, it's a pity—if I could only see the mother—she's a young creature—I might tell her some things."

"Mrs. Seaman," I exclaimed with vehemence, "Mrs. Montana is very ill? Upon her mother and myself, in her father's absence, devolves the care of his child. I shall therefore assume the responsibility of denying you admission to her presence : you may sit here if you wish; excuse me, I must go to Ala."

The little thing manifested no more consciousness of the blisters on her little temples than if they had been wisps of paper. She was sleeping soundly when I entered. The grandmother bade me go at once to the cottage to Stanley, who had been confined to the house for several days with a severe cold, and give her information to allay her immediate fear concerning our darling. I spoke words of comfort to Mary, whose heart-cry was, "Oh! that Raymond was here;" then took my way down the garden-path, where the snow lay cold and white. I inquired if she had been to Ridgely recently? She replied that she had not. A few commonplaces, and then I left her to return to my charge. A few rods from the cottage I met the mysterious stranger going there by way of our private road. I started, sprang forward with a sudden impulse, then retreated with an ejaculation, I do not now remember what it was; I only know I found myself then and there *face to face with Clyde Ingram!*—him whom I mourned far off in his Southern grave. Had the dead really come back, or was he only the ghost of a former time standing there white and still before me? He offered me his hand; I could not take it, but gazed at him with wild, streaming eyes, until I saw the old, proud smile curling his bloodless lips, and heard his sarcastic tones ringing out chimes in that cold, winter day. Were we two doomed to misunderstand each other to the bitter end? In truth, it seemed fated that we should do so.

"And so you will not give me your hand, Aljean! Oh! I have wished so much to see you! though perhaps you do right to remind me that even the relations of friend and friend, existing between us when we parted, are changed now, very sadly. When wounded and left for dead upon the field, I failed to remember for a time the bitter truth; I only thought it would soothe me to look upon your face once more : I forgot that you regarded me as a traitor. My country's enemy I have been, and am still! but yours— never! not even when you tore my heart-strings by giving your love to another. No, I did not hate you then. He has been by my side, my faithful friend ever since I saw you last. I sympathize with you both, and regret your inevitable separation for so long. As for myself, I felt I must see you again : I have cheated death for that purpose; I am here, and you scorn me! What little is left of my possessions I bequeathe to you with my last blessing. I am no longer proud, Aljean, *but you are.* This very instant we must part, never to meet any more. I shall go my way now, you have heard my bequest—farewell."

"Stay!" I almost screamed; "I do not comprehend one half that you say, Clyde Ingram; but the strange fierce tides of mingled joy and sorrow surging through my heart and brain threaten to unhinge my reason. You must not, shall not go. What you have been, I know : what you are, I care not. I have things to tell you you will think strange to hear: but not now—not to-day; little Ala Ray—Raymond's child—is dying! come with me to her : I cannot stay away longer, and I do not want to leave you here." So saying, I catched his hand and kissed it with burning lips: a strange, beautiful light seemed breaking over his wan face, but it darkened into a frown when he remembered all things, for he said :

"No, no, *I cannot go there!* that is why we have not met before to-day. I shall see Stanley—I was going there when I saw you." I gave him my hand; his face had resumed its wonted expression of bitter patience : he held my fingers tightly in his clasp with a look that said, I still must wait; then went his way to the cottage. Once more in my own room. I knelt and thanked God fervently that the great seal of silence which sat upon those years; a hopeless hope, was broken at last: even though death should set another more enduring on his lips, it would not be cruel as the first.

Three laggard days, slowly dragging through their weight of suspense and anguish, had passed, yet we waited still the opening of the golden doors and the passing of Ala's soul beyond. On the noon-time of the fourth she awoke from her death-like stupor. I wrote a few words upon a slip of paper addressed to Clyde, and sent Jamie with it to Ridgely.

When the beautiful eyes of the child unclosed from their trance-like slumber, she saw her father, who knelt beside her in his great anguish. With one last effort she twined her thin arms about his neck, kissing and talking softly in her sweet caressing tones, as though he had never been away. Mary was almost wild with joy when she heard the loved voice still so long. Oh! we could none of us realize that our darling was going, even when her breath grew short and quick in sudden gasps. As for the father, his soul seemed wrenched from him; his hope, joy, life almost, had been hung on that little frail thing. He exclaimed wildly—

"Oh! my child, my Ala, do not, do not leave me."

A dark figure crept into the room unobserved, and knelt reverently upon the opposite side of the little couch.

"See! see, papa, that dark man—I saw him in my dream." Raymond lifted his eyes when he heard that angel voice. A frown heavy, terrible, like a gathering tempest, followed his swift recognition of Clyde.

"Take his hand, dear papa; he loves you—I am sure he

does; a bright, beautiful angel told it to me." Slowly the gloom cleared away from that father's brow: then there came upon his face a bright, brief gleam of the old brotherhood, mingled with unspeakable surprise. By one joint, God-given impulse, the brother hands met and clasped over the little form, and with her last sight she saw that it was so   Then a glorious brightness came upon her little face, and the sinking sun poured its red floods into the chamber. Wide open flew the pearly doors of the New Jerusalem: all the heavenly harps were attuned! angels chanted the triumphal chorus when the little spirit passed therein.

What conqueror, even though his blood-stained wreath of victory was dearly bought, had done what this sinless child, with only her little, loving heart to prompt her, and God to point her mission out, had accomplished! She had abridged floods of sectional hatred, and with her small, weak hands, had drawn together two brother hearts, wide asunder as the stars! Her reward was well begun. But oh! for us, with our darling gone, woe, misery unutterable! we felt it in all its length and depth and breadth as silently we knelt there, until the last tinge of color faded from the western heaven: then in the grey of descending twilight we saw the wan whiteness of death upon the little face smiling to us sweetly through its pallor. The portals closed after her, and we with our great sorrow were left all alone in the darkness of the night.

We will not linger upon the days that followed, the nights of watching, and the funeral. Once, strong man as he was, the father's tears fell like rain, when, as his idol was being borne slowly down the garden-way to the churchyard, he saw a few modest daisies struggling to blossom in the snow: she loved daisies, and they seemed waiting to salute her as she passed. God's fingers had gathered one daisy ere the grass grew green and the myrtle upon the gilead sides where the birds sang blithe in spring-time.

"See, Jennie, it has all come to pass as she said; I am here: but she—oh! would that I had not been forced to tear myself away from her when she was so soon to leave me alone!"

Gathered by that little grave-side, Mr. Kingswell's voice uprose in prayer; a prayer so fraught with faith, so blent and tremulous with hope—so frail and yet so strong, it seemed to lay hold on the eternal throne. Then, like dropping water or falling leaves in autumn, came the lulling spell-like words that told of resignation which was inevitable. We took up our burdens of life again and went back to the lonely house, where, in many yesterdays, she had been with us: but now it would be so no more. It was long before our darling's footprints faded from the starry homeway o'er which she passed to God.

For a week after Ala's death, Raymond was confined at home by the illness of his wife, during which time Clyde Ingram had never once left Ridgely. Stanley had resumed her school duties; and I vibrated, as usual, between brother and sister. I was with Stanley when Mrs. Seaman called to express her virtuous indignation that Mr. Kingswell should entertain a renegade nephew, who had borne arms against his country; which sentiment, she avowed, was shared by the community at large; the expression of which had been prevented, or rather delayed, on account of the calamity which had befallen the household. I drew my breath hard, with a bitter sense of outrage, while I listened to the animadversions of this fractious woman, upon the character and acts of those, "the latchet of whose shoes she was not worthy to unloose." I thought of Ala, became calm and subdued. There are many like Mrs. Seaman in the world; one must learn, sooner or later, to deal with them leniently; so I did; just as though, with profane feet, she walked not into the sanctuary of our sorrow.

Miss Phœbe came from Ridgely, bearing a note addressed in the clear chirography of Clyde's uncle. She had gone daily, since his visit to the cottage, to see the boy who was the apple of her old eyes. Without asking to be excused, I hastily perused the lines which summoned us three to his side. My heart sank down with a new apprehension. I bade Miss Phœbe hasten dinner, that we might go immediately. Mrs. Seaman took her place at the table, so anxious to learn something more concerning the subject which lay nearest her heart.

"I presume you are going to see that young man?"

"Yes, madam, I certainly shall not fail to meet my adopted brother, Col. Ingram, whom we all esteem; despite his position, an honorable gentleman!"

The old lady was completely nonplussed; something in my manner suddenly checked her propensity to be inquisitive concerning a matter in which our family alone should have become involved.

To do the old lady justice, I must say she was not bad-hearted in the main; only meddlesome, sometimes. Of late, she had been particularly gracious to Stanley; had sought her society in many instances. I think the manner in which that young girl had gone on in her quiet round of patient duty-doing, commanded her respect, as it had won homage from those who had formerly denounced her so fiercely. Mrs. Seaman was the mouth-piece of the Wayburn social circle; when its heart warmed towards Stanley, she was the first to admit they had wronged her, and to ask of the young girl toleration and forgiveness. Stanley was grateful for this change, since it increased her capacity for usefulness in the community; grateful, too, that her friends were no longer submitted to humiliation for her sake. Now she enjoyed a favoritism stronger in proportion than had been the original persecution.

When Stanley came home at noon-time, we three took silently our way to Ridgely. I had not been there since winter had settled cold and bleak around the great square house.. Now there were no wreathings about window or colonnade; only a few daisies, struggling with the snow, like the hope that was in my heart.

The excitement of meeting us all once more, of coming back to the haunts of his childhood, had borne Clyde up wonderfully for a fortnight; now this prop had failed him. He lay, white and still, with lines of suffering about his mouth, though his eyes were clear and undimmed. The marked change struck me dumb, when we were ushered into his presence. He feebly held out his hand; I pressed it to my lips; his head fell forward on his breast in the effort to rise; it was then I saw, what I had not before known—the ghastly wound, his bright hair stained with gore. My soul grew sick within me; then I realized how much I had scarce consciously counted upon his recovery. I signed Clyde's uncle to come with me to the parlor, and tell me all that he feared; there is no agony like suspense.

" It is a fearful wound—by mere chance has he escaped death until now. The skull is broken; we fear concussion constantly; then the pressure is at times so great as to produce delirium. Poor boy, he is well aware of his danger. Be calm; any outburst may bring on the result we dread so much."

I could not speak, but pressed his hand, and returned to

Clyde. By tacit consent they all withdrew, leaving us alone together. I held my breath, that I might not lose one syllable of what he uttered:

"Ah! Jennie, all my hopes and schemes in this world have come to naught; life is a failure. I promised my sainted mother I should achieve something in the conflict with it; but I could not. Now I shall take my place with the rank and file of an army that is gathering fast, silently; we shall never more be placed on duty in mortal conflict. For me the service will soon be over; the solitary ship has long drifted o'er the blood-red tides, gleaming through this dark night of strife, without rudder or compass to steer it towards the port beyond. You could not love me, Jennie; yet you alone will be near me when I cast my anchor over the boundary line. Behold! light is breaking yonder on the further strand, with its calm white swelling slopes of peace. I once thought you loved Hayne; then again, Lane Austin; now I think neither one nor the other, yet fear to ask you the question I should have asked you long ago. Read to me from the book my mother loved; ah, would that I had loved it too!"

I knew not where I read, for through the mist of falling tears I could not readily see my way; but he seized upon one sentence: "What is bound upon earth, shall be bound in heaven."

"Jennie, I asked you a question once; I told you the answer was for all time. That, now, is a myth! fate and death are narrowing down the brief space that is left to us. I have a few more days of life, then a higher hand shall open wide the doors of my soul's prison. Now I repeat that question! not for this little span of days, but for all eternity must the answer be. Have you ever loved?"

Truly souls are laid bare by death, the lashing scourge of

mortality. My voice was clear as the sounding roll of some far victory, when I said :

"Clyde, I have loved some one for long years, patiently, hopelessly, silently. Ever since you came to me in the light of a morning long ago by the golden river side, in our youth—I have loved you."

For a long time his great joy was still, then it found voice :

"Ah! I see it all now! How much of suffering had been spared me if this glorious truth had been revealed ere I came to stand upon the failing sands of another shore— another river gliding near—and I, a battle-scarred soldier, will soon pitch my tent upon the further side. Yet I solemnly swear of the world of women I have loved you—only you—and have sought or cared for none other. How I have waited and longed·for this day of final triumph! Now I ask you to let the answering love which you this hour avow, stand revealed in sight of God and man ; be mine! give me leave to hope that I may claim you in the life to come : in the great peace in which friend and enemy shall stand side by side again." He held out both his hands to me ! Over the great abyss which before had seemed to separate us, I saw a bridge of flowers. To our lives of patient waiting death had brought a rich reward, the breaking up of those great immutable silences whose chains had bound us in their thraldom. I promised to be all that he wished ; by that bed of dissolution I knelt in union with him. The tocsin sounding his release from an earthly prison, and the roll-call of heaven, were our marriage bells ! the peal and the pœan of our wedded lives on earth—in death. Grand and glorious over the everlasting hills of Zion shone the promise that he would be mine for all eternity, who had been mine for one short hour here. No fate should henceforth blot out the memory of this one blissful truth.

As I knelt the full tides of the winter's sun, reddening as he sank, came in at the casement and wrapped us in its beams. My eyes wandered from terrace and spire to the far New Hampshire hills, with a coronet of sunbeams about each crest, and the bright river which ran at their feet. The current ran golden 'neath the floods of light, streaming, it seemed, through a wide, open door in the heavens. Now, as I look back into the fading long ago, receiving the full glory of that hour, I can count still the pulses of eternity that throbbed in it.

To us, tried and purged as we had been, death would be no barrier, only a little longer waiting the fruition of hopes upspringing in life's sunset hour. By eternity's brink we stood, Clyde holding my hand very tightly, while the sun sank lower. The sands were falling, and the golden river gliding on, on, bearing to a swift, sure end, his frail remnant of vitality.

Thus they found us when Raymond, who had been summoned at Clyde's request, came up a short time afterwards. There by his side I kept my place while on earth he had need of me; we propped him up with pillows while he spoke to Raymond of what lay heaviest on his heart—bravely, fearlessly.

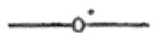

CHAPTER XXI.

"Death is the crown of life:
Were this denied, poor man would live in vain.
Death wounds to cure: we fall, we rise, we reign;
Spring from our fetters—fastened to the skies,
Where blooming Eden withers from our sight,
This king of terrors is the prince of peace."

YOUNG'S NIGHT THOUGHTS.

"RAYMOND, my brother, after all that has passed, we cannot meet as enemies in these last days of mine upon the earth. We learned our first lessons in life together, sheltered 'neath the same roof-tree. We have been friends from boyhood, yet are we bound by a still brighter link than this—it was woven by an angel's fingers—your child's. Notwithstanding all this, in obedience to the dictates of the powers you serve, by the authority vested in you, *I am your prisoner!* I have borne arms against the government whose loyal subject you are, whose protection I dare not claim! Do with me as you will. For the sake of all that has been and is, shrink not from your duty."

Raymond was fearfully pale, now that the issue, so long dreaded, was really come. He said not a word; only trembled visibly, as though the struggle between duty and the old love raged strong within him. It was evident these necessities had asserted themselves before, but his angel had joined their hands together. Must the pleading love of his dead child be set aside, and no shelter extended to his brother in his hopeless helplessness?

Clyde saw his struggle, and essayed to speak, with his thin hand resting on my bowed head.

"You have never asked me, brother, why I have subjected you to this fearful test. I had something I felt I must say

13

to this poor child. I was left for dead within the enemy's lines; I had nowhere else to go; I did not pause to inquire whether or not I would be an unwelcome guest in the house of my old friend; or that you, who had been reared in the home of my father, should feel it to be your sacred duty to send me forth an outcast, or retain me as your prisoner. When I came to Ridgely I did not expect to die here; I thought it would all be over; I should have said my say, and gone my way long since—this feverish wound has proved too strong for me. In the first instance, I meant only to remain here a few hours; but for the illness of the child, I should have completed my errand in your absence. Now, since I have told you why I am here, I will tell you how it came to pass.

"Oh! it was a fearful contest, that preceding my fall; the men fought grandly on both sides. I have led my braves through many a gauntlet of Federal shot and shell, but never were their breasts bared to volleys like those. A ball struck my horse; I fell with him; the wound on my head is a sabre cut, which left me entirely insensible. I wore no uniform, consequently I was left with the heaps of dead and dying on the slaughter-ground. The last thing I remember was my faithful horse laying his head upon the shoulder of the orderly who always groomed him when in camp, who lay dead by my side. Twenty days later, Col. Austin found them thus, man and beast; hence the supposition of my death. How long I lay unconscious I know not; when I awoke, as from a trance, there was a woman, stately and beautiful, bending over me; she assisted me to her carriage, then conveyed me to a house near at hand. It was Retta Austin, the Colonel's sister. During the reign of Gen. Butler, the family had removed to their plantation in Georgia. She informed me that Gen. Johnston had breakfasted there the morning upon which I left camp, proclaiming in angry tones the sentence which awaited me for having disobeyed orders; and pursued the foe to what he foresaw would be certain destruction. Retta was well aware a court-martial awaited me should I return to my allegiance, even were such a thing possible, with the whole of Sherman's army between them and me. She therefore set about preparing a complete disguise, which I adopted; then insisted upon my appropriating enough of her gold to insure me an unsuspicious passage North. Of course I am very much obliged to her for her kindness, though I believe the girl is half demon. She vaunted her hatred for the Yankees in a manner that quite surprised me. She even boasted of having broken the engagement between Stanley and Hayne. Her treachery has been amply repaid by the restless misery which consumes her now.

"I paused nowhere by the way, until I found myself at Montreal. There I lay prostrate for months, gradually growing more wasted. I asked my physician to tell me frankly what I might depend upon. He informed me I had not weeks to live. I motioned him to leave me, rose at once to prepare for my journey hither. You know the rest.

"Upon leaving Claremont you remember my regiment was encamped at Brightland. I received what I considered an excellent cash offer for my city property. I sold it to prevent an ultimate transfer to strangers. Claremont with its flowers and fountains, blue sky and distant stretch of sea, was purchased by an old friend of our family. He was a distinguished rebel; his property was confiscated and has since been converted into a barracks for the soldiery. If I had not sold it just when I did the loss would have been ours. Brightland I retained. Here is a deed, Raymond, executed two years ago. Brightland is yours! You can claim it should we ever have peace again. The gold for which I sold Claremont and its belongings—horses, furniture, conservatory, all things partaining thereto, amounting to fifty thousand dollars—you will find at Brightland. The old female servants, including Aunt Dinah and Hawsy, are there still! They are true, and will show you where the money is buried. Though for fear they may have been removed, I will give you a plot of the ground containing the deposit. Sand-banks are the only banks which in seasons of war do not discount their paper, more especially when the deposits are all in specie currency. Now I have said all I wish to say, nothing remains but the exercise of the power vested in you; you are my executor. See to it that the girls are put in possession of this money, and that it is properly invested for their future needs. I am your prisoner! If you fail to claim me as such I must go elsewhere to die; I cannot think of subjecting you to the censure—punishment perhaps—which an omission of this nature must necessarily bring upon you."

Raymond was agonized beyond expression; Clyde's consideration for him was so delicate, his generosity so great, even as his enemy his brotherly affection so strong! It would be worse than traitorous to set aside all these considerations and put the law in force. How could he do what it seemed needful to do? Why was this horrible alternative between duty and the old brotherhood presented? When I looked upon Clyde's pale face I could only exclaim:

"Oh! Raymond, you will not, you *cannot* do this thing. You say that Clyde is unchanged; when leagues divided you, you felt him to be your enemy. Now that you have ceased for the time being to view things from a national

stand-point—have allowed individual issues to assert themselves—you know that he has never been so in reality; that
what you and he feel as representatives of belligerent sections, affects very little those natural ties which are stronger
than life itself. That no conjuncture of circumstances
could ever make you less to each other than you now are.
Then wherefore exists a necessity for this thing?"

Oh! if, instead of the calculating heads which plan and
prosecute this war, the bleeding hearts of the revolution
were permitted to assert themselves, and obey the sweet
promptings of affection, in the opinion of those who suffer
peace would not be long in coming. Lips, now hopelessly
mute, might give utterance to their wild prayers; and the
hero hands that supplicate so dumbly while striking inevi-
tably those round whom their heart-strings fondly twine,
might give heed to the clamorings of voices louder than
the clarion notes of triumph. I speak of the many who
suffer for the crimes of those who deserve to suffer. Raymond left the room, but returned presently with the war-
worn banner he had held at Fredericksburg.

"Clyde, I would give all I possess to-day to have you
share our hospitality under the folds of this old flag, as a
friend to the country, whose symbol it is. Like yourself,
my brother, its days of service are over, but we retain and
love it still. You have poured your volleys into it while
we held fast the standard in many a fierce charge; but of
this we will not think to-day. Give homage to the old
banner during the remnant of your life, brother; be the
prodigal of our household! Receive our blessing and
God's joint birth-right to a higher inheritance than you,
in your noble generosity, have conferred upon us."

Clyde answered him, speaking very sorrowfully:

"You will, perhaps, discredit my words, though I tell

you solemnly, brother, I have no feeling of hatred for our
common country; and I love that old flag for the many
times that I have seen it proudly waving over the whole
land, and from the mast-head of ships in which we crossed
seas together, though I cannot in honor now swear
fidelity to that which I have desecrated by raising my hand
to strike it in the dust. I was in the Southern army because circumstances rendered it imperative that I should be
there. My lot was cast with them. I have fulfilled my
destiny. I do not feel myself to be a coward! And not
to save my own life, or to spare pain to those I love, would
I skulk behind an assumption of loyalty which my acts
have already disproved."

Raymond said no more on the subject; though they
talked almost gaily of the time that was long past and the
days that were ended.

Clyde waited; Raymond struggled with his stern duty
and his sorrow. One Sabbath morning, warm and balmy
in March, we sat with open casements listening to the
Wayburn bells. The sun shone brightly without, and in
our two hearts was joy unspeakable. Oh! it was so blissful to be beloved. Clyde drew me to him, saying:

"God is very good to us, Jennie." A closer nestling in
his fragile clasp was my only answer; there was a glamour
in the air about me; I thought I was dreaming, when I
heard voices inquiring for Mr. Kingswell in tones that were
loud and harsh. They were shown into the library adjoining; the door was slightly ajar, we could hear plainly all
they said.

"You have not been to church for many weeks; why is
this?" inquired the deacon, Mr. Seaman, who had a cold
in his head and talked through his nose most woefully. Mr.
Kingswell replied in tones that were courteous yet firm:

"During the illness of my little grandchild, my Sabbath services were given almost exclusively to her; later, I have had with me a relative who is so ill as to require my constant care. I think, Mr. Seaman, our first duty to God lies in these ministrations to our suffering fellow-men."

"It is evident you feel so, sir; perhaps you are right; as for myself, I cannot exactly appreciate humanity exercised at the expense of Christian principle."

"Excuse me, sir, I do not understand you; be kind enough to speak plainly. In the exercise of these holy duties I do not feel that I have made any sacrifices of principle, or failed in my duty to God."

"Let him alone: he is joined unto his idols!" exclaimed Elder Bridgewater, in guttural tones resembling distant thunder. "Come away, he will not hear us; he is wedded to his sin." I grew blind and sick at heart; remembering the conversation of Mrs. Seaman on one or two occasions, I knew to what the self-righteous Pharisee referred.

"I do not understand you, gentlemen; of what am I accused?"

"A few minutes since you did not deny having that man, that spy, that double traitor, Colonel Ingram, here under your own roof; and gave your care of him as an excuse for your omissions in the Church of God. Now you ask hypocritically, of what am I accused?"

"I certainly never meant to deny the fact that my nephew is here under my roof, and will remain here while he lives. Be he what he may, or rather what he might have been, Colonel Ingram is, I fear, fatally wounded, and beyond the power of harming any one." Mr. Kingswell's fearless avowal of these facts somewhat surprised them, and disarmed, in a measure, their malignity; at all events they

were slow to speak again. At length, the pompous old
elder, whose main characteristics were sanctity, gold spec
tacles, ebony cane, voice grim and guttural, with much tug-
ging at his neck-tie, delivered himself as follows:

"Notwithstanding all you say, Mr. Kingswell, painful as
it may be, we have our duty to perform. The church had a
called meeting yesterday evening, and they appointed a com-
mittee of **two** to wait upon you at your residence and inform you of the proceedings of said meeting. What I have
to say is this. Unless you expel from your domicil that
traitor, from your bosom that serpent, you will be accused
before the Church of God, and your fault dealt with in no
very lenient manner. Now, by the holy Church **whose in-**
terests you have served, of which you have long **been a**
consistent member, ponder well what I have said—let it
weigh——"

"Just this far, gentlemen, no further. I have, as you
say, lived long in the Church; I should regret that anything
should come to mar the harmony of my life there; yet I
have ever been influenced by a higher authority than the
law and creed of said Church. I have come this day to feel
as I felt once before, that an edifice claiming to be **the**
sanctuary of God may possess external evidence, but
nothing of the spirit of the Great Master, who cast, as you
did, no stone at the erring, whom you would not have
bidden as He did, to 'go and sin no more.' You would
drive such not only from the world's clemency, but from
God's. **Is your spirit** consistent with that of true Christianity, manifested by the old patriarch, who killed the
fatted calf when his prodigal returned? Is there any room
in your heart, filled full of altars reared to the God of the
upright, for the weary wanderer who perchance would lay
aside his sin and come back to the forsaken way, were your

strong hands but outstretched to receive him? any room for the exercise of that justice, which 'as ye mete to others shall be meted unto you again?' any charity for the unrepentant transgressor for whom a God died? If within His tabernacles on the earth I stand condemned for what I have done and am doing, then deal with me as you like: my conscience sustains me; to a higher tribunal will I appeal. God is not only just, and kind, and loving; he has not closed the doors of his great heart upon those for whom the way and the warfare proved too much. I have done. May the Father in his mercy strengthen and sustain me!"

Ah! and he will, dear noble heart. Here was manifest the spirit which all my life I had recognised and worshipped in Clyde's uncle. The high moral integrity which ever characterized his dealings with his fellow-men, was nothing compared to his soul of justice and charity. I crept close to him, kissed his hand reverently, then led him to where Clyde lay, calm-faced, patiently awaiting. He, too, looked and spoke proudly the man that was in him.

"Uncle, I am glad for the trial that has come to you, and the noble words that I have heard you speak. I am enabled now to see my way and duty clearly; no false scruples of honor shall deter me from the performance of that duty. As regards the great crime for which I stand condemned, I leave that to God. May my transgression be blotted out by this return to my allegiance. Send for my brother, his wish shall be respected; in due form will I swear to support the old flag; and ere I die we will shake hands once more under its starry folds."

Long and sweet was the conference that ensued. Thus came peace to our household. Sweet Ala Ray, what had not thy blessed influence accomplished!

Long protracted had been the struggle with duty in

Raymond's heart; he could not bring himself to arrest Clyde; his brother should be permitted to die in peace, even though he suffered court-martial for the omission.

He had promised his little daughter he would come home to stay when the daisies bloomed; he sent on his resignation, which was accepted previous to the expiration of his term of service.

His gratitude was boundless when he learned the purpose for which he was summoned a second time; his banner had spoken for him; his country was vindicated; so was his brother.

Not so, however, in the estimation of those self-righteous men who had expostulated with Mr. Kingswell in the morning. They returned at nightfall, with a detachment of home guards from a neighboring town, and demanded that Col. Ingram should be delivered up to them. Raymond, strangely moved, advanced to the leader, with drawn sword, bade him halt and await his commands. Messrs. Seaman and Bridgewater, from the rear, made use of some impatient and rather unchristian-like expletives, which, however, availed them little. Thus they kept guard until morning.

Within—ah! within, the man's spirit was leaving its clay; peacefully, gently, as the child who went before, his soul passed away. All night we watched, until the morning; then there was only the white face of the dead, and the morning of a new life. Very calmly he slept the pale sleep, and we spread the old flag over him as he lay there.

"Gentlemen," said Raymond, in a harsh, stern voice, advancing a second time to where the guard stood waiting, "allow me to conduct you to the prisoner."

They came into the death-chamber, followed by the

deacon and the elder, who looked so abashed and crest-
fallen, it was piteous to behold them.

"Gentlemen," continued Raymond, "this little handful
of dust is what you have been warring with for days and
weeks; bring your strength to bear upon it; scatter it to
the winds; he was a traitor, but one who came, when death
pressed him hard, to clasp the hand of his mother's son,
and die under the folds of the old flag. When you have
satisfied yourselves, you may withdraw; this prisoner whom
you sought is my comrade and *brother;* with the honors
of war he shall be buried."

And thus was buried Clyde Ingram, of Claremont.

———o———

CHAPTER XXII.

"'Tis morning again on the tents and the spears,
  But the soldier's voice is for ever still—
There's a form that is missed from our cavaliers;
  There's a sweet face blurred with its bitter tears;
    There's a new-made grave on the hill."
                            COL. HAWKINS, C. S. A.

THIS wail kept ringing through my heart, low and plaintive as the voice of spring, which came not as our Southern springs; true, the dun skies cleared into blue, birds
sang, and flowers upsprang at the sunbeam's touch, yet
there was in the air a haze as of slow falling tears; broken
wreaths of snow lay on the new-made graves long after we
counted the pulses of coming warmth; until the slopes
were green, and verdure clothed the far New Hampshire
hills, and distant fens gathered mossy sprays. I thought
how the cypress bloomed in coral clusters in our far-off

Southern home, while we gathered their black garlands in
another land. Where were the orange blossoms on our
home shore, from which the gulf rolled waves of green to
a wide, wide reach of sea? Alas! neither of us would
ever wear one little wreath of the bright symbols that had
grown about our youth. Stanley's white wreath—another
had worn it; my garland was of cypress. To us were left
only memories of the days that had been; that would be
no more; and—

OUR DEAD.

"Nothing is our own; we hold our pleasures
  Just a little while, ere they are fled;
One by one life robs us of our treasures;
  Nothing is our own except our dead.

They are ours, and hold in faithful keeping,
  Safe for ever, all they took away.
Cruel life can never stir that sleeping;
  Cruel time can never seize that prey.

Justice pales; truth fades; stars fall from heaven;
  Human are the great whom we revere;
No true crown of honor can be given,
  Till the wreath lies on a funeral bier.

How the children leave us—and no traces
  Linger of that smiling angel band;
Gone, for ever gone; and in their places,
  Weary men and anxious women stand.

Yet we have some little ones, still ours;
  They have kept the baby smile, we know,
Which we kissed one day, and hid with flowers,
  On their dead white faces long ago.

When our joy is lost, and life will take it,—
  Then no memory of the past remains,

Save with some strange, cruel things, that makes it
   Bitterness beyond all present pains.

Death, more tender-hearted, leaves to sorrow,
   Still the radiant shadow, fond regret;
We shall find, in some far bright to-morrow,
   Joy that he has taken, living yet.

Is love ours, and do we dream we know it,
   Bound with all our heart-strings, all our own?
Any cold and cruel dawn may show it,
   Shattered, desecrated, overthrown.

Only the dead hearts forsake us never:
   Love, that to death's loyal care has fled,
Is thus consecrated ours for ever,
   And no change can rob us of our dead.

So when fate comes to besiege our city,
   Dim our gold, or make our flowers fall,
Death, the Angel, comes in love and pity,
   And to save our treasures, claims them all.
                LITTELL'S LIVING AGE.

Yes, our dead were ours in truth; though a wide rough world lay between us, yet how brightly shone hope on the journey o'er which we should pass to join them in one of those far bright to-morrows, whose nights were under the eternal stars. There was no denying the space in my life; a space all shadowed by a grave in spring-time; though the chords of my soul were swept by a spirit-hand, and that space outstretching towards the broad everywhere in the dim-lying future, could be filled by no lesser radiance. I had loved him! There was glory in that one great truth, which no after prevarication could cancel or circumstance annul; the destiny of two souls lay in its wide compass. I knew that I lived on in that dead heart, passed beyond the reach of time and change. It was a higher will than chance that placed this burden on my life. There was enough of joy in this consciousness to palliate the hunger in my desolate heart. God, who is God of the vanquished, **as** well as of the victor and the fallen, was his God; in this trust there was a holy peace.

Another change had come to pass in Raymond's home; a little daughter was added to the household. Before Ala died the parents had wished for a son! Now they were glad it was otherwise. Little Jamie, Leah's child, had been adopted as their own; not to fill the lost one's place, we could **not** have borne that—but he had grown into our hearts strangely of late. Leah's gratitude was boundless, but William Kingswell never heard her thanks, though it was he who brought the matter about.

This spring-time brought home Frederick Seaman from a long tarrying over seas. He had made a great deal of money. **Not** daring to visit Leah in person, he wrote several letters, asking for her hand; proposing to relinquish all claims to the child, which bore its mother's name. Leah manifested the true dignity, latent in her character, by omitting to give heed to his proposals in whatever shape they came. He had wooed and won her once, and then betrayed her trusting love. For her faith in him she had endured years of ignominy and shame; he exhibited no penitence that he had caused her to suffer. She had been weak, very weak, but now she could be strong, for right was on **her** side. By our aid she had worked her way up from mazes of sin, and stood firmly in God's clear light once more. We were rejoiced to feel that our confidence was not misplaced.

Captain Bob Eldridge, on his death-bed, sent for William Kingswell. I was at Ridgely when the summons came. Poor old man, whose sense of shame was stronger than the ties of natural affection—who could never bring himself to exercise forgiveness towards others, not even his own kindred, now had need himself to be forgiven. He had come down to that last strait in life when we all feel more or less our dependence and reliance upon one another. When Clyde's uncle went to him I pleaded to go too; I had found my way by his side, up many a steep of suffering, since Clyde left me in the wide world, with no destiny only to work my way to him once more.

I had not seen Capt. Bob since we went to ask of him a home for Leah and her nameless child. Now I pitied the old man from my soul; over those stormy gorges of passion he had not found the pathway clear to God's love and peace. He had gone down hill ever since; the room yawned with the meagreness of its few articles of furniture. He lay upon a miserable pallet, made of blankets soiled and torn—the grey old miser, alone in crowds, and childless in sight of his children; in want, with plenty to make him independent. A few minutes after we entered, a young man came in, bringing a bowl of gruel from a neighboring restaurant. I observed him narrowly while he ministered to the feeble old man, who vouchsafed a few words to him in return for his kindness.

"Now lay me down, Fred." Then, turning to Mr. Kingswell, he said in tones broken with misery:

"Of all the friends and messmates who flocked about me in my days of prosperity, he alone has volunteered to stand by me in this bitter hour."

Ah! thought I, long years ago he had denied his only child that privilege, and Fred. Seaman was the cause thereof. He looked abashed in presence of Mr. Kingswell, and said, half-apologetically, with a dash of his old spirit: (I realized who it was that poor Leah so loved. Oh, had his prineiple been strong enough to sustain those generous and tender impulses, how different it might have been with both! Perchance they had not then come under the hard ban of the transgressor.)

"I found the old man on the street when I returned from abroad. He, you are well aware, is father to the woman who should have been my wife. I have come often to his shelter-tent, and shall continue to do so while he needs me, **which, I imagine,** will not be for long. He wished **to see** you—that is why I sent the message which you have so promptly responded to. I do not think he is quite satisfied that I am by his side, though if I had not chanced to be here he might have died alone. Mr. Kingswell, you are a good man, a God-fearing man ; you will acquit **me in** this matter of any motive save that of trying, in a very slight measure, to atone for the wrong done to parent and child. I do not want the wealth **that** he has hoarded; I could never be brought to touch **a** penny of it; I should accept nothing save that which he once refused to bestow upon me—which, after having won, I trifled away, because I had not moral strength to keep it. **This** gift and favor you may have it in your power to confer upon me ; at least, you may influence matters **to** that end, when I have repurchased my integrity, and earned an honest man's right to ask it of you, who, for a long time, have been her only friend. Almost six years ago, when you picked me up on the hillside, a miserable drunkard, and I heard your pitying words, **I resolved to do this** thing, though there were scores of good Pharisees crying: 'He is lost!' Ah, yes! Lost, with God's world around me, and my manhood within ; lost, because they refused to lift me from my fallen estate and stand me on my feet again; lost, because at the mandate of such, society had barred her gates against me, and against the woman whom passion, not love, had profaned; and upon the brow of each of us had written that damning word—outcast! No, no; not all lost! In the mazes of my beastly intoxication, I heard your words ringing clear in my understanding heart:

'When I see a man thus debased and fallen, I do not feel like thanking God that I am not as that man is, but that I have not been tempted as he has been.'

"Ah, sir, those words saved me! Not feeling strong enough to climb the steep passes to the world's favor here, I fled from temptation. Since I crossed the ocean I have not tasted ardent spirits. From my old boon companions, who did not forget me, I learned how the same disciple who had uplifted me in my sorrowful abasement, had taken to his own home the victim of my wrong. I resolved to show you that there is no man, however low he may have fallen, who, by a little timely aid, may not reform, if there are any to point the way. Had you spurned me, as did others of your set, I might now be consumed by those still fires which the waters of repentance sometimes fail to quench."

"Who dare be silent, when by chance they may speak so strong a word for God and man?" thought I, while young Seaman continued to talk:

"There is a secret which not even poor Leah knows; the old man may tell you—I have done;" though he stood still holding his hat as though there was something he would say. Then in a husky voice, through which trickled the tears that were in the hazy air of that spring-time, he continued:

"If you will allow me, I would like to ask you about Leah, though I feel that she is much too good for me. I should not come a second time to seek her, did I not be-

lieve her, of all the women I have ever known, the most virtuous—the most upright by nature. No man, unless by
the same avenues of her strong love through which I led
her, could ever win her as I did. Knowing this, I supplicate of you the gift of her hand in marriage. I will not
ask this of her father; had he not once denied Leah to me,
it might have been different. My mother is anxious and
willing now to receive her as my wife. As for the child, I
am glad for his sake that your son has adopted him; I
have forfeited the right to claim him. I shall hear your
decision."

"Nobody shall claim the right to provide for that child
except myself," exclaimed Captain Bob, almost fiercely.
"My money shall be his! Since poor Alice died, and
Leah left me, I have toiled on for his sake to this end. My
old, desolate heart yearned over him; but I gave no sign,
for he was in William Kingswell's house." Then turning
to Clyde's uncle: "Send the girl away—I have something
I must say: the night is coming on, and I would be alone
with you."

It was growing late and we left them, Fred and I—the
righteous and the unforgiving together—and came down
the hill trampling the daisies of spring beneath our feet.
I had been both pleased and affected at the young man's
recital; so much so, I promised to use my influence with
Leah for his sake. Thus it came about, that this man,
whom I had long held in superstitious horror, aloof from
my thoughts even, because of his wrong to my friend,
now that I had met him face to face, and saw suffering
where before I had seen only sin; had recognised his generous self-abnegation, his tender love and manly truth;
I found myself espousing his cause ere I was aware of it.
I had come, reader, to feel what we all must, should those

in whom we have an interest err and fall—to separate the sinner from the fault, and not confound the first wrong step which may be retraced, with an after career of abandonment. I trust none of us can have sympathy or affiliation with hardened guilt; yet it is only Christian-like to discriminate between those who sin from impulse against principle, and those who have no principle to violate.

During our walk home, Fred told me what I was puzzled and confounded to hear, exhorting me, at the same time, not to repeat it until the season came in which it might be revealed. That night, with Stanley's golden head lying close to mine, looking over the starry way to heaven, I pondered of that strange revelation.

Mr. Kingswell prevailed upon Captain Bob to see Leah. Thus, in the presence of God and the dying, she and Fred renewed their vows. Little Jamie, too, was brought by Raymond to kiss the withered cheek of his grandsire. He returned home carrying a bag well filled with gold coin, which the old man had given him with his own hand just before he passed away. After that conference with William Kingswell, Captain Bob Eldridge seemed well contented to go, and waited patiently for the time to come when his master should call him. I know not what Clyde's uncle said to him from time to time, but the messages were those of peace, which came with its golden tides coursing like the river of my dream which broke its billows, now, on dim, far shores of the eternal. The members of that widely-sundered band were drawn together by the shining links of that peace, bound fast for time to come. Then by the grave in the field where the poor of Wayburn were buried, another grave was made, and two white stones reared side by side in the spring-time : the voice that had prayed that strange, solemn prayer of faith when Ala slept, was up-raised here.

After a few days—in the old church, in the bright village green—Leah and Fred were married. In the very presence of Mr. Seaman and those who had dared to cry her down, she became the wife of this young man, who belonged to one of the first families in the place. Notwithstanding the array of hollow smiles and malicious home-thrusts incident to such occasions, there were many who were rejoiced that it was so, and who gave it as their opinion that Leah had only been justly dealt by. Mrs. Seaman said she always felt that Leah was a good girl, and ought to be encouraged; so my friend, bearing no resentment, accepted the proffered hand of the woman who had always treated her in her neighbor's house as in her own, as a menial, whose presence she could barely tolerate. But that was all passed now; Leah was justified by the world that had renounced her.

I met Clyde's uncle in the graveyard, one afternoon. He led me to a seat, very tender in manner; he saw the tears upon my cheek.

"Jennie, I honor you for those tears; I know how true to the dead your heart is, but you will, in time, become reconciled to the decree of Providence. You will love again; you will marry."

I was wounded; he felt that I was, for he took my hand, saying:

"I must tell you the story of my youth; I believe there is some such cross in every life. We learn to bear it; grow accustomed to the burden; it is but just and right that it should be so."

"Such a cross in every life? Surely not in yours?"

"Yes; one that well nigh drove me mad."

"Long years ago, in a seaport town, I lived with my pious parents and only sister, in an old homestead, very quaint and curiously wrought, after the Puritan fashion. My father was generous and high-souled, a kind husband, a strong staff to my mother, who was blind. He had brought her from Scotland; a minstrel of wondrous beauty, he seemed to love her more for her entire dependence on him. In my sister there was early manifest a strange disposition to wander from the home-ways; whenever she heard a snatch of a song our mother had sung to us, she would follow the sound until she found the singer. Once or twice she lost herself in the vain attempt, and we were compelled to summon assistance in seeking her out. Alice grew up very beautiful! Hers was a strange, classic beauty, superb in repose, and when animated is what men will dare all things and die for. Several gentlemen of wealth and refinement, in our circle, sought her hand; she gave heed to none of them, for her heart was untouched. It remained so until a stranger of great beauty—a wonderful singer, a sailor by occupation—knowing that we would never consent to the arrangement, sought her clandestinely. They had met by chance; the acquaintance was well begun ere our knowledge of it. With that perverseness which had always characterized her, my beautiful sister gave to the untaught sailor that which others had sought for in vain. He laughingly boasted of having won

"'The girl who gave to song what gold could never buy.'

"We forbade him to see her again; then came the sequel: she fled with him, leaving no line to relieve our suspense. I had never believed his intentions to be honorable towards my sister; now, of course, we feared the worst, and the shame bowed me to the very dust. My grief was purely selfish; I was engaged to a beautiful girl, whose parents withdrew their sanction to our union because of the ignominy that had come upon our house.

"In my fierce sorrow, I thought only of my own hard loss, and did not pity, as I should have done, our poor, blind mother, who sat helplessly, day after day, moaning with hands outstretched piteously towards the sea, over which we supposed Alice had gone; and the old father, who stooped lower daily with the weight that was growing upon him. Ere long, we received a taunting letter from Alice's betrayer, which I did not answer. Then one from her, in which she made no mention of her fault, even spoke as though she had not committed one, telling me she was very happy in her European home. This so exasperated me, I wrote to her bitterly, angrily, that she should never again manifest to me, by word or deed, the humiliating fact that we abode in the same world together. I afterwards regretted my harshness, when repentance was of no avail; and not until other years with their trials came, did I realize how unkind I had been to my parents and to her. The grass grows green upon their graves now; that old home has long been desolate.

"Oh! how I mourned my broken dream! Sorrow passed, leaving me only despair. I was too proud to supplicate for the hand that had once been given me; yet only God knew what I suffered in the sundering of those bright bonds. She had been brought to believe that I no longer wished that she should be my wife. Nothing but this reflection could have induced her to relinquish me; my coldness and silence confirmed the belief incited by the doubts of her parents.

"They made known their wishes; she, gentle, yielding,

became the wife of a rich and elegant Southerner. I thought my heart was broken! I fled before the profanation of my high hopes. I left home—came away from the hated scenes. Here, in this lovely spot, through its vales of quietness, by the rolling river-side and the light of morning on those far hills, I found my way to God after a few years. When the Father had given me strength to go, I went home and remained until the old people were gone. She, too, was gone, my beautiful Edith, with her proud, haughty husband, to his southern home. Her grave is there now, under the flowers of this spring-time.

"Long afterwards, when it was little triumph to know the fact, I learned how deeply she had loved me. She wrote, on the death of her husband, telling me all; asking me to be a father to her husband's son. That son was *Clyde Ingram!* She afterwards married your uncle; Raymond and Stanley were *her* children. I loved them, but not as I loved Clyde—he was my own: his youth was passed with me here. You, Jennie, have often called me Clyde's uncle! I was your own as much as his. Shortly after Edith's second marriage, I married Mary Mellville, whom I met on my return home, and brought her back with me to Wayburn. She has been a good and true wife, and we have lived happily in the performance of our duties to each other and to God. There was in my feeling for her none of the wild, clinging tenderness of the former passion, but something deeper, truer, more enduring than the first. She is very dear to me now. Towards my son, the best beloved of my heart, I have performed the last duty. He never knew quite how well I loved him, or how I prayed after he had taken that one wrong step that he might come back to us, if only to die. My prayer, thank God, was granted.

"As for my sister, I am rejoiced to know she did not fall. Captain Bob Eldridge, whom we knew, was Alice's lawful husband; and Leah, the homeless outcast, to whom we gave shelter, was her child.   Jennie, I have often read that sacred promise, 'Cast thy bread upon the waters and it shall return after many days.' Who could have guessed that little act of kindness would be thus requited; that we were extending charity to those of our own household!

"Then we two came and stood by the graves; every life is growing fuller of them in these battle-days; the land seems one great burial-place.

"Our baby minstrel is singing to-night!   I often hear her little voice, and fancy I see her sweet eyes looking to me from the world of light: the radiance nestles and warms my soul."

For me the altar-fires of another love, too, were burning as we came up the broad street to Ridgely. I saw the fair round moon far over the New Hampshire hills, and the bright river ran crystal clear to the distant sea. The lights of our home shone sweetly as we came from the shadows without into their brightness.

---o---

CHAPTER XXIII.

"Thou art the friend
To whom the shadows of long years extend."
BYRON'S CHILDE HAROLD.

IT was the anniversary of Stanley's birthday. Our cottage was lovely to see; we had woven wreaths for its pictures, and in each vine-trellised window we placed a nosegay of flowers from the garden walk, over which an angel's feet had lately passed. Miss Phœbe, arrayed in her favorite gown, was preparing tea for our expected guests.

First came Leah and Frederick, serenely happy; then Raymond, proud and handsome, with Mary, on whose face was the bloom of her youthful beauty, bringing their bright-haired boy and baby girl; a happy family, sorrow-chastened, but happy still. Then came Mr. and Mrs. Kingswell, calm, serene, as usual.

Stanley was engaged in conversation with George Seaman, younger son of our old friend, who had avenged Stanley on his mother, by falling in love with her. The old lady, however, strongly urged the matter, and devoted all her energies to bring about this union. She worked assiduously. Miss Phœbe maliciously insinuated that she seemed more anxious after becoming aware of Clyde Ingram's legacy to us. I could not fail to observe how intently she watched them, from a settee, over her round, bowed spectacles; her countenance evincing the satisfaction she could not conceal. Well, she might have gone further, and found for her son no lovelier bride. Stanley was very beautiful that night. She wore a muslin of pure white, relieved only by brooch and pendants of jet; her curls flowed; again the bright crimson shone through her clear cheeks, and her eyes were bright as stars, lighted with a hope she could not have defined, and did not understand. Here beau-cavalier remarked this, and she answered him gaily:

"It is my dress, I presume; well, I have worn black for three years, and worked hard; I feel free to-night, mysteriously happy; why, I cannot say."

"I wish I dared to hope that my presence——"

He ceased to speak. Mr. Milverton came in; in my greetings of him, I failed to perceive, for the rooms were

14

filling rapidly, that a stranger hadstepped in at the bay-window, which opened on the garden path. He stood holding his hat, heavily shrouded with crape, silently regard-ing the scene, himself unperceived. His hungry eyes were fixed on Stanley, as she gracefully crossed the room, with young Seaman, to welcome Milverton. He heard the officious mother say:

"Oh, yes! I am sure they will be married very soon; of course Miss Montana will not refuse my son; I know she thinks the world of him, and he worships the very ground she walks on."

Just then the young man restored her fan, which she chanced to let fall. She thanked him, with a slight inclina-tion of her queenly head, and the smile so radiant it dazzled him more than her words. Both were misconstrued by the haughty stranger, who, in a paroxysm of intense pain, retreated, unrecognised. Milverton soon made known to me the facts in the case; then I went into the garden to search for the renegade, whom I found pacing the walks like a madman. After shaking his hand warmly, and expressing my pleasure that we had met again, I said reproachfully:

"Cousin Warren, is this your return for the love of that heart that was so true to you, even in its hopelessness?"

"Ah, Jennie, you know not how madly I love that woman; as a girl she was never half so dear to me; now to see an insipid villain sueing for her smiles; and I cast off, forgotten."

"Warren, for Heaven's sake, desist; are you deranged? remember Stanley had no right to cherish of you the frailest memory. By so doing she would sin less against another than her own peace of mind. You forget she does not know that you are free; I myself was not aware of it until you came here to-night."

"That is sufficient reason for her having eschewed the memory of her former friend."

"Warren, you are as unreasonable as ever; she is coming. I bade Milverton send her to me here: conceal yourself in the summer-house."

He obeyed. She came singing down the garden-way, her golden waves of hair brightening in the moonlight. How like a time of old breathed the enchantment around us to-night.

"Well, Jennie darling, what do you happen to want of me? I left Mr. Milverton to play hostess in my place, while I came in answer to your summons."

"Oh, a fit of musing blues, perhaps, drove me forth. I have been thinking of that first summer so long gone, and of the other things that have so changed since then."

"Try not to think about it at all, dear; it only makes you sad. I try not to do so."

"Nevertheless, that old dream of yours, Stanley, you have not forgotten."

"Oh! would that I could forget it, or that the memory was not so hopeless; for, Jennie, a vision often crosses my daily work, of how another head is pillowed on the heart that should have been my own. It is very hard to think of, though. I am afraid I shall never be strong enough to live and remember no more 'what might have been.'"

Ah! cypress flowers entwined with her orange wreath; these withered where the fountain showered its diamond spray in drops that were countless as the tears we wept for that shadowy, unreal "might have been."

"Think of it no more, dearest, all that was so vain in the past; greater happiness awaits you; a joy that will not leave you, dear, as that did. Do not start, do not scream. Warren Hayne is a free man—his wife has been dead for fifteen months—he is yours; you shall see him within this hour."

I thought she was going to fall, she was so pallid. She clasped her hands wildly over her brow, unable to comprehend her bliss, then said piteously:

"Oh! don't, Jennie; it has always been so vain."

"Do not **say** it is vain any more, Stanley; come to my **heart,** my own darling; it shall be your home henceforth; none shall ever take it from you **now.**"

She ran into the arms outstretched, and was clasped to **his true** heart.

"Warren, **am** I dreaming, is it true, shall it be at last, then ?"

"**Yes,** darling; pleasant dreams of a bliss too long deferred, though blissful **yet;** I thank God for my joy and your love."

The old **caressing tones**—how like music they were as he talked on.

"**We shall have** another wreath **of** Northern orange **blossoms,** darling, **for** your golden hair. Ere we go back where I may look upon the faces of the good people assembled in your cottage home, you must name the day which will make me the happiest of men. I want to congratulate Mrs. Seaman! how cruel I am to have spoiled her plan of calling you daughter. Well, well, it matters little; I have not forgotten her propensity to interfere with others less deserving than myself."

The moon came up, as I had seen her many a time, cheery **and bright, above the** New Hampshire hills. Those two passed down the garden-way, the glory round them, while I knelt in the silence and thanked God fervently.

Milverton had announced Warren's arrival. When we reëntered the house all eyes were turned upon Stanley, who, flushed with her happiness, leaned gracefully upon the arm of her betrothed. Even Mrs. Seaman saw how it would be.

The morning came—the morning of their bridal; mists paled, and the noon welled in its tides of glory; softly fell the evening-time. Ah! those Wayburn bells! they had chimed the hour of worship and the hour of death; they had tolled when our graves were made—the graves where slept our dead. We never loved them more than in this hour of calm happiness in which we passed down the aisles of the lighted church, in view of the congregation assembled to witness the marriage ceremonies of Warren and Stanley. Then they two went forth bound together for time. Who would have thought it would all have ended thus!

Hoping much, I promised to go with Stanley to her new home; we were to leave Wayburn, with its sun-lighted paths; its melting mists and hills of splendor; its nights, with their watching stars; the graves that were wearing their summer green, to live again in the world of fashion, whose doors were once more opened to us. There was a way, God's way, in which Cousin Warren had never walked; by the strength of his love for his wife we must lead him there.

There was a merry party assembled in the square house at Ridgely upon the day succeeding the marriage. The cottage, with its belongings, was Mr. Kingswell's bridal gift to Leah. She and Frederick were established in their new home ere we took Miss Phœbe to New York to live with us.

The patient reader who has gone with us through hours of discipline, who has smiled with us when gay, and wept with us when the grave-clods were falling, knows which most to hope or to fear for our future. It all rests with God.

CHAPTER XXIV.

PEACE AND HOPE.

"Tho' close the tie that bound them, yet hath Heaven
A closer tie to the true-hearted given."

A YEAR has gone by! A year full of momentous events, which would in themselves constitute a nation's tragic history. The armies of the Republic are being disbanded and the soldiers mustered out. Many, during the four years of war, have been mustered anew into the service of their God. The red tides have ceased their coursing through our land. Far-rolling over the crimson sea of revolution came the white billows of peace. By the grave-side of our illustrious dead were the hearts in the whole land bowed down and once more united *under the stars* of our victorious banner. Once more the Southern braves came to rally round the old standard, whose constellations beam upon the broad fields where sleep the dead—men of the North and the South peacefully together—under the stars of heaven, and the tattered flag waves over them. In the broad noonday of our renewed prosperity, I see the arching bow of promise spanning the heavens. There shall be no more waiting; no more tears and death; no more sacrifices upon the altar of country; no more souls added to those still fires of patriotism, which flamed so fiercely in those long nights of strife.

When postal communication was partially reëstablished, there came a letter from Uncle Montana. During the first year of the rebellion, he barely existed in a Southern prison; he was incarcerated for his Union sentiments. Upon the acquisition of New Orleans by the Federal forces, he told his story, and was released and placed in the service of the Government. During the three years of hard work, filling a responsible position, he laid by a sum of money which enabled him to re-purchase Claremont of the authorities for a tithe of its original value. It was uncle's desire to take us home again. The Brightland slaves **were in** the Southern service; but Aunt Dinah, Hawsey, and many more of our female servants, were anxious that we should become reëstablished in the old home once more. We **would** go South in the autumn; the money which I inherited from Clyde I would cheerfully expend in having **the** old things back as near as possible to what they were. I resolved to spend my summers with Stanley; she and I together would visit Raymond and Ridgely; then we should all go to Claremont for the winter. I was almost happy in making plans; of course, we might expect some deviations from our former style of living. For instance, we could never have again what death had taken from us.

Lane Austin accepted the universal amnesty offered by the President, and came North to see us. My soldier had availed himself of that offered by Christ—the amnesty **of Heaven.** I was glad to see Lane, until he took my hand confidentially, telling me that he had loved me all his life. I answered earnestly:

"Lane, there **is one other who has loved me thus, who** loves me still, in that far world, beneath whose stars I **stand** in this night of my sorrowing for him on the earth. **Yes;** he loved me, and I him, when

> "'He went forth
> His princely way among God's **stars, in slow**
> And silent brightness.'

"**I** promised to join him in the glory yonder; I shall

keep my word. In the far-reaching solitudes of my widowed heart no other idol shall ever come."

I was right. God had given me, in answer to my lifelong prayer, that little hour of love, while the sun went down. I could sit in the shadowy twilight with my memory, in whose powerful echoes, says Lamartine, "there is only——always!" waiting for the day-dawn, whose stars should sing together the song of triumph over the death which came between us.

I wore no black for him who wore the white insignia of peace. My love had donned the snowy vestments of immortality. I saw the heavenly robes of the redeemed descending on the pale sleep through which his life rippled out. Again, at morning, beside a golden river, we should stand together—the bright-flowing river of everlasting life!

Oh, my love! though from the silence of thy death there comes no sound, yet solemnly I feel how

> " Immortality o'ersweeps
> All pains, all tears, all time, all fears, and peals
> Like the eternal thunders of the deep,
> Unto my ears this truth : *thou liv'st for ever !* "

THE END.

NEW BOOKS

And New Editions Recently Issued by
CARLETON, PUBLISHER,
NEW YORK,
413 *BROADWAY, CORNER OF LISPENARD STREET.*

Victor Hugo.

LES MISÉRABLES.—*The best edition,* two elegant 8vo. vols., beautifully bound in cloth, $5.50 ; half calf, $10.00

LES MISÉRABLES.—*The popular edition,* one large octavo volume, paper covers, $2.00; cloth bound, $2.50

LES MISÉRABLES.—In the Spanish language. Fine 8vo. edition, two vols., paper covers, $4.00 ; cloth bound, $5.00

JARGAL.—A new novel. Illustrated. . 12mo. cloth, $1.75

THE LIFE OF VICTOR HUGO.—By himself. 8vo. cloth, $1.75

Miss Muloch.

JOHN HALIFAX.—A novel. With illustration. 12mo. cloth, $1.75

A LIFE FOR A LIFE.— . do. do. $1.75

Charlotte Bronte (Currer Bell).

JANE EYRE.—A novel. With illustration. 12mo., cloth, $1.75

THE PROFESSOR. —do. . do. . do. $1.75

SHIRLEY.— . do. . do. . do. $1.75

VILLETTE.— . do. . do. . do. $1.75

Hand-Books of Society.

THE HABITS OF GOOD SOCIETY ; with thoughts, hints, and anecdotes, concerning nice points of taste, good manners, and the art of making oneself agreeable. The most entertaining work of the kind ever published. 12mo. cloth, $1.75

THE ART OF CONVERSATION.—With directions for self-culture. A sensible and instructive work, that ought to be in the hands of every one who wishes to be either an agreeable talker or listener. . . . . 12mo. cloth, $1.50

New English Novels.

RECOMMENDED TO MERCY.— . . . 12mo. cloth, $1.75

TAKEN UPON TRUST.— *In press.* . do. $1.75

THE GOLDEN RULE.— do. . do. $1.75

Mrs. Mary J. Holmes' Works.

'LENA RIVERS.— . . . A novel.	12mo. cloth,	$1.50
DARKNESS AND DAYLIGHT.— . do.	do.	$1.50
TEMPEST AND SUNSHINE.— . do.	do.	$1.50
MARIAN GREY.— . . . do.	do.	$1.50
MEADOW BROOK.— . . . do.	do.	$1.50
ENGLISH ORPHANS.— . . . do.	do.	$1.50
DORA DEANE.— . . . . do.	do.	$1.50
COUSIN MAUDE.— . . . do.	do.	$1.50
HOMESTEAD ON THE HILLSIDE.— do.	do.	$1.50
HUGH WORTHINGTON.— . . do.	do.	$1.50

Artemus Ward.

HIS BOOK.—The first collection of humorous writings by A. Ward. Full of comic illustrations.   12mo. cloth, $1.50

HIS TRAVELS.—A comic volume of Indian and Mormon adventures. With laughable illustrations.   12mo. cloth, $1.50

Miss Augusta J. Evans.

BEULAH.—A novel of great power.   .   12mo. cloth, $1.75

MACARIA.—   do.   do.   .   do. $1.75

A NEW NOVEL.—*In press.*   .   .   do. $1.75

By the Author of "Rutledge."

RUTLEDGE.—A deeply interesting novel.   12mo. cloth, $1.75

THE SUTHERLANDS.—   do.   .   .   do. $1.75

FRANK WARRINGTON.—   do.   .   .   do. $1.75

ST. PHILIP'S.— .   .   do.   .   .   do. $1.75

LOUIE'S LAST TERM AT ST. MARY'S.   .   .   do. $1.75

Josh Billings.

HIS BOOK.—All the rich comic sayings of this celebrated humorist. With comic illustrations.   .   12mo. cloth, $1.50

Mrs. Ritchie (Anna Cora Mowatt).

FAIRY FINGERS.—A capital new novel.   .   12mo. cloth, $1.75

THE MUTE SINGER.—   do.   .   .   .   do. $1.75

A NEW BOOK.—*In press.*   .   .   .   do. $1.75

New English Novels.

BEYMINSTRE.—A very interesting novel.   12mo. cloth, $1.75

THE SILENT WOMAN.—*In press.* .   .   do. $1.75

Geo. W. Carleton.

OUR ARTIST IN CUBA.—A humorous volume of travels ; with fifty comic illustrations by the author.   12mo. cloth, $1.50

OUR ARTIST IN PERU.—*In press.* $1.00

Pulpit Pungencies.

A new comic book of immense fun.   12mo. cloth, $1.50

A. S. Roe's Works.

A LONG LOOK AHEAD.—	A novel.	12mo. cloth,	$1.50
TO LOVE AND TO BE LOVED.—	do.	do.	$1.50
TIME AND TIDE.—	do.	do.	$1.50
I'VE BEEN THINKING.—	do.	do.	$1.50
THE STAR AND THE CLOUD.—	do.	do.	$1.50
TRUE TO THE LAST.—	do.	do.	$1.50
HOW COULD HE HELP IT?—	do.	do.	$1.50
LIKE AND UNLIKE.—	do.	do.	$1.50
LOOKING AROUND.—	do.	do.	$1.50
WOMAN, OUR ANGEL.—	do. *In press.*	do.	$1.50

Richard B. Kimball.

WAS HE SUCCESSFUL.—	A novel.	12mo. cloth,	$1.75
UNDERCURRENTS.—	do.	do.	$1.75
SAINT LEGER.—	do.	do.	$1.75
ROMANCE OF STUDENT LIFE.—	do.	do.	$1.75
IN THE TROPICS.—	do.	do.	$1.75
THE PRINCE OF KASHNA.—	do.	do.	$1.75
EMILIE.—A sequel to "St. Leger."	*In press.*	do.	$1.75

Orpheus C. Kerr.

THE ORPHEUS C. KERR PAPERS.—Comic letters and humorous military criticisms. Three series.   12mo. cloth, $1.50

Edmund Kirke.

AMONG THE PINES.—A Southern sketch.		12mo. cloth,	$1.50
MY SOUTHERN FRIENDS.—	do.	do.	$1.50
DOWN IN TENNESSEE.—	do.	do.	$1.50
ADRIFT IN DIXIE.—	do.	do.	$1.50
AMONG THE GUERILLAS.—	do.	do.	$1.50
A NEW BOOK.—*In press.*	do.	do.	$1.50

T. S. Arthur's New Works.

LIGHT ON SHADOWED PATHS.—A novel.		12mo. cloth,	$1.50
OUT IN THE WORLD.—	do.	do.	$1.50
NOTHING BUT MONEY.—	do.	do.	$1.50
WHAT CAME AFTERWARDS.—	do.	do.	$1.50
OUR NEIGHBORS.—*In press.*	do.	do.	$1.50

Robinson Crusoe.

A handsome illustrated edition, complete.   12mo. cloth, $1.50

Joseph Rodman Drake.

THE CULPRIT FAY.—A faery poem.   12mo. cloth, $1.25
AN ILLUSTRATED EDITION.—With 100 exquisite illustrations on wood.   Quarto, beautifully printed and bound, $5.00

Epidemic Cholera.

A handy-book for successful treatment.   12mo. cloth, $1.00

Cuthbert Bede.

VERDANT GREEN.—A rollicking, humorous novel of English student life ; with 200 comic illustrations.   12mo. cloth, $1.50

Private Miles O'Reilly.

BAKED MEATS OF THE FUNERAL.—A new comic book of songs, speeches, essays, banquets, etc.   .   12mo. cloth, $1.75

LIFE AND ADVENTURES—with comic illustrations.   do. $1.50

M. Michelet's Remarkable Works.

LOVE (L'AMOUR).—From the French. .   .   12mo. cloth, $1.50

WOMAN (LA FEMME).—   do.   .   .   .   do. $1.50

J. Sheridan Le Fanu.

WYLDER'S HAND.—A powerful new novel.   12mo. cloth, $1.75

THE HOUSE BY THE CHURCHYARD.—   do.   do. $1.75

Rev. John Cumming, D.D., of London.

THE GREAT TRIBULATION.—Two series.   12mo. cloth, $1.50

THE GREAT PREPARATION.—   do.   .   do. $1.50

THE GREAT CONSUMMATION.—   do.   .   do. $1.50

Ernest Renan.

THE LIFE OF JESUS.—From the French work. 12mo. cloth, $1.75

RELIGIOUS HISTORY AND CRITICISM.—   8vo. cloth, $2.50

Popular Italian Novels.

DOCTOR ANTONIO.—A love story. By Ruffini. 12mo. cloth, $1.75

VINCENZO.—   do.   do.   do. $1.75

BEATRICE CENCI.—By Guerrazzi, with portrait.   do. $1.75

Charles Reade.

THE CLOISTER AND THE HEARTH.—A magnificent new novel— the best this author ever wrote.   .   .   8vo. cloth, $2.00

The Opera.

TALES FROM THE OPERAS.—A collection of clever stories, based upon the plots of all the famous operas. 12mo. cloth, $1.50

Robert B. Roosevelt.

THE GAME-FISH OF THE NORTH.—Illustrated. 12mo. cloth, $2.00

SUPERIOR FISHING.—   do.   do. $2.00

THE GAME-BIRDS OF THE NORTH.—   do. $2.00

John Phœnix.

THE SQUIBOB PAPERS.—A new humorous volume, filled with comic illustrations by the author.   12mo. cloth, $1.50

Matthew Hale Smith.

MOUNT CALVARY.—Meditations in sacred places. 12mo. $2.00

P. T. Barnum.

THE HUMBUGS OF THE WORLD.—Two series. 12mo. cloth, $1.75